MOMENTUM IS A LIE

MOMENTUM IS A LIE

A Novel

Harry Holland

MOONFLY PRESS

Atlanta

This is a work of fiction. Names, characters, places, and incidents are either the product of the author's imagination or are used fictitiously. Any resemblance to actual persons, living or dead, events, or locales is entirely coincidental.

Published by Moonfly Press, Atlanta

HarryHollandStories.com

ISBN 979-8-9961659-0-2

ISBN 979-8-9961659-1-9

ISBN 979-8-9961659-2-6

ISBN 979-8-9961659-3-3

ISBN 979-8-9961659-4-0

First edition 2026

For Julie — who took every momentum-filled turn with me,

and always knew purpose was the true destination.

"Many are the plans in a person's heart,
but it is the Lord's purpose that prevails."

— Proverbs 19:21

CHAPTER 1

USE SOMEBODY

The party has been going on for hours, and I have found the only place in the house where nobody is performing.

It is December 2008, three months after Lehman, and every other room is full of men in tuxedos doing what men do when the ground shifts beneath them — talking slightly too loudly about everything except the thing they are all thinking about. The market. The losses. The specific silence where certainty used to be. My father's world, already gone, still performing behind a good suit and a full glass.

Somewhere in that room is Big. My grandfather — William Chaffee II, Big Will to everyone who knows him, just Big to us — is eighty-one years old and still the largest presence in any room he enters. In the seventies he moved the textile mills to North Carolina when everyone said Connecticut would hold. In the nineties he moved them offshore when everyone said loyalty would. Right both times. He's probably near the fireplace with a bourbon and the face of a man who has already assessed everyone present and filed his conclusions — tall, well over six feet, dark-haired gone fully white, with the jaw and the set of the eyes that people have always said I inherited. Looking at him is like looking at a version of myself that has already decided everything.

My father is also in that room. Trying to be him.

I have slipped away from all of it.

My father's study smells like old books and wood polish and the ghost of every cigar he has ever smoked in here. Someone has dimmed the lights without being asked, which is what happens at parties when people are loose and willing to let the unexpected happen.

There are maybe eight people sitting around — friends of friends, a couple of older kids I half know from school, Sarah Whitmore who I have been trying not to stare at all night, and Q, Andro Quimby — my best friend since forever, and I have my father's Martin in my lap and I am playing and singing and for approximately the last twenty minutes I have not thought about a single thing that has been making me miserable.

This is what music does for me. The only thing that can. It is my armor. I play "Use Somebody." I don't play it perfectly — there's a chord transition in the bridge I still haven't fully nailed — but I play it honestly, which is better than perfect, and the people in the room are quiet in the way people get quiet when something is actually reaching them. Dark-haired, broad through the shoulders in the way of someone who has been rowing since he was twelve — not quite the finished version yet, still a little unresolved around the edges, but the bones of it are there. Sarah Whitmore is looking at me in a way she has never looked at me in the hallway at school. I file that away for later.

I am sixteen years old, and for twenty minutes on New Year's Eve, I am exactly who I am supposed to be.

Nobody in this room wants anything from me except this. The music. The honesty of it. Not the name, not the school, not what I'm going to do with my life, not whether I'm living up to it or falling short. Only this.

I hadn't understood until right now how long I'd been waiting for that.

The door opens.

I know before I turn around. There's a particular quality to the air when my father enters a room. A pressure change. The way people who've been relaxed suddenly become careful without knowing why they're doing it. He is not a large man — Big got the size, and somehow I got it too, passing Bill entirely. What my father has is precision. Even at a party. The stillness of someone who has learned to make a room careful without filling it. My body knows it before my brain does — shoulders tightening, breath going shallow, the old familiar calibration clicking into place. I have been reading this room my entire life.

Wearing his tuxedo, with his bow tie loosened, his face achieves a specific color after several hours of drinking—it's not quite red, more like the blood has risen to the surface of everything, and his skin struggles to contain what occurs beneath it. He takes in the room. Takes in me with the Martin. Takes in the people watching me with the Martin.

Something moves across his face that I don't have a word for at sixteen. I'll have a word for it later. The word is unbearable.

"Will."

Just my name. The way he always says it. Like a verdict.

"Hey Dad." I keep my hands on the guitar. "We're just—"

"Outside."

Sarah Whitmore looks at her hands. The room does the collective thing rooms do when something private becomes public — everyone simultaneously finding somewhere else to look. I set the Martin carefully against the chair. I follow him out through the french doors onto the terrace.

The cold hits hard. It is about fifteen degrees and the terrace flagstones are glazed with ice and the sound of the party disappears behind the closed door the moment it closes. The sky is completely clear. In a few minutes it will be a new year.

My father stands at the edge of the terrace looking out at the dark lawn. He doesn't turn around when he speaks.

"In my study," he says. "With my guitar."

"I'm sorry, I should have asked—"

"Performing." He says the word like it's obscene. "Like some kind of—" He stops. Takes a drink from the glass he's carried out with him, scotch with one ice cube. The ice clicks. "You think those people came here tonight to watch you perform?"

"Dad—"

"You think this is—" He turns around now and his eyes are bright and wrong in the way they get and I take one automatic step backward which I hate myself for immediately. He gestures back toward the house, toward the party, toward everything. The gesture is too large, means too many things. His business. The house. The life he is currently losing piece by piece — not only because of Lehman, not only because of the crash, but because of decisions made long before any of that, decisions nobody will ever let him blame on the market. "You think any of this runs on guitar playing?"

"No. It doesn't."

"Then what the hell are you doing in there? Making a fool of yourself in front of my friends? In my house? With my guitar?"

"They liked it," I say. "They were listening."

"Nobody was listening. They were being polite. That's what people do when a kid makes a spectacle of himself — they smile and they wait for it to be over." He steps closer. "Curious about their real thoughts? There goes Bill Chaffee's son, the one who confuses hobbies with jokes."

I don't respond. I know better — the architecture of these moments — you keep quiet, you absorb, you wait for it to pass. I have been doing this my whole life. I have learned the specific geography of his anger, where it peaks, where it levels out, how long it takes to run through him and leave. I have logged more hours studying my father's moods than I have studying anything else in sixteen years. It is the primary education of my life.

"You're seventeen years old—"

"Sixteen."

He stops.

I don't know why I said it. It came out before I could decide whether to let it. That single correction, delivered in a voice that was steadier than I felt, and now the air on the terrace has changed in a way that is familiar and terrible.

"What did you say to me?"

"Nothing. Never mind."

"What did you say to me." Not a question this time.

"I said I'm sixteen. Not seventeen."

The silence is very complete. Behind us the party continues in its sealed world — music, laughter, the clink of glasses — indifferent to what is happening twenty feet away on a frozen terrace.

"You think this is funny?" His voice has dropped. Quieter is always worse. I learned that young. "You think you can stand there and—"

"I think you don't know how old I am," I say. And something breaks open in my chest as I say it, something that has been building for a very long time. "I think you've never known. I think you don't know what grade I'm in or what I'm good at or what I care about or anything about me except that I'm not what you wanted."

The words hang in the frozen air.

I have never said anything like that to him. Not once. Not in sixteen years of learning to be small and still and quiet and careful. I don't know exactly where it came from. I know it cannot be unsaid.

He looks at me. Something shifts in his face — not just anger, something way older and more intense. "You're exactly like him," he says.

Not a compliment.

He moves fast. Faster than I expect.

The punch catches me in the stomach — not a shove, not an open hand, a closed fist driving the air out of me completely — and I fold forward, hands on my knees, the cold flagstones swimming in my vision. My body knows this. Some part of me that is older than thought knows the specific quality of this pain, knows how to receive it, has been receiving some version of it for as long as I can remember. That is the worst part. Not the pain itself but the recognition. The way my body didn't even flinch in anticipation because it has learned there is no point.

I stay bent for a moment. Breathing. Waiting for the world to level out.

Then I straighten up.

And something happens that has never happened before. I look at him — really look at him — and I realize that I am taller than him now. That his shoulders, which have loomed over me my entire life, are actually not so broad. That the man in front of me is smaller than the man I carry around inside me. The man on this terrace is thinner than I remembered, his tuxedo slightly too big at the shoulders, his face in the cold moonlight showing its age in a way it doesn't under the warm lights of the party inside. He is shorter than Big by four inches — and I have an inch on Big, darker through the complexion, heavier in the face — something Mediterranean in the bone structure that skipped a generation in this family. He looks nothing like his father. He has always known that. He looks, suddenly and completely, like someone who has been running a bluff for a very long time.

He pulls his hand back again.

He swings.

I hit him first.

Not a shove. Not a defensive gesture. A punch, hard and clean, with everything I have in it and everything I have been absorbing for sixteen years. He goes down on the icy flagstones with a sound I will hear for the rest of my life — not a dramatic sound, not a movie sound, just a dull human thud of a body hitting a cold surface — and he sits there looking up at me with a look I have never seen on his face before.

I have never seen him surprised before.

I am breathing very hard. My stomach still hurts. The cold is extraordinary.

The french door opens behind me and Q's head appears. "Quart," he says. Just that. His name for me since we were ten — short for the Fourth, which is what I am, which he has always found funnier than I do. He is broad through the chest at sixteen, dark-skinned, with the easy grin that will always be on his face — the grin of someone who was loved without conditions from the beginning and has never once needed to protect himself from a room. He takes in my father on the ground. He takes in my face. He doesn't say anything, doesn't ask anything, doesn't make it worse by treating it as the enormous thing it is.

"Come on man," he says. "Let's go inside."

I look at my father one more time. He is getting up, slowly, with the careful movements of someone checking to see what's broken. He doesn't look at me. I don't help him.

I go inside with Q. Not back into the study. We walk further down the terrace and enter the main event.

The countdown is already happening. Ten. Nine. Eight. The room is packed and loud and full of champagne and people reaching for each other and the new year arriving whether anyone is ready for it or not. Confetti falls. Someone blows a horn directly beside my ear. Happy New Year!

Q puts his hand on the back of my neck briefly. That's all. Just his hand there for a second, then he hands me a drink and he's gone.

Nobody notices. There is nothing to see — there never is. My body has always known how to absorb what happens to it without leaving evidence. The party swallows me whole.

I stand at the edge of the room for a moment, still breathing hard, and look for her.

She's across the living room, exactly where she always is at these things — the center of it, naturally, effortlessly, the way a flame is the center of whatever darkness surrounds it. She's in vintage Chanel and her hair is still perfect and she is laughing at what the man beside her said, head tilted just so, one hand light on his arm. Marci is a half-step behind her, glass in hand, watching the room the way she always watches rooms —

cataloguing, assessing, deciding what needs managing.

My mother has not looked toward me. I have been watching to see if she would.

She hasn't.

I don't know if she knows. I don't know which version is worse — that she saw what was happening and stayed, or that she didn't see it at all. I have been trying to solve this equation for most of my life and I am standing in the middle of my parent's New Year's Eve party with a bruise forming on my ribs and no answer that makes anything better.

She laughs again. The room laughs with her.

Big is near the back of the room. I can see him from here. He is not laughing. He is watching the chair my father has not returned to. He has the expression he gets when he is deciding what he has already decided.

Elizabeth Prescott, at the absolute peak of her powers, in her own house, on New Year's Eve, untouchable. She is fifty-one and looks forty, which she has always treated as beside the point. The bone structure is what it will always be — those cheekbones, that jaw — her hair is dark gold, worn up, and the dress is the exact shade of green that makes every other color in the room look like it's trying. She is the reason my father built this house. She is the reason he is still standing in it.

Q finds me again near the bar a little later.

He doesn't ask how I am. Q never asks how you are when he can see how you are. He just picks up two glasses of whatever is being passed, hands me one, and we drink standing there watching the party like it's happening on television.

"You okay?" he says, after a while.

"No."

"Good," he says. "Me neither."

We drink.

The thing about Q is he never makes you explain yourself. He just arrives and stays and that is enough. It has always been enough. I have known him since we were six years old and in all that time I don't think he has ever once asked me to be something I wasn't. In a life full of people asking me to be things I'm not, Q is the only place I have ever been able to put the performance down.

We drink more.

The party moves around us — my mother laughing her particular party laugh, the one she saves for people she wants something from, the guests all shiny and animated and performing their own versions of fine — and somewhere in the third or fourth drink the thing that has been very tight since the terrace begins to loosen in a way that isn't good, isn't safe, isn't going to end quietly.

"I want to do something," I say.

Q looks at me. He knows my faces the way I know his.

"How bad?" he says.

I think about the terrace. The cold. My father's fist. The particular expression on his face before he swung. I think about the Martin in the study still leaning against the chair where I left it and the way Sarah Whitmore looked at the floor.

"Bad," I say.

Q says nothing. Then he refills both our glasses.

"Okay," he says.

By around one thirty we are seriously drunk and stripped down to our underpants.

This was not entirely planned. What was planned was somewhat less than this. But plans have a way of accelerating when you are young and furious and have nothing left to lose in a particular house on a particular night, and somewhere between the fourth drink and the sixth the tuxedos came off and here we are.

The band is playing a standard — something my father probably requested, safe and appropriate and completely without edge — and I walk through the crowd in my boxers with Q right behind me and the room does something extraordinary. It parts. Not because we're frightening, though maybe we are a little, but because there is something about two teenage boys in their underwear moving with absolute purpose through a room full of people in black tie that creates an involuntary path.

I step onto the small bandstand.

The guitarist — older guy, patient face, has seen things — looks at me with an expression of profound resignation. I pick up the band leader's microphone. The band trails off uncertainly, one instrument at a time, until the room is very quiet.

I can see my mother across the room. She has gone very still in the specific way she goes still when something threatens the performance she has been maintaining her entire life. Her smile is still technically present but it has stopped meaning anything. Beside her one of her friends — a woman whose name I have never learned despite years of the same parties — puts a hand on her arm.

My father is not in the room. My father is somewhere putting himself back together after the terrace. That is almost a shame. This is for him too.

I look out at the room. Greenwich's finest in their black ties and their jewelry and their careful expressions.

"Hi," I say into the microphone. "I'm Will. I live here."

Q is beside me now. I can feel him close. He puts a hand on my arm — steady, present — and I know he is going to try to pull me back from this and I know equally that he is going to fail because I am already gone, already past the point where the sensible thing and the true thing are the same thing.

"My mother," I say, "is a wonderful actress."

The room shifts.

"She's been performing tonight for all of you and she is very good at it, as we all know. I also want you to know that the performance you've been watching all evening has absolutely nothing to do with what actually happens in this house."

"Quart—" Q says quietly.

"She is a phony," I say. The word lands in the room like something dropped from a height. "A beautiful, talented, completely constructed phony. And my father—"

Q tries. He actually grabs my arm and pulls and for a moment I wobble and almost stop and then I look at my mother's face — the smile finally gone now, something raw and almost real underneath it, something that might be the actual her if she ever let it out — and I keep going.

"My father is an asshole."

The room exhales.

Somewhere in the back I think I see Big set down his glass. His face does not change.

"He is a spectacular, world-class, bankrupt asshole and I want every single person in this room to know that before the night is over because I think honesty is important. I think—"

The band leader gently takes the microphone.

Q takes me by both arms and moves me firmly off the bandstand and through the crowd and the crowd parts again.

As Q moves me through the crowd I catch Big's eye for just a second. He is not angry. He is not embarrassed. He is looking at me the way he looks at things he has already made peace with. Then the crowd closes between us.

I let him take me because I have said the true things, I have said them out loud in my parent's house with their friends watching, and something that has been building for sixteen years has been released into the stifling party air and I feel simultaneously better and completely destroyed.

We are in the front hallway.

Q's giving me this look I can't quite figure out. Not quite pride. Not quite horror. Something that contains both.

"Keys," he says.

"What?"

He nods toward the front door where the valets have been parking cars all evening. Through the narrow window beside the door I can see them — the cars lined up in the cold, Porsches and Mercedeses and one spectacular Aston Martin catching the moonlight.

"Keys," he says again.

We take two cars.

Not carefully. Not responsibly. We take them the way two drunk sixteen year olds with nothing left to lose take two very expensive cars on a frozen Connecticut road at one thirty in the morning, which is to say we take them completely and without apology.

The cold hits us when we come through the door and it is extraordinary and clarifying and we are in our underwear and none of that matters because Q has a fistful of keys from the valet stand and we are running across the frozen gravel and the night is enormous and clear and full of stars.

Q takes the Aston Martin without hesitation. I take a Porsche — black, low, something a hedge fund manager bought to remind himself he was still alive — and I turn the key and the engine catches and the sound of it fills everything.

We go.

Not anywhere specific. Just away. Down the long driveway and through the iron gates and onto the dark road and it is starting to snow — soft and indifferent, first flakes catching in the headlights — and the cold air comes through the windows I have opened because I am sixteen and invincible. The road is ours tonight, we have claimed it. Q's headlights appear in my mirror and disappear and reappear as I take corners faster than the road was designed for.

I don't think about my father.

I don't think about the terrace or the mic or my mother's face when the smile finally failed.

I just drive. Fast and cold and naked and free, through the dark Connecticut night, with my best friend's headlights in my mirror and the road running out ahead of me and for this specific window of time, maybe twenty minutes, maybe less, I am not anyone's son. I am not anyone's disappointment. I am not the boy who was punched on his father's terrace or the boy who grabbed a microphone in his underwear or the boy whose father's guitar is leaning against a chair in a study where nobody is playing it.

I am just moving. Fast. Through the dark.

It ends, as these things end, not with a crash exactly but with a Porsche in a ditch on Close Road and Q's Aston Martin at a forty five degree angle across someone's lawn and the two of us standing in the cold in our underwear looking at what we've done with the particular clarity that arrives when the alcohol meets the cold air meets the adrenaline and burns everything clean.

Q looks at the Aston Martin on the lawn.

"That one's on me," he says.

We start walking back.

* * *

My father wakes me at seven fifteen.

Not by knocking. He opens the door and turns on the overhead light and that is how I know this is not a conversation. The overhead light in this house has always meant something specific. It means the performance is over and what comes next is real.

I am face down on my bed still in my boxers. My head is a construction site. My stomach still aches from the night before — a deep, settled soreness, the kind that has been there before and knows how to make itself comfortable. Through the window the January sun is gray and flat and unforgiving.

He stands in the doorway. He is dressed. Pressed shirt, dark trousers, shoes that have been polished. He has shaved. He looks like a man who slept perfectly and rose early and has been thinking clearly for several hours, which is the most frightening version of him, the version I have spent my whole life dreading more than the drunk version, more than the loud version.

The drunk version is weather. This version is architecture.

He doesn't come into the room. He stands in the doorway and he lets the silence do its work.

"Get up," he says.

I get up.

"Downstairs. Every room. Every glass, every bottle, everything left in them. You drink it."

I look at him.

"All of it," he says. "Every drop that's left in every glass in every room in this house. You finish what your guests left behind. Then you clean up. Every glass, every plate, every ashtray. Then you shovel the driveway. The whole thing."

The driveway is a quarter mile long.

"Dad—"

"Every drop," he says. "Start with my study."

He holds my gaze for a moment longer than is necessary. He wants me to understand: this is not anger. Anger would be easier. This is something colder and more deliberate, something that has been constructed specifically to fit the dimensions of what I did last night, punishment as craft, humiliation as methodology.

Then he turns and walks back down the hall and his footsteps are very even and unhurried on the stairs.

He wants me to start with the study. I am going to start with the sitting room.

I lay on my bed in my boxers in the dim light.

My stomach hurts. It will hurt for three days. I know this. I have a working knowledge of how long these things last.

Somewhere down the hall my mother's door is closed.

It will stay closed all day.

I drink what's left in twenty-three glasses.

Some of it is wine. Some of it is scotch. Some of it is things I can't identify, melted ice and lipstick on the rim and the specific sourness of a drink that has been sitting since three in the morning. I go from room to room with the systematic thoroughness of a person under orders who understands that deviation is not an option.

The study is last.

The Martin is still where I left it. In the flat morning light it looks smaller than it did last night. Everything looks smaller in the flat morning light.

I pick up the two remaining glasses from the side tables. I drink them standing there. I look at the guitar. The room went quiet last night when I was playing. The way that felt. The way nothing else has ever felt quite like that.

I leave the Martin where it is and go to find the cleaning supplies.

The driveway takes me nearly six hours.

It is the kind of cold that gets into your shoulders and stays there. The snow is heavy and the driveway is long and by the second hour my back is a single sustained complaint and my head has moved from construction site to something geological, tectonic and deep. My stomach registers every movement of the shovel. I took both shovels from the garage before I started — the heavy one for the packed ice near the gate, the lighter one for the fresh snow in the middle. I have done this before. I know this driveway.

Somewhere in the second hour I put the shovel down, walk to the hedgerow, and vomit into the snow. Quietly. Efficiently. Then I pick the shovel back up. My father checks on me once. He comes to the front door and stands there and looks at my progress and goes back inside without speaking.

I shovel.

Somewhere in the third hour I hear a car on the gravel. The particular sound of Big's old Mercedes. I look up.

He parks outside the gate. I can hear the engine cut. A minute passes. Then he comes through on foot, in his coat and his cap, carrying the extra shovel from the gate post. He doesn't look at the house. He walks to where I am.

Standing there in the January light I can see what people mean when they say it. Same height. Same build. Same jaw. He is eighty-one and I am sixteen and we are made from the same template, two generations apart.

He walks to where I'm working and starts in without a word.

We work side by side. He doesn't ask what happened. He doesn't say anything about last night. He just shovels.

By the end of the third hour the nausea comes back. I set the shovel against the wall, crouch down with my hands on my knees, and let it happen again. Big keeps working. Doesn't stop. Doesn't look over. The sound of his shovel on the stone doesn't change rhythm.

I stand back up. We keep going.

At some point my father appears at the front door again. He stands there watching the two of us. Big doesn't look up. He just keeps working, steady and unhurried, like my father isn't there at all. When we reach the gate Big stops. He sets the shovel down and looks at me directly. "Good work," he says. Just that. Then he walks back to his car.

There's maybe a quarter of it left. I pick up the shovel and finish it alone.

I look back at the front door. My father is still there. He has watched the whole thing. His face has the expression I will spend years trying to understand — not anger exactly. Anger held so long it has become something else.

He goes back inside without speaking.

At some point Q calls. I let it ring. I don't have language yet for what happened last night or what is happening now. Q will understand. Q always understands. By the time I finish the light is already failing, the January afternoon collapsing into early dark, and I stand at the end of the driveway and look back at the house. Every light in every window. The warm yellow glow of a life that looks from the outside like everything anyone could want.

I lean the shovel against the stone columns at the entry gates.
I stand there until the cold gets in.
I go inside.

CHAPTER 2

ON THE EDGE

That was eighteen years ago.

This morning the sky's still dark. Thin ice splinters beneath my shoes. Rain knifes sideways across the New York-bound platform.

The crowd's sparse. Ghosts chasing the 6:04.

I stand on the yellow edge, collar up, hands buried in my coat. A distant squawk cuts the air — the train. Three headlights burn through mist.

The edge feels clean. Quiet. Not an exit — just the one honest place on the platform where the performance hasn't reached yet.

I don't move. Not forward. Not back.

The doors hiss open. I grab the last seat in the back.

The black glass gives me back what it always gives back — dark brown hair that does what it wants, hazel eyes that read differently depending on the light, a jaw that looks like it's already made a decision. The rowing build visible even in a coat. I look like someone who belongs here. I've been practicing that since I was twelve.

I slide in my earbuds. Kings of Leon. Use Somebody.

I've played it a hundred times. Today it hits different — the way it did in my father's study, the way it did when everything changed. I let it play and don't think about that.

The song takes me somewhere else.

I'm six years old, chasing fireflies with Q on the lawn below the terrace. My parents somewhere above us. Ice clinking in glasses. My father's laugh drifting down – the early one, before the drinks pile up and the laugh turns into something else entirely. Q cups one between his palms, opens them, watches it go.

Fifty-six minutes to Grand Central. Enough time to prep a pitch that might save my job. Some regional bank in the Carolina woods. The numbers don't work but I'm not paid to make sense of them. Just to sell them.

The suits around me are locked in screens. Dead-eyed. Execution mode.

My phone buzzes. Liz.

"I'm on the train. Yes. I'll do it when I get home. Let it go, please. Later."

I was fourteen when I stopped calling her Mom. I chose Liz — the one name she hates, the name my father used in public exactly once and paid for with two weeks of silence. At galas it was Lizzy. In the press it was Lizzy. In her Greenwich circle always Lizzy, the name that belonged to the icon and the Oscar and the magazine covers. But to me, since I was fourteen and understood for the first time what was happening in that house and who was choosing not to see it, she's been Liz. One syllable. Clipped. The smallest act of refusal available to me. She knows what it means. She's never acknowledged it.

The train screeches into the tunnel. Darkness takes the windows. I pause the music but leave the earbuds in.

Grand Central swells into view. I wait until the car empties.

"Chaffee!" someone calls. I don't turn.

"Will! Will, buddy!"

Nate Myers. Shaggy hair, lopsided smile. He played rhythm guitar while I sang lead at Brunswick. He hasn't aged. I've aged ten years since Tuesday. He grins and walks toward me. I nod and move into the crowd.

* * *

Sutter Rowe. Twenty-three floors of glass and steel at Park and 54th. Today I'm supposed to save a deal I don't believe in for a company I don't respect.

I walk through the door. I always do.

The lobby is cold. Sleek marble, too much glass. The only color a Sol LeWitt mural, large and vivid and completely ignored. Below it, Lou Garcia at the security desk.

"Morning, Will."

"Morning, Lou."

The elevator opens on twenty. Half-lit floor, monitors flickering. One screen alive. Daren Kwan — compact, quick-handed, almost always in a hoodie regardless of the occasion. His grandparents came over with nothing and built something in the San Gabriel Valley; his parents made sure he never had to think about that twice. He doesn't. He just works. Protein bar. Model already halfway built.

"You're early," I say.

He doesn't look up. "Technically you're late. I didn't leave last night. Seen the texts?"

"Better off not."

"We're dead. Client pushed the deadline. Numbers don't clear. Ames is already asking questions."

Priya Desai arrives. Crisp blazer, phone in one hand, coffee in the other. Her parents are both research scientists at the CDC in Atlanta — the kind of household where precision is a baseline, not an achievement. She is the first in her family in finance and she carries that the way you carry something heavy until you stop noticing the weight. Her eyes move fast. "Ames is copying half the floor on those emails. He wants blood."

"Where's Nico?"

Daren smirks. "It's only 7:45."

Right on cue Nico Calderon strolls in — lean and precise, with his mother's Santo Domingo eyes and his father's New York economy. He is not the typical face you see on a floor like this and he has always moved through it like he knows exactly that — not apologetically, not aggressively, just with the specific awareness of a man who earned every inch of the room and remembers exactly what it cost. Tailored coat over one shoulder, sunglasses still on. He slides into his chair like arriving was the actual work.

"Cut the shit, Kwan. I'm here."

"Command performance on 22 at eight."

Nico grins. "Fake it till you break it."

* * *

Floor 22 is warmer. Quieter. Thicker carpet. Shouting leaks from behind a glass wall.

We step into a conference room dense with stale air. Managing Directors down both sides — red eyes, no smiles.

At the head: Martin Halbridge. Senior Managing Partner — trim, early sixties, silver hair kept short, the posture of someone long since comfortable at the head of a table. His hands are always still. To his right, Philip Ames — my boss, the kind of man who measures everything in decimal points and posture.

“Cherry Point is blowing up,” Ames says. “Will, run new scenarios.” No greeting. Just command.

I tap my screen. The deck flares up.

“Southeast arrives at ten,” Halbridge says. “Two hours to clean this up.”

"Clean how?" I ask.

Ames: "Make the numbers work."

Translation: lie beautifully.

"If this deal implodes, we lose almost ten million in fees." He doesn't say the rest of it. We all know — a seven-figure bonus for him.

Daren types like he's defusing something. Priya's already building scenarios. Nico scrolls with one eyebrow raised.

"The Fed called Charlie," Ames says. "He's got until Friday to find a white knight. Our job is to get him his number. Southeast pays up, we all win."

Charlie Lawrence. Chairman of Cherry Point Bank. Old-school southern banker, all charm and golf-course bravado. The kind of man who still calls everyone son while the floor burns beneath him.

No pressure.

Daren exhales. Priya stops typing. Even Nico glances up.

I stare at the deck. I've made plenty of deals I didn't believe in. But this time I can't locate who I'm trying to convince — Southeast, Charlie Lawrence, or myself.

Outside the glass walls the floor hums — Managing Directors in private offices with skyline views, wrapped in the calm that comes from control. Different stakes up here. Different rules.

The room measures you whether you speak or not. Failure has a hierarchy. I know where I rank. I'm the lead on this deal.

I gather my laptop. "Let's get to it," I say, voice thin.

We file out. As the door closes, Ames asks if I'm aligned.

I say yes.

The yes comes slow.

We descend in silence. No one meets my eyes.

The floor number drops.

Back on 20, the floor is louder than usual. Every team in motion. Zack Holleran's crew in full armor — Zack leaning back like he owns it, Monica at the edge of a desk, Jamie hunched over his monitor. Zack is dark-haired, fit, and good-looking. He carries the kind of attitude that makes you want to punch him in the face — unless he's on your team, at which point it reads as unshakeable.

Zack looks up. Smiles. "Morning. Heard Cherry Point's going beautifully."

Laughter from his cluster. Someone taps a slow sarcastic drumroll on a desk.

We walk past, heads high. But Zack's voice follows like smoke.

"Must be tough, trying to shine up that pig with two hours and a bottle of Febreze."

More laughter.

I stop at our cluster and set my laptop down. Daren catches my eye. Small shake of his head — not worth it.

Priya exhales through her nose. "What a clown," she mutters, just loud enough. Across the floor Monica raises an eyebrow. Zack leans back further, hands laced behind his head.

"Don't worry," he says. "If Southeast passes, I'm sure the FDIC will be happy to step up." That one hits.

"Ignore them," I say. "We've got two hours."

Daren mutters, "We'll be the ones dead if they figure out what's under the hood."

We grab our laptops and retreat to a small conference room—our makeshift sanctuary. The room is dim, the sort of light that makes even bad ideas feel sacred.

We spend fifteen minutes arguing about language.

"Exposure."

"Concentration."

"Sensitivity."

If the deal works. The bank survives.

None of that belongs in the notes.

This isn't the part where anyone pretends not to understand the stakes.

It's the part where we decide who carries them.

I think about testing the boundary.

I don't.

"Footnote," I say.

No objections.

Ninety minutes gone. Red ink everywhere. Priya marks through the deck. Daren flips slides like he's grading a midterm.

Priya drops her pen. "This bank's a dumpster fire. We're dressing up a corpse."

"We're selling the turnaround story."

"There is no turnaround story." Daren doesn't look up. "Their Tier 1 capital's a joke. The credit book's radioactive. Lawrence is playing chicken with the Fed."

I close my laptop. "You think I don't know that?"

Silence.

"Southeast needs market share. If we frame it right—"

"Frame it?" Priya cuts in. "You mean spin it until we believe our own bullshit?"

She's not wrong. But I'm past justifying.

"If you want clean and pure, join the Peace Corps. Otherwise, find the angle."

Nico deadpans, "There's always an angle."

Daren snorts softly.

"Belief isn't part of the job," I say. "Persuasion is."

Nico leans forward. "The rural footprint. Stickiness. Underserved market — Southeast has no presence down there."

The table quiets

"That's not nothing," Daren says. "We bury the crap. Let the coverage team discover it."

Priya gives Nico the smallest nod.

"Nice tweak," I say.

He shrugs. "Just trying to keep my job."

"Aren't we all."

"We frame it as mission-aligned," I say. "Responsible expansion."

"Pull back on housing, push consumer-loyalty numbers," Priya says. "Rural doesn't scare them — headlines do."

I pick up my phone. "Show time."

* * *

The Southeast team arrives on time and unamused. Eric Lane — sharp, personable. Maya Hollis — ice-cold strategist. Dan Clemens — senior, quiet, already disappointed. Ames and Halbridge sweep in together.

Charlie Lawrence trails behind them, tie slightly askew, face drawn from too many sleepless nights.

Halbridge opens with a practiced smile. "Appreciate you making the trip through the sleet." Eric grins. "We've seen worse." Halbridge settles back. "Let's get started."

We sit. The kind of quiet that precedes a verdict.

Priya takes the wheel. "As you'll see, Cherry Point offers direct access to an underpenetrated footprint — particularly in rural Carolina markets where Southeast currently lacks exposure."

I pick it up. "They're not polished. But they're embedded. Strong community trust, margins you're not seeing in your Tier-1 markets. What they need is scale and structure. What you bring."

Maya asks about concentration in manufactured housing.

I almost say the honest version. Almost.

Charlie jumps in. "Those borrowers know us. We know them. It's not flashy banking, but it's loyal."

Ames cuts him a look. Let the bankers talk.

He quiets. Folds his hands.

Dan keeps flipping. "Margins are impressive. What's driving the losses?"

"Operating costs — legacy infrastructure, community footprint. But that's the opportunity. Southeast runs a leaner model. Close the overlap, digitize, and you've got instant efficiency."

Numbers on screens. Risk notes. Regulatory chatter. Every time Charlie's eyes flick toward me there's weight in them. Not panic. Stakes. This is the last hand he has to play and everyone at the table knows it.

At a natural pause I lean in. "Clock's ticking. The Fed won't grant extensions."

Eric nods. Maya's expression doesn't change.

When it ends Charlie shakes Eric's hand with both of his, thanking him twice, voice steady, eyes tired. He straightens his jacket as though it might keep something from slipping. The kind of man who built something that was supposed to last and watched it slip.

The door closes behind the Southeast team. The room deflates.

Charlie lingers by the window. "They were polite. Too polite."

"They'll come to the table."

He gives a small tired smile. "I've been in enough rooms like this to know when the deal's drifting."

I don't answer. Because he's right.

Halfway down the hall: "Chaffee." Halbridge falls in beside me, eyes forward. "Your line with Clemens — about the Fed's deadline. Smart. Created urgency without drawing blood."

Not a compliment. An assessment. From him that's more than most.

"Thanks."

"You don't waste words," he says. "Rare here." He peels off down another corridor. No handshake. No smile.

The afternoon grinds. I call Eric from a huddle room — no deck, just a drink invitation, The Astor Bar at 7:30. He says yes.

By six the day has a particular quality — the kind that comes when you've been performing something difficult for twelve hours and can feel the seams.

The bar is warm, golden — built to make trouble feel far away. Van Winkle for Eric. Rye for me. Something clear and unforgiving for Nico.

We toast and make banking chatter. Rate trends. Old Lehman war stories.

Then Eric shifts. "So," he says, "what am I not seeing in Cherry Point?"

I roll the glass between my hands. "You saw the deck. Strong footprint, loyal base, great cross-sell potential. It's not flashy, but it's solid."

Eric waits. "And?"

I hesitate just long enough. "There's some exposure in the manufactured-housing book. Older credits. Long tails. Military families, small contractors, people who depend on the local economy running right."

He nods slowly. "Meaning it works right up until the day it doesn't."

"Meaning it needs scale and structure. Southeast could bring that. Clean it up without losing what works."

Eric studies me. "So it's not a clean asset."

"It's workable. With the right discipline behind it."

Nico snorts into his glass. "So basically it's like buying a used car lot that also sells weed — cash flows, but a weird cross-sell." He grins at no one in particular.

Eric doesn't smile. He leans forward, eyes knife-sharp. "That's cute. Seriously — what am I missing here, Chaffee?"

Eric's waiting. The polished version is right there. Structure. Scale. Synergies.

Then I stop pretending.

"Look," I say. "Cherry Point has impressive elements. But a meaningful slice of the book is tied to narrow, sometimes fragile markets — borrowers with no margin for error, people the traditional system priced out or walked away from. They perform, mostly, but the underwriting favors convenience more than caution."

Eric's jaw clicks. "You mean predatory?"

"I mean products that, if you buy them and roll them into a regional book, you have to be ready to defend in public. Not just to regulators, but in the press. High rates, targeted geographies, exactly the kind of thing that turns into headlines you don't control."

A silence.

"So if we buy it," Eric says, quieter now but harder, "we'll have to explain why these loans exist, who benefits, and why the pricing is justified."

"You need the compliance playbook up front — clear documentation, revised underwriting, aggressive loss reserves, community outreach. If you can show remediation and transparency, you reduce the risk. Roll it together without those controls and you'll be defending emails on cable news."

He stares at me like he's weighing whether I've sunk the deal or saved them from a mess they don't want. "That's useful," he says finally. "Thanks for being direct."

Relief shows up first. Shame isn't far behind, just quieter.

Eric stands, shakes our hands, disappears into the lobby.

Nico orders another round like nothing happened. I watch condensation slide down the glass.

"Subtle."

"I didn't lie."

"No. You opened a window and let the storm blow in."

"You disagree?"

He thinks. "No. But I'm not pretending I did it for the other guy."

We sit a little longer — drinks untouched.

Outside, the street glows. Steam from manholes. Headlights indifferent.

"Think they'll walk?" Nico asks.

"I wouldn't blame them."

We walk a block in silence.

"He would've found out anyway," I say.

"Maybe," Nico says. "But it didn't have to be you."

At the light I glance over. Unreadable — half bemused, half tired.

"You trying to make me feel bad?"

He shakes his head. "I don't think you need help with that."

I laugh. It dies in my chest. The light changes. We cross. Grand Central ahead, lit up.

"My dad lost everything in '08," he says.

I look over. His voice is flat. Almost gentle.

"Small construction business. Steady work, nothing flashy. He leveraged too much right before the crash. Thought he timed it right. He didn't. Bank called the loans. Deals vanished. He kept showing up to job sites afterward, like movement could stop the fall."

He pauses.

"I was ten. He started popping oxy. I started figuring out how to get out."

I nod without speaking. Ten. Early to understand that the person who was supposed to protect you is the one you need protecting from. I know something about that.

"He thinks I came to Wall Street to avenge him," Nico says. "Maybe I did. I came to become the guy who saw it coming. The one who didn't get caught."

We pass a bar with the door propped open — somebody inside playing acoustic guitar, the sound warm and unpolished. It catches for a second, a song I almost recognize, and something tightens in my chest before I can stop it. We keep walking.

"You weren't sabotaging," Nico says. "You were refusing to cover for it."

"I used to think this job would fill the parts that never stayed filled," I say. "Like if I got good enough, won enough, I'd stop faking it."

Nico exhales — half sigh, half laugh. "Still playing the part?"

"Always."

At the corner he stops. "I'm cutting west."

"Alright."

He turns, then pauses. "For what it's worth, you did the right thing tonight." A silence. "But if you're doing the right thing just to prove you're not the wrong kind of person — it's still about you."

He slips into the crowd before I can respond.

I stand there awhile, staring at Grand Central lit up ahead.

Nico's father showing up to empty job sites. Still moving, as though movement could stop the fall.

My father on Court Street in Brooklyn, the particular stillness of a man who lost everything twenty years ago and has been tending the wreckage ever since.

He lost everything in 2006 — two years before Lehman gave men like him a story to tell at dinner parties. My father never had that luxury. His was already gone.

My great-grandfather built it. Big took it global. Bill couldn't keep it. His own decisions — built on the Chaffee name, dependent on it, finished when the name stopped being enough.

Big was still alive when it happened. That's the part that doesn't get said. My father didn't fail in private — he failed in front of his father, the one man whose verdict he had been building toward his entire life. And Big said nothing. Not disappointment, not consolation. Just the particular silence of someone who had seen this coming and said nothing, because nothing was left to say.

The drinking wasn't about the failure exactly. It was about what the failure meant — that he was never going to be the man his father was, and now everyone knew it.

I stand at the Grand Central entrance for a long moment. I walk past the Metro North. Greenwich.

I find the subway steps on 42nd Street and go down.

The F train runs express through the dark.

His building is simple. Four floors, brick, no doorman. The F train audible somewhere below. I watch the same black window and see the same face looking back at me. But something has changed — moved the way a room changes when you weren't watching, something you feel before you can name it.

His name on the directory in the lobby. I take the elevator to four. I knock. He answers the door in his pressed shirt — or it was pressed this morning. By ten at night the collar has gone soft. He steps back. I come in.

The years have done their work. The face I remember had edges — jaw, cheekbone, edges that suggested the world owed him something. That's gone. The drinking has redistributed itself slowly across twenty years of Court Street evenings, settling and softening everything. His hair is fully white now. He moves more carefully than he used to — not frailty, more like a man who has learned the cost of momentum and decided against it.

The apartment is exactly as it always is — immaculate, contained, the Persian rug from the Greenwich study anchoring the living room like the last piece of a life that used to be larger. The cognac sofa. The amber lamp. A glass of scotch on the side table his father has likely been drinking from since lunch.

He crosses to the bar cart, pours two fingers into a second glass, drops one ice cube, and sets it on the table across from his chair without asking whether I want it.

We sit. He settles across from me.

"How's the deal?" he says. Not looking up. The way he asks about my life — as if he already knows it's going badly and wants to hear you say it.

I tell him. The bank, the loan book, the manufactured-housing exposure. Ames's directive. What I said to Eric Lane at The Astor Bar. All of it.

He listens without interrupting. That's new.

When I finish he picks up his glass.

"You told him what made you feel clean," he says. Not unkind. Just precise.

"There's a difference between that and what he needed to know."

"He needed to know what was in that book."

"Maybe," he says. "But the deal is dead. Ames is going to come for you in the morning. Lawrence is going to blame you. And the man you told is going to use exactly what you gave him to walk away clean while you take the fall." He sets the glass down. "You chose feeling right over getting the deal closed." He shakes his head. "Pick one."

"I know."

"Do you?" He looks at me directly for the first time. "Because you came here at ten o'clock on a Tuesday night. Which means part of you thinks I'm going to tell you that you did the right thing."

I don't answer.

"I'm not going to tell you that."

The F train passes somewhere below. That particular vibration traveling up through the building.

I look at the scotch in my hand. I came here because I did something that felt true and I wanted someone to confirm it. My father is not going to confirm it.

He lifts his glass.

“The opportunity,” he says, “is what you see when you’re in the room that nobody else has seen yet. Find that. Get there first. Don’t wait for permission.”

He says it like a philosophy that should be self-evident. Like the reason everything fell apart was that he stopped believing it hard enough.

Big used to say something similar. The difference was Big had already proven it by the time he said it. Bill learned the philosophy without the track record. He inherited the words. Not the instinct. I finish the scotch. Stand. He doesn't stand with me.

"Good night," I say.

"Good night, Will."

In the elevator going down I think about what Nico said about doing the right thing and making it about me. Maybe my father and Nico are saying the same thing from opposite ends of the same corridor.

I come up out of the subway on 42nd Street. The city doing what the city does. I walk to Grand Central and find the last Metro North to

Connecticut.
    The train rocks north through the dark.

CHAPTER 3

ELEGANT ROT

From Greenwich station my Uber winds through the dark bends of Round Hill Road.

Her house. Limestone facade, the hedgerows still immaculate from the road but yellowing underneath where the gardener doesn't reach. A roof gutter pulled loose on the east side, left that way since August. The gravel drive freshly raked — appearances maintained in the places that show and quietly surrendering in the places that don't.

Elegant rot. The slow and dignified unraveling of a life built on being seen, now entering the years when being seen requires more effort and returns less.

I push the front door. It groans.

I moved back three years ago — bad breakup, job that wasn't working, the usual reasons. I told myself it was temporary. I'm still here.

Then the soft click of claws on stone. Blue pads in from the hallway, ears low, tail wagging — a large golden retriever going gray at the muzzle, with the patient eyes of a dog who has been through enough with one person to have stopped needing to be explained things. He doesn't bark. He watches, measuring which version of me came home, then positions himself against my leg.

I brought him home two years ago from a rescue in Stamford. Liz looked at him the way she looks at anything that doesn't fit the room and said absolutely not. He's been here ever since.

"Hey, bud."

He nudges my hand and trots away.

Two Oscars on the mantel — separated by sixteen years, the first when she was the discovery, the second when she was undeniable. The Leibovitz photographs still on the walls. The name still means something in certain rooms. But the rooms are smaller than they were and the calls from Marci are further apart and the scripts she's sent now are for the mother, the grandmother, the woman who knew the icon when she was young. Supporting roles. Character parts.

Liz doesn't say any of this out loud. She doesn't have to. The house says it.

From the living room, voices. Not the television — actual voices. Liz in performance mode and underneath it, quieter, the sound of someone typing.

I hear my name before I reach the doorway.

Not spoken — implied. The particular cadence Liz uses when she is building a case and the case is about me. The rising inflection on certain words. The careful deployment of pauses. I have been listening to this particular music since before I understood language and I can identify the key and tempo from forty feet away.

I go in.

Alex is directly across from her with the laptop open and her fingers not quite moving. Liz's personal assistant — six months in. She stopped typing a minute ago, I'd guess, when the subject moved from the gala to me. Her face is doing the thing I've noticed it does when she's absorbing something she hasn't yet decided what to do with. Still. Professional. Present in a way that gives nothing back.

Alex sees me come in. Liz doesn't. She is mid-sentence and

sentences, for Lizzy, are not interrupted by entrances.

"— which is exactly what I said to Marci, and Marci agrees with me, that the Sutter Rowe positioning is simply not right for someone with William's profile. You don't go to Stern and end up—"

"The Sutter Rowe thing," I say pleasantly, coming further into the room, "is called investment banking. Hi, Lizzy."

She turns. Recalibrates without missing a step. "William. You look exhausted."

"Long day." I drop into the armchair across from her, not beside her. Beside her would mean I'm joining her orbit. Across means we're having a conversation.

"What are we talking about?"

"I was just telling Alex—"

"About my career trajectory." I take a nut from the bowl. "You can say it in front of me. I'm thirty-four, not fourteen."

A flicker. She wasn't expecting directness. She recalibrates again.

"I'm simply saying that for someone with your name—"

"My name is Chaffee," I say. "Which is Dad's name. Yours is Prescott. Always has been." I say it like it's nothing. "So if we're talking about the weight of a name, yours is the one with leverage right now."

The room is very still.

Across from Liz, Alex has gone completely motionless. Her eyes have moved from Liz to me and back with the careful calibration of someone who is not going to betray attention but cannot stop paying it.

Liz opens her mouth. Closes it. I have about four seconds before she finds the response and I need to be somewhere else before she does.

"Speaking of which," I say, leaning forward slightly, elbows on knees, dropping into the register I know she responds to — warm, interested, focused entirely on her — "I saw the piece in the Times last week. The retrospective. They used a photograph from the Cannes profile."

The shift is immediate. Subtle but immediate. Her shoulders release a fraction. The cocktail glass lowers.

"That photograph," she says.

"In a retrospective piece about what the industry used to be, you were the only person who still looked like the industry needed you."

"It was a good photograph," she allows. Trying not to respond to it. Responding completely.

"It was a great photograph. And the quote they pulled — about instinct versus technique — that's the one that follows you. That's the quote people remember."

She sets her glass down. Something has happened to her posture — still perfect but different, less like a weapon and more like a woman. She is Elizabeth Prescott and someone has just reminded her of that without requiring anything from her, and the relief of it, however brief, is visible.

"Marci thought the piece undersold the early work," she says.

"Marci's protective. That's her job. But the early work doesn't need selling anymore. It's established. What that piece did was position you for what comes next." I lean back. Easy. Finished. "Which is more useful."

Liz looks at me — a real look, not a performance. The one she occasionally produces when she forgets to be Elizabeth Prescott and is briefly just my mother.

"You always know what to say," she says.

"I know what's true," I say. "It's usually the same thing."

I stand. Pick up my jacket.

"I had her hold dinner," Liz says, gesturing toward the hallway. "The housekeeper. She was hovering."

"She has a name," I say. "It's Hana." A small Filipino woman in her sixties who has been running this household longer than I can remember. She moves through the kitchen with the quiet authority of someone who has nothing to prove. She doesn't speak much. She leaves food. The food is always exactly right.

A flicker across Liz's face. She absorbs it without changing. Alex's fingers pause on the keyboard for exactly one beat. Then continue.

"The Cannes photograph," I say. "Frame it somewhere people actually see it. Not the study — the study gets no light."

I go.

I'm at the kitchen counter when I hear footsteps and Alex appears in the doorway. She has her laptop under her arm. She stops when she sees me and something moves across her face — that flicker I've been trying to read for six months, the one that gives just enough and no more.

"She's happy," Alex says. "She's going to spend the next hour telling me about Cannes."

"Good. That'll keep her busy."

Alex doesn't move, which is unusual. She is always going somewhere, always with the next task already in motion.

"Can I ask you something?" she says.

"Sure."

"How do you do that?"

I look up. "Do what?"

She gestures back toward the living room — the whole scene, the shift, the ninety seconds it took. "That. You walked in and she was—" She stops. "And then she wasn't."

"She needed to be reminded of who she is," I say. "When she's in that mode she's forgotten. You give it back to her and she stops needing to take it from somewhere else."

Alex is quiet for a moment, absorbing that.

"You've been doing that your whole life," she says. It isn't a question.

"Since I was about twelve," I say. "You learn the instrument."

She looks at me with the expression I have never been able to fully decode — making some assessment I don't have access to. Then she nods, once, and opens her laptop.

"Cannes," she says, half to herself, moving to the table. "Got it."

She sits down and starts typing and I pour a glass of water and the kitchen is quiet and something has shifted in the room in a way that neither of us mentions and both of us know.

I take my time — shower, change. An hour passes. On the way back down I slow at the landing.

The house has shifted. Liz's door is closed — she always retreats when the performance has run its course. The living room is quiet, the cocktail glass left on the side table like a prop forgotten after a scene.

Then, from somewhere toward the back of the house, music. Soft and unhurried. Something with a melody I almost recognize. I follow it.

The kitchen light is warm and low. Alex is at the counter with her laptop open — still working, always working — one earbud in, the other out, a half-eaten plate beside her. She hasn't heard me yet. She's reading something on the screen, one hand wrapped around a coffee mug, and she's humming. Barely. The shape of the melody more than the sound itself.

For a moment the house feels almost real.

I clear my throat. She looks up — half a second of surprise, then level, then a small smile.

"Hello, Will."

It's the first time all day I've heard my name without an expectation attached to it.

"Hey." I lean against the doorframe. "Don't let me interrupt."

"You're not." She closes the laptop halfway. "I was just finishing notes from your mother's session. She wants three letters drafted by morning." "She also wants me to find the cell number for the High Pond board chair so she can call him directly."

"She'll want to do that first thing."

"I know." Something changes in her expression — not quite amusement, not quite resignation — something she's chosen not to name. "I'll manage it."

That's the thing about Alex. She always manages it. She's twenty-six years old, going to law school three nights a week on top of this, building something deliberate and patient out of proximity to a woman who treats her as furniture — and she does it all without a word of complaint and without ever quite letting you see the full picture of what she's actually doing.

"You eaten?" she asks.

"Not since this morning."

She nods toward the refrigerator without looking up from her screen. "Hana left roast chicken. It's cold now but you can warm it up."

I find the plate on the second shelf, pull it out, sit back down. She doesn't make anything of it. She's already back in the laptop, cursor moving, the small sounds of someone working through something that requires real concentration.

I eat. She works.

"How bad was today?" she asks, not looking up.

"On a scale of what?"

"On a scale of you arriving home looking like you lost something expensive that may not have been yours to begin with."

I almost laugh. "That specific."

"You have a tell." She glances up briefly. "The tie. You loosen it exactly this much when things went wrong." She holds up two fingers close together. "More than that means something went catastrophically wrong. Less means you're just tired."

"Six months and you've been studying my tie."

"I study everything," she says simply. "It's the job."

We sit for a while. The house quiet around us. Outside, the trees move in the wind.

"Your mother mentioned the NYBC panel again," Alex says. NYBC — the cable business network.

"She mentions it every week."

"I know. I schedule her weeks." She lets it sit before continuing. "For what it's worth — I think she mentions it because she's proud of you. In the particular way she has of expressing pride, which is mostly indistinguishable from criticism."

I look at her. "That's a generous read."

"Maybe." She sips her coffee. "Or maybe I've just spent six months translating her." She holds my gaze a moment — steady, direct, giving nothing extra. "Either way. You should eat more."

I look down at the plate. I've eaten most of it without noticing.

The music from her phone is still playing — something slow, a particular quality that catches in my chest without me being able to name why.

"What is that?" I ask.

She glances at her phone. "Bon Iver. You know it?"

"Vaguely."

"You're an indie rock person."

I look at her. "How do you know that?"

"Your commute playlist. You leave it on your phone on the kitchen counter sometimes." She shrugs. "I wasn't snooping. It was just there."

"Use Somebody."

"Every morning, apparently."

Something in that settles somewhere I wasn't expecting. She knows the song. She knows I play it every morning. She knows it without having been told and without making it into anything — just another observation, another data point, filed away with everything else.

"There's a guitar," she says. Not pointed. Just there, in the conversation, available. "Saw it when I was looking for one of your mother's scarves she wanted to wear for an interview. Back of the hall closet."

"I know."

She waits. Doesn't push. Goes back to her laptop.

I sit for another moment. Then I stand, find the closet, find the case behind the coats and the spare linens. Dusty. Latches stiff. I carry it to the study.

The study smells like cedar and lemon polish. Late light pools across the floor in long gold strips. I sit in the old leather chair by the window, open the case, and look at it — my father's guitar, gathering dust for years in a closet nobody opened.

I pick it up.

My fingers find the chords before I tell them to. Something I wrote in college, never finished, never played for anyone. The notes spill into the quiet the way they always did — like they'd been waiting in there all this time, patient and unchanged, holding the shape of something I put down and never came back for.

I don't hear Alex come in. At some point I look up and she's in the doorway, laptop closed under her arm, shoulder against the frame. Not performing attention. Just present the way she is — steady, present, actually listening.

Blue appears from somewhere and curls at my feet. He thumps his tail once and goes still.

I play through to the end of what I have. Let the last chord hang in the room and fade.

"That was yours," Alex says.

Not a question.

"Yeah."

"You didn't finish it."

"No."

She looks at the guitar, then at me. Something moving quietly behind her eyes that she's deciding whether to say. She decides not to.

"Why'd you stop playing?" she asks instead.

I set the guitar carefully against the wall. "Someone told me it wasn't practical."

She nods slowly. Doesn't offer the reassurance I didn't ask for. Doesn't tell me I should play more, that I'm good, that it's not too late. She just receives it and holds it and says nothing, which is somehow the most respectful possible response.

"I have three letters to draft before midnight," she says finally. "And a board chair cell number to track down for your mother."

"Go," I say.

She pushes off the doorframe. Pauses.

"You should finish it someday," she says. Not insistent. Just true, stated once, left there.

Then she's gone — back down the hall, back to the work, the laptop already open before she's out of my sight.

I sit in the study with the guitar across my lap and Blue at my feet.

I put the guitar back in the corner and go.

CHAPTER 4

DAMAGE CONTROL

I wake to the smell of coffee.

Blue is at the foot of the bed watching me with the patient attention of a dog who has been awake since five. I shower, dress, come downstairs.

The kitchen is warm. Hana has been in already — scrambled eggs on the stove, plates set, coffee made. She moves quietly through the back of the house the way she always does, present without intruding.

Alex is at the table.

Laptop open, her own plate half-eaten beside it, a highlighter in one hand and a contracts textbook flat on the table. She's been here a while — longer than me, probably longer than Hana. She's in the sweatshirt she wears on early mornings, the Wesleyan one, hair pulled back. She glances up when I sit down — the small acknowledgment, professional and easy — then back to the page.

I pour a coffee, take a plate from the stove, sit across from her. Hana moves somewhere in the back. Outside the kitchen window the lawn is still gray with cold.

After a few minutes Alex closes the textbook and reaches for her coffee.

"Your mother wants to do an interview," she says. "Thursday. She's been emailing Marci about it since six."

"Marci won't let her."

"Marci is trying to make it happen." She checks her phone. "There's a journalist from The Atlantic Standard, the magazine she's been in contact with. Wants to do a piece on the house."

"The house?"

"The AmFlix role. What she's working on now. The Greenwich life as backdrop." She says it neutrally — not mocking, just reporting. "I've been pulling together some background. She had a contact in Caracas years ago, apparently. A director she worked with in the nineties. I've been trying to track down the connection for the timeline."

"Caracas," I say.

Something in my voice makes her look up.

"Have you been?" I ask.

"I grew up there." She says it the way she says most things — simply, without making it into anything. "Came here for college. Haven't been back."

"You want to?"

A moment. She considers it honestly rather than reflexively. "I grew up wanting to make it worth not going back," she says. Then she opens the laptop again.

I'll think about that. The coffee is good. The house is quiet. Hana comes back through, refills the pot without being asked, disappears again. Outside, the lawn is getting lighter.

For a few minutes it feels steady. Real in a way the rest of my life hasn't felt in longer than I want to count. Part of me wants to ask what she sees when she looks at me. The other part already knows. And isn't ready for it.

"You're going to miss the 7:04," Alex says, without looking up.

I look at the clock. She's right. I finish the coffee, leave the plate for Hana, and go.

The next train is fuller than the 7:04 — I've missed the window when people are still half-asleep. Everyone on this one is already somewhere. Someone's reading the Journal. Someone else is on a call they're pretending is private. I find a window seat in the back and let the city come at me.

My phone has a message from Ames. WHERE ARE YOU SEE ME. No punctuation. All sting.

I know what it means. He's already priced what I'll pay.

I put the phone away. Look at my reflection in the glass — blurred, not quite right, the face of someone performing composure and not quite landing it.

My roommate blasting indie rock through the walls while I sat on the dorm floor with my old Gibson, writing. Then the back room of a bookstore café in Waterville where I cut a demo — me, a four-track, a borrowed mic. I wanted to transfer to Berklee. Thought I could make people feel something for a few minutes at a time. Make music and live cheap. That was the whole dream.

I stayed. Swapped music rooms for Econ electives. Filed the demo away.

The train brakes. Grand Central. I sit until the car empties. Then I stand, jacket over my shoulder, and walk out into the city.

* * *

The floor knows. I can feel it before I clear the elevator — that particular shift in air pressure when a deal has died and nobody wants to say it first.

Daren catches my eye across the bullpen. Tilts his head toward the glass conference room at the end of the hall. I go.

Ames is inside. Standing. Jacket off. Sleeves rolled. Already positioned.

"Southeast passed," he says. No setup. Just the cut.

I nod once. "Did they say why?"

"Reputational risk in the manufactured housing segment." He goes to the window, hand on the sill. "Sound familiar?"

I don't answer.

"You want to tell me why they're using language we never put in the deck?"

"I had a drink with Eric last night. I gave him the full picture."

A pause that stretches a moment too long.

"You gave him the full picture," he repeats. "The part we chose to downplay."

"He would've found out eventually."

Ames walks toward me — not fast, but with verdict energy. "You think you're the only one who sees the risk? The rest of us don't wake up knowing exactly what we're selling?" He stops. "The difference is we know what we're here to do. You want to be clean and clever at once. Doesn't work here."

"Cherry Point is dead. Lawrence is threatening a press release. My ass is on the line with Halbridge." He picks up the deck and sets it back down. "I'm not shielding you from the fallout this time."

A moment. Then: "Halbridge likes you. So you'll survive this. But next time you want a moral epiphany, have it when there isn't a ten-million-dollar fee on the line."

He turns back to the window. Yelling would have been easier. I walk out without another word.

Ames's door closes behind me.

I stand in the hallway for a moment. The carpet. The frosted glass. The low hum of the floor doing what it does. Then I go back to my desk.

The Miami file is open where I left it. SunCoast Bank, forty-three branches, a balance sheet that tells one story and a deposit base that tells another. I have a call at eleven with their CFO. I have a deck to finish by three. I have a follow-up to send to the credit team before end of day.

I do all of it.

The eleven o'clock runs long. The CFO is cautious in the way CFOs at small regional banks are cautious — he's heard the pitch before, from someone else, and it didn't go the way that someone promised. I am patient. I am measured. I say the right things in the right order and by the time we hang up I have a second call scheduled for Thursday.

Priya stops by around two with a question about the deck. I answer it. She looks at me for a half-second longer than the question requires, then goes back to her desk.

The deck goes to the credit team at 2:58.

I eat something at my desk. I don't remember what.

By four the floor has thinned and the light through the windows has gone flat and gray and I am still at my desk reading a term sheet I have already read twice without retaining a single number. I read it a third time. The numbers stay where they are.

At five-thirty I close the file.

I pass my desk without stopping. Daren, Priya, Nico — they clock me. Nico falls in beside me in the hallway. Doesn't ask. Just matches my pace. "You owe us a drink, saint."

* * *

The Tank is a dive — cheap wood-paneled walls, the floor tacky under us, Lord Huron bleeding through the speakers. A place that forgets you the moment you leave.

Nico and I take a corner booth. Tequila for him, rye for me.

Twenty minutes in, Priya shows — work heels still on, hair down, laptop bag still over her shoulder like she walked out mid-sentence. She slides in beside me, drops the bag, orders a whiskey.

"I thought you had Miami prep," I say.

"I do." She picks up Nico's drink, takes a sip, sets it back. "Thirty slides. Talked Daren into finishing them."

Daren barrels in an hour later with a guy in a zip-up hoodie and wire rims. Startup eyes — like he's not sure this was a mistake. "Slides are done, by the way — you're welcome," he says, already moving toward the booth. "Ran into this guy outside — we play basketball on Sundays. Will, Ian Cato. Smartest guy I know who doesn't work in finance. Yet."

Ian offers a quick handshake. "Heard you're the guy to talk to if you want something taken seriously."

"Define seriously," I say.

He grins, loosening up. "This place some kind of underground club for investment bankers?"

Nico: "More like rehab than a club."

Priya lifts her glass. "Step one — admit you hate your job."

Ian laughs and slides in. "Seems like you're skipping straight to step twelve."

I catch the bartender's eye. Five shots land on the table.

"To survival," I say.

Nico clinks. "Selective memory."

Priya: "And whatever comes next."

Daren lifts his last. "To the ones who still show up."

We drink. The burn is sharp.

"Let's see if we can ruin your life with ambition," I say to Ian.

Daren waves the bartender back over. Another round arrives. The air eases. We trade the usual late-night survivor talk — office politics, bad coffee, the standard decompression. Then somewhere after the first beer Ian leans forward.

"I actually built something," he says. "Not sure what to do with it. Daren said you might help."

He pulls a folded notepad from his jacket. "A payments platform. Skips traditional rails. Targets underbanked users. Distributed identity verification — blockchain architecture without the crypto noise."

He starts explaining — slow at first, then faster as the spark catches. Smart. Maybe brilliant. I listen. Nico watches. Priya rests her glass against her cheek.

"So you basically built another Tap."

Ian shakes his head. "Tap serves merchants. Optimizes interchange for the seller. This serves the person on the other side — the one the system was never built for. We don't charge people for moving their own money. We make money the way a bank should — a share of the interest on savings balances, a cut when someone qualifies for a better loan than they could get anywhere else. The healthier they get, the more they save, the more they need from us. Different incentive. Different bet."

I file that away. It's a real answer, not a pitch.

Daren orders another round. Then — of course — leans back. "Okay. Truth time. If you were a tree, what tree would you be?"

Priya groans. "No."

"I'm serious," Daren says. "No metaphors. Just tree vibes."

"Palm tree," he starts. "Lazy man's tree. Always looks like it's on vacation."

Priya: "White oak. Stubborn and solid. Takes forever to fall."

Nico, eyes down: "Baobab."

Daren squints. "What the hell's a baobab?"

"Stores water. Hard to kill. Never needs permission to be what it is."

Ian fidgets. "Japanese maple. Not the biggest, not the flashiest. But beautiful if you look close."

They look at me. I finish my drink. Think too long. "Sycamore. Messy. Doesn't know what to do with itself half the time. Used to be something. Still stands tall, even though it doesn't know why anymore."

Silence. Not awkward. Transparent.

"You said you built this thing," I say.

He nods. "Started in college. Side project. My mom runs a laundromat in Crown Heights. No bank account. Never trusted the system. I was trying to make something that worked for people like her." His leg bounces. "If it worked for her, maybe it could work for others." His voice drops slightly — like he's not sure anyone believes that anymore.

He's not pitching. It's much more personal than that.

"Where'd you go to school?" I ask.

"Cooper Union. Engineering. Paid my way tutoring stats and writing code for people with better résumés."

I raise my glass. "To making things that matter to someone."

He grins. "And finding someone dumb enough to believe in them."

We drink. Long after the night dissolves — laughter, cab searches, half-meant promises — I'm still thinking about what Ian said. Not the tech. The reason he couldn't let it go.

* * *

The last Metro North north is half-empty. I find a window seat and watch the city thin out — lights giving way to dark, the suburbs arriving in stages. Someone two rows up is already asleep against the glass.

Ian's voice running underneath the train noise. My mom runs a laundromat in Crown Heights. It worked for her, it could work for others.

I think about that. The specificity of it. Not the market, not the addressable users, not the TAM. One woman in Crown Heights who doesn't trust the system. That's where he started.

The train pulls into Greenwich at twelve forty. My Uber makes its way through the dark — Round Hill Road quiet, the hedgerows black against the sky.

The house is still. Liz's door closed. Blue meets me in the hall, tail steady, and follows me upstairs.

The guitar case is on the floor by the desk where I left it. I sit on the edge of the bed and look at it for a while. The latches still stiff. The dust still there from the hall closet. I open it. The guitar is exactly as it was — my father's Martin, older now, strings dull from years in a closet. I tune it by ear the way I always did. It takes longer than it should. I play for a while. Nothing finished. The melody I started at Colby and never completed, the one that surfaces sometimes without warning. The last time I played it someone was in the doorway. Tonight there's no one. Blue stays at my feet, tail lifting once, then still. The house doesn't stir. Liz's door stays closed.

Nobody needs anything from me right now. Ian's leg bouncing under the bar table. The particular energy of someone who built something because he had no choice. I used to know what that felt like. I play until my fingers remember where they are. Then I set the guitar against the wall and lie back.

I go straight to 22. Blinds closed. A thin stripe of light across the floor. Ames sits behind his desk — immaculate, still — like he's been waiting. "Close the door." I do. He keeps his eyes on the screen. A minute passes. Maybe two. He slides the deck across the desk. Our deck. The Cherry Point deck. That's all he gives me. "I went too far," I say. "I'll recover on the Miami deal—" He raises a hand. "A total lapse of sound principles," he says. "You stepped outside the lane we operate in. Halbridge is demanding action." "I'll make it up on SunCoast—" "That's not going to cut it. He wants blood and it isn't going to be mine." He leans back, fingers steepled. "We're also taking your VP title. Effective today you're back to Senior Associate." For a second, everything lists a few degrees off center. I bend forward in the chair. Pull myself back up. "Come on, Phil. I've poured everything into this place. One mistake—" "We're limiting the damage," he says. "You know we can't let a stunt like this slide." Silence. He nods at his desk. Meeting over. "Anything else?" I ask. Voice level. "Close the door on your way out." The click behind me is louder than it should be. I stand in the hallway. The bullpen hum rolls back in around me. Everyone else keeps moving. I'm the only one standing still. I walk down the hall. Southeast was never really buying. The numbers never lined up. Priya raised the same concerns. By the end of the hall, the weight has doubled.

Then Halbridge steps from a glass-walled room. He spots me. He nods once, the way senior partners nod when they have already moved on to the next thing, and continues down the corridor.

I leave the building without a word. I don't head home. I don't check my phone. I walk. Fifth Avenue looks painfully composed for a day like this. Wind off the park, sharp and directionless. I follow the sidewalk north, past the storefronts and the tourists, the midday city indifferent. I call him before I decide not to.

It rings three times. He picks up on the fourth ring. Waiting, as always, without wanting you to know it.

"Will."

"Hey, Dad." I keep walking. "They took the title. Effective today. Back to Senior Associate."

A pause. Not the pause of a man processing bad news. He already knows what I did — I told him three nights ago in his Brooklyn apartment. This is the pause of a man tallying the damage.

"They demoted you," he says.

Not — are you okay. Not — I'm sorry. Just that.

"Senior Associate. Reporting to someone who was beneath me six months ago. Ames made sure everyone on the floor knew by noon."

"You did this to yourself," he says. The way he used to say things when I was sixteen and had said something he considered foolish. Not angry. Beyond angry. Tired of a son who kept misunderstanding the basic rules. "Will. You knew what would happen."

"I know."

"You're in the business of moving capital. Not saving people from decisions they were going to make anyway." The ice clicks in his glass — even now, even at this hour. "You want to do good in the world, you do it with the money you've made. You don't do it on Sutter Rowe's dime."

I don't answer.

"Senior Associate," he says. The words flat and specific. "That's a significant step back."

"I know."

"Do you?" His voice shifts — not warmer, just more deliberate. "Because I'm not sure you do. I'm not sure you understand what you've actually lost here. Not just the title. The positioning. The trajectory. The years it took to build that and the months it will take to rebuild it if you're lucky." Another pause. "If they keep you at all."

The park entrance is ahead of me. I stop at the corner and let a cab pass.

"I hear you," I say.

"I don't think you do," he says. "I think you feel righteous about it. And that's the most dangerous thing you can be in this business. Righteous and broke look the same from the outside."

He hangs up before I say anything else. No goodbye. Just the click, then the city noise rushing back in.

The park entrance. Wind off the reservoir finding the gaps in my jacket.

I called him because some part of me thought — what? That this time would be different. That he would say something that sounded like a father talking to his son rather than a man explaining the rules of a game to someone who keeps losing.

It wasn't different. It never is.

I go into the park.

Bare branches, the reservoir catching the low sun. A cellist plays near Bethesda — notes hollow and measured, the right sound for the wrong day. I find a bench and sit.

I sit. I don't move. I don't think.

I used to come here after finals at Stern — walk the loop with earbuds in and try to feel like myself again. I remember the sensation of it, the specific quality of that relief, but I can't locate it today. The same trees. Different weight.

The sun is low when I finally stand.

I head south. Back toward the train. Back toward Greenwich.

CHAPTER 5

SOMETHING THAT BREATHES

I wake up early. The house is still — Liz's door closed, the hallway dark, Blue a warm weight at the foot of the bed. Outside, the lawn is covered with frost.

I lie there for a while with the ceiling and the quiet and the specific feeling of a day that hasn't started yet. Senior Associate. I've been saying it to myself since yesterday, testing the weight of it. It doesn't get lighter.

I shower. Find coffee. Hana has been in already — the pot warm, the kitchen set. I stand at the window with the mug and watch the frost on the grass catch the early light.

By the time Liz surfaces I'm two cups in and dressed. She moves through the kitchen in her robe without looking at me, which is its own kind of communication. I don't push it.

Alex comes downstairs at nine, already on a call. She gives me a small nod crossing to the study. Professional. Whatever yesterday was, today she has work to do.

It's Saturday. The day has the particular quality of a weekend in this house — slower, less purposeful, Liz's schedule loosened but not gone. She has a lunch she comes back from quieter than she left. Alex works anyway.

She always works on weekends.

By late afternoon, the house had changed.

I hear it. Not shouting — Lizzy doesn't shout. That would be beneath her, and besides, volume was never the point. What I hear is the particular register of her voice when she has decided to be surgical. Low. Controlled. The voice that says I am not angry, I am simply telling you the truth, and if the truth hurts that is not my problem.

I push the door open.

Alex is standing in the center of the room with her laptop against her chest like a shield, and her face is doing something I have never seen it do in six months — it has gone very still and very careful in the way of someone who is deciding, in real time, whether to stay or leave or say the thing that would end this conversation permanently.

Liz is on the chaise. She hasn't moved. She has the posture of someone who believes the geography of a room is a form of argument.

"—which is exactly what I mean," she is saying. "You had one call to make, Alex. One confirmation. Marci caught it — barely — or we would have had cameras at the house yesterday for a live interview no one knew was canceled. And honestly, this is not the first time I've had to wonder about your judgment. Because I know that wasn't something required in the career you had before you came to work for me."

Alex sees me in the doorway.

She makes a face that's not quite relief, more like someone caught being hurt and wanting to hide it. She closes it down immediately. Professional. Practiced. Then she says, quietly, "Excuse me," and walks toward the door and past me and I step aside and she is gone down the hallway before I can say anything.

Then I close the door and turn around.

Liz is already reaching for her cocktail. She takes a sip with the composure of someone who has concluded a difficult but necessary conversation and is now moving on.

"What did you just do?" I say.

She looks up. Mild surprise. "I'm sorry?"

"I heard the end of that. What did you say to her?"

"I was addressing a professional matter," she says. "Which is none of your—"

"She's been here over six months," I say. "She runs your life. She does it well." I stop.

"I know that voice, Lizzy. I grew up with that voice. Whatever just happened in here — what was it?"

She turns to face me. "She failed to confirm a cancellation with Marci. A talk show conflict that could have been avoided. It made me look sloppy. Like I have a rookie running my schedule."

"So you addressed it."

"I was being honest with her. The entertainment industry is not forgiving. I told her she was lucky to have this opportunity — that not everyone would have taken a chance on someone with her background."

"Her background?" I say.

"She worked in clubs before this. Cocktail waitress. Other things." Liz picks up her glass again. "She told me. I think she thought it made her seem resilient. I simply reminded her that not everyone in this industry would see it that way."

"You were using it," I say. "She told you about herself — something she worked hard to get past — and the moment she made a mistake you handed it back to her as a disqualification." I look at her.

"You've done this before. You did it to Dad. You did it to me. You find the thing a person is most privately proud of surviving and you make it sound like proof they don't belong."

The room is very quiet.

Liz sips her cocktail.

"I was preparing her for how this industry works," she says finally.

"You were protecting yourself," I say. "Because she's better at this than you expected and it unsettles you. That's all this was."

I don't wait for the response. I open the door and go.

She's not in the kitchen.

I check the hallway, the small office off the back where she sometimes works late. Then I see the terrace door slightly ajar, cold air coming through the gap, and I go out.

She's at the far end of the terrace — the garden side, the stone balustrade with the lawn dropping away into the dark below — with her arms wrapped around herself and her laptop set down on the stone beside her. Her breath comes white in the cold. She hasn't heard me yet.

I stand there for a moment. I know this spot. I know what it is to stand at the edge of a terrace in this house and breathe cold air and try to decide what to do with something Liz just put inside you.

I go back inside and come back with two glasses of wine and a coat from the hook by the kitchen door.

She turns when she hears me. Looks at the coat. Looks at the glasses.

"You didn't have to—"

"I know," I say.

I set the glasses on the balustrade and hold the coat out. She takes it without arguing, which tells me something. Alex doesn't accept things easily. She puts it on and wraps it around herself and picks up one of the glasses and we stand there looking out at the lawn. The light is going — that particular Saturday evening quality, the sky still holding color at the edges.

"I should have confirmed the cancellation with Marci," she says finally.

"Yes."

"I assumed. I shouldn't have assumed."

"No."

She looks at me. Expecting something softer. I don't give it to her.

"That's the mistake," I say. "One mistake. What she did with it has nothing to do with the mistake."

Alex says nothing. Her jaw is set in the specific way of someone who has been crying and is finished and is not going to discuss it.

"She told me I was lucky," Alex says. "That not everyone in this industry would take a chance on someone who —" She stops. Looks at the lawn. "I danced in clubs for two years when I first came here. Before Wesleyan. I told her that. I thought we were having a moment."

"She used the word resilient. Like she was complimenting me."

"You were," I say. "She was too. That doesn't mean she won't use it. Those things aren't mutually exclusive with her."

Alex considers that. Files it.

"How do you live with that?" she asks.

"You stop trusting the moments," I say. "You let yourself have them and then you don't give them any weight. You enjoy them for what they are and you don't build anything on top of them."

She tilts her head. "That sounds exhausting."

"It is."

Silence. Below us the lawn is dark and still. Somewhere across the property a branch moves in the wind.

"She said she'd be a bad reference," Alex says. "She said don't count on her to pave the way."

"She won't follow through on that."

"How do you know?"

"Because she needs you more than you need her and she knows it. The threat is the control mechanism. It only has power if you hand it power."

Alex turns to look at me directly. Something has changed in her face — the professional composure is still there but there's something behind it now, some calculation running, some reassessment.

"You know her very well," she says.

"I've had thirty-four years."

"Is it always like this?"

I think about New Year's Eve 2008. The terrace. My father's fist. Liz across the room not looking toward the doors. "Not always," I say.

"Sometimes it's different."

She absorbs that. Doesn't push.

We stand there in the cold for a while longer. The glasses are nearly empty.

"I need your help," Alex says.

Not a request. A statement of fact, delivered with the directness of someone who has weighed it and decided.

"With her," she says. "I need to understand how to manage her well enough to stay in this position for another eighteen months without —"she gestures back toward the house, toward what just happened, "—without that. I have a plan and I need this job to execute it. I'm not walking away and I'm not letting her do that again."

I look at her. In the cold, in the dark, with the borrowed coat and the near-empty glass and the jaw still set from whatever happened in that room, she is one of the most determined people I have encountered in a life full of determined people.

"Okay," I say.

"Okay?"

"I'll tell you what I know. It's not a short conversation."

She nods. Looks back at the lawn. "I have time," she says. "I have three letters to draft and a casebook chapter to read before midnight. But I have time."

Something in the way she says it — the complete matter-of-factness of it, the total absence of self-pity — does something I wasn't expecting.

"Start with the scheduling thing," I say. "That specific thing. I'll show you how to make sure it never happens again in a way she'll believe was her idea."

Alex almost smiles. "That's very specific."

"She needs to believe everything was her idea," I say. "That's the whole map."

She picks up her laptop from the balustrade and holds it against her chest again — not as a shield this time, something different. Then she gives me the expression I can't figure out.

"Thank you," she says. And means it. And goes inside.

I stand on the terrace a little longer. The cold is extraordinary. The lawn is dark. The house behind me glows with all its expensive lights, its fraying edges, its doors that close when things go wrong.

I pick up both glasses and go in.

* * *

The week passes the way demotions do — in the small details. Priya runs the Miami call and I'm on it but not leading it. She's good. Clear, surgical, no wasted motion. I find myself listening more than talking, which is new.

Daren slides a revised sensitivity analysis across my desk on Wednesday afternoon without comment. I look up. He's already back at his screen. No ceremony. Just the work continuing.

Nico stops by once. Leans in the doorway. "You eating?" he asks.

"When I remember to."

He nods. Leaves. That's the whole conversation.

I think about Ian more than I should. The notepad. The laundromat on Nostrand Avenue. The specific way he said if it worked for her, maybe it could work for others — not as a pitch line but as something he'd been carrying a long time and had finally set down on a table.

By Thursday the floor has found its new normal. So have I. Mostly.

Thursday. Conference room B sits off the main floor — glass walls, long table, the faint smell of burned coffee and dry-erase markers. Zack's already there. Jacket off. Sleeves rolled. Standing, not sitting — a small courtesy that feels intentional.

"So," he says. "You're reporting to Priya."

I nod. No defense. No explanation.

He exhales through his nose. "Tough seat. She's sharp. Also very careful about whose mistakes she owns."

"Look," he says. "These things happen when a firm needs to signal control. You became available." He lets that sit. "You've got two choices.

Ride it out. Play supportive lieutenant. Hope it resets." Marcus exhales. "Or you don't."

He slides a single-page brief across the desk. Clean. Hard problems. Real leverage.

"Come over to my team. You and me — we'd be lethal."

"That's not subtle," I say.

"Neither was the demotion."

I skim the page. Serious work. The kind that doesn't get applauded but decides outcomes.

"And the catch?"

"You stop caring how things look," he says. "You stop explaining yourself. You let the results speak — even when they're ugly."

"And if they're wrong?"

"They won't be." A silence. "Not if you listen."

I slide the paper back.

"I appreciate the offer."

Zack's eyebrow lifts. "That's not an answer."

"It is. Just not the one you want."

"Why?" he asks. No edge. Genuine curiosity.

"Because if I do this," I say, "I won't just be opting out of reporting to Priya. I'll be opting into becoming you."

Zack studies me. Then nods once. "That's usually how opportunities work."

I stand. At the door he adds quietly: "People who pass on protection usually regret it."

"Maybe," I say. "But at least I'll know what I'm exposed to."

For a moment — just one — respect crosses his face briefly. Then it's gone.

* * *

Nico falls in beside me through the revolving doors without asking. We head south toward Grand Central, our unspoken escape route. Midtown noise folds around us.

"You alright?" he asks eventually.

"Sure." Then: "You ever sail?"

He looks at me like I just switched languages. "Closest I got was a busted ferry to Staten Island."

"My father had an old sloop. Thirty-eight feet. Halcyon. Teak deck, brass winches, smelled like salt and canvas. He'd take me and my buddy Q out when it was warm enough — cast off before sunrise, stay out for days. No pressure. Just wind and the boat and the steady rhythm under us."

"Sounds like a vibe."

"He'd chart while I sat the tiller. Q would lie on the bow yelling about pirates on the horizon." I watch a cab run a light. "I don't remember what we talked about. Mostly we didn't. We were just ourselves out there."

I smile. "Being unneeded, but wanted."

Nico nods.

"We'd end at Block Island. Quiet coves, slow days, nights under the stars. No cell service. No noise. Q's grandfather tapped his dad to oversee their West Coast investments. My dad drank more. We stopped going."

Nico lets it hang.

"What happened to the boat?" he asks.

"She took it in the divorce," I say. "Liz. Not because she wanted it — because it would cut him deep. Then she sold it. Said it smelled like mildew and failure."

"Christ."

I smile. "Bought it back with my first big payout. It's down at the club."

"Sentimental and expensive," Nico says. "Bold."

We stop at Grand Central. People split around us like current around stones.

"The times I felt most like myself were never the ones I chased," I say.

Nico nods. Lets the quiet settle. Then: "So what are you going to do?"

I look across the avenue. "Something that breathes," I say.

He doesn't ask what that means. We stand there a moment longer. Then he heads downtown and I find the stairs to the Metro North.

CHAPTER 6

GOD'S GLITTER

Back in Greenwich the house is silent — except for sporting dogs barking somewhere far off, a backcountry echo. Blue lifts his head when I come in, then drops it with a sigh.

Liz is in the sitting room. Alone. Hands empty, face bare. Staring at an old photo on the mantle like it might say something new.

"You okay?" I ask from the doorway.

She doesn't turn. "I didn't hear you arrive. Please tell me you didn't walk from the station."

"Uber."

She looks over. Her eyes are clearer than I'm used to — tiredness showing through. The armor she wears in every other room isn't here tonight. I don't know if she forgot it or left it on purpose.

"We almost named you Samuel," she says quietly.

That catches me.

She sits by the fireplace, studying the picture. "Your father never liked his own name. Said William sounded too much like a question."

I wait.

"I didn't know," I say.

She exhales softly — almost a laugh. "Of course not. He told me in a rare unvarnished moment. Said Samuel belonged to a man who'd made his peace. William, to someone still looking for the right to be himself." She sets the photo down gently. "I like William, though. It suits you." She says it the way you'd say something true that cost you nothing and everything at the same time.

"Safer that way," I say. She doesn't deny it.

She studies me until I feel seen instead of managed.

"You look like your grandfather when you walk into a room and pretend not to care," she says.

She pauses. Something shifts in her face — not grief, but rather the specific look of someone who has been carrying this a long time. "You were always more his than Bill's," she says. "He chose you. Deliberately. And Bill has always known it."

She looks at me directly. "It wasn't fair to either of you. But especially not to Bill."

I don't answer. There's nothing to say that wouldn't make it smaller than it is.

She looks past me. "Big was iron," she says. "Bill was something softer that kept trying to be iron and couldn't sustain it. He was emotional. That was his problem — not that he cared, but that he couldn't manage what he felt."

"He was still trying," I say. "Even at the end. Even when it was too late."

"I know," she says. Not gently. Just honestly. "That was the hardest part to watch."

Her eyes flicker — surprise, or grief she hasn't touched in years.

"I just—" I go on, because stopping feels worse. "I could never tell which version of me you were waiting for. A version like him? Or one that would save me from what he became."

She looks away — out the window, toward a yard that isn't as perfect as it used to be.

"And?" she asks, voice low.

"And I couldn't do both," I say. "I couldn't hold his breaking and your expectations at the same time. I wasn't strong enough for that."

For the first time in my life, she doesn't correct me. Doesn't deflect. Doesn't tighten her jaw into the Prescott mask.

Instead she exhales — small, shaky, almost human.

"I didn't know what to do with either of you," she whispers. "Your father or you."

I stand near the window. The garden's gone to shadow, hedges dissolving into night.

“Do you remember when he had this house built? When we moved here from New Canaan? The evenings on the terrace. The way the lawn sloped down to the tree line.”

A smile ghosts her mouth. “Of course. Romantic.”

“Was it?”

Her smile holds. Her eyes don’t.

“You and Dad used to sit out there at night with cocktails. Music. Fireflies. Picture-perfect, at least from a distance.”

She breathes out — half laugh, half sigh. “I remember.” “They always ended the same though.” “Did they?”

“Too many martinis. Fights about money. Him losing it. You spending it. He’d snap. Sometimes violent. You’d go in. He’d stay out there, alone in the dark, pouring another.” She blinks. Slow.

“I used to watch from the window,” I say. “He’d just sit. Not moving. Staring into the dark like he was waiting for something to come out of it.”

A long quiet breath. We wait in it.

Then, barely above a whisper: "He always needed a fire to stand in."

I swallow. "And you—"

The rest catches in my throat. I try again.

"I used to hope he'd stay out there all night. So I could sleep."

Liz's face shifts — just enough to show she heard the fear under it.

I take a breath. "Did he ever—?" I stop. "With you."

The question hangs there. Incomplete on purpose. Both of us knowing exactly what I mean.

Liz looks away — toward the window, toward nothing.

Her silence is an answer I can't quite name.

"Some things," she says finally, "you learn to live around."

Just that. Not a defense. Not an indictment. The answer of a woman who managed and survived and never named it.

I sit on the arm of the chair across from her. Quiet.

She turns back, something gentler breaking through the surface. "You're not your father," she says. "You carry things he couldn't. You always have."

No performance. No jab.

I nod, not trusting my voice.

The room settles around us.

I start for the doorway. Halfway there, she speaks again. Smaller. "Those nights—" I stop.

"I watched him too. From upstairs. I just didn't know what to do anymore."

I let the words land.

"None of us did," I say.

I was sixteen. Maybe seventeen. The years blur at the edges.

We were stretched out on the lawn, backs against the steps, the house glowing faint behind us. Inside, my parents were having their usual evening cocktails — voices drifting through open doors, ice clinking, words rising just a shade too loud. The kind of noise that doesn't hold. Q was beside me, knees pulled up, grinning at nothing. We'd been working through a joint the way we always did when the house got loud.

"You see that?" he said, pointing. Fireflies blinked on across the grass. Not all at once. One here. One there. Like the night couldn't decide where to start.

He laughed — too loud — then caught himself. "Shit," he

whispered, clapping a hand over his mouth. “Sorry.”

I tried to focus on one. Just one. But every time I did, another flickered somewhere else, pulling my eyes away.

“You ever notice,” he said, squinting, “they don’t stay put?”

I nodded like this mattered. Maybe it did.

I cupped my hands around one when it flashed close. Felt the warmth of my own breath trapped inside. For a second, there’s light — then nothing.

I opened my hands.

Gone.

“You kill it?” Q asked.

“No,” I said. “I don’t think so.”

He grinned. “Figures.”

For a moment everything feels lighter than it should. Then just as fast, that feeling slips. The lawn is still the lawn. The house is still loud. The light keeps blinking on and off, indifferent.

Another memory drops in. Older. Cleaner.

The Berkshires. Big, Q, and me. I was maybe twelve — old enough to feel the weight of being included, young enough not to know why it mattered.

Big had driven us up himself. No driver. Just the three of us in his old Land Cruiser, gas station sandwiches, Big humming a tune he couldn't name. We set up camp badly — the tent half-collapsed before he showed us how the stakes actually worked. He laughed watching us. Not at us. With us. There's a difference and he was one of the few people I knew who understood it.

That night we laid on our backs in the grass, the three of us, the stars and the pines holding the sky.

"God's glitter," Big said.

Q snorted. I smiled. The kind of thing a man says when he has stopped needing to sound impressive.

He passed me a Coke like it was contraband. Handed Q a

marshmallow with a wink. The fire had gone low and none of us moved to build it back up. We were just there — no house, no party, no performance. No one in that field was failing anyone else.

Big didn't say anything about my father that night. He didn't have to. The absence of it was its own kind of statement.

I fell asleep to the fire and his low voice talking to Q about things I couldn't follow and didn't need to.

I have never told anyone about that night. Not because it was private — because some things stay clean by staying unspoken. But somewhere in the Berkshires there is a field where for one night nothing needed to be fixed or proven or survived.

The morning feels staged.

I come down the stairs in gym shorts and a half-zipped hoodie, earbuds in. Blue pads out from the kitchen, tail swishing like we're headed somewhere that matters.

Sun spills through the leaded glass like it forgot where it was. The dining room smells faintly of coffee and stale Shalimar. Liz is already seated — magazine in one hand, espresso in the other, robe knotted tight like she's bracing for combat.

I pull out my earbuds.

"I sent Hana to the market on Putnam," she says, as if there's only one. "They carry the white asparagus, thank goodness."

I grab a banana from the silver bowl and head for the door.

"Where are you off to?" she asks, too casually.

"Gym."

Liz studies me. "You know, High Pond has an excellent new trainer. You should make better use of your privileges."

"Too many rules. the Y has what I need."

"Everything except the right people." She looks at me over the magazine. "You're a member at High Pond, William. They expect you to be visible."

"They'll have to adjust their expectations."

She sets the magazine down — slow, deliberate. "When your father joined, it meant something. The waiting list was six years."

"Yeah. And they blackballed him from the finance committee when he was at his lowest."

Liz waves it off. "That was ancient history. The club is one of the few things in this town that hasn't turned into a yoga retreat."

It's too early to take her on. I sit across from her. She turns to the window, studies me.

"Everyone's meeting this afternoon for tennis and cocktails. You should come. It'll be good to be seen."

"Seen by who?"

"Oh, you know. The Chases, the Hardings, that new couple who bought the Irving's place. You'll play a few sets, have a drink, make an impression."

I lean against the cabinet. "You want me to come play social doubles with your friends?" "If it helps, bring someone along," she says, smoothing her napkin. "Just — please — don't bring one of your drunken rowing friends."

"You think that's my social circle?" Her look sharpens. "I think you could do better than pretending you're still one of them." Then, softer: "Please try and dress like you care. Everyone remembers your Brunswick days."

They do. I was captain. We beat Hotchkiss in the New England Prep finals. Twelve wins, one loss, first singles. Liz in the front row for every match, sunglasses on, smile rehearsed. She didn't love the sport — she loved the applause. I was proof the Chaffees could still produce someone polished.

That season bought me a kind of grace in her world. Just enough to spend the next decade losing it.

She folds her napkin. "Four o'clock. Don't be late."

* * *

Alex is already outside when I get to the Y — lacing up on the front steps, headed out. I fall in beside her without asking.

It's cold enough that our breath shows between us, but not enough to keep us inside. Mason Street runs quiet through downtown, last patches of snow clinging to stone walls. Gravel crunches under our shoes.

Alex runs beside me, sleeves pulled over her hands, breath steady. She doesn't seem to notice the cold. She runs like someone who has done this her whole life — not as exercise but as oxygen.

"You run a lot?" I ask.

"When I can." She glances over. "My brothers and I used to race on the beach back home. There was a park nearby — volleyball, soccer, anything that kept us moving."

"Caracas."

"You remember," she says, smiling faintly. "We didn't have much. Just the noise of the city and the noise of people who cared."

I match her stride.

I think about Liz at the High Pond terrace this afternoon. The careful smiles, the managed impressions, the performance she's been perfecting for forty years. Then I think about Alex beside her and almost smile.

"Hey," I say. "You ever play tennis?"

"A little," she says, in the vague way that hides a truth.

"Come with me today. Liz's doing one of her tennis and cocktails events. It's a show worth watching."

She laughs — low and genuine. "I don't think your mother and her friends are looking for someone like me on the guest list."

"We'll see. I could use a friendly face."

Alex's eyes narrow just enough to make me wonder what I've signed up for. "Careful," she says. "My serve is more impressive than my smile."

"That's a dangerous line."

"I figured." She picks up her pace. "That's why it'll be fun."

She surges ahead, gravel scattering under her shoes. For a moment I just watch — the way she moves, certain and loose, like someone who doesn't need an invitation to belong anywhere.

When I finally catch up, I'm the one out of breath.

By afternoon the High Pond Club hums with late-winter restraint — too cold for real tennis but too proud for silence. The courts are damp clay, raked and waiting for spring. White fences, hedges just starting to green, the faint sound of approval in every laugh.

Liz is on the terrace wrapped in a cream shawl, martini catching the pale sun. Around her, people talk in low approving tones — the voices, the scent, the quiet ranking system that has never changed and never will.

When she spots us walking up the path her smile tightens like a stitch pulled too far.

"How charming," she says. "You've brought... help."

"She's playing," I say.

Something flickers behind her eyes — surprise, then calculation. "Oh," she says. "How... fun."

The first few rallies feel ceremonial. Cold air, soft thud of ball on strings, breath showing. Alex moves well — too well. Balanced, patient, reading everything.

By the third rally I realize I'm not warming up. I'm being studied.

A few members wander closer, coffees steaming in gloved hands. Someone remembers I captained Brunswick's state championship team, that I made semis at NESCACs before spreadsheets replaced scorecards. I can hear the murmurs — nostalgia tinted with curiosity.

Then Alex slides forward and drops a forehand crosscourt that kisses the damp baseline. Clean. Precise.

"Nice shot," I say.

"Just finding my rhythm," she says, smiling through her breath.

The small crowd chuckles — half amusement, half disbelief.

Her next serve breaks wide with heavy spin. I reach late. Forty-fifteen. She paints the corner again. Game.

By the third set she's taking me apart — angles I don't see coming, touch that's almost casual, control that never wavers. Her focus is pure calm. Mine is performance fraying at the edges. A few of Liz's friends in cashmere lean forward on the terrace, whispering.

"Remind me — isn't that your assistant? She's quite good," one comments.

Liz stirs her drink. Doesn't answer.

When it's over I'm bent over my knees, laughing through the burn. Alex's breath fogs once, steady.

"Good match," she says.

"Define good."

"You play like someone afraid to lose," she says.

"And you play to win."

She shrugs. "My father said everyone should learn at least one beautiful thing. For me, it was this."

Up on the terrace Liz claps once — sharp, brittle. "Well," she says. "How unexpected."

Alex smiles, warm and unbothered. "Thank you, ma'am."

The small crowd disperses. Liz lingers, watching the lines on the court like she's reading bad news.

As we walk off, clay dust on our shoes, Alex bumps my shoulder.

"You really were captain?"

"Yeah."

"Guess titles don't help much once the game starts."

I laugh — the sound cutting through the cold.

For a moment the noise of the club falls away. Just the two of us, side by side, breath rising.

Liz approaches. She offers a tight smile — the kind meant for cameras that aren't there. "Well," she says, brushing invisible lint from her sleeve, "that was... spirited."

"Thank you for hosting," Alex says. Still calm. Still gracious.

Liz's smile doesn't reach her eyes. "Of course, dear. William, do see our guest out? I'm staying for a drink."

Translation: don't come back inside until she's gone.

"Sure," I say.

Alex holds her expression.

I've seen Alex do this before — receive what Liz intended as a small wound and simply not bleed. Most people flinch. They recalibrate. They look for the exit. Alex just takes it in and sets it down somewhere the room can't see, and by the time she looks up she's already past it. It's the kind of self-possession you don't learn. You either have it or you perform it, and performance always shows around the edges.

Alex has it clean through.

Outside the wind is sharper now, carrying that damp coastal cold that seeps through wool. The parking lot is half-empty, hedges brittle with frost.

"I didn't mean to make it awkward," Alex says as we reach the cars.

"You didn't," I say. "You were perfect. That's what made it awkward."

She laughs, breath fogging.

"You're not used to losing, are you?"

"Not really. Not when my mother's watching."

We stop beside her old sedan — the kind that looks out of place against a row of Range Rovers and Jaguars. She opens the door, then pauses.

"I'm sorry if that—"

"Don't be," I say. "You didn't just beat me. You reset the whole damn club."

Her smile softens. "Then maybe it needed resetting."

She gets in, starts the engine, heater coughing to life. I stand there longer than I should, watching her taillights disappear past the frozen hedges.

* * *

Later that night the house has gone still. No chatter. No roles to play. Just the low hum of the old Sub-Zero and the soft patter of light rain against the windows — steady, almost shy.

A breeze slips through the cracked window above the sink, carrying in the smell of wet leaves and cold stone.

Alex is in the kitchen, barefoot, wearing one of my sweatshirts over her tennis clothes — she must have grabbed it off the hook by the back door. She's at the table with the laptop open and a coffee going cold beside it — the contracts textbook closed for once, something different on the screen, the posture of someone working through a thought rather than a problem. The rain ticking lightly on the copper gutters outside. Blue is curled on the rug, tail lifting once when he hears me, then dropping.

"Can't sleep?" I ask.

"Not after that look your mother gave me."

I laugh quietly. "She'll find another target by morning."

"Maybe. But that was worth it."

Hana has left rice and braised ribs on the stove — she always leaves food. I find a pan, warm it properly, find two plates. I slide one in front of Alex without asking and sit down across from her. She looks at the plate, then at me. Then she closes the laptop.

The lights are low — just the under-cabinet glow, soft gold. The rain steady on the gutters outside.

"You ever think," I say, "how crazy it is that the most honest moment of my week happened at Liz's uptight club?"

She looks up. "You weren't pretending out there."

"Neither were you."

"I used to play for control," I admit. "Now I don't know what I'm trying to win."

Alex sets her plate down. "Maybe it's not about winning."

She steps closer, the air between us quiet but charged.

"Maybe it's about remembering you're still allowed to feel something honest."

I reach up, brushing a smudge from her cheek — not flour, just the impulse to touch her face, finally, after months of not.

"You're good at reminding me."

"Somebody has to," she says. Eyes steady.

For a long second, neither of us moves. The night holds its breath.

Then she leans in — slow, certain — and the world goes quiet.

I reach for her before I think too much — one hand at her jaw, the other at the small of her back. She doesn't pull away. The kiss is slow, quiet, intentional. The kind that doesn't ask for anything except truth.

When we finally break, she keeps her forehead against mine, breathing shallow.

"You sure?" she whispers.

"I've never been."

Her laugh comes soft — half nervous, half free. "We're both going to regret this."

"Then let's at least regret something that won't evaporate."

The rain picks up. The wind rattles the pane. Blue shifts on the rug, sighs, settles again.

The night folds around us — unhurried, human, alive.

* * *

The first thing I notice is the light — gray and quiet, letting the morning form at its own pace.

Alex is already up. The sheet folded neatly where she'd been. Somewhere down the hall, water running and Blue's paws on the tile.

She's on the small porch off the kitchen, coffee in both hands, still in the sweatshirt from last night. She doesn't turn around when she hears me.

I go back inside, pour a coffee, and bring it out. She makes room without being asked. I sit beside her. Blue follows, turns twice, and settles at our feet like he belongs there.

We let it settle for a while. The garden is quiet they way things are quiet after rain. A bird works somewhere in the hedges. The coffee is good.

"Hey." I look at her. "You okay?"

She looks at her coffee. "I think so." She glances over. "You?"

"Yeah."

We drink. Blue lifts his head once at something in the hedges, decides against it, and drops back down.

After a while she says, quietly: "This can't happen again."

I look at her.

"I work for your mother," she says. Still looking out at the garden. "I live in this house. I can't—" She stops. "I can't afford to make this complicated."

"It doesn't have to be."

She turns then. Not unkind. Just certain. "It already is."

She sets her coffee down, stands, pulls the sweatshirt around her.

"I'm sorry," she says. And means it.

Then she's gone. Blue watches the door. I don't move.

* * *

It's been a few weeks.

Feels longer. Time drips and disappears at the same time.

I've spent most of it buried in SunCoast files, nodding at Priya's instructions, pretending the title I used to cling to isn't still echoing somewhere.

Liz is quieter than usual. Not cold — absent. Like the air after a storm. Still, not calm.

Alex is gone by the time I come down. I hear her sometimes — a door, her voice on the phone with Liz, footsteps on the stairs. We don't quite land in the same room. I don't know if that's her doing or mine.

We haven't really talked since that morning. Not from regret — hesitation. We both stepped to the edge of something and backed away. I took too long to say something that mattered. Maybe it was too soon. Maybe she expected more. Or less. I don't know.

She's back in her rhythm. I've disappeared into mine. Not distance — drift.

Blue stays close. He's figured out something changed, even if I haven't.

I haven't reached out to Ian. Not yet. The idea sits in the back of my mind like a card I haven't played.

* * *

I knot my tie twice before it sits right. Tasha Reyes — relationship manager at Stanhope, one of the old-guard banks, someone I've known since my first year out of Stern — texted three times today. A launch party. Founders, editors, a little brand oxygen, she called it. I told her I wasn't in the mood. She told me that wasn't an option.

The loft is wide and staged — exposed brick, track lights angled to make everything look intentional. Once it was raw. Now it has a trust fund and a Parsons degree.

I wasn't going to this thing. Tasha from Stanhope — one of the old-guard banks — insisted. Nothing formal, she said. A few founders, a few editors, a little brand oxygen. Skipping it would have said more than showing up.

I'm halfway to the exit when I see her.

She's laughing, eyes narrowed, wine glass dangling from easy fingers. The dress is vintage — worn like she found it in her grandmother's closet and it happened to fit perfectly. She is tall, light brown hair catching the room's light, with the particular posture of a woman who learned to take up space correctly rather than apologetically. Her eyes do most of the work — quick, measuring, never quite at rest. She has the ease of someone whose family stopped counting money before she was born. Her voice, when it reaches me across the room, carries the faint soft vowels of the Carolina coast — not performed, just there, the way an accent stays when you stop trying to lose it.

She looks like she isn't trying. Her cheekbones say she doesn't have to.

Of course Tasha knows her.

"Blake Caswell," she whispers. "Long pedigree, glossy résumé. CODA editor — the fashion monthly that shapes careers. Knows everyone. She saw your name on the list — asked about you before you walked in."

I blink. "What?"

"She knew you were Lizzy Prescott's son. Said your mother made half of Milan care about the Oscars." Tasha nudges me. "Go say hi."

"I don't do that."

"You do now."

So I go. Not ready. Curious.

She smiles like we go way back. "William Chaffee. Your mother's a legend. She didn't just wear the clothes — she made them mean something. Commanded a room without a word. That kind of presence doesn't fade."

"She keeps people talking," I say. "That's the trick."

I offer a hand. She toasts instead. We drink to nothing.

"I grew up watching her redefine the red carpet," she adds. "And here you are — same cheekbones, less makeup."

I laugh. "Give it time."

She circles a half step, changing the angle — the move of someone who has been reading rooms since before she could drive.

"Blue-blood polish," she says, "and something else. Unbuttoned."

"Best or worst compliment I've ever gotten."

She laughs — the kind that turns heads. She wears it the way she wears everything. "Best," she says. "You're dangerous."

I raise my glass. "Appreciate the scouting report."

"Colby?" she asks.

"Yeah. One of the kids pretending not to want Wall Street while applying to internships."

She twirls the straw in her drink, eyes drifting toward the terrace. "I never thought about Colby," she says. "Small schools weren't on my radar."

There's a pause — just long enough to hear what she didn't say. I nod once, slow. "Yeah. I figured."

She looks back, resetting herself. "Where'd you go?"

"Brown," she says, with the shrug of someone who assumes you already knew. "Art history. Hated studio art."

"Bold."

"Self-aware. I like beautiful things. Doesn't mean I should make them." She glances around. "These parties always feel like someone's networking in a linen jumpsuit."

"Wouldn't be Chelsea without a soft-launch founder pitching equity over mezze."

She laughs and lifts her near-empty glass.

"Vodka soda?" I ask.

"Ketel One."

I return with a vodka seven. She takes it, smiling like she's politely sipping someone else's order at a wedding. "This isn't a vodka soda."

"Nope."

"But it's cold and has bubbles."

"Halfway there."

She studies me over the rim. "You're lucky you're not boring."

We drift toward the terrace. Café lights overhead, bass just enough to feel. She tucks her hair, laughing at what I say about the line at the door.

"You'd think they were handing out prizes."

"The prize is getting in before the guy with the beanie and the podcast."

"Tragic we beat him. He had opinions."

"On tequila," she says.

"Underprepared, then."

She lets her eyes run down my jacket and back up. "Smart choice. It works." Then she leans in just enough. "Don't waste that face on finance forever. The world has better uses."

Then she's gone. Not dramatic. Not conquest. Just gone — absorbed back into the room like she was never quite standing still.

I finish the bourbon and leave.

I don't sleep.

Somewhere between the bourbon and Blake's exit, I loop back to Ian's pitch — rough around the edges, something beating inside it anyway. Not because of the deck. Because it points to a door I've been walking past for years.

CHAPTER 7

SAWBUCK

I find Alex in the kitchen on my way out.

She's at the table in her Wesleyan sweatshirt, contracts textbook open, her coffee going cold beside the legal pad. The notes are dense, compressed — the handwriting of someone who doesn't waste margin space. She's been up for a while. She is compact and precise, dark hair pulled back with a few strands loose in the way that suggests she stopped fighting it years ago. Her skin is the warm brown of the Venezuelan coast. She looks younger than she is until she speaks, at which point she looks exactly the right age.

I'm already in my row clothes — thermal compression underneath, hoodie over it, gloves tucked in the pocket, ready to move. I grab a coffee from the pot Hana has out and stand at the counter.

Alex looks up briefly. Then back at the page.

"She came at me again last night," she says. Not dramatic. Just true.

"I heard some of it."

She nods. Doesn't elaborate. She states and waits, which is more effective than most things.

"Meet me at Putnam after the row," I say. "Eight thirty. I'll tell you what I know."

She looks up again. The assessment running. The decision made.

"I'll be there," she says. And goes back to the textbook.

I take the coffee and go.

* * *

The Mianus has thawed just enough. Ice clings to the banks, thin shards drifting on black water. Our oars pivot in the locks as we slip through — silent, rhythmic. The closest thing I have to feeling present all week.

Graham grunts at the cold — thick through the neck, ruddy from the cold, rowing like it owes him something since prep school. Tucker tells the same joke he always tells, lean and loose in the way of a man whose family has had money so long they've forgotten what it felt like not to. Beau rows with effortless form, already somewhere else in his head — probably a dinner reservation he hasn't made yet.

Steam lifts off the water. No one says much. Just breath. Just catch, slide, release. I like it this way — the ache in my shoulders, the rhythm that asks for nothing but presence.

Tucker breaks first. "Remember when we used to do this half-drunk?"

Graham: "Still counts as cardio."

Beau: "Only if you didn't puke before the sprint."

We laugh — tired, familiar, easy. For a little while I'm not selling anything. Not pretending to be worth listening to. Just a guy in a boat with people who knew me before the mask.

"This is where we pretend it counts as therapy," Tucker says, still pulling. "Cheaper than a shrink. Worse for the joints."

"Tuck," Graham mutters, "you're the only man I know who talks this much before seven. Shut up and pull."

I smile. Not much. Enough.

The river bends west and the sun hits the surface just right — soft gold on the water, frost bright on the reeds. Beau in profile. Tucker laughing. Graham grinding like his life depends on it.

When we reach the dock I'm raw — muscles tight, skin flushed, head quiet. Graham pitches egg sandwiches. I make excuses and peel off before the war stories start.

I like the walk. The air that sharpens your breath and makes everything feel earned. March bites through my gear as I cut up Field Point toward Belle Haven.

I slow at the dock.

Halcyon sits under canvas at the end of the second pier — lines coiled, brass gleaming through the wrap, teak deck invisible under the winter cover.

Big taught me to sail on this boat. Not the mechanics — the mechanics you can learn from anyone. He taught me to read it. The way the water changes color before the wind shifts. The particular chop that means the tide is running against you. The sound the rigging makes when you need to pay attention.

We were out past Watch Hill the summer I turned nineteen. Just the two of us — he'd sent the crew home, which is what he did when he wanted to talk. He was at the helm and I was on the bow and the wind had gone soft and we were just drifting in the last of the afternoon light.

"Your father never learned to read the water," he said. He wasn't looking at me. He was looking at the horizon the way he always looked at things he'd already made peace with. "He always thought he could outthink the conditions."

I didn't say anything. I knew he wasn't finished.

"The water doesn't care what you think," he said. "It only cares what you do."

He never said anything else about it. He didn't need to. That was Big — one line, delivered once, that you carried for the rest of your life whether you wanted to or not.

There are things you buy back that you can't explain to anyone.

This is one of them.

I stop. The sound of something waiting.

I keep walking toward Putnam.

The Nutmeg Café sits between a minimalist denim boutique and a shop where every mannequin looks unimpressed. The bell gives a tired chime. Burnt coffee and buttered toast — same as high school.

Alex is in the third booth down. Soft blue sweater, hair back, both hands around her mug. She looks up when I come in and something settles in the room.

I slide in across from her — still in my row clothes, hoodie, hair damp from the cold. Debbie sets my coffee down without asking. She's been doing that since I was fourteen.

"You made good time," Alex says.

"Wind was with us." I blow on the steam. "Can't feel my fingers."

She laughs. "You're the only person I know who thinks rowing in the dark in March is fun."

"Graham says it builds character."

"Does it?"

"The kind that needs Advil."

She grins and waves Debbie over with the ease of someone who knows small kindness matters. When the order's in she turns to me and waits.

"Tell me what I'm dealing with," she says.

So I do.

I tell her how Lizzy works. Not the surface version — the architecture. The way she identifies a person's weakness and stores it until she needs it. The way an attack always arrives dressed as honesty, as concern, as I'm telling you this for your own good. The way she escalates when she feels threatened, not when she's angry — anger she can manage, threat she can't.

"She used the dancer thing," I say.

Alex's jaw tightens slightly. "I told her that in — it was a good moment. We were having a drink after a long day. I thought—"

"She was genuine in that moment," I say. "That's what makes it worse. She can be both things at once. The connection was real. The file she kept was also real."

Alex looks at the window. Processing.

"The threat about the reference," I say. "She won't follow through."

"How do you know?"

"Because you're the best thing she has right now and she knows it. The threat is the control mechanism. It only works if you believe it." I pause. "Stop believing it."

"That's easier to say than to—"

"I know. But here's what's true. You have eighteen months left on whatever timeline you're running. She has maybe two years of relevance in the spaces you actually need access to. You outlast her. You don't need her goodwill. You need her contacts and her name on a door you've already figured out how to open."

"You've thought about this," Alex says. Not a question.

"I've thought about her my whole life."

Her expression shifts— not sympathy exactly, more like recognition. Like she's adjusting a calculation.

"What do I do when she comes at me again?" she asks.

"You give her something to be proud of," I say. "Not about you — about herself. She escalates when she can't see herself clearly. You redirect her toward her own reflection and she forgets what she was doing."

"That's what you did with the Cannes photograph."

"Every time," I say. "Since I was twelve."

She sits with that.

"You've been doing this your whole life," she says. Not an accusation. Something more careful.

"It's the instrument," I say. "You learn it or you don't survive the house."

"And you're still in the house," she says.

I don't answer that. She doesn't press.

We order. When the food arrives we eat in the comfortable silence of two people who have run out of performance and found something easier underneath it. Debbie refills the coffee. The avenue wakes outside — dog walkers, European SUVs, ponytails going somewhere fast.

"Do you miss it?" I ask. "Venezuela."

She thinks about it the way she thinks about most things — actually. "Sometimes I miss the noise," she says. "Everyone in everyone else's business. You always knew where you stood." She turns her coffee mug. "Here people are very private about their catastrophes."

"What about your family?"

"My mother. Two brothers." She hesitates. "They're fine. We talk on Sundays." She says it the way you say something that's both true and incomplete.

"Law school. The bar. Then entertainment law — not the glamorous side, the contractual side. The side where artists actually get protected." She turns her coffee mug. "I watched smaller artists — people just coming up — sign things they didn't understand. Good people being taken advantage of because nobody was in the room who understood both the art and the contract. Artists at your mother's level have the infrastructure. The ones coming up don't. That's who needs the help."

"That's the job you're building toward."

"That's the job," she says simply.

"And you're using her to get there."

She meets my eyes. "I'm using the access. There's a difference."

"Is there?"

"Yes," she says. "I do the job well. She gets what she pays for. What I learn is mine." I tilt my head. "Is that so different from what you do every day?"

That hits somewhere specific. I don't have a clean answer for it.

She smiles — small, quick, gone before it becomes anything. "I should go."

She pulls on her coat. A soft gray scarf, edges worn. Loops it and tucks it in.

"It's Ash Wednesday," she says.

"I missed that."

"I'm going to church." She stands. Then pauses. "You're welcome to come."

"I don't think I'd belong."

She leans close — not a touch, just near enough. "You do," she says. "You just don't know it yet."

Then she's gone. The bell rings. Her warmth hangs in the air a moment longer than it should.

My phone buzzes on the table. Liz.

Six o'clock. I need you here. There's a role I'm looking at.

No good morning. No how are you. Liz, being Liz.

The warmth drains. The coffee's cold.

I turn it over — the gap between what just happened in this booth and what just arrived on my phone. You do belong. You just don't know it yet. The words hang in the Formica light, not sentimental. Certain. The way she says most things.

I leave with the smell of bacon in my gear.

* * *

I make it to the office by ten thirty. Late enough for people to draw their own conclusions.

The floor is full buzz — lights too sharp, keyboards moving fast. The team is knee-deep in the Miami deal. Nico leans against the window with coffee black as resentment. He lifts the mug when I walk in — no turn, just acknowledgment.

Priya doesn't look up. A tight exhale through her nose and a sharper click of the keyboard — her version of a lecture.

Daren is in a hoodie with headphones draped around his neck, deep in a model. Spreadsheets open, code running, market data blinking — everything in motion.

"Morning," I offer.

Priya glances over. Crisp nod. Daren gives a thumbs-up.

"SunCoast call at eleven," Priya says. "Still need to tighten market-share metrics. Daren's running EPS accretion. Nico's reworking revenue growth and synergies."

"And you?" I ask.

"Making sure we don't embarrass ourselves."

Fair.

Nico breaks from the window. "You look human."

"I rowed."

"Early-morning absolution. Good for the soul."

"Better than bourbon."

"Debatable," he says. But lets it go.

The SunCoast call runs until two. I lead the market-share section, Priya takes valuation, Daren walks their CFO through EPS accretion without losing him. Their team asks good questions. We answer well. When we hang up Priya exhales through her nose — her version of a standing ovation.

I text Ian from my desk.

Will: Free at two thirty? Brew on East 54th, between 2nd and 3rd.

He responds in four minutes.

Ian: Yeah. See you there.

***

Brew is a couple blocks east — exposed brick, communal tables, everyone pretending not to eavesdrop. Half full with freelancers and new dads. Ian's in the back nursing a cold brew, hoodie half-zipped under a peacoat, glasses pushed up. He is compact and serious — West Indian coloring, Trinidadian from his mother's side, the particular warm brown of the

Caribbean. His hands are a programmer's hands, quick and precise. He looks like he's been squinting at code since sunrise. He waves.

I grab a latte and slide in.

"Appreciate you meeting," he says. No posture. Just ease.

"Needed a break from the holding cell I built for myself."

He laughs. "Still dragging out the Cherry Point thing?"

"Pretending it was a deal."

He tilts toward the window. "Weather's teasing spring."

"Still cold enough to trick you into forgetting your coat."

"March does that. Makes you think baseball's around the corner."

"You follow it?"

"Yankees," he grins. "My mom put the games on in the laundromat — tiny TV on a milk crate by the register. Every spring meant something. Even the bad years." He looks at the table a moment. "You grow up with that — you don't forget where you came from."

"Crown Heights," I say. "Brooklyn."

"Yeah. She still runs the place." He keeps going — quiet pride in the telling. "She'd let people run tabs when they couldn't pay. Kept detergent behind the counter for kids who came alone. Gave people somewhere to sit when the power got cut." He glances up. "I didn't realize how much it meant until I saw who kept coming back, years later."

I nod.

"She built something people leaned on without thinking about it," he says.

We do the small talk — commute, weather, bullpen woes — then I nod at his notepad. "You still want my help?"

He straightens. "Yeah. I wasn't sure you meant it, but yeah." He taps the notepad once, like he's deciding where to start.

"You know the kind of person who cashes their paycheck at a check-cashing place instead of a bank? Pays three percent just to touch their own money?"

"Sure," I say.

"Why do they do that?"

I think about it. "Banks make it hard. The minimums. The fees. The paperwork assumes you have a fixed address and a clean credit history."

"Right. So I built a way around it." He opens the notepad. "Payments platform. No traditional rails. The identity verification runs on distributed architecture — blockchain logic without the crypto noise."

"What does that mean practically?"

"It means Mila — my mom's neighbor, no bank account, system never worked for her — can send and receive money, pay bills, get paid for work, without handing three percent to a guy behind bulletproof glass every two weeks."

"And the backend?"

"That's where it gets interesting." Smart. Maybe brilliant. He's not selling. He's telling the truth.

"Most fintechs rearrange the same incentives," he says. "Optimize fees, dress it in UX, call it disruption. It's extraction — just smoother. I want to flip the stack. Use the core mechanics of banking but align incentives to long-term financial health, not quarterly profit."

"That sounds expensive."

"Break it up. Start with commercial DDA and savings. Then credit. Then income smoothing. Micro-underwriting, behavioral signals, shared upside." He says it like the idea's been sitting on the table, waiting for someone to pick it up. "It's not rocket science."

"You're building it now?"

"Bits and pieces. Some code. Some partners. What I need is someone who knows how to pitch it. Get it in front of capital."

That registers.

"You've got reach," he says. "Relationships. Credibility. You know how to play the game." He smirks. "Looks to me like you're ready for a different kind of game."

I watch a drop of espresso cling to the rim of my cup.

"I'm not trying to sell you," he says. "Feels like you want something that breathes."

He stands, swings on his backpack. "If you want to jam sometime, text me. We can whiteboard. No pressure."

"Ian."

He turns.

"What's it called?"

"Sawbuck," he says. "Old slang for a ten. Kind of a joke. Kind of not."

He's gone.

I hold the name. The pitch. The clarity of it — half-baked maybe, possibly naïve, but more spark in it than anything I've handled in a long time.

Not sure I want to build it with him.

Or claim it before someone else does.

That's the thought I don't finish.

The thought stays with me all the way to Grand Central.

CHAPTER 8

TAKE CONTROL

She's at the kitchen table when I come down. Casebook open, coffee going, the particular posture of someone who was up before I was and has already accomplished things. She looks up when she hears me on the stairs.

"Morning," she says.

"Morning."

We haven't talked about it. Not in the weeks since. She drew a line on the porch that morning and I've been respecting it the way you respect something you don't fully agree with but understand is right. She goes back to the page. I pour coffee.

I want to say something. I've been composing it since I woke up — some version of what I mean that isn't an explanation or a request, just the true thing said out loud. But I stand at the counter with my coffee and the moment passes and she turns a page and that's that.

"I'm heading into the city," I say.

She nods. "I'll be here."

I take the coffee and go.

* * *

The diner sits on a corner in Astoria — the kind of place that hasn't changed since the seventies and doesn't intend to. Formica counters, coffee in ceramic mugs, a pie case with two kinds of pie and no apologies about it. Halfway between Brooklyn and midtown. Neutral ground.

My father is already there when I arrive. Corner booth, back to the wall. Of course. A cup of coffee in front of him and the Post folded to the sports page. He's in a pressed shirt despite the neighborhood, despite the hour, despite everything. That never changes.

He looks up when I slide in across from him. Studies me for a moment.

"You look better than you sounded on the phone," he says.

"I feel better than I sounded on the phone."

The waitress comes. I order coffee. My father waits.

"So Rube," he says. "Tell me."

My father used "Rube" the way some men use "kid" — affection wrapped around disappointment, fear wrapped around love.

I start slowly. I've been turning this over for weeks and I'm still not sure I have the right language for it. I tell him about Ian — the Cooper Union degree, the laundromat in Crown Heights, the mother who never had a bank account. I tell him about the platform. Distributed identity verification. Payments that skip traditional rails. An infrastructure built for people the system was designed to exclude.

My father listens without interrupting. That alone is unusual.

I keep going. I tell him about the food trucks testing it in Brooklyn, the gig workers paying three percent just to cash a check, the traction that shouldn't exist yet but does. I tell him what I see — the gap in the market, the timing, the specific moment in fintech when the regulatory environment is actually favorable to something like this.

I watch his face as I talk.

Something is happening in it that I don't see often. The calculation is still there — my father is always calculating — but underneath it something else is kindling. He leans forward slightly. His coffee goes untouched.

"The underbanked market," he says. Not a question. Working through it.

"Sixty million Americans," I say. "Most fintech ignores them because the margins look thin until you understand the volume. Ian's model flips the incentive structure — he makes money when the user succeeds, not when they fail."

My father sits with it. I can see him placing the pieces.

"And the founder," he says. "You trust him?"

"He built it for his mother. He's been testing it for two years with no funding, no institutional backing, just conviction and code." I pause. "That's either naïve or the most honest thing I've seen in this business."

"It's both," my father says. Then: "What's the IP situation?"

I tell him. He asks about the competitive landscape. I answer. He asks about the regulatory pathway — FDIC, OCC, state licensing requirements. I've done enough research to hold the conversation and he knows it. He can tell when I'm bluffing and I'm not bluffing.

The questions get sharper. Faster. He's leaning fully forward now, elbows on the Formica, coffee cold beside him.

I realize, somewhere in the middle of his third question, that my father has not looked at me this way in my adult life. It's the look his father probably got when he brought home a real idea. The one Bill spent his whole life trying to earn.

Not at a deal. Not at a pitch. At me. Listening. Engaged. The full weight of his attention aimed in my direction without judgment or correction or the quiet machinery of disappointment running underneath everything he says.

It is the thing I have wanted since I was eight years old chasing fireflies on a lawn while he sat on the patio above me. And it is happening now, over terrible coffee in an Astoria diner, because I am describing a way to take something from someone who trusted me with it.

I push that thought down. Not away — down. I'm aware of it. I file it.

"The problem," my father says, "is the founder."

"Ian."

"Ian doesn't know what he has. You said it yourself. He's been building this for two years with no institutional backing — which means he has no idea what it's actually worth. No idea what the right terms are. No idea who should be in the room when the real money shows up." He picks up his coffee. Finally. Sips it. Sets it down. "You do."

I don't say anything.

"You've been in those rooms," he says. "You know the landscape. You know the players. You know what this is worth and what it could be worth and the distance between those two numbers." He looks at me directly — the look I have been waiting for my entire life, the look that says I see you and what I see is formidable. "Will. You need to take control of this before someone else does."

"It's his company," I say.

"It's his idea," my father says. "There's a difference. Ideas need infrastructure. They need capital, relationships, positioning, execution. Ian has an idea and some code and a story about a laundromat. You have everything else." He sets the glass down. "This is what you've been building toward. This is the room. The question is whether you're actually looking."

The last line hits with a specific weight. I've heard it before. In a Brooklyn apartment, amber light, expensive scotch.

My father is watching me.

"What would you do?" I ask.

He almost smiles. Not quite. But almost. "I would get in front of this before it gets away from you. Structure the relationship correctly from the beginning. Make sure your equity position reflects the value you're actually bringing." He pauses. "And I would do it now. Before he talks to anyone else. Before he understands what he has."

He says it without malice. As strategy. As the way the world works to a man who has spent his life believing the world works this way and failing at it and still believing it. He sounds, I realize, exactly like Big probably sounded when he was deciding which way to move the mills — certain, decided, the decision already made before it was spoken. The difference is Big had already proven it. My father learned the philosophy. He never quite got the instinct.

I let it sit.

The diner hums around us — short order cook calling out numbers, a TV above the counter with the local news on mute, a couple in the booth behind us arguing softly about something domestic and real.

My father reaches across the table and puts his hand briefly on my arm. He has not touched me with affection since I was a child. The gesture is awkward, slightly stiff — the gesture of a man who doesn't do this and knows he doesn't do this and is doing it anyway.

"I mean it," he says. "You're smart enough for this. You've always been smart enough. You just kept getting in your own way."

I nod. Don't trust my voice.

I stay for awhile. He asks about Lizzy — the old way. I tell him she's the same. He makes a sound.

When I stand to leave he stands too. We shake hands across the table — the handshake distance, the conversational arm's length. His grip is deliberate and holds a moment longer than usual.

"Get the deal done, Will."

Same words. Different register. For the first time in my memory they sound like something other than a verdict.

I walk out into Astoria. The light is thin and low off the elevated tracks, the street smelling of coffee and exhaust and something frying. Something loosens in my chest — the specific feeling of being seen by the person who was supposed to see you.

* * *

That evening I meet Ian at Corsini. Low jazz, polished wood, shadow — the particular quiet of a room where money feels comfortable. I didn't tell him why I picked Corsini. I want to see how he fits among the polished surfaces. The idea holds. I'm still testing the man behind it.

The host barely looks up, gestures to a back booth. Ian is already there with a Negroni and a menu he's trying to memorize.

"You look like a guy about to convince himself the second-cheapest bottle is the fiscally responsible choice," I say, sliding in.

He grins. "Only because I can't pronounce the expensive one."

His hoodie has become a collared shirt. My navy jacket is wrinkled from the walk from the office. Two versions of trying, meeting in the middle.

Menus disappear too quickly. Drinks land faster.

Ian glances around the room — dark walnut floors, white tablecloths, the soft clink of old money being comfortable. "Never been anywhere like this," he says. "My mom would steal the bread basket."

"My mother would send it back if the crust wasn't perfect."

He laughs. Nervous at first, then not. "Yeah. Different planets."

"Different and somehow the same," I say. "We both ended up here."

He nods, loosening. "You from New York?"

"Connecticut. Which is basically New York with better lawns and worse emotional boundaries."

That gets a real laugh. The kind that turns a room into a conversation.

He takes a sip of his Negroni. "Only time I ever left Queens as a kid was to go back to Trinidad. Spent most of my time working around my mom's laundromat in Crown Heights."

"Sounds honest," I say before I can stop myself.

He shrugs. "Harsh too. But yeah — honest."

Not forced.

We talk through dinner. Ian eats like someone who is present with what's in front of him, not self-conscious about it. I watch him and think about Gloria's back room, the careful shelves, the photograph.

I lean in. "So. Sawbuck. Still tinkering?"

His eyes change. Focus sharpens. "Past tinkering. I'm piloting. Early, but it works."

"What's the hook?"

"Ease. Dignity. You scan a code and pay, deposit, or get credit — no bank, no form, no shame." He looks at me directly. "No shame. People miss that part." He says it like it's the whole thesis.

"My mom knows her business," he says. "Banking didn't know her. Fees, rejections, arrogance. I watched her cry behind a change machine after a ten-dollar overdraft cost her a hundred." He pauses. "So I built something that wouldn't do that."

"Tell me how it actually works," I say.

He does. No bank charter — they're not replacing a bank, routing around the parts that fail people. The bank handles regulatory compliance — KYC, AML, custody. Sawbuck owns the customer interface, the rails, the trust layer, the UX. A wrapper around a banking engine that puts the user first. Onboarding through local programs — food trucks, bodegas, childcare collectives. Virtual wallets, QR payments, faster access, fewer fees, no minimums. Then micro-credit, savings tools, reputation scoring built from actual behavior rather than credit history.

"Not trying to be a bank," he says. "Trying to be what people thought banks were."

There's a sharpness under the idealism. He finishes his branzino and leans back.

"Where do you want to go with it?" I ask.

"Build it right. I don't want to sell out before it proves it matters."

"You need backing."

"I need someone who gets it," he says, holding my eye a moment too long. "Not someone chasing headlines."

Compliment. Challenge. Both.

"There's something real here," I say. "The right people would pay attention."

Something shifts in his face. Not enthusiasm — something more careful. He sets down his glass.

He repeats the word carefully. "Frame it?"

I hold that. Ian built this for his mother, for Gloria, for the people the system didn't provide options to. And I'm about to tell him someone needs to drive the car. I know what that means. I file it next to the other thing I filed this afternoon.

"You've got the engine. Someone has to drive the car."

He knows exactly what I mean. He doesn't say it.

"What if I bring two people into the conversation?" I say. "Your buddy Daren — sharp, technical, won't bullshit you. And Nico, my senior associate — clean instincts, a finance brain that isn't trapped by finance."

Ian considers. "Think they'll get it?"

"If they don't, they're not who I think they are."

He half-smiles. Not convinced. Curious. "My space," he says. "Near the High Line. Closer to reality than a boardroom."

I raise my glass. "To something happening."

He clinks. There's a flicker in his face — hope, or something sharper that might cost us both.

At the door he pauses. "Named it for my mom. Sawbuck." A silence. "She used to say that's all we ever had — a sawbuck and a prayer."

"Then let's make it worth a lot more," I say.

We shake hands. No smile this time.

* * *

My head buzzes on the Metro North home — something building that I'm not ready to name.

I'm going home to think.

Somewhere past Harlem-125th I take out my phone. I open it.

Then I type.

Will: Good to meet you the other night. I owe you a proper drink.

I put the phone away. She'll respond or she won't. I'm not sure which outcome I'm hoping for.

She responds before the train reaches New Rochelle.

Blake: I wondered when you'd get around to that. Thursday?

I read it twice. Then:

Will: Thursday works.

Greenwich approaches through the dark window.

CHAPTER 9

OPENING DAY

Ian texts me on a Thursday.

Opening Day Saturday. Yankees. My mom's place if you want to see Sawbuck in the wild. No agenda. Just the game.

I read it twice.

I type back before I think about it.

I'll be there.

He sends the address. Nostrand Avenue, Crown Heights. I know the neighborhood by reputation more than presence — one of those parts of Brooklyn that Manhattan acknowledges but doesn't really know.

* * *

The 4 train deposits me at Nostrand Avenue on a morning that can't decide if it's still winter. The sky is the particular gray of early April in New York — not threatening, just noncommittal. I walk half a block with my hands in my jacket and the city changing register around me immediately. The storefronts carry Trinidadian and Jamaican flags alongside the hand-lettered signs. Roti shops and doubles carts and a parlor with a West

Indian flag in the window. The smells coming from the restaurants are specific and serious. Nobody is performing anything for anyone.

I find the laundromat between a Salvadoran bakery and a cell phone repair shop. The sign above the door says GLORIA'S in hand-painted block letters, the paint faded to a soft gold. Through the glass I can see the machines running, a few customers with their phones out waiting, and at the back a small television mounted high on the wall showing the pre-game ceremony at Yankee Stadium.

Ian is outside, leaning against the wall with a beer, already watching me walk up. He's in jeans and a worn Cooper Union hoodie. No peacoat. No glasses case tucked in the pocket. This is the version of him that exists when nobody needs anything from him. He reached into a cooler and hands me a cold one.

"You found it," he says.

"The 4 train is underrated."

He laughs. Opens the door and holds it.

The laundromat smells like warm soap and something cooking from the back — rice and something sweet underneath it. The machines run in their own rhythm, a low mechanical percussion that fills the space without dominating it. Six or seven people are already settled in — plastic chairs pulled into a loose configuration facing the television, coffees and paper cups, a couple of the regulars who have clearly been doing this for years. An older Trinidadian man in a Yankee cap nods at Ian as we come in. A woman with two children spread a blanket on the floor between the machines. Someone has strung a small Yankees pennant above the TV with tape.

"You do this every year?" I ask.

"Every year since I can remember," Ian says. "She started it when we got here. People just showed up and it never stopped."

He says it the way you describe something that doesn't require explanation. This is what we do. This is who we are.

A door at the back opens and Gloria Cato comes through carrying a tray of food — roti, small paper plates, a bowl of something that smells extraordinary. She is a compact Trinidadian woman in her late fifties, hair wrapped in a bright orange cloth. Ian has her eyes — that's the first thing I notice. She moves through her own space with the settled confidence of someone who built this from nothing and has never once needed to announce that fact. She sets the tray down on the folding table by the wall and begins arranging things without looking up.

Then she looks up.

Her eyes go to Ian first — a quick private assessment, the look a mother gives a son that says I see you and I'll ask you later. Then to me. The assessment is slower. Not unfriendly. Thorough.

"Ma," Ian says. "This is Will. He's — we're working on something together."

The pause between we're and working is small. I hear it. She probably hears it too.

"Will," she says. Her voice has the particular music of Trinidad — the vowels longer and more deliberate than American English, a rhythm underneath the words that makes everything sound considered. "You hungry?"

"I could eat," I say.

She nods, which means something. She hands me a paper plate and turns back to the table.

* * *

The game starts at one.

By one-fifteen the laundromat is fuller — a dozen people now, maybe more, the plastic chairs occupied and a few people standing along the wall. Gloria moves between the back room and the front, refilling things, checking machines, stopping to say something to the regular customers in the easy shorthand of people who have known each other for years. She calls the older man in the Yankees cap Mr. Sylvester. She crouches to talk to the children on the blanket. She manages the room the way a good host manages a room — present everywhere, conspicuous nowhere.

Ian sits beside me. We watch the game with our beers and with the specific attention of someone returning to something they didn't know they'd missed.

I watch Sawbuck.

Two customers pay for their wash using the platform — I recognize the interface from Ian's demo, the clean verification flow, the transaction completing in seconds. Neither of them thinks about it. They tap, it works, they go back to the game. A third customer — older woman, heavy bags, moves like her feet hurt — fumbles with her phone and Ian is up before I realize he's moved, beside her, helping without making it a thing, the transaction completing, her saying thank you without quite looking at him the way people thank someone they've come to rely on.

He comes back and sits down.

"How many regulars use it?" I ask.

"About sixty percent of her customers now," he says. "Took eight months to get there. First few months people didn't trust it. Then Mr. Sylvester tried it because I asked him to and told everyone it worked." He nods toward the man in the cap. "He's basically my unpaid ambassador."

"Does he know that?"

Ian smiles. "He absolutely knows that."

On the television, the Yankees strand two runners in the second. The room makes its collective sound — not despair, just recognition. This is how it goes. This is the ritual. You show up and you absorb it and you come back next year.

Mr. Sylvester says something in Trinidadian Creole that makes the room laugh.

"What did he say?" I ask.

"He said the Yankees have had him on an emotional roller coaster since 1978 and he doesn't know why he keeps coming back."

"Didn't they win a few Series since then?"

Ian grins. "Exactly. He's never forgiven them for making him care."

* * *

In the fourth inning Gloria sets out more food — curry chicken this time, the smell filling the whole laundromat — and I watch her move back and forth from the kitchen, carrying things, setting things down, quietly tracking that everyone has enough.

By the fifth inning the paper plates are stacking up on the folding table and I can see her starting to gather them. I stand without thinking about it.

I pick up the tray and the stack of plates and the empty cups and carry them through the door at the back.

The back room is small and warm and organized with the precision of someone who learned long ago to make a small space work. A deep industrial sink. Shelving with supplies stacked in careful rows. A small table with two chairs. On the wall above the table, a photograph — a younger Gloria holding an infant, somewhere tropical, the light the specific gold of late afternoon near water.

I set the tray down by the sink and start rinsing plates. Gloria comes through the door behind me and stops for a moment, assessing.

"You don't have to do that," she says.

"I know," I say. And keep doing it.

She moves beside me without ceremony and starts drying what I rinse. We work in the comfortable quiet of people who have found a shared task.

After a moment she says, "You're not from here."

"Connecticut," I say. "Greenwich. I live there with my mother."

She makes a small sound. Not judgment. Calibration. "Long way from Greenwich to my laundromat on Opening Day."

"Ian mentioned what you'd built here," I say. "I wanted to see it."

She lets it settle. Through the wall I can hear the game — the crowd noise, the commentator, a burst of reaction from the front room.

"He's been building that thing for two years," she says. "Working at night, on weekends. Every time I talked to him his head was somewhere else." She sets a dried plate on the stack. "I used to worry. Thought maybe he was chasing something that would never catch." She pauses. "Then I saw it work. Right here. Customer came in, no account, no card. Ian had her paying for her wash on her phone in two minutes. She looked at me like —" Gloria stops. Searches for the words. "Like someone had finally done something that made sense."

I hand her another plate.

"That customer," she says. "She's been coming here fifteen years. Pays cash every time because that's all she has. Banks don't want her. Credit cards don't want her. She's sixty-three years old and she has never had anyone build something for her." Gloria pauses. "Ian did."

I look at the photograph on the wall. The young Gloria, the infant, the golden light.

"Is that him?" I ask.

"Six weeks old," she says. "Trinidad. We came the next year." She looks at it too. "I wanted him to have more than I had. I didn't know what that meant exactly. I just knew it meant here."

"Did it work?" I ask.

She considers this properly — not the reflexive yes a mother performs, but a real answer. "It worked different than I thought," she says. "I thought more meant bigger. More money, more space, more of everything America tells you to want." She sets the last plate down. "Ian built something small. Something specific. Something for people like me." She turns to face me. "That's more than I knew to ask for."

From the front room a roar goes up — someone has done something worth roaring about. Through the door I can hear the room coming alive, Mr. Sylvester's voice above everything else, and then Ian's laugh, and then what sounds like half the laundromat talking at once.

Gloria smiles. The real one — not the one for managing a room, the one that belongs to a woman watching her world work the way she built it to work.

She says something then in Trinidadian Creole — soft, almost to herself, the words running together in a way that sounds like a prayer or a blessing or both.

"What does that mean?" I ask.

She looks at me for a moment. "It means — God does not give you the future you planned. He gives you the one He planned."

She goes back through the door to the front room.

The game noise comes through the wall. The warm soap smell. The precise organization of her shelves. The photograph of a young woman holding her son in Trinidad in the golden afternoon light.

I dry my hands and go back out to watch the rest of the game.

* * *

The Yankees win 4-2. The room disperses slowly — the way people leave a place they were glad to be in, reluctantly, with promises to return. Mr. Sylvester shakes Ian's hand for longer than a handshake needs to last. The woman with the children folds her blanket. Gloria moves through the space collecting things, restoring order, already preparing for tomorrow.

Ian and I stand outside on Nostrand Avenue in the cooling afternoon. The roti shop next door has turned its lights on. The street is still busy, the neighborhood running at its own Saturday pace.

"Your mother is remarkable," I say.

Ian looks at the laundromat window. "She built something people lean on without thinking about it," he says. "I just wanted to make it easier for her to run." He pauses. "Then I realized how many people were like her. And how nobody was building anything for them."

I nod.

"She liked you," he says. "She doesn't do that automatically."

"I liked her," I say.

A car passes playing something with a good bass line. Down the block someone has a sound system going — the particular bass of soca that belongs to this neighborhood on a warm afternoon.

"So," Ian says. He's not looking at me. Looking at the laundromat. "Are we doing this?"

I think about Gloria's prayer. I think about a woman who has been coming to this laundromat for fifteen years, paying cash because that's her only option, and the look on her face when something finally made sense.

"Yeah," I say. "We're doing this."

Ian nods once. Something settles in him — a decision confirmed, a weight accepted. He's still not fully sure about me. I can see it. He's choosing to proceed anyway, the way you choose to trust someone when you need to and hope the choice holds.

We shake hands on Nostrand Avenue in Crown Heights on Opening Day with the roti shop lights on and the laundromat behind us still warm from the afternoon.

I take the subway back to Manhattan.

The term sheet. My father's voice. The 4 train runs express through the dark and I watch my reflection in the black window. I look like someone who has made a decision.

I open a group text to Nico and Daren.

Will: Meet up? Something to run by you.

No questions. Nico replies: High Line. What time?

Eight.

Daren sends a yawn emoji and a thumbs-up.

* * *

Just before seven I'm heading south. Nico wanted the 23rd Street entrance. Eight a.m. is apparently "ungodly" and he wants credit for showing up vertical.

I grab coffee from a vendor who hands it over like mornings are fragile.

Nico arrives first — coffee in one hand, half-eaten bagel in the other, sunglasses on despite the pale sky.

"Morning? Outdoors?" He squints at me. "I left my coffin for this. Feel honored."

"Couldn't sleep."

"Bold strategy."

Daren arrives two minutes later, earbuds in, granola bar half gone. "Text me this early again and we're done."

We fall into step without agreeing on a direction. Skyline to the right. A breeze pushes down the path like it has somewhere to be. Nico launches a theory about Trader Joe's being a social experiment — never the same thing twice, chaos disguised as calm, training us to accept unpredictability.

Daren lifts an eyebrow. "You've been listening to Rogan again."

"So," I say, hands in my pockets. "I want to run something by you both."

Nico glances over. Daren finishes chewing.

"Sawbuck," Daren says. "Ian's thing. From the bar."

Caught. "Yeah."

Daren grins. "Told you he was brilliant."

"He's testing with food trucks," I say. "The concept works. Underbanked, cash-reliant — people the system was never built for. I've been running the numbers. I can see the shape of it."

Nico keeps his voice even. "Where's the capital coming from?"

"Have to figure that out still. We'll need a seed round. Probably me and my friends, a few family offices who I owe a call. Keep it lean. See if it breathes."

"You partnering with Ian?" Daren asks.

"He's got the concept. I've got the network. I wanted the three of us to whiteboard it first."

Nico slows. "You think it's real?"

"I think it's needed. Someone else takes the swing if we don't." I pause. "I'm not asking you to jump. Just look." Daren nods. "I'm in for a session."

"Ian's got a space downtown," I say. "Let's do it there."

Nico hesitates. "If we're doing this, it's not for show. Not theory and buzzwords."

"No decks. No pitch. Just a whiteboard."

We stop where the old tracks show through the grasses. The breeze cuts. No toast, no glass raised — just the three of us standing in the middle of something none of us is naming yet.

Feels like a beginning I'm pretending isn't one.

At 20th Street a staircase drops between rusted rails and wild grass.

"I'm headed down," Nico says, tipping his coffee.

"Same," Daren says. "I need actual food."

"I'll keep going," I say.

We do the half-wave men use when no one wants to hug. They take the stairs, already debating the nearest deli. I keep walking.

I don't want to go home. There's nothing at the office. So I let the streets pull me east — past shuttered galleries and flower stands setting out their buckets — until the grid loosens and the buildings stop trying.

At Bryant Park the trees are still bare, branches reaching into pale morning. The breeze has just enough bite to remind you it isn't spring yet.

I find a chair and sit.

My phone buzzes—an old thread from Liz: Brunch tomorrow. Noon at the club. Dress accordingly.

The city moves around me — dog walkers, a kid on a scooter, low conversations at corner cafés. Nobody looking for anything. Nobody pretending not to.

I stay until the cold works through my coat. Then I get up and go.

CHAPTER 10

THE BOX

Sunday. Noon. I'm in the Jeep, inching up North Street toward High Pond.

The engine coughs like a smoker. The dash rattles over every seam. I chose it on purpose — dragging a piece of my former self to brunch to see if he still fits.

At a red light I adjust my collar, catch my reflection: button-down, navy sport coat. Appropriate, per Liz.

The lot is full of Range Rovers and G-Wagons. My Jeep doesn't belong. I park anyway.

Inside, nothing's changed. It never does. The terrace is pristine — white tablecloths, striped awning snapping in the breeze, silverware chiming under low conversation.

Liz is at her usual table under the heaters, already holding court with no one. Cream wrap, tortoiseshell sunglasses she only takes off for cameras.

"You're on time," she says, eyes on her phone.

"Miracles happen."

A waiter appears. I order eggs and a Bloody Mary. She adds a Chardonnay.

"I may have something," she says. "Supporting, not a lead. Tasteful. Period. AmFlix. Marci thinks The Review if we spin it right. And The Monthly wants to revisit icons — Gwynth, Meryl, me."

She shrugs like those names share oxygen.

Then Liz stops.

"You seem lighter."

"I've been working on something."

I give her enough — the shape of it, the purpose, the edges of Sawbuck.

She leans in a fraction. Closer to genuine attention than I've seen from her in years.

"Strong," she says. "Clean. I like it."

No conditions. No redirect.

She raises her glass. "You're finally learning how to turn your cleverness into something meaningful."

I let that sit.

She butters her toast with surgical precision. A pause that has been prepared.

"I had coffee with Blake Caswell the other day," she says.

I look up — just a fraction too late.

"Did you," I say, reaching for my glass like it's nothing.

"Remarkable woman," Liz says, setting the knife down carefully. "Sharp. Knows everyone worth knowing. Grew up with real money — the kind that's had time to develop manners."

She lifts her glass.

"She's the kind of woman who makes things happen without making a scene of it. You don't find many of those."

The flag snaps in the wind off the green. I wait.

"She asked about you," Liz adds. Casual as weather. "More than professionally."

"I'm aware."

"Good." She tips her glass slightly. "She'd be an asset, William. Not just personally. For what you're building. She understands how the right story gets told to the right rooms. That's not nothing — especially for something that needs credibility before it has it."

"I know what she brings."

"Do you?" She sets the glass on the rail. "From where I'm sitting, you seem distracted. By things that don't move you forward."

"Blake understands your world," she says. "She was born adjacent to it. That matters more than people admit."

Then, lighter — almost an aside:

"Alex has a way about her, doesn't she?"

I don't respond.

"Quiet. Steady," Liz continues. "The kind of woman men mistake for simple until they realize they're the ones being read."

She folds her napkin.

"I'd be careful, Will."

"That feels a little out of left field," I say, trying to keep it even.

"She seems earnest," Liz says. "But you understand how that reads."

She lifts her sunglasses, looks at me fully — clear-eyed, maternal in the coldest way.

"If you're serious about building something significant, it matters who stands beside you. Someone with access. With a name that opens doors or a rising New York financial star."

Condensation slides down my glass.

"Sleep with whomever you like, William," she says. "If you want to be taken seriously, date someone who hasn't had to earn attention taking off her clothes in smoke filled rooms."

"That's not who she is," I say. "And you know that."

The words land quieter than I expect. Final.

Her expression changes. A question forms. She doesn't ask it.

She holds my gaze a moment longer than usual, then sets her sunglasses back in place. She knows better than to push.

A long pause.

Then I laugh — not at her. At something further back.

"What?" she asks.

"Dad said the same thing when I wouldn't date girls from around here. You threw a bread basket at him after the Crawfords because he called them boring."

She's quiet, then laughs softly.

"That man had the emotional range of a decorative pillow," she says. "But he was right about the Crawfords. The daughter was wallpaper — thin and painfully beige."

"She's on two foundation boards now."

"Exactly," Liz says, finishing her wine. "Beige always endures."

For a moment there's warmth. Real. Unscripted.

"You should dress like this more often," she says.

I glance down — navy sport coat, open collar, jeans, loafers.

"Like someone who belongs here?"

She smirks.

"Like someone who doesn't need to prove he does."

The sunglasses slide back on. The moment passes.

I hold onto the laugh a second longer than I should.

* * *

I get the tickets through Halbridge's assistant. Four seats in the club level, third base side, the kind of box that has its own door and a server who appears before you ask. I don't tell Ian how I got them.

I take the Yankee Clipper from Greenwich — a Metro North special that runs directly to the stadium on game days. The train fills up at each stop, Stamford and Harlem-125th, fans in pinstripes and replica jerseys, a particular energy that belongs to this ritual and nothing else. Ian is waiting at the Yankees-East 153rd Street platform when I arrive, Yankees cap on, looking like he belongs here in a way I never quite will.

He takes in the stadium with the look of someone who has been here thousands of times in one form and never like this. He has a hot dog in his hand before we reach the seats.

"Your seats or the firm's?" he asks.

"Does it matter?"

He thinks about it. "A little."

"The firm's," I say. "I wanted you to see what the upside looks like."

He nods once. Files it.

The game is already in the first. The stadium is the particular loud of fifty thousand people doing the same thing at slightly different times — the wave of sound when contact is made, the collective groan, the specific silence before a pitch that matters. Ian watches it the way he watched the Opening Day game at his mother's laundromat — fully, without performance, like the game is actually happening to him.

I watch him watching it.

We eat. The server appears with drinks. Ian is polite to her in a specific way — not the politeness of someone remembering their manners, but the ease of someone who has always known that the person bringing your food is a person. I notice it and don't say anything.

In the third inning, with the Yankees down one and the crowd settling into its patient discontent, I say: "I want to talk about structure."

Ian looks over. He knew this was coming. He's been knowing it since Corsini.

"Okay," he says.

I lay it out. Not the pitch — the actual numbers. The equity split I'm proposing, the rationale behind it, what I'm bringing and what it's worth and what happens to Sawbuck in the next eighteen months without someone who knows how to move through the institutional landscape. I've been doing this for ten years. I know how to make a number sound like logic.

Ian listens. He watches the game while he listens — not distracted, just anchored to something real while I talk about something abstract.

"That's a significant ask," he says when I finish.

"It reflects significant contribution."

"Or significant leverage." He says it without heat. An observation.

I don't flinch. "Both, probably. That's how this works."

He watches the field. Below us a Yankees batter works the count full. The stadium leans in collectively.

"You know what I keep thinking about?" Ian says.

"Tell me."

"The woman at my mom's laundromat. The one who's been coming for fifteen years. When I showed her the platform she looked at me like—" He stops. Starts again. "Like something finally made sense. Like someone built it for her instead of around her." "I don't want to lose that." His voice drops. I don't care about the valuation. I care about that look."

The batter hits a line drive into the gap. The stadium erupts. Ian watches the runners move with the same attention he gives everything.

When the noise settles I say: "You won't lose it. That's the whole point. The platform works for her right now with fifty users. Imagine what it does for her with five million."

"If it still works the same way."

"It will work better."

"You sure?"

"I'm sure that without capital and infrastructure and the right relationships, Sawbuck stays exactly what it is right now — something that works beautifully for fifty people and never reaches the fifty million who need it." I pause. "And someone else builds a worse version and gets there first."

That one sticks.

Ian turns his beer in his hands. He hasn't eaten the second half of it.

"I need a lawyer to look through what you've put together," he says.

"Absolutely."

"Someone I choose. Not someone you recommend."

"Of course."

"And I want founder protections. IP stays mine. Mission language in the operating agreement — we're not pivoting to serve a different customer base without my vote."

I nod. "All reasonable."

He looks at me. The particular look of someone who is making a decision they're not entirely sure about but have decided to make anyway. The look Ian's mother probably gave the first customer she let run a tab.

"Okay," he says. "Let's do this."

We shake hands in the box seats on the third base side at Yankee Stadium with the game tied in the fifth and the crowd making its particular sound and below us in the Bronx and across the river in Brooklyn a woman named Gloria Cato is running a laundromat on Nostrand Avenue where her son built something for people like her.

I think about her exactly once.

Then I think about the term sheet.

* * *

We stay for the whole game. Yankees win 5-3 on a walk-off single in the ninth. The box empties around us, the stadium lights still blazing.

Ian finishes the warm second half of his beer.

"Good game," he says.

"Good game," I say.

We take the elevator down and part ways outside the stadium — he goes to the subway, I go to the train.

My father's voice underneath everything: Get in front and make sure you get what you deserve.

Do it before he knows what it's worth.

I take the Metro North back from 153rd Street, changing at Harlem-125th for the New Haven Line to Greenwich. The train thins out past each station — the fans peeling off first, then the late commuters, until somewhere past New Rochelle it is mostly quiet and I am sitting with my phone and the window.

Alex's name is in my contacts. I've looked at it three times this week without pressing it. Not because I don't know what to say — because I do, and saying it means deciding something I haven't decided yet.

You around tonight?

Nothing. The suburban stations ticking past. Larchmont. Mamaroneck. Harrison. The particular rhythm of going home.

Somewhere past Rye my phone lights up.

Cos Cob. The little pub on Sound Shore. Can you come?

No explanation. No preamble. Alex, who always has context, sending none.

I get off at the Greenwich station and walk to my car.

* * *

The pub sits on the sound side of the Post Road — dark wood, low beams, a fireplace that's been burning since Eisenhower. The kind of place that was built to last and has. Brass fittings on the bar. A chalkboard with six beers and no apologies about it. Two or three people at separate tables, each of them comfortable in the way of regulars who stopped needing to explain themselves here years ago.

Alex is on the second stool from the end.

She's still in work clothes — the blazer she wore to manage whatever Lizzy needed today, the dark trousers, the low heels. But the blazer is unbuttoned and her hair is down and she's holding a glass of white wine with both hands the way you hold a glass when you need something to hold. She looks like a person who has been keeping it together all day and stopped somewhere between the car and this stool.

She doesn't look up when I sit down beside her. She knows it's me.

"Hey," I say.

"Hey."

The bartender comes. I order a rye. He goes away.

I wait. Alex looks at her wine. The television murmurs. Outside,

Sound Shore Drive is quiet, the harbor dark beyond it.

"I failed the paper," she says finally.

I don't say anything.

"Contracts. My strongest subject." She turns the glass slowly. "Professor Elman. He's brutal but fair — everyone says that, and I believed it, and he handed it back today with a C-minus and two pages of notes and one line at the top that said 'this reads like it was written by someone who wasn't fully present.'" She stops. "He wasn't wrong."

Her eyes go to the wine glass. Not to me. I watch her decide something — not about the paper, about whether to let herself be in this. She almost doesn't. I can see the moment where she nearly reaches for the practical version, the already-past-it version. Then she lets her shoulders drop, just slightly, and the effort of the last few weeks shows in her face the way it does when someone stops performing composure.

"I worked so hard to get here," she says. Quiet. Almost to herself. "Not just the scholarship. All of it. The visa. The move. Convincing people I belonged in rooms I wasn't sure I belonged in." She turns the glass again. "One bad grade doesn't undo that. I know that. I just — I don't always know that at eleven-thirty on a Thursday."

"When did you write it?"

She gives me a sideways look. "Oscar week. The Paris trip fell through so Lizzy wanted to do the whole thing locally — the pre-show, the after-party at Vantage Artists, the Harper's Bazaar breakfast, the meeting with the Times Style section." She shakes her head. "Four days. I wrote it at two in the morning in a hotel room in Midtown while she was at a dinner. I thought I could do both."

"You do do both," I say. "Every week."

"Not that week." She takes a sip of wine. "And now it's on my record. And if my GPA drops below a certain threshold I lose my scholarship." She catches herself. "Which I need. Because I don't have a trust fund and law school is—" She stops. "I'm not asking you to fix it. I just needed to be somewhere that wasn't the house."

The bartender sets my rye down and disappears.

I stay with it for a moment. Not reaching for the redirect. Not looking for the angle. Just sitting with what she's actually said.

"Can you appeal?" I ask.

"Maybe. But Elman doesn't reverse grades. He's known for it."

"Can you talk to him? Not appeal — just talk. Tell him what was happening."

"Tell a law professor that I was too busy managing a celebrity's schedule to focus on contracts law." She gives me a look. "That's not exactly the argument."

"It's not the argument you'd make to a professor," I say. "But it's the truth. And sometimes the truth is worth saying even when it doesn't win."

We sit for awhile. The bar does its quiet thing around us. Someone feeds the jukebox a song from the nineties that neither of us comments on.

"Can I tell you something?" I say.

She nods.

"There was a school in Boston. Berklee. Music conservatory." I look at my glass. "I had the application. I'd already written most of it. Senior year. I was going to transfer — leave Colby, go to Berklee, finish the demo I'd been working on, see what happened." I pause. "My father sat down with me and explained why it was a fantasy. Not cruelly — carefully. Music's a hobby, not a future. He said it like he was doing me a favor." I take a sip. "I listened. I tore up the application. Enrolled in Econ. Worked on my GMAT instead of the demo."

Alex is very still.

"The demo is still on a laptop or a disc somewhere," I say. "In the attic probably. I haven't looked for it." I pause. "Now I'm building something that might actually matter. But I never stopped hearing it."

"Why are you telling me this?" she asks.

"Because you built a plan," I say. "A real one. You're executing it under conditions that would break most people. And one bad paper in one brutal week doesn't change what the plan is or who you are." I turn to face her. "You're not someone who wasn't fully present. You're someone who was present in too many places at once. Those aren't the same thing."

She holds my gaze for a long moment.

"That's the most you've ever told me about yourself," she says quietly.

"Yeah."

"Why tonight?"

The Yankees game. Ian's hand. The term sheet forming in my head on the train ride home. The specific feeling of becoming the man my father always wanted and finding myself in a bar in Cos Cob because a woman I care about texted and needed someone.

"Because you needed it," I say. "And it was true. And I'm trying to say true things more often."

She nods slowly. Turns her glass.

"My father had a line or two about faith," I say. "Same delivery. Same certainty." I look at my rye. "We were driving somewhere — I was maybe twelve, the radio was low — and he said it was a good book like it was written by Hemingway or something. He said People just got confused about what kind of book it was." Alex waits.

"Faith is for people who can't handle uncertainty," I say. "That was the other one. Smart people learn to sit with the not-knowing." I pause. "He said it once. He only needed to say things once. It just settled in and I never examined it. The same way I never examined the Berklee thing until tonight."

"Do you believe that?" she asks. "What he said about faith?"

I think about it honestly. "I don't know," I say. "I've been carrying it so long I'm not sure what's his and what's mine anymore."

She looks at the harbor through the window. "My abuela prayed every morning before sunrise," she says. "Before the neighborhood woke up. Before anything was asked of her." Alex is quiet a moment. "She was the steadiest person I've ever known." She doesn't say anything else. She doesn't need to.

* * *

By six I'm back at it — emails, research, a few stabs at the Sawbuck deck. Too soon. I close the laptop.

I take Blue out before seven. Early-April chill, the damp kind that finds your collar and stays. Dew along the stone walls. The hedges still half-asleep.

Blue trots ahead, leash loose, glancing back now and then to confirm I'm still in the world with him.

I didn't sleep. Not really.

Last night keeps replaying — her shoulder brushing mine waiting for the Uber, the quiet ride home, the moment we stepped through the door and both pretended we weren't waiting for the other to say something. Alex drifted toward the back hallway. I took the stairs. We split without speaking.

I take out my phone.

You doing okay—

Delete.

Can we talk?

Delete.

I stand in the driveway staring at a blank screen like it might tell me what I mean. Blue sits beside me, patient, unimpressed. A breeze moves through the trees. I put the phone back in my pocket and keep walking — past the stone pillars, past the quiet driveways, past the neighborhood I've spent years measuring myself against.

My footsteps echo. Her absence walks with me.

CHAPTER 11

BURN RATE

It's nearly noon when I badge into Sutter Rowe. Weekend quiet. Phones asleep, lights dimmed. A handful of us on SunCoast—trying to unwind leverage ratios, deal protections, and Fed pressure points before Monday's partner call.

Priya's in a glass-walled conference room, hair tied back, AirPods in, locked on her spreadsheet like it's a chess match. Daren's cross-legged at the far end, hoodie up, half-eaten bagel on a napkin. Nico leans back in a swivel, boot on the table, flipping printouts like someone else's exam.

I rap the glass twice. Nico looks up first. No smirk today—just a nod.

"Thought you found religion," he says.

"Not exactly," I say, stepping in. "Running behind."

Priya pulls one bud out. "We reworked the model. Biscayne National and BankFirst are at the table—both light on price."

"I'll read in."

I open my laptop. SunCoast loads—the model, the emails, the tension. I work it for twenty minutes. Then I minimize it. Behind it all, one word keeps circling.

Sawbuck. Still a whisper. Getting louder.

I crack a fresh deck. White screen. Blank title.

Marco, my roommate at Colby, used to say: If the song's authentic, the rest takes care of itself.

I type: Sawbuck: Fund Potential, Not Paperwork.

Delete.

We back possibility before paperwork exists.

Delete.

We see you before the world does.

I leave it. For now.

Priya slices through bidder questions like they owe her money. Nico's eyes drift between the memo and the window, wrestling something unspoken. Daren crunches like he cares.

I'm supposed to redline LOIs, clean up a slide Halbridge wants, and review Ames's sensitivity markup—while quietly sketching a startup I'm not supposed to be thinking about.

The name started as a placeholder. Now it's an earworm. In the notebook margins:

The same lines. Still wrong.

Wrong tone. Still wrong. Try again.

Priya stops by with a question about the SunCoast sensitivity markup. She's holding the printout, marked up herself, halfway through the answer. She doesn't need me. She stopped needing me weeks ago and we both know it and neither of us has said it.

"I'll look at it shortly," I say.

She nods. She doesn't believe me. She goes back to her desk and opens the file herself. That's the whole picture. That's what this has become.

I close my laptop.

The decision was made somewhere I wasn't watching and I'm just catching up to it now.

I knock on Halbridge's door at nine-thirty.

* * *

He's at his desk with his jacket on, reading something in a folder the way men of his generation read things — fully, without distraction. He looks up. Closes the folder.

"Will," he says. "Sit down."

I sit. He waits. He's always been good at waiting.

"I'm leaving," I say.

He nods once. Not surprised. Not performatively unsurprised. Just receiving information he had already considered.

"Tell me about it."

His office is the kind of room that stops accumulating things after a certain point — not sparse, just settled. No awards on the wall. A framed photograph I've never been close enough to read. A window facing east that lets in gray morning light and nothing else.

I've been in this room four times in five years. Always as a supplicant.

So I do. Not the pitch. I tell him the truth — Ian Cato, Cooper Union, the laundromat in Crown Heights, the platform built for people the system designed to exclude. The traction. The timing.

Halbridge listens the way he listens to everything — fully, giving nothing back until he's ready.

"You believe in it," he says. Not a question.

"I do."

"And the founder?"

I look at him. "He's exceptional."

Halbridge holds my gaze. He's been in enough rooms to know when someone is telling a partial truth and choosing not to press it. He chooses not to press it.

"You came in here to tell me, not to ask me."

"Yes," I say. "But you said you were around if I wanted an old dog's perspective."

Something shifts in his face. He picks the thing he's been thinking rather than the thing that's appropriate.

"This business takes things from people," he says. "It took things from you. Some you let it take. Some it just—" He pauses. "The ones it just took — those are worth going and finding." He picks up his pen.

He sets the pen down. Looks at me in a way he hasn't before — not appraising. Something closer to honest.

"Whatever you're building, build it because it matters to you. Not because it would have mattered to your grandfather."

The room is very quiet.

"How long have you known?" I ask.

"Long enough," he says. "Go. Do it well. Don't burn it down on your way out."

I stand. We shake hands — not the handshake distance. Something closer.

"One more thing," he says. "The founder. Whatever you've structured — make sure it's something you can live with in ten years."

I nod. I don't answer. He opens his folder and goes back to reading.

In the elevator going down I keep expecting the feeling to change. It doesn't. Whatever he said landed somewhere specific and it doesn't lift.

* * *

Ames takes four minutes.

I close the door. I say I'm resigning, effective two weeks from today. He says he's sorry to hear it. His face says he isn't. I tell him I'll have a full handover to Priya by end of the day. He nods. He picks up his pen.

“Clear out your desk and turn in your security cards right after you get Priya what she needs.”

That's exactly what I will do.

I walk through the floor slowly. Not making a production of it.

Daren pulls one earbud out. Looks at my face. "You did it."

"I did it."

"Come with me," I say. "When you're ready."

He grins. "Ask me again in six months."

Nico raises his coffee mug from the window. "To the ones who still show up."

"Different address," I say.

"Same idiots," he says. "Probably."

Priya looks up from her screen. Composed. Professional. Something underneath it that might be respect.

"I'll have everything to you today," I say.

"I know you will," she says. Her eyes go back to her screen.

A few hours later, I take the elevator down. Lou at the lobby desk. I nod and hand him my access badge. He nods back.

Outside, the city does what the city does. I stand on the sidewalk with my jacket over my shoulder and the April sun on my face and Halbridge's words running underneath everything.

I start walking.

Two missed calls from Liz.

A text from Blake.

The Canal House rooftop. 9:30. Dress to get in.

Open air, twenty floors up, one of those rooms that earns its reputation quietly.

I let it stand. She's already been to Marci. She's had coffee with my mother. And now this.

I go anyway.

***

The car smells like old fries and a losing battle with the vents. The driver hums along with the radio, tapping the wheel. He catches my eye in the mirror. "The Canal House, boss?"

"Yup."

"Easy," he says.

I watch the city change register through the window — FiDi to Meatpacking, hard edge to curated cool. Different worlds. Same act.

At the door I trade whatever I actually am for the version that gets through it. Buttoned jacket. The right kind of smile. I've done this so many times it doesn't require thought.

That's the problem with it.

The rooftop is the kind of softly lit where everyone is pretending not to watch. Low conversation, glassware, a playlist someone overpaid to feel effortless. I'm halfway through a rye when I spot her.

Blake is already seated — sleeveless black dress, hair half-up, shoes off, a cocktail in hand like she's been waiting for the city to catch up. She smiles when she sees me. Half invitation, half something else.

"If it isn't the man I mistook for his mother's cheekbones."

"Still one of the stranger things I've heard at a party."

She gestures to the seat. I sit.

"I thought you'd bail," she says, sliding her shoes back on.

"Not my style."

"Good." She picks up her glass. "You've been on my mind."

"Compliment or warning?"

"Both."

I look at her. "You've been to Marci."

She doesn't flinch. "I have."

"And coffee with my mother."

"Also yes." She holds my gaze. "And you still came."

"I wanted to see what you'd say about it."

"Nothing," she says. "There's nothing to explain. I saw something worth moving on and I moved." She sets her glass down. "That bothers you?"

A silence. "No."

"Good." She signals the waiter. "Because this is how things start to move."

She orders a Negroni. I switch to rye, neat.

"To second impressions," she says, lifting her glass.

"And slightly improved situations."

She settles, legs crossed, shoes off again. "So. What's your deal, Will Chaffee?"

"Which version?"

"The one that isn't rehearsed."

I watch the city through the glass, then her. "You ever build a life that looks exactly right from the outside and can't remember how much of it you chose?"

She doesn't smile. "Exhausting."

"It is. But it photographs well."

"You deflect well," she says.

"And you interrogate like you're on deadline."

"Comes with the job." She turns her glass. "Legacy profiles. Stories that mean something to readers who pretend they care."

"And you? What do you care about?"

She holds my gaze. "People who know what they want and make it happen."

She waits. "Why'd you say yes tonight?" she asks.

"I wanted someone to ask me a question I didn't already have an answer to."

She studies me. "Last time you looked like you'd escaped a hedge fund hostage situation."

"Accurate. I walked away from Sutter Rowe." I leave the rest of it there. "Building something instead."

No concern. No pause. Just interest.

"Good," she says. "You seem ready for something more."

We let the music blur for a minute.

Then she talks — Winston-Salem, debutante balls, gowns heavy with expectation, parties where last names matter more than eye contact. Growing up inside a tobacco fortune, everyone knowing your family before they know you.

"That town can smother you with politeness," she says. "Like you're born into a script someone else already wrote."

Then New York. Paris. Runways that were battlegrounds. Casting directors who never looked up. Editors who remembered her mother more than her.

Not glossy. Survival with good lighting and better lipstick.

"People think they know me," she says. "I've reinvented more times than I can count."

"You're not who they think."

"Neither are you," she says.

It hangs there.

I look at her past the angles and the polish. Ambition, yes. Also something lonelier. Familiar.

I reach for her hand without deciding to. She lets me.

For a moment the rooftop falls away. No noise. No pressure. Just two people who have been performing for so long they've almost forgotten what they're performing for.

When we kiss it isn't fireworks.

I don't know what I'm looking for when I go into the study. Something to occupy my hands, maybe. I open the low drawer that hasn't been opened in years — old files, lacrosse team photos, Colby yearbooks, the paper archaeology of a life I stopped tending.

Under a box labeled MBA Apps a slim jewel case with a fading label.

Demo WC – Colby.

I turn it over. Marco dared me to blow off studying and record it. I almost mailed it to a few places. Instead I filed it away. Along with everything else I didn't chase.

The study speakers still paired to my father's old Bang and Olufsen. I slid in the disc. Converted the tracks. Pressed play.

Guitar and voice. Hesitant at first, then stronger. Not perfect. Raw. I turned it up. I remembered that basement room — Marco smuggling two mics and a battered mixer from the campus theater, furniture pushed aside, one desk lamp, cold air coming through the window we couldn't fully close.

We laughed through the second take. I forgot lyrics. My voice cracked. I played the bridge twice. We kept two tracks, dubbed them to the only blank disc I had, labeled it in Sharpie.

My voice was younger on the recording. Rough. But I remembered every word, every chord. How it felt to write without thinking about who might hear it.

In that basement room I wasn't performing for anyone. Not my father. Not the market. Not Sutter Rowe.

Just this.

But morning doesn't wait. The light shifts. The world moves. I shower, pull on jeans and a flannel, then swap them for something cleaner—charcoal slacks, a navy sweater, boots I haven't worn in months. Casual, but presentable. Still me, dressed enough to pass. No tie.

Enough said.

* * *

Two hours later, I'm in a warehouse loft on West 26th, dry-erase marker in hand like I'm twenty-five again and still believe work can save me. Ian's barefoot in sneakers, hunched over a fold-out table. Gear piled everywhere – monitors glowing, paper scattered, energy drinks close. The room carries damp hoodies and ambition.

"So," he says. "Here's what I've got."

He launches—data rails, underwriting layers, embedded guardrails. The aggregation is real. Early, messy, but real. The vision isn't yet—at least not in a way an investor can taste.

I start sketching boxes and arrows. "Forget mechanics for a second. What's the story?"

He blinks. "Like... the tagline?"

"No. The thing I can pitch in two sentences. The line that makes a managing partner lean in instead of glazing over."

"A new way to align financial health with profitability?"

"Too soft. Again."

He thinks. "We use behavioral data to make access to money safer for the person traditional scoring screws."

"Better." I nod. "Say it like you believe it. And don't say people. Say her. Make it intimate."

He scribbles, muttering. I pace, adrenaline kicking.

Then it hits.

"We're not building a product," I say. "We're building agency. Control.

The relief of swiping and knowing it won't decline."

His eyes spark. "Yes. Exactly."

I write on the board: SAWBUCK We see potential and fund it before you ask.

Under it: Anticipate. Align. Empower.

It sounds like bullshit. Good bullshit—the kind that gets a second meeting.

Ian stares. "That's... actually good."

I grin. "Right. It has to feel inevitable. Not another fintech. Systemic—like it always should've existed."

Ian smirks. "Not vague at all."

"We're not a bank," I say. "But we fund. That's the paradox. We don't wait for people to come to us—we already know who they are."

Ian nods. "We're not underwriting—"

"We're unlocking," I say. "Potential traditional underwriting misses because it never shows up on paper."

Ian rubs his jaw. "Cool. How do we not get sued? Or audited into oblivion?"

"Our bank partner will carry that," I say. "We plug into their rails and make them smarter. They hold the deposits. We generate the demand."

Ian taps. "We monitor repayment through real-time performance—point-of-sale, inventory turns, customer data. Tech makes risk transparent."

He turns his screen. "Basic structure: revenue triggers mapped to predictive cycles by merchant type and flow timing."

"That's what seed wants to see," I say, grabbing a marker. "But it has to land."

I draw a triangle: Velocity at the top. Trust bottom left. Predictive Cash Flow bottom right.

"This isn't plugging gaps with loans," I say. "It's seeing businesses the way their future customers will—before the P&L catches up. Before the paperwork exists."

"Needs a hook," Ian says. "Tagline-clean."

I smile. "That's what I do," I say. "Grounded, not app-y. A bridge between legacy finance and possibility."

Ian deadpans. "TED Talk voice unlocked."

"Not the goal," I admit. "We back growth before anyone else sees it. See what's coming. Bet on what matters."

Close. Not it.

I draw three columns: Markets. Merchants. Movement.

"Let's clean it up," I say. else:

We fund before you ask. We don't erase it.

We work for hours. Map flows. Draft outlines. I sketch personas; he sketches features. Laughter. Momentum. A little hope. It feels like momentum. I know the investors to call. I know how to dress this up. I know how to make them want it.

He has the heartbeat.

I have the voice.

Something clicks into place.

* * *

214 Water Street is a four-story brick warehouse with a dented metal door and a freight elevator that groans like it's ready to retire —a place startups go when they're too broke for glass towers and too proud for co-working spaces Before loft conversions made it creative space it was a warehouse. The lobby still smells faintly of varnish and old rope.

Our floor has exposed beams, uneven hardwood, windows that rattle in the wind off the East River. Ian calls it startup charm. I call it rent we can barely make.

We've been here two months since Nico and Daren walked out of Sutter Rowe.

And I'm still here.

Everyone else is gone. Even Ian—when he's focused—kills the lights by eight. But I stay.

Laptop open. Slack silent. Trello boards untouched.

Another seed investor passed this morning—polite, vague: Too early-stage for us right now. Keep us posted.

I don't even forward the email.

The dev team in Uruguay is two sprints behind. Beta testers aren't logging in. The only meaningful traction we've got is a PitchDeck post someone's cousin liked — the tech blog everyone in the space reads. I stare at the dashboard mockup we overpaid for clean, sleek, and hollow. It looks finished if you don't click too deep. That's the trick. We learned quickly where not to linger.

In the notebook beside the keyboard, in my own handwriting from last week:

We see potential where others see process.

We fund before they ask.

Not a bank. A bridge.

Wrong tone. Still wrong. I close the notebook.

The days blur.

We sharpen our pitch, re-cut the model. Nico tightens the narrative; Daren stress-tests the assumptions.

I rehearse until it no longer sounds like me.

* * *

The Uber crawls downtown, headlights smearing across the glass as the city slips into its night self—garlic, rain on asphalt, people chasing something brighter than they feel. I let it move me.

Blake pulls me into a night that feels more staged than spontaneous—Saga sixty-three floors up, all glass, candlelight, and curated shadows. She slips through the room like someone born for reflective surfaces: silk that moves like water, a low-smoked perfume you catch only in pieces, the kind of poise that looks effortless but is absolutely engineered. She knew half the room, and the other half pretended to know her. Next to her, people assume I belong.

Over martinis, she asks what's happening with Sawbuck —"the real thing," she says, brushing her thumb along her glass as if she is coaxing the truth out of it.

"Burning through our cash," I tell her. "Dev costs and tech build are eating us alive. Early, messy, but maybe something."

Her eyes lit the way expensive things catch light—sharp, intentional.

"Then stop hiding it."

"It's not ready."

"Nothing worth anything ever is," she says. "But you know what is ready? The part people care about." She thinks for half a breath, then:

"Your mother's name still opens half the doors in this city. Why aren't you using it?"

I shake my head. "Because it's hers. And she'd weaponize it."

Blake smirks—perfect, practiced.

"Every legacy is a weapon. The trick is deciding who gets to aim it."

She tosses out angles faster than I can track—founder profiles, underdog narratives, "the son of an icon building something with purpose." Half of it feels insane. Like she sees a future I hadn't signed off on.

The bill comes. She covers it with one fingertip, looks up at me like she is letting me in on something rare.

"Let me think on it," she says.

In the gold-lit elevator ride down, I catch our reflection—her polished, intentional; me unsure which version of myself she is selling back to me.

* * *

By the time I walk into the office the next morning, it's pushing eleven. The place is humming—bright overheads, keyboards firing, half-finished coffees abandoned in rows. No one looks up, but everyone notices. Nico spots me first from the window side. He doesn't say anything—just lifts an eyebrow over his mug, the closest thing to you good? I'm going to get.

Daren doesn't even hear me come in—AirPods in, whispering to his screen like he's negotiating peace with a spreadsheet. I drop my bag, try to pretend arriving at eleven isn't another crack in a week full of them.

Last night's orbit—the drinks, the people, Blake's style—still clings to me like perfume I didn't ask to wear. Everyone's chasing. I'm still searching.

The cash we're burning isn't venture money. Not a bank loan. It's what's left of what my grandfather left me—capital meant to anchor a life, not bankroll a gamble. I told myself it was an investment in a future worth building. Now it feels like betting the last of the family silver on a long shot.

Runway: a few weeks. The number in my head: one hundred million. Enough to build the bench, make the product real, and convince the market we're not just another pretty pitch. Until then, every meeting feels like a wager.

Blake's voice echoes: It's about winning. Ian's voice lingers too, quieter—his hesitations when I pushed the tech team build.

I've circled this for weeks. Investors keep looking past the deck and right at me, measuring whether I'm the one who can deliver. They're right. I'm the only one who can sell this in a room of people who don't care about mission or the underbanked unless it pays.

Ian believes in Sawbuck like it's a cause. I believe in it's a tool, maybe even a blade—and blades need to be pointed in the right direction.

My father made it sound clean: push Ian into the build, put my face on the front, bring in people around him so the machine runs if he walks. Cold, sure—but getting harder to argue with.

I once swore I'd never be like my father—making quiet decisions that cost other people more than they cost him. And here I am, in a quiet room, deciding whether to cut loose the guy who started this.

Not fixing. Not hesitating.

The decision doesn't feel theoretical anymore.

It's dark now. The place has thinned to the three of us—Nico, Daren, me. Daren's buried in a model, hoodie up, barely blinking.

I pour a drink I don't really want and carry it to the window. Below, traffic is thick enough that the brake lights glow like embers in a dying fire.

Nico leans back, eyes on my glass.

"You ever notice how speed messes with your sense of direction?" he says.

"At sea?" I ask, thinking of the sail.

"In life."

I force a grin. "We'll keep it straight."

He doesn't look convinced. He turns back to his screen. The glow flickers across his face. The thought stays with me, low and steady, like a current shifting under the surface. I finish the drink in two pulls and set the glass down harder than I meant to.

I stand there a long time, watching brake lights fade.

I don't go to my desk. At the far end, I duck into a glass-huddle room with a sticky door and an un-erased whiteboard. I close it behind me, sit, and scroll to a name I haven't tapped in years.

The tech needs more than we have. Not marginally more — significantly more. Building the bench, making the rails production-ready, getting to the point where the product can handle real volume. I've been running the numbers in my head for three days and they keep landing in the same place. We need a serious backer. Someone with real capital and the patience to let it breathe.

Q's name sits in my contacts like a door I haven't opened in a long time.

We haven't really talked in three, maybe four years—just a couple of casual social media exchanges. Last time I saw him was his West Village wedding; I drank too much at the rehearsal dinner and left before dessert. His family has the kind of money that doesn't sweat recessions. Third-generation wealth that somehow dodged the curse mine didn't—backcountry Greenwich real estate, a High Pond Club board seat, and a trust that probably throws off more daily interest than Sawbuck's seed ask.

It isn't just cash. It's access. If he buys in, others follow. That's how that world works. I can hear him now, half laughing, half curious:

So, Chaffee—what's the play? The play is survival. Tech bench. Burn rate. Runway. Less than three weeks before we're out of both.

"Alright, Quimbo," I mutter. "Let's see if you're still good for a favor."

I hit call before I can overthink it.

"Quart," he says—warm, surprised. "Man, it's been too long. How the hell are you?"

"Better than I have a right to be. You?"

"Busy. Kids are feral. House is a construction zone. Business is good. Surf's been decent when I can sneak away."

"Still riding the same beat-up board from high school?"

"Hell no. Upgraded. Kept the old one, though."

I smile. "You were always sentimental about gear."

"Coming from the guy who still wears his Colby beanie in June?"

"Guilty."

The pause after that is just long enough to feel the weight of why I called.

"I'm going to be in your neck of the woods next week," I say. "We should catch up. Grab dinner. My treat."

"Will Chaffee buying? Must be serious."

"Just overdue." I keep it light, but the shape of the conversation I need is already forming.

"So next week? We catch up—and a drink to celebrate or fail spectacularly?"

"Absolutely. Tuesday night?"

"Let's make it happen."

I hang up. Seed planted. A possibility—and right now, that's what I need.

CHAPTER 12

OLD BUDDY

Tuesday. I fly to LA not because I have to. Because the thing I'm thinking about building needs an anchor that isn't just Ian's conviction, my grandfather's money and my father's voice. Someone who knew me before all of it. Someone who will ask the question I don't want to answer and make me answer it anyway.

The hotel is Q's choice. The lobby carries the quiet of a place where money has stopped needing to announce itself.

He's at the bar when I walk in. The same easy grin he had at sixteen on a frozen Connecticut road with a Porsche belonging to a friend of my father's in a ditch behind us.

"Will Chaffee," he says, standing. "I thought you'd gone witness protection."

"Not quite." We shake, then hug. The hug of two people who don't do it enough.

He orders bourbon straight. The way we drank before we knew better. The first minutes are the years we didn't talk — his move to LA, the family office, the foundation, the deals that hit and the ones that didn't. He asks about Liz. I tell him she's the same. He makes the sound everyone makes about Liz.

"You remember sophomore summer?" he says. "Your parents' house. Pool house roof. You with the acoustic trying to play "Wish You Were Here" for three girls who were more interested in your mother's wine cellar."

I laugh. "We drained it."

"And bribed the responding officer with your dad's cigars." He shakes his head.

"God, we were stupid."

"Resourceful," I say.

"Same thing at fifteen." Q tilts his head. "Different now," he says. He's not smiling.

"Whatever happened to Sarah Whitmore?" he says.

"I have no idea," I say.

"You finally asked her out. Junior year. She said yes." He shakes his head. "You missed the date. Music gig." "I don't remember that."

Q holds his drink up. "To Sarah Whitmore."

We drink

By the second round we've covered the years and the names and the distances between who we were and who we became. He knew my father when he was still standing. That sits between us the way it always does —present, unaddressed, not uncomfortable.

There's a pause between stories. Just big enough.

"Q," I say. "I've got something I want you to hear."

He sets his glass down. Amber catching the bar light. His eyes change.

"Go for it," he says.

I tell him about Sawbuck. Not the deck — the story. Founder's mother, the laundromat in Crown Heights, the sixty-three-year-old woman who finally had something built that works for her. The platform. The traction. The window. Somewhere in the middle of it we order off the bar menu without looking at it. By the time I finish the entrées have arrived and neither of us has touched them.

Q turns his glass. "Sounds noble," he says. The same two words he always uses when he's reserving judgment.

He's quiet a moment. The bar light on his glass.

"Founder's mother. The laundromat in Crown Heights." He nods — not approval exactly, something more careful. "That part I believe. That part's worth protecting." He looks at me directly. "Don't let the rooms talk you out of that. Whatever else this becomes — don't lose that part."

"It is. And it's working."

"How much?"

"One hundred million seed. You'd be in early right after my money, founder's terms."

He nods slowly. "Your dad ever tell you how many times he pitched my old man?"

"I was there for one of them."

"So was I." He picks up his fork. Puts it back down. "Quart, what happened at Sutter Rowe?"

There it is. The question I came here for.

"I left," I say.

"I know you left. Why?"

I look at him. Q has known me since we were eight years old. He knows exactly who I am when I'm performing and he knows the difference.

"Because I couldn't keep selling something that felt like a performance," I say. "And Sawbuck felt like the first real thing I'd touched in years."

"And the founder? This Ian. What's he getting?"

"He gets the infrastructure and the capital to scale what he built."

"And what are you getting?"

"A stake in something that matters."

Q holds my gaze for a long moment. Reading the full sentence, not just the words.

"Is it clean?" he asks. Quiet. Specific.

"It's structured correctly," I say.

He hears the difference. He doesn't press it. That's Q — he asks the question, gets the honest answer, decides what to do with the space between what you said and what you meant.

Q turns his glass. Quiet for a moment — not thinking about what to say, but about something far earlier.

"Early days of the family office I had a founder. Real thing — the actual article. I put my name behind him, structured it right, gave him everything he needed." He sets the glass down. "Lost him by year three. Not the money — he stayed. But the man I'd believed in was gone. A stranger showed up in the same suit." He looks at me. "Best investment I ever made financially. Still think about him."

He picks up his fork. "You learn to read that gap early or you learn it late."

"Send me the deck," he says. "I'll have my guys look at it. If the numbers hold I'll talk to Lauren and Wes." He picks up his fork. "And Will — whatever you here, make sure it's something you really want."

We eat. We drift to easier ground — his kids, his wife, a house in Malibu he describes with the embarrassed pride of someone who still can't quite believe his life.

Later, when the bill is settled, I find myself at the piano in the corner of the bar. I don't decide to sit down. I just sit down.

Muscle memory takes over. Something low and slow — Billy Joel, half-forgotten, the chords coming back before the melody does. Q appears at my shoulder. He leans over and starts singing the chorus, hopelessly off-key, pounding the lid in time.

The bar turns. A few people smile. Someone claps along.

When we wind down Q throws his arm around me in a mock bow and we take the moment like we earned it.

Outside, the LA air is cool and the palms move in the dark.

"Text me when you're back in town, Quart," Q says as we leave the hotel.

"I will."

He gets in his car. Rolls the window down. "The founder. Ian." He holds my eyes. "Don't lose him."

The window goes up. The car pulls away.

The piano still humming somewhere in my hands. The long flight home and somewhere in New York a platform called Sawbuck running on Nostrand Avenue.

I didn't come for the music.

I came for the ask.

Both are true. That's the problem.

In the Uber to my hotel my phone lights up.

Blake: Back in the city Friday. Dinner?

Simple. Direct. Like she already knows the answer.

Will: Friday works.

LA sparkles around me.

* * *

The bar is on Court Street, three blocks from the F train. My father's suggestion. A place that has been on the same corner forever and doesn't need to announce it — dark wood, decent scotch, a bartender who knows returning customers by their drink and doesn't ask about the gaps between visits.

He's in the corner when I walk in. Dark jacket despite the hour. Glass already in hand. He catches me coming in and nods — as if he'd been expecting me and wasn't sure yet what I'd brought.

I sit across from him. Order rye. The bartender sets it down and disappears.

"Quimby is coming in," I say.

I say it directly, without preamble, because that's the language my father respects and because I have been rehearsing this moment since the plane touched down at LaGuardia. I want it to land the way it felt when it happened — clean, real, earned.

My father absorbs it. The machinery running — calculation, assessment. He takes a sip of his scotch.

"Tell me," he says.

So I do. All of it. The hotel bar, the pitch, Q's questions and how I answered them. The term sheet arriving three weeks later. One hundred million, two tranches, founder's terms. The cap table, the structure, the valuation. Ian's equity position and my own. I tell him everything because I want him to see the whole picture and I want the whole picture to be what makes him lean forward the way he leaned forward in the Astoria diner.

I watch his face as I talk.

He doesn't lean forward.

He listens with the stillness of a man filing information rather than receiving it. His glass stays on the table. When I finish he lets it sit.

"The Quimbys," he says.

"Q's family office. He runs it now. They've backed—"

"I know what the Quimby family office has backed," my father says. "I knew Q's grandfather. I knew his father." A pause that closes the door on that subject. "The Quimbys' money always comes with strings, Will."

"Q is my oldest friend."

"Q is your oldest friend," he says. "The family office is a different entity. When Q's team sits across from you with term sheets and board seats, they are not your friend's family. They are capital with obligations to its own interests." He picks up his glass. "Your oldest friend and the institution that just wired a hundred million dollars into your company are not the same thing. The sooner you understand, the better."

"The terms are founder-friendly," I say.

"The terms are what they are until they need to be something else," he says. "Seed terms don't survive contact with an A round. What's founder-friendly at one hundred million becomes negotiable at five hundred." He sets his glass down. "And when the Quimbys decide the terms need to change, Q will be in a room with his family's money managers and his fiduciary obligations and you will be surprised to discover which one he chooses."

"You don't know Q," I say.

"I know the Quimbys," he says. Simply. Finally.

Silence.

"What about the founder?" he says.

"Ian."

"What's his position now?"

I tell him. The equity split. The operational structure.

My father absorbs it. Nods slowly. "And he accepted this."

"He understood the value I was bringing."

His expression shifts. Not disapproval — something more complicated. "The founder always thinks he understands the value the money is bringing," he says. "Until the money is in the room and the value starts making decisions." He leans back. "You've put yourself between Ian and his company. When it goes well he'll be grateful. When it doesn't — and something always doesn't, Will, that's not pessimism, that's the business — he'll remember exactly how the structure was built and who built it."

"I know what I'm doing," I say.

"Do you Rube?" He says it without heat. "Because what I'm hearing is a man who took a significant equity position in a founder's company, is about to bring in outside capital with its own agenda, and is now sitting in a bar in Brooklyn telling his father about it like he expects to be congratulated." He leans forward. "I'm not going to congratulate you. I'm going to tell you what's coming."

I look at him.

"Q's terms will tighten at the A round. Ian will eventually understand what you took from him. And when both of those things happen at the same time, you'll be the man in the middle with obligations in every direction and loyalty from none of them." He sips. "That's not a prediction. That's arithmetic."

I came here for something specific. The lean forward. The hand on the arm. The look that felt like faith in the Astoria diner.

What I'm getting instead is a forensic examination of everything that could go wrong, delivered in the voice of a man who has been right about the wrong things his entire life.

"So what do you suggest?" I ask.

He stares at me for a moment. "Stop waiting for permission," he says. "Stop needing people to see what you're doing before you act. Stop—" He pauses. "Stop performing for an audience that isn't paying you back." He puts the glass down. "Trust yourself. Not Q. Not Ian. Not anyone. The only person you can trust is yourself."

He says it like wisdom — the philosophy of a man who has lived by it his entire life and cannot see what it cost him.

"You're right," I say.

And I mean it. In this bar, in this light, with his voice doing what it always does — finding the place where my fear lives and speaking directly to it — I mean it completely.

He nods once. Drinks.

He asks about valuations and dilution and what happens to my position if the A round terms shift. Not about Gloria. Not about the people the platform was built for. Just the numbers.

I answer all of it. I am good at this. I have always been good at performing competence for my father.

When I stand to leave he walks me to the door. Court Street in the Brooklyn cold, the F train audible somewhere underneath us.

"One more thing," he says. "Ian." He looks at me steadily. "Men who feel displaced have a way of becoming problems."

He says it like management advice, not a warning about himself.

He doesn't say it like a warning about himself.

I walk to the subway.

On the F train back to Manhattan I sit in the window seat and feel the thing I always feel leaving my father — worse than when I arrived, carrying something I didn't come for, unable to put it down.

He might be right about Q. He's probably right about Ian. Right about all of it, maybe.

And he is sitting alone in a bar on Court Street having delivered that wisdom to his son, and he will walk home to his small immaculate apartment and pour himself one more scotch, and the rightness of everything he said will keep him excellent company.

I think about Ian on the platform at 153rd Street in his Yankees cap, looking like he belonged there in a way I never quite will.

I think about Gloria's back room. The photograph. The smell of clean laundry.

I think about Q at the piano, arm around my shoulder, the bar turning.

The train runs express through the dark.

* * *

Blake picks the restaurant. Of course.

It's a place in the West Village that seats thirty and doesn't take reservations except for people who don't need to make them. Low light, paper on the tables. She's already seated — dark green dress, the Carolina accent she's stopped trying to flatten, a glass of something white in front of her.

She clocks me coming in. I slide in across from her and she pours me a glass without asking.

"LA suited you," she says.

"It was work."

"It's always work with you." She says it without edge. "What are you building?"

I tell her where things stand — the platform, the traction, the early users coming through the food vendors and the after-school programs in Brooklyn. The verification flow, what makes it different from every other fintech play trying to serve the same market. What I'm building and why the window is open right now and won't stay that way.

I don't mention Q.

Blake listens the way she does everything — fully present, nothing wasted. She turns her wine glass slowly. When I finish she's quiet for a moment.

"Sawbuck," she says. Trying the name.

"Old slang for a ten. Ian named it for his mother."

She nods. Still turning the glass. I can see her thinking — not about whether the business is good, she's already decided it's good. She's thinking about something else. "What?" I ask.

"You know who your mother is."

"I've been aware of that for some time."

"I mean her brand. What she represents. The specific way her name still moves in a lot of rooms in this city." She leans forward slightly. "Elizabeth Prescott's son leaves banking to build a financial platform for the underbanked. That's not a business story. That's a cultural story. That's a cover."

Something shifts in her face.

She smiles.

"Yeah," I say. "It's what you do."

"Stories that mean something." She holds my gaze. "And I've been trying to find the right angle on your mother for a very long time. She and her handler can be evasive."

"Marci. Absolutely. That's become her primary function. Unless Liz sees a real opportunity."

"Exactly. And this is the right leverage," Blake says. Not cruelly. Just as fact.

I let it settle. The restaurant hums around us.

"You're describing a piece that uses Liz's legacy to launch Sawbuck," I say.

"I'm describing a piece that gives your mother the retrospective she's been angling for since the Oscars dropped her from the A-list," Blake says. "And happens to also be about her son and what he's building and why." She sips her wine. "Everybody wins."

"Except it isn't that simple with her."

"Nothing is simple with women like your mother. But women like your mother want to be seen. Give her the cover. She'll give you the platform."

She's right. That's just Blake. She's usually right.

"This is also how you raise your seed round," she says. "The right story in the right rooms before you're ready to pitch."

"Seed is pretty much covered," I say.

She tilts her head. "Really." Not a question. Filing it.

"But platform users are another matter. And Series A is eighteen months away." I lean forward. "The right cultural story now — Elizabeth Prescott's son, what he's building and who he's building it for — that's exactly the kind of credibility that moves institutional investors."

Something changes in her face. More than interest now. "That's actually the better story," she says. "Seed is table stakes. Series A is legitimacy. That's the piece."

"Good luck getting access," I say. "To her, to the house, to the whole thing."

"All I need is you," she says. Simply.

The word hangs there. Both meanings present. Neither disclaimed.

We eat. We talk about other things — her childhood in Winston-Salem, the weight of a name everyone knows before they know you, the way old tobacco money taught her to recognize performance from fifty feet. She tells me about Paris, about a casting director who looked through her for three seasons until she learned to look through him first.

She tells it without self-pity.

"You grew up in it too," she says. "The performance."

"Since before I could name it."

"Then you know the only way out is through." She refills her glass. "Or you find someone who sees it the same way and you stop performing for each other."

"Is that what this is?" I ask.

She smiles — the real one, only partially curated. "I haven't decided yet. Have you?"

We walk out into the West Village night. She has a car coming. I have a car coming. We stand on the sidewalk in the particular closeness of two people who have had an honest conversation and aren't sure what to do with it yet.

She kisses me — not the performative cheek kiss, the real one — and steps back.

"Talk to your mother," she says. "Warm her up to the idea. I'll handle Marci."

"Marci is not handleable."

"Everyone is handleable. You just have to find what they actually want." Her car pulls up. "That's the whole map."

She gets in. Gone.

I walk.

* * *

Three weeks later, the huddle room at Water Street feels even smaller with all of us crammed inside. Daren claims the corner by the whiteboard, laptop open, screen glowing with the model. Nico leans against the glass wall, coffee in hand, giving the street outside a casual surveillance. Ian sits opposite me at the table, elbows on the wood, pretending he isn't keyed up.

Q's face fills the screen. He is leaning back in a chair that belongs in a Malibu beach house. Beside him are Wes Greer and Lauren Keeley from the Quimby Family Office — Wes with the silver hair and clubroom smile, Lauren with the look of someone who could spot a flaw in a diamond.

"Will," Wes says after the greetings. "We appreciate how responsive you and your team have been. Every request, every follow-up — you've kept the process moving." He straightens a cufflink. "We've finalized our view on the seed."

My shoulders tighten. "And?"

Q grins like we're still seventeen, sneaking bourbon from his father's cabinet. "We're in with terms, Quart. Quimby Family Office will lead, and we'll bring in two other family offices we like to invest with alongside us."

Lauren continues — calm, surgical. "One hundred million, in two tranches. Given the risk profile, we're not doing this for the twenty-five percent you proposed. We'll require fifty-one percent ownership and full control of the board, with Mr. Quimby as chairman."

For a second the words just hang there. Daren stops typing. Nico raises an eyebrow. Ian sits back, arms crossing.

Wes is the closer. "It's a swing for the fences, guys. But you've got the drive, and we like the idea. Just — don't try to bunt."

Q adds: "Brother, this isn't standard for us. Don't make us regret it."

We wrap with a little banter — a nod to our dinner in LA, a joke about my history of dating models — but the impact of the terms doesn't move.

When the call ends, we don't say anything right away.

"It's a lifeline," Ian finally says. "We take it."

I feel the terms tighten in my chest. But I force a smile, because that's what a leader does. "Yeah. It's a go."

Ian stretches his arms above his head, almost in relief he leaves the space to grab a coffee. I stay in my chair.

My father was right about the strings. He is always right about the strings.

I accepted them anyway. Because the alternative is watching

Sawbuck die with clean hands and nothing to show for it.

* * *

Q sends the formal term sheet the following Tuesday.

One hundred million, two tranches. The terms are real. The commitment is real. And whatever the last remaining argument I had with myself about whether this was serious — it just ran out.

I put my phone face-down on the desk.

Not a bad Tuesday. Not a good one. Just a Tuesday with thin light coming through the floor-to-ceiling glass and the floor running at its usual pitch — keyboards, calls, the quiet percussion of people executing things they've stopped believing in.

CHAPTER 13

WHAT I TELL MYSELF

One hundred million in the bank—almost—is something. Enough to keep the lights on, pay the engineers, even upgrade the IKEA desks. But I know better than to mistake this for stability.

This is runway. And runways only matter if you have liftoff. I step into the bullpen. Ian's at his stand-up desk with a knot of engineers, sketching code on a legal pad like he's storyboarding a heist. Daren is buried in spreadsheets. Nico taps out emails with his usual one-hand, one-coffee rhythm.

I walk to the whiteboard wall, grab a marker, and write in block letters: SERIES A — Q1. Ian glances over from his stand-up desk. "We haven't even closed seed." "Seed keeps us alive," I say. "A makes us serious." He nods — genuine enough — but there's something quiet in the way he watches the board before heading back to his team.

The marker squeaks against the board. The room is very quiet.

Q's voice echoes—fifty-one percent... control of the board... I'll be chairman.

Everyone on our side smiled like it's a win, but I can feel the other part of it—the part that means this company isn't really ours anymore.

Ian's in the other huddle room, animated, walking a couple of new hires through their sprint schedule. He's in full founder mode—pacing, gesturing, explaining the big vision like it's the first day all over again. The energy fills the room. But it's not what I need right now.

Energy won't be enough.

I tell Daren and Nico I want to run through something later—just us.

I wait until the place thins out, until the overhead hum is the loudest thing in the space. Then I text them: Stay. Need to talk.

When they show up to the huddle room, the office is mostly dark. Nico leans against the far wall, hands in pockets, watching me like he's not sure if this is a meeting or an ambush. Daren drops into a chair with his laptop open, the glow lighting his face like a campfire.

"We've got the seed," I say, drawing a thick circle at the top of the whiteboard. "One hundred million is enough to build, but if we want to survive after launch, we start shaping the Series A story now."

The AC kicks off with a loud clank, filling the silence. Nico's still leaning there, expression somewhere between curious and concerned. He doesn't say a word. But I know that look—like he's watching the waterline creep higher and wondering if I even notice.

Daren looks up. "The tech's not finished. Ian—"

"Ian's doing his part," I cut in. "But investors don't just buy tech. They buy belief. They buy trust. We need them to see us as inevitable before they even see the platform."

Nico shifts his weight. "And by us, you mean... you."

I meet his eyes. "I mean Sawbuck. But yeah—there's always a face. That's how this works."

His eyes hold mine a second too long. Not an argument—just a quiet acknowledgment that he knows exactly what I'm doing. Daren says nothing, already building new slides.

I write three words on the board: Access. Trust. Impact. Underline them twice. "This is what we sell. Access for the underbanked. Trust in the product. Impact they can measure."

Daren's typing now, probably building the first slide in his head. Nico just watches me—measuring whether I believe my own pitch, or if I've just practiced it enough to make it sound like I do.

I cap the marker. "Deals close on trust," I say. "Investors trust people they know."

Daren nods. "You want me to rework the deck around those three?"

"Yeah. Start tonight."

We work until the hall lights go dark and the cleaning crew starts on the bathrooms. Deals don't close on tension; they close on trust. That's the note I leave hanging in the air as I shut my laptop.

I take a break and head home to shower and eat before getting back to it.

* * *

We're not formally raising yet. I'm building the story — gauging the room, making sure the right people have heard the name before we go to market.

By the time we walk into Brighton Capital I'm buried under polish — tailored suit, crisp logline, the steady voice I use when I need a room to believe something before the numbers earn it. They've already heard about Sawbuck. I made sure of that. Jessie, a junior partner, had texted the week before: Heard you left Sutter Rowe for a startup. Should we be taking a look? I waited a day to reply. Just long enough.

Ian arrives flustered. Daren already has the deck up — tight branding, clean TAM slide. I wave off Ian's lateness and we go in.

They shake Ian's hand. Polite, not warm. Then they turn to me. The energy shifts. Curious in the way people are when they don't want to be wrong. I've pitched here before. Won here before. They remember that.

I open the deck.

"Imagine a platform that uses behavioral signals — not just credit scores — to help people anticipate financial stress before it hits."

They nod. I keep going. "We're not just giving people tools. We're giving them timing. Precision. Predictability. The kind of confidence that breaks cycles."

Ian jumps in — API layers, consent frameworks, embedded underwriting logic. It's impressive. But their eyes drift back to me.

He's doing it right — careful, precise, faithful to the build. I step in anyway. Not to correct him. To simplify him.

By slide eight I've become the translator. Ian's voice fades. I finish his sentences — not to undercut him, but to land the message. I tell myself that.

The room is with me. Heads lift when I speak. Pens stop moving. The attention swings back to me. Rooms like this always find their center.

This is the part I'm good at.

Then a senior partner leans back. "What stage are you at?"

I could say we're early. I could say we're still learning. "Post-seed," I say smoothly. "Tech's built. We're structuring the cap table now. I'm leading the round."

Ian glances at me. Quick, uncertain. I don't look back.

The deck clicks to the final slide. Ian finishes the demo, still breathing hard, still hopeful. Across the table Brighton's team sits in silence. I can feel it before they say it.

Jessie clears her throat. "It's a compelling idea. Really is. But I'm struggling to get conviction around your ability to deliver the tech."

The senior partner: "We've been burned by this exact story before. Execution is everything. And your technical bench feels thin."

Ian starts to respond. I let him. I don't help.

He tries again. "We've got early partnerships—"

"We know. But we'd need more confidence in the build."

It's over.

We thank them, they thank us. The glass door closes.

I tell myself they didn't get it. I don't ask whether I let them misunderstand.

* * *

Nothing on the elevator down.

Not when Ian talks about reworking the demo. Not when Daren calls Brighton risk-averse.

Outside, Madison is loud and clean and moving on without us. It doesn't care what we just lost.

Nico shoves his hands into his pockets. "Well, that was uplifting."

Daren exhales. "We're officially the band no label wants but everyone compliments."

I try to laugh. The kind that tightens instead of easing.

Ian's quiet, hands in pockets. "They're wrong. They don't get it."

But I'm not sure.

A few blocks together, the city pushing around us. Then Nico bumps my shoulder once. "Text if you need us. Or whiskey. Or both." He and Daren peel off toward the subway, arguing about whether a burrito counts as two meals or one.

* * *

Ian and I keep walking. The city noise stretches between us.

He talks about next steps, who else we should circle back to. His voice is steady. Technical. He's already rebuilding the model in his head. That's how I know he hasn't felt it yet. Or maybe he has — and he's waiting to see if I'll say something first.

We stop at a crosswalk. Traffic hisses past. A delivery bike cuts too close.

"For the next round," I say, casual, like I've already decided this ten times, "I think it makes sense if I handle the narrative."

Ian turns toward me. "The narrative?"

"The story investors need to hear."

The light changes. We don't move right away.

"I can walk them through the architecture," he says. No edge. Just offering ground. "If they understand how it's built—"

"They don't need that level of detail yet," I cut in.

The word yet hangs between us. Even I'm not sure what it's buying me.

We start walking again. My phone buzzes — something from Blake — but I don't check it.

"This round needs a single voice," I say.

I don't know why I choose that phrasing. I just know it reads clean.

Ian slows. Not angry. Not shocked. Just recalibrating.

"So what am I now?" he asks.

I look at the traffic instead of him. Yellow cab. Black SUV. A guy jogging in place at the corner like he's late for a life he still believes in.

I don't answer.

That's answer enough.

We stop outside a bank branch with marble columns no one notices anymore. Ian adjusts his backpack strap — precise, like the world still deserves good handling.

"I meant what I said," he tells me. "About believing in this."

I nod. Because I did too. At least once.

"Did you know they had concerns about the tech?" he says.

I shrug.

"They didn't ask the right questions," he pushes.

"That's not how this works."

Hurt flashes across his face. "I built this from scratch, Will. I believe in it. I thought you did too."

I don't answer. Because right now I'm not sure.

A delivery truck rumbles by. When it passes the silence feels heavier.

"Ian—" I start.

He turns. There's no accusation in his face — just a tired kind of understanding, the kind that hurts more than anger ever could. "You knew they were worried about the tech," he says. "Before I did."

I don't answer fast enough.

He adjusts his backpack strap, shifts his laptop under his arm. No big exit. No flare of temper. Just acceptance. He turns east. Disappears into foot traffic.

No scene. No door to slam. Just another guy absorbed by the city.

I stand there longer than I need to. My thumb hovers over Alex's name.

I pocket the phone and start walking. Faster now.

* * *

The next room smells faintly of leather and old coffee. Ian in a side chair, deck up, introductions made. I speak first.

When Ian starts walking them through the architecture, I simplify him — not because he's wrong, but because I know where the room is going. His careful answer becomes my cleaner one.

Nico watches from the far end of the table with the look he's been giving me since Brighton.

When it breaks, I'm the one they shake last.

In the hallway Ian falls in beside me. "You didn't let me answer a single question."

"We didn't have time for the long version."

"The long version is the version that's true." He stops. "You sold them a different company than the one we're building."

"I sold them the company they'll fund."

He watches the elevator doors close between us.

The doors seal. The elevator drops.

No nodding heads. No curious eyes.

I lean back against the wall, adrenaline still fizzing in my chest. Ian's face the last thing I saw — tight, hurt, scared.

Not the pitch. Not the handshake. This.

I'm not giving it back.

* * *

Two blocks east. I've been walking without deciding to. The city keeps moving around me — cabs, shoulders, the indifferent percussion of people who know where they're going. At a light I stop. The crosswalk signal flashes. I look up at the building across the street — glass and steel, nothing like it — and something drops loose in my chest. The kind of memory that doesn't ask permission.

Someone brushed past my shoulder. And then I was somewhere else.

His office was on the third floor of a brick building downtown — the kind with brass numbers by the door and a lobby that smelled like floor cleaner and old air. His name was still on the directory when I arrived. That didn't last.

Inside, the lights were on but no one was working. Desks stripped to bare laminate. Filing cabinets yawning open, drawers tagged with orange stickers. Cardboard boxes folded and stacked like they were waiting their turn. Two men I didn't know unplugging computers. They moved carefully. Not cruel. Just thorough.

My father stood near the window, jacket on, tie loosened, phone in his hand like it might still ring if he stared at it long enough. When he saw me he straightened a little.

"Hey, Rube," he said. Too bright. "You made good time."

He didn't ask how school was. I didn't ask what was happening.

A woman in a gray blazer stepped out of his office carrying a framed photo. She checked a list, set it gently into a box. "Sir, we'll need access to the board room next."

"Of course," my father said. "Take whatever you need."

I followed him into his office. The shelves were bare except for a dust outline where books used to be. His desk clean in a way that felt unnatural — no papers, no pen, no coffee ring. The window behind it looked out at another building close enough to touch.

"They'll take the signage down this afternoon," he said. "Building management's already approved it." He tried to smile at that. It didn't quite form.

In the hallway, through the glass, I saw a maintenance man unscrewing the nameplate by the elevator.

Not my father's name.

My great-grandfather's.

The screws came out easily. The plaque resisted for half a second, then gave. The wall behind it was lighter — untouched by years of hands and passing eyes.

My father turned away before it came off. He pressed his thumb to his eye, quick, like brushing away dust. Then his hand stayed there.

His shoulders dipped — not much, just enough. He exhaled, and something in him gave up pretending. He didn't sob. He didn't make a sound.

But his face folded in on itself, and I saw it — the exact moment the math finally stopped working.

I didn't move. I didn't touch him. I stood there, hands at my sides, learning something I wouldn't understand for years.

He wiped his face with the heel of his palm. Straightened his tie. "Alright," he said, forcing the word into shape. "Let's go."

We walked out together, past the boxes, past the desks, past the men unplugging what's left.

I didn't carry anything. Neither did he.

That evening I went to Big's house. I don't remember deciding to — I just ended up there, the way you end up somewhere when you don't know where else to go.

He was in the study. Bourbon in hand, The Financial Record open on his knee, the television on low. He looked up when I came in. He knew. Of course he knew. Big always knew before you told him.

He didn't say anything about it. He didn't ask how my father was or what had happened or what it meant. He just moved the newspaper and said — "Sit down, Will."

I sat. We watched the news for a while without speaking. At some point he got up and came back with a Coke for me. He set it down on the side table without making it a thing.

"Your great grandfather built that business from nothing," he said finally. His voice was the same as always — level, deliberate, level, deliberate — a voice that had been making peace with things for a long time. "Your father tried. That's not nothing." He pauses. "It just wasn't enough."

He turned back to the television. The conversation was over.

I understood something sitting there that I still don't have full words for. Big wasn't angry. He wasn't disappointed in the ordinary way. He had seen this coming for so long that what I was watching wasn't grief — it was a man who had already done his grieving and was simply waiting for the facts to catch up.

* * *

Back on Madison the light has changed. I'm standing at the corner where Ian disappeared into the crowd.

My father pressing his thumb to his eye. My great grandfather's name coming off the wall. The version of himself he needed to become settling back into place.

I walk two blocks south and go home.

Seven years after the business failed, Big died. I was twenty-one, junior year at Colby. The call came on a Tuesday morning in October — my father, voice careful and clipped, the way he delivers facts he doesn't want to hold. He went in his sleep. No suffering. The funeral was in Greenwich, small, the way he would have wanted.

Three weeks after the funeral his attorneys called. There was a letter. The inheritance — the number was larger than I expected — had been placed in a trust and a foundation specifically designed to keep it protected. Protected from creditors. My father's creditors. Big had been thinking about this for years. The paperwork was meticulous. He had done his grieving, filed his conclusions, and made his arrangements.

The letter at the bottom said simply: for Will's work.

He left it to me and not to my father. That was the decision. Not an oversight, not an accident of timing. Big had watched Bill lose the company he'd been handed and he had made his judgment. The estate structure wasn't just protection from creditors — it was a statement.

I didn't know what that meant yet. I sat in my dorm room with the letter until it got dark. My father knew this was coming. He had known for years— not the specific number, maybe, but the decision. Big going around him in the most permanent way available. Not cruelty. Just the final verdict of someone who had decided long ago.

I used that money for Stern. And then to seed Sawbuck. By the time Q came in it was nearly gone.

* * *

The house is quiet when I get back. Liz is out. Blue meets me in the hallway. I crouch and let him lean into me.

There's a light on in the study. And something playing — guitar and voice, low, coming through the half-open door. I stop in the hallway and listen.

I know what it is before I reach the door. The Colby demo. I left it in the player months ago and forgot about it.

Alex is sitting on the floor, jeans, her Wesleyan sweatshirt, hair down, elbows on her knees. Blue pads in past me and settles on the rug. She doesn't look up. She's listening.

The track runs through to the end with that soft analog click you don't hear anymore.

The room holds it.

She picks up the jewel case from the desk. Looks at the label. Sets it back down carefully, like it's something breakable.

"When did you record this?" she asks.

"Years ago."

She doesn't say anything. She sits with it for a moment.

"This is the Colby demo," I say. "The one I mentioned at the pub in Cos Cob."

She picks it up carefully, the way you handle something that's been waiting a long time. Turns it over.

"You listened to it recently, though. What did you think?"

"That it was better than I remembered," I say. "Which made it worse."

She sets it down. "What I don't understand," she says, "is why you never went back. Not when you were twenty-two and someone talked you out of it — I understand that. But after. When you were old enough to know the difference between someone else's judgment and your own."

I think about it honestly. "Momentum," I say finally. "You get far enough down one road and the other one stops feeling like a road. It just becomes a field."

"And now?"

"Now I'm building something that might actually matter." I pause. "But the demo's still in the attic."

She looks at me. Not at the disc, not at the speakers. At me.

"It sounds like you," she says. "Without the armor."

I laugh. "Back then that was the only part of me I didn't have to fake."

Blue shifts on the rug and puts his head on his paws.

Alex holds the thought. When she speaks it's careful, like she's choosing between several true things and picking the one that costs her something too.

"That's different from choosing badly," she says. "That's having a choice taken."

I look at the speakers. The disc still spinning.

"It matters," she says simply. "I hear it in there. It still matters."

The room goes quiet — soft, specific, the particular quality of a silence between two people who have just said something true in each other's presence.

She stands. "Hit replay," she says. "It deserves to be heard again."

She goes. Blue stays.

I hit replay.

At some point I stop hearing it and start sleeping — the chair, the lamp still on, Blue a warm weight against my feet. When I wake up the disc has cycled through twice more and the house is completely still.

I pick up my phone.

You sail?

Three dots. Then:

Never learned.

Tuesday. Early. I'll teach you.

A longer pause this time.

Okay.

I set the phone down on the desk next to the jewel case. Outside, the Connecticut night. I don't go upstairs. I close my eyes again and let the disc run.

* * *

The yard has woken her up for the season — nothing fancy, just enough to make sure she floats. The wind sharpens as I reach the dock. Halcyon rocks gently against the fenders — same teak, same worn brass cleats, the same quiet welcome she has always had.

Alex appears at the top of the ramp, cheeks flushed from the wind, hair pulled back, eyes steady.

"It's a beautiful morning to be on the water." she says as I help her onboard.

"Watch your step at the rail. Once you're on, you're on." I tell her.

She nods once. We step aboard. I cast off the lines and talk her through it — tiller, sail, where to put her weight. She listens the way she listens to everything, fully, without performing attention. When I hand her the tiller she takes it carefully, then steadies. She doesn't pretend to know more than she does. She doesn't pretend to know less.

The Sound opens up ahead of us. The chop softens. The wind finds its rhythm.

Alex keeps one hand on the tiller, the sun on the curve of her shoulder. She looks grounded. Like she trusts the moment to hold.

I miss the wind shift.

The sail luffs — that soft, defeated flutter that means you've lost it — and the boat falls off her line. I know what to do. I've done it a thousand times. I hold the tiller anyway and let the moment run longer than it should, the boom swinging loose, the Sound opening flat and gray ahead of us.

Alex doesn't say anything. She shifts her weight the way I showed her — automatically now, like she's been doing it longer than an hour — and the boat steadies under us even before I bring her around.

I trim the sail. We find the wind again.

I've been quieter than usual since we cleared the harbor. She's noticed — she notices everything — but she's given me the water and the wind and the particular grace of not asking.

"So what's going on?" she says. "Why did you invite me for a sail on a Tuesday?"

I watch the water. The bow cutting through. A gull somewhere behind us working the wake.

"Is everything okay?" she asks.

"Investor stuff," I say.

She doesn't press it. Not buying it either. Just leaving the door open the way she does — quietly, without making it a thing.

"Or," she says, "we can just sail."

I look at her. The wind has caught a strand of hair across her face and she pushes it back without breaking her eyes from the horizon. Easy. Like she belongs out here.

"Yeah," I say. "Let's just sail."

But I tell her anyway.

"Another investor passed. Execution risk. Code for: we're not convinced you can pull this off." I look out at the water. "I didn't expect the no's to pile up this fast."

"That doesn't mean the idea's wrong."

"No." I let my hand rest on the rail. Smooth. Familiar. "I dragged Nico and Daren onto this. If it goes sideways it's on me."

"Because you care about them," she says.

"Because I sold them a vision I still believe in most days. But there's a whisper now. A what if."

Alex adjusts the sail — I told her how, fifteen minutes ago, and she remembered. The boat leans, steadies.

The wind tugs the sail. The boat cuts cleanly.

"Out here," she says, turning back to the horizon, "you can't hear the noise."

I don't answer. The teak is warm under my hand. Something loosens that has been tight for days.

We don't talk for a while.

We don't need to.

* * *

Back at the club the sun hangs low above the treeline, a gold streak across the water. I kill the engine and toss the stern line. Alex hops up without a word, tying off the bow with the same quiet confidence I've watched her use with Liz — steady, certain, like she's already decided nothing here is going to rattle her.

Two club attendants make their way down the dock — white polos, clipboard, long-handled brush.

"Evening, Mr. Chaffee. We'll take it from here."

I glance at Alex. She raises an eyebrow just slightly.

"We've got it," I say. "Appreciate it though."

They nod and turn back toward the boathouse.

Alex is already pulling the cockpit cushions to air. I grab the hose and start rinsing the deck. She coils the sheets and wipes the rails. We fall into rhythm — a gull somewhere over the Sound, the last light slipping behind the trees, her humming softly under her breath. Spanish.

"Haven't had a moment like that in a while," I say, drying my hands.

She tosses me a bottle of water. "Because of the wind? Or because we didn't capsize?"

I grin. "Both."

We sit on the dock with our legs over the edge. Salt in the air. Just the soft lapping of the water and the quiet satisfaction of having nothing to prove.

* * *

At home the sky's darkened to deep indigo. We come through the side door still carrying the smell of salt and wind. Blue trots over, nails clicking across the hardwood.

Alex smiles down at him. "Someone missed you."

I hang the keys on the hook. "Thanks for today."

She looks up. "You don't have to thank me. It was nice."

For a moment neither of us moves. Her hair tangled from the wind. I stop myself from closing the small distance between us.

"I'm going to head up," she says softly. "Shower, warm up."

"Sleep well."

She turns to go, then glances back — holding my eyes a moment longer than necessary. Something in it almost said. Then she disappears down the hall.

I scratch Blue behind the ear and go upstairs.

I don't turn the light on. I sit on the bed with the wind still in my hair and the salt still on my arms. On the dresser the leather notebook — investor notes, pitch revisions, half-formed taglines. I flip it open. The words blur in the dim light.

Ian's optimism still rings in my head. How this is just part of the grind. How the right investor is out there.

I used to think momentum was everything. Keep pushing. Keep building. Don't stop. Don't look down.

Now I'm looking down.

Nico and Daren are still in. Ian still believes — God, Ian still believes. But I'm not sure I do. Not in the wide-eyed late-night whiteboard way. If I don't believe — really believe — what am I dragging them toward?

I fall asleep without undressing, watching the ceiling fade into shadow.

CHAPTER 14

FOUNDERS

We go back to Brighton two weeks later. Nico has rebuilt the TAM slide, Darren has tightened the merchant data, and I've rewritten the opening to lead with Ian's architecture instead of the market size. Sheila Rosen listens the whole way through this time. Then she thanks us for coming back and passes again. Same reason, different language. I walk out onto Madison and stand on the sidewalk for a moment. Then I grab an Uber back to Water Street.

Third coffee, staring at the dashboard mockup. Alex's name on the screen.

Alex: Blake Caswell met with your mother and Marci this morning. Lizzy said yes to the CODA piece. Thought you would want to know.

I read it twice.

That's all she sends. No context. No editorial. Just the fact, delivered in her specific register — precise, neutral, deliberately not telling me what to do with it.

I put the phone down and look at the ceiling.

Blake went without telling me. Got to Liz without me in the room. And it worked.

The first time — Marci, the early conversation, before the story had shape — I let it go. Blake was moving, I understood that, and nothing had been agreed. This is different. This is Liz saying yes. This is the piece becoming real. And I found out from Alex.

Then Blake calls.

"She said yes," she says. No preamble.

"I heard," I say. "Alex texted."

A silence. "Alex is efficient."

"Tell me how it went."

She does. The Greenwich house, the sitting room, the way Lizzy had arranged the geography before Blake arrived. The 1994 Oscars detail — framed not as a fashion moment but as a shift in cultural power. Lizzy listening with the stillness of someone deciding whether the person across from her understood the difference between flattery and accuracy. And then the moment Lizzy's posture changed.

"Marci pushed back," Blake says. "Approval on photographs, final quote sign-off, timeline flexibility. Standard Lizzy terms. I agreed to all of it."

"They're reasonable," I say.

"She knows that. She wasn't trying to control the piece. She was trying to know she could trust the writer." Blake continues. "The piece will run in the October issue. Access visits start next month. I'll need time in the house, time with her, time with the archive."

Another pause. "And I'd like to understand Sawbuck properly. For the piece to land I need to understand what you're building and why."

"I can make that happen."

"I know." Her voice shifts slightly — the business register softening a fraction. "How are you doing? With everything."

My eyes go to the notebook on my desk. The wrong-tone taglines. The dashboard that looks finished if you don't go deep.

"Getting there," I say.

She doesn't press it.

"Why didn't you tell me you were going?" I ask.

Not long. "You would have tried to help," she says. "Briefed me. Told me which version of her to expect. And then whatever I got in that room wouldn't have been mine."

"That's not—" I stop.

"What?"

I stare at the dashboard. "That's not why I would have done it."

"I know," she says. "But it's what would have happened."

The line is quiet for a moment.

"You managed me," I say.

"I moved," she says. "There's a difference."

I laugh. She said my line back to me again. She keeps doing that.

"It worked," I say finally.

"It worked," she says. Then: "Talk soon."

She's gone.

The CODA piece is real. Blake moved without me. It worked. Those three facts arrange themselves in my head and I'm not sure in what order they matter

* * *

That evening Alex is at the kitchen table when I get home. Contracts casebook open, coffee going cold the way it always does. She looks up from whatever she was doing.

I sit down across from her.

"You set up the meeting," I say.

"She reached out through Marci. I put it on the calendar."

"She asked you not to tell me."

"Yes."

I nod. That's the truth and I knew it before she said it. "What did you see?" I ask.

Alex considers it properly — not performing the consideration, actually doing it. She closes the casebook.

"She came prepared," she says. "Not the Wikipedia version. The actual work — things about your mother that took real time to find." She pauses. "Your mother responded to being seen rather than being pitched. Most people who come into that room are pitching. Blake was observing."

"And Liz felt the difference."

"Immediately. About twenty minutes in your mother's posture changed — just slightly, the performance went down a register." She smiles slightly. "That almost never happens," she says.

The Cannes photograph redirect. The instrument. Since I was twelve.

"What was the moment?" I ask. "What did Blake say?"

"She said your mother changed what the red carpet meant. She didn't say she wore beautiful things. She said she made fashion into a language the culture had to learn to read." Alex continues. "Your mother had been waiting to hear that for thirty years. Blake knew it. And she said it like it was obvious — not as flattery, as fact."

I stay with it.

"One more thing," Alex says.

She has my full attention.

"When Blake was leaving she said your mother was extraordinary. I said yes." A moment. "She looked at me the way people look when they're recalibrating what they know about a room. She's very good at reading people, Will. She saw that I'd been there for the whole meeting. She knows I see things."

The implication settles without needing to be stated.

"And?" I ask.

"And nothing," Alex says. "She left." She opens the casebook. "She's very good," she says, not looking up. "I hope you know that."

I'm not sure if it's a warning or a compliment.

Maybe both.

I leave her with her casebook and her cold coffee and go upstairs.

* * *

In Midtown, the air's sharper, the sidewalks already crowded. I ride the elevator to the thirty-fourth floor, the same weight I couldn't shake last night. Inside the glass conference room, the team from Grayson is already flipping through our deck like they're looking for a reason to say no.

The pitch ends.

Daren closes his laptop like a casket. Nico leans back, staring at the ceiling as if the answer's written there. Ian's already halfway out the door, muttering something about "next time."

I don't move. Just sit there, fingers pressed to my temples, listening to the scrape of chairs on carpet.

It's not just Grayson. It's the last four. Same reason every time: confidence in the tech. Confidence in the team. Which, translated, means confidence in Ian.

Elevator down. Forty-five floors of silence.

Ian holds his laptop like a shield. Daren checks his phone. Nico glares at his reflection in the mirrored wall.

Outside, Park Avenue buzzes, steady and indifferent. Inside me, something cracks.

"They didn't even give it an honest shot," Ian says. "They're just chasing names."

"No," I say. "They didn't believe we could execute. That's three in a row now."

"Then they're wrong."

"Or we're not ready."

Ian looks at me like I've betrayed him.

"I've been killing myself building this. You said it yourself—it's a good idea."

"It is," I say. "But no one's backing ideas anymore. They're backing people. Confidence. Execution. And right now, we're not selling any of it."

Daren exhales. "We should rewrite the product slide. Again."

"Let's just get back," I mutter. "We've got an idea no one believes in and a pitch that pretends they should."

Nico stops walking.

"That's not the problem," he says.

I turn.

"The problem is the pitch is starting to pretend something about us that isn't true either." He's not angry. He's worse than angry — he's precise. "We keep repositioning around Ian's work like it's a liability. It's not a liability. It's the only thing we actually have. Every time you sand that down to make the room more comfortable, you're selling something we don't own."

"I'm framing it—"

"You're replacing it with something easier. That's not framing." He starts walking again. "Ian sees it. I see it. The rooms see it. That's why we're three for nothing."

Nobody says anything the rest of the way back.

* * *

The office is empty except for the low hum of the HVAC and the soft buzz of my monitor. Outside, the city is washed in late-afternoon gold — that particular light that makes everything look more expensive than it is.

I've been sitting here for thirty minutes without opening a file.

Daren appears in the doorway. Jacket still on. Hasn't gone home.

"You're going to push Ian out," he says. Not a question.

"I'm going to restructure the narrative," I say.

"Same thing." He leans against the frame. "I'm not saying you're wrong about the pitch. You're probably right that Ian in front of investors is costing us. But Will—" He stops. Starts again. "He built it. The actual thing. If you take his name off the deck, you need to know what you're doing. Because that's not framing. That's something else."

"It's a business decision."

"Sure." He pushes off the frame. "Just wanted to say it out loud. So someone had."

He goes.

I let that land. Then I open the file.

My father's voice from the Court Street bar runs underneath everything the way it always does. Make sure your position reflects the value you're actually bringing. Men who feel displaced can become problems. Build the bench before you need it.

It isn't advice anymore. It's architecture. The bones of a decision I've been constructing for months without admitting I was building it.

I open the Sawbuck site. The About page loads — the photo from the launch party. Me mid-laugh, jacket slung over my shoulder. Ian leaning into the camera, beer in hand, eyes lit the way they get when he's talking about something real. The caption underneath: Founders.

I hover over the edit button.

My name goes first.

Then I lift a line from his bio and move it into mine: Will Chaffee is the Founder and CEO of Sawbuck.

His title stays. Co-Founder.

A small change. Almost invisible. The kind of thing you could explain in a dozen ways — administrative, structural, investor-facing, necessary.

The kind of thing that looks like nothing and means everything.

I feel it.

I open Slack. Ian's green dot glows beside his name. I start typing, keeping the tone easy: We need to build a stronger tech bench. Not because you're doing a bad job — just what investors expect. More depth. More proof we can scale. I frame it like I'm protecting him. Freeing him up to focus on vision.

The truth is I'm already picturing the room without him.

I send it. Then I rework the pitch deck — my voice in the opening, my story, my framing. Every slide tightened for investors who don't care about idealism. Only return.

By late evening the office has emptied. The Sawbuck logo glows in the dark. My coffee cup catches the light, rim still wet. I look at it and think about my father the night he told me the family business was finished. Sitting in that office downtown while men unplugged computers around him. His grandfather's nameplate coming off the wall.

He said you can't rebuild once the world stops believing in you.

I'm not ready for that to be true here.

But I know Ian will see this for what it is. And when he does, there's no walking it back.

I take a long breath, close the laptop, and leave the logo glowing behind me.

I took the last train north. The car was almost empty. I watched the city lights thin out and tried not to think about what I'd just sent.

I didn't sleep much.

* * *

In the morning I was back before anyone else. The office smelled like cold coffee and overnight air conditioning. I made a fresh pot, sat down, opened the laptop. The Slack message was still there. Ian's green dot was gone — offline, already in transit, on his way in.

I had maybe an hour.

I open my laptop and pull up the Series A pitch. The sections Ian drafted are fine. Fine won't get us funded.

I start stripping it down — rewriting headlines, tightening the story until it doesn't just sell the product. It sells me. By the time Daren and Nico walk in, I've added three new slides, a closing statement, and a photo of Ian at his screens—with me in the frame, hand on the back of his chair.

But I know what I'm doing.

Ian isolates me near the window before the morning gets away from us. “I’ve been talking to some engineers,” he says. “Two guys I think could be the right build. Want to loop you in before I move.”

I barely look up from the screen. “Glad you’re here,” I tell him. “We’ll need the build polished in the next three weeks if we’re going to start soft-circling Series A investors.”

He nods. But I can see it — the way he's registering that we means me.

By afternoon the office feels too small. Ian's in the huddle room with his new hires, talking sprint timelines and backend optimization. I'm in my corner, polishing the pitch for the fifth time, pretending the sound of their laughter doesn't irritate me. Most days we work like a team. Other days the distance between us is hard to measure.

That's the thing about momentum. Once it builds, no one asks what got buried underneath.

* * *

When I step back into the bullpen the next morning, Ian's at the whiteboard, hoodie sleeves shoved up, laptop open, a tangle of charger cables spilling off the long table. He's sketching a diagram — so absorbed he doesn't hear me come in.

He turns, marker in hand. "Mapping a new workflow for the onboarding API. If we get the right back-end guy, we can cut processing time by—" He stops, frowns. "You serious about building out the team?"

"Yeah," I say, easy. "Investors want depth. You've been saying we need more horsepower — I'm putting pieces in motion."

His eyes narrow — not angry, just connecting dots I didn't want connected. "Right. Depth."

I gesture at the board. "This is good. Keep pushing. I'll handle recruiting."

A half-beat too long passes before he turns back. "Sure. Whatever works."

We talk through the morning in bursts — all business. He's cooperative, but there's a tightness in his voice that wasn't there yesterday. When I head to the restroom, he's still at the board, erasing an arrow he drew ten minutes ago.

In the mirror, I look at my own face for a moment. This is how you run a company, I think. You anticipate. You make hard calls before the market makes them for you.

Walking back, I can feel it — the space between us widening. A shift so small it's easy to miss.

A few hours later I clear out for the night. Ian's still at the long table, voice pitched low as he and Daren grind through specs. I don't say anything. I've already said what I needed to.

Outside, the evening heat wraps around me, thicker than morning. Sidewalks hum — cabs, dripping AC units, a stray bass line following me down the block.

The logo is still glowing upstairs.

I don't look back.

CHAPTER 15

A FACE REDEFINED

The Uber pulls into the motor court. I nod thanks, watch the taillights fade. The house is dark except for the gas lantern flickering above the front door — blue and still, throwing soft shapes across the stone. I don't go inside.

I call her from the motor court.

She answers on the first ring, brisk, skipping the hello. "We're locked for Thursday. Interview in the morning, shoot in the afternoon at your mother's place. Crew of six: photographer, two assistants, lighting, stylist, hair and makeup. Camilla Thorne will interview. She's sharp."

A pause that isn't a pause.

"We'll want you and Lizzy together, a few solo shots, some candid garden work. If weather's bad we stage inside. Your mother's house is perfect either way. I've got images and designer lists from her publicist. She's signed off on everything. Expect wardrobe racks everywhere."

I can already see it. Lizzy holding court, every lens tilting toward her, light falling just so. My face in frame because they need a second prop.

"Sounds like you've got it handled," I say.

"I do," she says. "You just show up and smile. And try not to look like you'd rather be somewhere else — this is a big moment, Will."

For who? I want to ask. Instead I thank her and hang up. The motor court. The road quiet. Somewhere across the sound in the distance Long Island glittering like it means something.

The machine doesn't care. CODA will run the story. Investors will read it. People who can wire nine figures without blinking will start taking my calls. If they come for Elizabeth Prescott and stay long enough to hear my pitch, that's still a win.

Sawbuck needs to be more than a sentimental footnote in a feature about my mother's dresses. Numbers. Case studies. Something that looks like inevitability.

I go inside.

* * *

The sitting room smells faintly of lilies and hairspray. The CODA crew is already set — lights on stands, cables taped down, garment racks lined with dresses Lizzy insists still have their moment.

Camilla Thorne stands in the corner reviewing her notes — a lean British woman in her forties, watchful, dark hair, reading glasses she removes when she wants you to know she's paying full attention. The photographer, André Besson, paces near the bay windows muttering to his assistant about light angles — French, fifties, silver stubble, always composing the room he's standing in. Blake is at the fireplace in black cigarette pants and a champagne silk blouse, talking to Marci Gold like they've known each other for years — Marci small and silver-bobbed, sharply dressed, the particular authority of a woman who has managed talent in Hollywood long enough to have outlasted four agencies and every prediction about her retirement. Her laugh cuts clean through the room.

Alex moves through the edges of it all — clipboard in hand, earpiece in, coordinating the crew's schedule with the quiet efficiency of someone two hundred shoots deep who doesn't need to raise her voice. She catches my eye across the room. A small nod. Back to work.

"William," Liz says, brushing a hand over her gown as if checking for wrinkles that aren't there. "Blake has been keeping me company. She's an absolute dear."

Blake smiles like she already knows how this ends. "We're making sure your mother gets the cover she deserves."

Before I can respond, the set producer waves us toward the makeup chairs. Lizzy sits like a queen, already holding court with Marci and Blake. I have my own chair. André's assistant powders the shine off my forehead and tells me to sit up straighter.

Camilla turns from the window. "We'll start with the joint interview, then break for stills. If you can both sit together on the sofa, we'll roll right into the conversation as we shoot."

"Lizzy by the window," Marci says, her voice carrying. "Natural light will do half the work." She gestures toward the armchair. Doesn't ask.

I sit where she points. Liz angles toward me just enough for the cameras, her hand ghosting the top of my shoulder.

* * *

Camilla starts with Lizzy — career, favorite collaborators, the changes she's seen in fashion over thirty years. Lizzy sparkles, tossing out names and stories with practiced ease. When Camilla finally turns to me, Blake lingers at the periphery, leaning against a lighting rig, eyes on me like she's measuring the cut of a suit.

"Lizzy, the piece will celebrate your career, but also explore how your legacy intersects with William's work. How do you see that connection?"

Lizzy laughs lightly, like the answer is obvious. "Style and vision transcend industries. Whether it's couture or fintech, you either have an eye or you don't. William has always known how to carry himself."

A makeup artist dabs at my cheekbone. The camera clicks.

Camilla glances at me. "Will, you're building a technology company — a world that couldn't be further from couture — but you grew up watching your mother define style for a generation. How do those worlds intersect?"

I think of saying I don't reconcile it. Instead I smile for the cameras.

"Presence is presence," I say. "You grow up watching someone command a room, you learn early what people respond to. With Sawbuck, we want to change the perception of who gets to be bankable. It's about aiming that understanding somewhere useful."

Lizzy doesn't wait. "And of course, we share the same standards." She smiles for the camera.

The lights flash. My jaw tightens.

Camilla doesn't blink. "Some would say your mother's name opens doors that might otherwise stay shut. How do you respond to that?"

The room pauses. Even the makeup brush in my peripheral vision pauses.

"Doors stay open because of what we do once we're inside them," I say.

Marci leans from her folding chair. "That's quotable." She taps it into her phone.

Across the room, Blake's expression barely moves — except for the faintest upward curl at the corner of her mouth.

Camilla keeps going — Oscars, mother-son dynamics, fashion as legacy. Then she pivots.

"I always knew he'd do something newsworthy," Lizzy says, not missing a step. "Though I thought it might be a Grammy, not a tech startup."

Camilla's eyes lift. "A Grammy?"

"Will had real talent," Lizzy says, leaning back as the makeup artist dabs at her cheek. "Music. He was extraordinary."

I shift in my seat.

Camilla turns to me. "Do you miss it? The music?"

The question hangs in the room. The lights are on me. Blake is watching from the lighting rig. Liz is waiting with the expression she uses when she has just handed someone something they didn't ask for and wants to see what they do with it.

"I'm focused on what's ahead," I say.

The polished answer. The safe answer. The answer that photographs well.

My father's voice underneath it, as reliable as weather: Music is a fantasy, William. For people who can't handle the actual world. I was seventeen. I folded the Berklee application, put it in the recycling, and went back to whatever the house was doing. He never knew what it cost.

Somewhere in the back of the room I hear Alex pause her quiet movement between the crew. I don't look toward the sound.

Marci cuts in, steering it back. "And what's ahead is a fintech solution with the potential to change how underbanked communities manage money. That's the actual story here."

Camilla makes a note, but her eyes stay on me a half-second past comfortable.

"Will — how do you reconcile building something so pragmatic while being raised in a house where image was everything?"

I give her the answer that sounds like honesty without being it. The camera clicks. My face on the monitor looks alive — jaw set, eyes bright, the perfect founder mid-sentence. Standing there I cannot find the pulse beneath it.

She flips to a new page. "Your personal history — Stern, Wall Street, now this startup. Was this always the plan?"

"That's how it reads now," I say. "I've always had this idea in my back pocket — something that could level the playing field for people who just need a fair shot. Sawbuck was waiting for the right time, the right team, the right momentum."

The words sound polished. Solid. Like I've been rehearsing them for years.

I let the camera catch my profile. I give Camilla the practiced smile.

She glances at her notes. "Last one, Will — our readers will want to know — anyone special in your life?"

Blake is three feet away, reviewing proofs on her tablet.

"It's all Sawbuck right now," I say. "Building something like this takes every ounce of focus. The rest will have to wait."

The crew laughs politely.

Blake doesn't look up from her tablet. But she goes very still for exactly one second.

* * *

André is suddenly everywhere — tugging a curtain, adjusting a reflector, crouching to check how the light hits Lizzy's cheekbones. "The window light is gorgeous right now. Mother-son shot first. William, stand here. Lizzy, turn toward him but keep your eyes at me. Yes — elegant. Close."

Lizzy glides into place like she's been doing this her entire life. Which she has. Her arm loops lightly through mine, her other hand resting just so on her hip. Blake stands behind André watching the monitor, giving small nods of approval.

"Lift your chin, William. Yes. Good. Now softer — imagine you're proud of each other."

The crew chuckles. Lizzy delivers a warm smile for the lens. I try to match it. I feel like I'm standing in someone else's life.

"Perfect. Now let's bring Blake in — the power circle look."

Blake steps forward without hesitation, taking her place beside Lizzy. André steps me back half a pace — just enough that the new framing makes them the focal point. I watch it happen. The light shifting. The camera lingering on them. The subtle slide from participant to accessory.

Alex is in the doorway.

She has a clipboard that an assistant handed her, something about the afternoon crew schedule. She pauses when she sees the three of us under the lights — Lizzy radiant, Blake sharp and composed, me half in shadow— She takes us all in and closes whatever she's thinking before I can read it.

Then Blake steps toward me during a lighting adjustment, two fingers straightening the edge of my jacket collar, her hand staying a moment longer than necessary. Low enough for only me to hear: "Hold still."

Alex's eyes move from Blake's hand to my face.

It is a fraction of a second. It is completely legible.

She turns and walks away without a sound, the clipboard under her arm, already back to the work that is always waiting for her.

André keeps firing. Blake and Lizzy lean slightly toward each other, the shutter running, and I hold my pose and think about what I just saw in Alex's face and what I am choosing not to do about it.

* * *

The CODA crew packs up. Lights folded, makeup kits snapped shut, the echo of clipped instructions fading down the drive. The silence after is almost jarring — like stepping out of a crowded room into cold air.

She doesn't announce it. She just doesn't leave — still at the fireplace when the crew wraps, still there when André packs his cameras, still there when Marci gives Liz a long goodbye in the foyer and the house goes quiet.

The last car from the shoot leaves at seven. Blake stays.

I find her outside. She has her heels off, standing in the grass in the last of the evening light. The cigarette pants, the champagne blouse. The Hudson Valley still around her. She doesn't hear me come out.

"You were good today," I say.

She turns. Something moves across her face and then settles. "I'm always good."

"I know." I come to stand beside her. "That's not what I meant."

She looks toward the tree line. August light going copper at the edges. I've never seen her still like this — without an agenda, without the next thing already assembled.

"My mother was at a shoot like this once," she says. Not to me. Just out loud. "I was eight. She came back and told me the camera had struggled with me. Too much forehead. Eyes too close." She turns the heels in her hand. "I was in the background of one shot."

I don't say anything.

"I spent the next ten years learning how to stand so that wasn't true." She says it the way you'd say something you've turned over so many times it no longer has edges. "And then I realized the problem wasn't my face. The problem was that she needed something to be wrong."

The grass. The copper light. The shape of hills going dark.

"Blake—"

"Don't." She says it quietly. No heat. "I'm not telling you that so you'll say something." She glances at me — not the managed version, not the woman who ran this house today like a production. Just her. "I'm telling you because this is the kind of shoot where things like that come out."

She puts her shoes back on, one hand on my arm for balance. The professional composure returning not all at once but in layers — the shoulders, the chin, the particular stillness that makes her so good at this.

"The CODA piece is going to change the conversation around Sawbuck," she says. "The investor interest is already there. You just need to be ready to move when it comes."

I watch her rebuild the distance.

"What do you want from this?" I ask. Not the platform — her.

She looks at me for a moment. Something almost arrives. Then she smooths the front of her blouse and picks up her bag from the garden chair.

"The same thing you do," she says. "Something real."

She walks back inside. I stand in the grass a moment longer.

I'm not sure either of us knows what that means anymore.

* * *

Blake makes her exit efficiently, a kiss on my cheek, already on her phone about the city. "André wants a few shots at the Sawbuck office. I'll set it up." And then she's gone, the particular energy of her departure leaving the room slightly emptier than the crew did.

I find Liz in the sitting room. Barefoot in silk pajama pants, a glass of red wine balanced on one knee. Lights low, the fireplace doing the work André's lighting rig did all morning but differently — warmth instead of performance.

She looks up, and for once there is no production in her eyes.

"You handled yourself beautifully today, William," she says. Her voice is gentler than I can remember it being in years. "You didn't hesitate. Steady."

I ease into the chair across from her. "I'm not sure I felt that way."

"Doesn't matter," she says, almost smiling. "You made it look easy." She studies me in the firelight. "I was proud. Genuinely."

The word sits between us. Unfamiliar. Not unwelcome.

I don't trust it to stay.

But I stay with it for now. The firelight. The wine. The particular quiet of a house after a long performance has ended.

I let her believe I'm steady. Let myself believe it for as long as this lasts.

* * *

Morning light is soft in the kitchen. Alex is at the table with her casebook and her coffee, the familiar posture of someone three hours ahead of everyone else. Hana has left food on the counter.

I sit down across from her. She doesn't look up right away.

"You were good yesterday," she says.

"I stood there. Lizzy and Blake ran the show."

She looks up then. "You were present. That's what people notice — who stays present when everything around them is performance."

Both things at once. Alex usually means both things at once.

My phone is on the table. Blake's name on a message I haven't opened. I pick it up under the table — old habit from Sutter Rowe, the thing you check before you're ready to act on it.

Alex glances over. Catches enough. "Busy morning?"

"Just following up," I say. I give her a smile that doesn't quite land and step into the hallway to call.

Blake picks up on the second ring. "Morning. How's my cover boy?"

"Still recovering."

She laughs — easy, warm, already three steps ahead. "You were perfect. Lizzy was perfect. André's sending selects today and I've already talked to Camilla about the copy. The feature's going to land exactly where we want it." Then: "I told you — you photograph well."

"Camilla was sharp," I say. "Some of those questions—"

"That's her job. And you handled it." Another pause — different quality.

"The Grammy comment. Did that land wrong?"

My eyes find the wallpaper in the hallway. The old pattern, the house that has held its shape through everything. "It was fine," I say.

She hears what I'm not saying. "I'll talk to Camilla about how much of that thread makes the piece."

"Don't," I say. "Leave it."

"Okay," she says. Then: "Sawbuck office this week for André. I'll send times."

We hang up.

When I come back to the kitchen, Alex is rinsing her mug at the sink, shoulders turned. The casebook is closed. She doesn't ask who I was talking to. She doesn't ask about anything. She rinses her mug, shoulders turned, moving with the calm precision of someone who sees everything and is deciding what to do with none of it.

"Have a good day," she says. Not cold. Not warm. Somewhere that used to be warm and has learned to hold a different temperature.

She picks up her bag and goes down the hall toward her room.

I stand in the kitchen with Hana's food going cold on the counter and the light coming through the window and the specific quality of a silence that used to feel

like comfort and now feels like something else entirely.

CHAPTER 16

THE STORY IS WORKING

When he catches my eye he grins. "We're close, man. Another week and the beta's ready."

I nod. But I'm thinking about whose name carries the room. He wheels his chair toward me. "You didn't loop me in on the Brighton follow-up," he says. No heat. Just a fact.

"It wasn't planned."

"That's not better." He swivels, facing me fully. "You brought Nico and Daren in. You reframed the whole deck. The language, the positioning — that came from you, not me."

I sit. "We were losing momentum. Brighton passed. Others too. I thought we needed a reset."

"A rebrand."

"A version people listen to."

Ian leans back, folds his arms. "You mean a version that sells." I don't fill the pause.

"You used to talk about your dad," he says, quieter. "How he lost everything. How you swore you'd never end up like that. I thought Sawbuck was your way of doing something different. Something that meant something."

I want to say it still is. I'm not sure anymore.

"You said this was about people like my mom," Ian adds. "You remember that?"

"I do."

He looks away, jaw tight. "Now we're quoting customer lifetime value to hedge fund guys. They don't care about people like her."

"They will once they see how big the market is."

Ian's laugh is small. Not cruel. Just tired. "There it is."

"What?"

"That's a pivot, man." He exhales, rubs his face. "I brought you something warm," he says. "And you put it under glass."

I stay quiet. Part of me agrees.

"You're good at this," he says. "You know how to win a room. I just don't know if we're building the same thing anymore."

Neither of us moves.

"I don't want to lose this," I say.

"Then stop remaking it without me," he says. "I'm still here. But you're treating me like a placeholder."

We sit there. His guys pretend not to listen. The hum of laptops. The overhead lights. Tension that doesn't need raising to make itself known.

Eventually I stand. "Let's talk later."

Ian doesn't answer. He nods once and turns back to the screen.

* * *

It's after eleven when I get home. The house is mostly dark except for the kitchen — that specific warm strip of light under the door that means Alex is still working.

She's at the table with the casebook open, a highlighter in her hand, her laptop pushed to one side to make room for a printed contract she's been annotating in the margins. The coffee beside her gone cold again. She doesn't look up when I come in.

I open the refrigerator. Hana's food. I set two plates on the table. I find a pan, turn on the low burner.

"You don't have to do that," Alex says, still reading.

"I know."

She turns a page. I heat the food. The kitchen settles into the quiet of two people past the point where silence needs filling.

After a while she sets down the highlighter. “How was your day?”

“Which part?”

“Whichever part you’re thinking about right now.”

I eat for a moment without answering. “I have to change Ian’s role,” I say. “Move him out of the investor-facing work. Put him back in the product.”

She doesn’t react immediately. “Does he know that?”

“He knows something is coming.”

“That’s not the same thing.”

“No,” I say. “It isn’t.”

She looks at me. Not judgment — something more careful than that. “Is it the right thing for the company?”

“Yes.”

“Is it the right thing for Ian?”

I don’t answer. She doesn’t push. She just waits, the way she always waits — as though she has the time, already knowing what the silence means.

“It’s the thing I can defend,” I finally say.

A moment. Then she picks up the highlighter and goes back to the contract.

She doesn’t say what she sees.

My phone buzzes on the counter. Blake’s name.

I pick it up. Step toward the hallway to take it.

Alex doesn’t watch me go. She’s back to the highlighter, in the next clause, further down the path she's been on since before any of this started.

I answer the call in the hallway. Behind me the kitchen light stays on.

* * *

Monday morning. Brew, before the rush. Ian is at the table, coffee in front of him, phone face-down. He knew this wasn't a casual breakfast.

I grab a latte and sit. Don't open with anything soft.

"I want to restructure your role," I say. "Product and engineering — full ownership. Best seat in the house for what you built. But the investor meetings, the A round conversations — I need to own those."

Ian looks at me. He doesn't look surprised. He looks like a man who has been waiting for a fact to finish arriving.

"You're taking me out of my own company's story," he says.

"I'm putting you where you're strongest."

"That's a good line," he says. Flat. "You come up with that this morning?"

I don't answer.

He looks out the window. The street coming alive outside — deliveries, dog walkers, the Manhattan morning energy that doesn't care what's happening inside any given room.

"You know how many guys like you pitched me before you?" he says. Finally. Quietly. "Before and after I met you. Word got around about what I was building. They came in talking about capital, contacts, the whole thing. Just like you. Every one of them had a plan. Every one of them had a reason why they needed to be out front." He wraps both hands around his coffee. "I knew what that meant. Knew it would end up gutting the thing that made Sawbuck worth building in the first place. So I said no. Every time."

He leans forward.

"You came in and talked about my mom's laundromat like you

understood what it meant. Talked about the people we were building for like they were real to you. And I thought — this one's different. This one gets it." He sets the cup down. "That's on me."

The words land and stay.

"Ian—"

"No." Not angry. Just done with the soft version. "I built this for people who can't get a fair shake from the system. And now the system is inside the building. Inside the pitch deck." He picks up his coffee. "You want the role restructured. Fine. But don't dress it up."

Silence.

"Are you out?" I ask.

He looks at me for a long moment. "No," he says. "I'm not out. I believe in what this can be. Even still." He sets the cup down. "But I'm not going to pretend this is what we said it was going to be."

He picks up his phone, stands, pulls on his jacket.

"I'll see you at Water Street," he says.

He walks out. I watch him go through the window — head down, backpack, moving through the morning like a man who has made a decision he'll have to live with.

* * *

Liz calls on Tuesday. The Nantucket cottage needs to be checked before they close it for the season — storm shutters, water lines, the usual. Two hours each way. I tell her I'll handle it.

I invite Alex the same afternoon. Casual, practical. Come up for the day. I could use the company. I have groceries delivered to the house before we arrive — clams, two ribeyes, things for a salad, a bottle of something white and something red.

She says yes without asking why.

* * *

We take 95 north out of Greenwich in the late morning, the September sky the particular shade of blue that only happens when summer has fully given up. Alex has her feet on the dash, a coffee in both hands, reading something on her phone. Blue is in the back, nose pressed to the crack in the window.

She doesn't fill silence the way most people do. I've noticed that about her. Most people treat quiet like a problem to solve. Alex just lets it be there.

We pick up Route 6 east at Providence, following the Cape Cod signs. By the time we reach Hyannis the afternoon is leaning.

"You come here very often?" she asks.

"Used to come every summer until I was about fifteen. Then less."

"Why less?"

I watch the road. "Other priorities. The usual reasons."

She doesn't push it. Goes back to her phone.

* * *

The ferry out of Hyannis takes forty minutes. Alex stands at the rail watching the island come into shape through the gray. Blue presses against her leg. Neither of them moves.

The house sits on a bluff above the water — gray shingle, white trim, a wraparound porch that faces the Atlantic. The hydrangeas have gone brown at the edges. The lawn furniture is stacked and covered in canvas.

Alex steps out of the car and stands for a moment looking at the water.

"It's beautiful," she says. Not performing it. Just saying it.

"It's even better in the summer."

"Everything is."

I unlock the front door. The house smells like it always does at the end of the season — sunscreen and cedar and something faintly damp.

Alex walks through slowly, touching things lightly. The old barometer by the door. The ship model on the mantle. A framed chart of the coastline that's been there since before I was born.

"Who decorated this?"

"Mimi, Liz's mom. Liz hasn't changed anything. She wouldn't know how."

Alex looks at a photograph on the console — my grandmother on the porch, young, laughing at something outside the frame.

"She belonged here," Alex says.

"She did. It was in her family forever."

* * *

I go through the house methodically — storm shutters, water shutoffs, the boiler. Alex helps without being asked, checking windows, testing latches. We move through the rooms in easy parallel, the house revealing itself in the particular way houses do when the season is over and no one is performing for anyone.

By three o'clock the house is squared away and the light off the water has gone that low gold that means the afternoon is turning.

I start on dinner.

The kitchen faces the water. I set Alex up with the white wine and the clams while I get the grill going on the porch. She rinses them at the sink, tapping each one the way I showed her, discarding the ones that don't close.

"This one," she says, holding one up.

"Gone."

She sets it aside. "How do you know how to do this?"

"Mimi. She'd make them every Sunday in August. Same kitchen."

"She taught you to cook?"

"She taught me that cooking for someone is different from feeding them."

Alex considers that. "What's the difference?"

"Feeding someone is just logistics. Cooking for them means you thought about what they'd like before they asked."

She looks at the clam in her hand. Sets it in the bowl.

Outside the grill catches and the smoke goes sideways in the wind off the water.

* * *

We eat on the porch as the light fails — clams first, then the steaks, a salad Alex made while I was at the grill. Blue sits between us with the focused attention of someone who has been promised nothing but remains optimistic.

The water goes from gold to gray to a color that doesn't have a name.

At some point, the conversation slows, and we sit with our glasses, contemplating the quiet of a place closing down for the season. A buoy bell somewhere. The neighbor's boat in its cradle.

"Can I ask you something?" Alex says.

"Sure."

"What are you actually building? Sawbuck. What is it really for?"

I look at the water. Not the investor answer. Not the pitch. She's not asking for that and she would know the difference immediately.

"Honestly?"

"That's what I'm asking for."

"What reason?"

I don't answer right away. The buoy bell again, further out.

"My father lost everything," I say. "His father's company, the name on the wall, all of it. I was there the day they took the nameplate down. I watched his face when the math stopped working." I look at my glass. "I've been afraid of that my whole life. The specific version of it. Standing in a room where something with your name on it doesn't exist anymore."

Alex doesn't say anything.

"So I think — I think part of why I've been pushing so hard, taking the meetings, letting Blake build the story around me — I think it's less about Sawbuck and more about making sure there's enough between me and that moment that it can never happen." I stop. "Which is not a good reason to build a company."

The water is dark now. Just the lights of a few boats and the buoy and the neighbor's porch light through the trees.

"My mother used to say," Alex says quietly, "that the thing you build out of fear always has fear in the foundation." She pauses. "She said you can feel it in the walls eventually."

I wait.

"She said the only things that hold are the ones you build because you can't not build them. Not because you're running from something. Because the thing itself won't leave you alone."

"Did she build something?"

Alex looks at the water. "She rebuilt us. After Caracas. New city, new language, new everything. She didn't do it because she was brave." A beat. "She did it because we were there and we needed it and there was no one else."

I don't say anything. The buoy bell one more time and then quiet.

"The laundromat woman," Alex says. "Gloria. You told me about her once."

"Ian's mom."

"Is she still the reason? Even a little?"

I think about it honestly. "Yes," I say. "Even a little."

"Then build from that," she says. "Not from the other thing."

She's not looking at me when she says it. She's looking at the water. But her hand is on the table between us, close enough that it isn't accidental.

I don't move. Neither does she.

The season is over. The house is closing. Somewhere in the city the

CODA issue is already at the printer.

We sit there until the cold comes in off the water and Blue finally gives up waiting and goes inside.

* * *

The October issue drops on a Thursday.

I'm on the 6 train headed downtown when my phone erupts. Slack pings. Email dings. A dozen texts in fast succession. I scroll through expecting bad news — another round of investor ghosting, some user-churn spike.

Then I see it.

Lizzy. Her cover shot impossible to miss — silver silk and practiced grace, framed by the headline: Elizabeth Prescott: A Legacy in Motion. Buried three pages in, there's me — navy suit, half-smile — standing behind a glass conference table.

The caption: William Chaffee, founder of Sawbuck, a new financial platform built on access, trust, and impact.

The photo's clean. The copy's cleaner. Every paragraph has Lizzy threaded through it like gold stitching. The subhead does exactly what Blake said it would:

Sawbuck isn't just another fintech startup — it's a modern answer to legacy, built by a man whose family redefines glamour.

I exhale. It reads legitimate.

The article paints me as a fourth-generation pioneer. It name-checks Lizzy four times, calls Sawbuck ethically modern, and casually mentions our Series A round as if already closed. It isn't. By the time I step off the train, my inbox has ten new intros, a calendar invite from a VC who wouldn't return my calls two weeks ago, and a message from a luxury brand's innovation team asking if we're open to partnership.

I'm two blocks from the office when my phone rings. I pause on the sidewalk.

"Hello, Liz."

"William." A moment, and I can already hear the smile. "I saw it." Of course she did.

"It's well written," she says, voice like silk over scotch. "Camilla captured the tone perfectly. Your quote about financial dignity — very strong."

"You think so?"

"Oh yes. And that bit about my Oscar dress — divine." Then, quieter: "I'm very proud of you."

It hits sideways. Not the way I wanted.

I grip the phone a little tighter. "Thanks," I say quietly.

"Don't waste this," she adds. "Ride the wave. Call the right people. Make it matter." She hangs up without goodbye.

Surrounded by hurried commuters, I let it feel like a win for a moment. People are noticing. The buzz is starting. Sawbuck might actually work.

And maybe Liz is finally proud of me.

But beneath the rush, a familiar crack. Because she's not proud of me. She's proud of the version that reads well — glamorous, curated, adjacent to fame. The article didn't break through because of me. It broke through because I finally played the part she always cast me in.

* * *

Back at Water Street the place is buzzing — keyboards rattling, Daren arguing with a vendor on speaker, Nico pacing with his headset on.

“We’ve got a meeting with Langford Partners next week,” I say, dropping my bag. Nico pauses mid-sentence. Daren pulls his headphones down.

“Trevor Langford?”

“Yeah. They are coming in hot. I have a call with them at nine. Need you both to join me.”

A low whistle from Daren. "That's huge."

Ian emerges from the huddle room, sleeves rolled, a faint red mark on his temple from leaning into a monitor. "Who's Trevor Langford?"

"Private equity. Big in fashion, looking to branch into fintech. Blake sent them an early release of the CODA piece."

Ian nods. I see it — the flicker between confusion and distance. He's still catching up to the room we're in.

Nico claps me on the back. "That's your Series A right there."

"It's a start." But my voice is already pitching the future — how we'll package the story, what numbers we'll show, how to make Langford feel early enough to brag but late enough to pay a premium. I feel Ian's attention land on me. I keep talking.

Ian starts to say something. Daren cuts in. "We should mock up a Langford-specific deck."

"Exactly. Nico, you and I run point on the narrative. Daren, refine the model for Langford's eyes. Ian—" I hesitate just long enough for him to notice. "—keep the tech moving."

He forces a smile. No one argues.

* * *

Ian is at his desk when we come in from the Langford call. He has his headphones around his neck — the ones he wears when he doesn't want to be interrupted but also wants you to know he's there. He looks up.

"Good meeting?"

"Productive," I say. "Blake's intro paid off."

He nods. Waits. The old Ian would have asked what came next, what he needed to build toward, how the tech roadmap aligned with the pitch.

This Ian just waits.

"Langford wants the full deck by Thursday," I say. "Nico and I are going to tighten the narrative section. Daren's running a fresh model."

"You need anything from me?"

The question has a shape to it. Not passive — specific. He's asking whether I'm going to include him.

"Keep the beta clean," I say. "We need the merchant retention numbers solid before Thursday."

He nods once. Puts the headphones back on.

I pull up the Langford deck.

* * *

It's past one when I make it back to the house.

The sitting room light is on. Liz is there, the only light a brass lamp by the bar cart, something pale in her glass.

She doesn't look up. Just smiles with the satisfaction of a woman who believes the world has finally caught up to her expectations.

"I've been reading the media around our story, William," she says, still not looking at me. "This"—she taps the iPad—"is exactly what I've been trying to tell you for years."

I step into the room but stay standing.

She looks up. "The quotes were perfect. You came off thoughtful. Strategic. Not too eager. And that photo—whoever picked it knew what they were doing. The lighting made your eyes look less tired."

"Thanks," I say, not meaning it.

She waves a manicured hand. "And the part about me—Blake is brilliant. Not overdone, but enough to remind people who you come from. Legacy matters in this world, Will. Especially now."

I cross my arms. "The legacy part is certainly being covered."

"Be thankful for that. Everything's about lineage in this town. You're not just some founder—you're the son of Elizabeth Prescott, who wore McQueen before he was McQueen. That matters to people."

She sips her cocktail, unbothered.

"CODA readers don't care about fintech," she continues. "They care about story. And this? This one lands."

There it is.

Just: finally worth reading.

I sit across from her. "Do you know what the company actually does?"

She frowns, like I've asked her to recite chemical formulas. "Something with payments. Access. It's disruptive, right?"

I don't answer. Because she doesn't care.

Not really.

She cares that it sounds powerful. That it sounds important. That her name is in CODA again, even if it's through me.

She reaches for her phone, already moving on. "I'll forward this to Anne at Chanel. She was asking about you the other day."

I stand. "Don't."

She glances up, surprised. "Don't what?"

"Don't use me to rebrand yourself."

Her eyes narrow. "That's an ungrateful thing to say."

"I'm not trying to be ungrateful. I'm trying to be authentic."

"Being visible does matter, William. However, sometimes perceived value is as deep as anyone gets."

I don't respond. Anything I say will spiral into another cold war.

The room goes quiet. Liz looks at her drink. Something shifts in her face — not the performance, not the armor. Something older and less managed.

"You remind me of your father," she says quietly. "The year before everything fell apart."

I don't answer.

"I'm not talking about Sawbuck," she says. "I think what you're building matters. Leaving Sutter was right." She leans back. "I'm talking about how you're carrying it. Bill carried things the same way — like the weight was proof he was serious. Like if he pushed hard enough, held on long enough, the thing he was afraid of would stop being true."

"I'm not him."

"No." She looks at her glass. "But I watched one person I loved disappear into himself one late night at a time." Her eyes move toward the hallway. "And I notice the things that distract you."

"She has nothing to do with this."

"She has everything to do with this," Liz says. Not cruelty. Something more careful. "Not because of who she is. Because of what it means that you won't let yourself have it properly. You're doing what your father did — reaching for something real and making sure it can't reach back."

A floorboard creaks in the hall. I glance toward the archway — Alex, a shadow, still and silent. Then gone.

Liz stands. Sets her glass on the cart. "Good night, William." She goes upstairs.

The sitting room smells faintly of her perfume — sharp citrus with something colder underneath.

I don't go upstairs. I cross the hall into the study.

The room is dark except for the streetlight coming through the curtains. I don't turn on the overhead. I find the lamp by the chair and leave it at that.

Blue is already in here, curled on the rug.

The bookcase. Third shelf — a photograph — me, my Dad, Q on the Halcyon. I'm maybe fourteen. Q is grinning at something off-camera. My father has his hand on the boom, looking out at the water. He looks like a man who knows exactly what he's doing.

I haven't looked at it in a long time.

I sit on the floor. Same carpet. Same window with its view of ivy and stone. I slide in a disc and lay back for a moment as the music plays. Then the memory surfaces.

A bar off the Post Road in Port Chester. Cracked leather booths, '70s rock. I was sixteen, barely passing for legal. My father nodded at the bartender and two bourbons appeared like we'd been doing this for years.

He raised his glass. "To surviving the American Dream."

I clinked without knowing what I was agreeing to.

The bourbon burned on the way down but I didn't cough. He noticed. Something like pride in his eyes. We didn't talk about the bankruptcy. About leaving the attorney's office with a folder and nothing else. That night he didn't want to be the man who lost everything. He just wanted to be a guy at a bar with his son.

"You ever wonder what it'd be like if we just left?" he asked, swirling the ice.

"Packed a bag, took the old sloop up the coast, left it all behind."

"The Halcyon wouldn't make it past Nantucket," I said.

He laughed. An honest one. "You're probably right."

A Led Zeppelin song came on. He tapped the rim of his glass to the beat. "Your mother hated this kind of music. Called it poor people's poetry."

"She still hates it," I said.

He looked at me, something soft settling in his face. "You're not like her. Not really like me either. You've got too much heart, Rube." He knocked back the rest.

"That's why I've always loved you."

He never said it again.

"Love you too," I said. I rolled my eyes so neither of us had to sit with how much I meant it.

We ordered burgers. Talked about the Yankees like the world hadn't fallen apart. He told me about sweeping floors at Big's factory in Bridgeport. "Can't run a place if you don't know how it smells when the machines run hot."

It was the only night that felt even. No scolding. No performing. Just two guys in a bar trying not to feel like failures.

Later, stepping into the cold, he grabbed my shoulder. "Rube — don't forget this. Not the drinking. Not the jokes. Just the feel of it. You and me."

I nodded.

I didn't forget. I didn't.

* * *

I wake clear — showered, shaved, dressed with precision. The house quiet. Liz left at six for the other coast. Blue watches me from the kitchen doorway, head tilted, as though he doesn't recognize this version.

Espresso. Messages. The day assembling itself.

Alex is at her usual spot at the table in the kitchen when I come through, casebook open, coffee cooling at her elbow.

Blake's text comes in while I'm standing there.

Dinner tonight. You need some fun. And so do I.

Alex sees me read it.

"She checks in a lot," she says. Not accusatory. Just noticing.

"She's good at knowing when to," I say.

Alex nods, back to the casebook. "I think she cares about you," she says. "More than the story." She says it like a conclusion she's arrived at slowly, after watching carefully. Like she's decided to be generous about it.

I hold her gaze a moment. Then I drop to the text.

"Yeah," I say. "I know."

I should pass. I need to focus, clear my head, get the Series A narrative where it needs to be. But when I see the restaurant — Five Central, one of those rooms that knows exactly what it is — quiet, precise, the kind of place that makes the city feel worth staying for — I already know my answer.

By eight-fifteen I'm in the car heading into the city. Navy suit, no tie. The road steady under the wheels.

* * *

She's waiting in the bar. One kiss on the cheek, a glass of champagne in my hand, and whatever guilt I'd been carrying starts to dissolve.

The first glass goes down too easily. The second even easier. Midnight arrives without anyone noticing. By dessert the night is already spinning. SUV to the Meatpacking District. A bar without a sign. Then another place where the walls sweat and the DJ's bass line presses into my ribs like a dare.

We end up at a place called Space 10:10 — just off SoHo, unmarked door, shadow and pulse inside. Glass walls fogged from bodies and heat. Blue light coiling up the walls, pooling around mirrored tables and velvet booths.

Blake knows everyone, or they know her — air kisses, whispered names, hands on my back guiding me deeper in. The table refills itself. Champagne arrives before we sit.

When Blake disappears to the bathroom, the hedge fund guy beside me moves closer, palms cupped around something white. Not a question. An offer.

I don't hesitate. Just part of the night.

When Blake returns, the room feels smoother. Edges gone.

My father used to say the night has a price.

I'm just not counting yet.

* * *

I wake to glass and sunlight. Blake asleep, hair across the pillow. My phone on the floor. A single text from Ian, 1:14 a.m.: Need to regroup on the deck. Call me when you're up.

I stare at it longer than I should. Last night I didn't think about Ian, or Sawbuck, or seed capital, or burn rate. I didn't think about anything beyond the next drink, the next hit, the next laugh.

And the truth is, it felt good. That's the problem.

I walk to the window. From this high up, the city is winning. There's a pit under it — a low, grinding awareness that I'm drifting into waters my father used to warn me about. The kind where you don't realize how far you've gone until the shore is gone. He used to say the current feels safest right before it takes you.

I could text Ian. I don't. I let myself believe it's fine.

It can wait.

* * *

By 8 a.m. I'm in the back of another black SUV, head against cool glass. Blake's perfume still on my collar.

When we hit the Merritt I check my phone. One more text from Ian. I put it face down on the seat.

We pull into the drive. Blue meets me at the door, tail wagging slow. He sniffs my jacket once, then falls in beside me like we're picking up an old conversation neither of us remembers how to finish.

We walk the side yard in silence. Dew on the grass. A bird breaks the morning with one sharp call, then nothing.

Inside, Alex is at the kitchen table. laptop open, coffee going, already into her morning like the night before didn't happen to anyone.

"Hey," she says.

"Hey."

She reads me in one look — Blake's perfume, yesterday's suit, the particular quality of a man who went somewhere and came back less than he left. She doesn't say anything. Just goes back to the page.

I stand at the counter with my jacket still on. I have the words. I've had them for weeks. I open my mouth and close it and pour a glass of water and go upstairs.

CHAPTER 17

THE HABIT OF IT

A year goes fast when people decide to believe.

Nobody planned for what the CODA piece actually did.

Blake had framed it as a profile of Liz — her legacy, her philanthropy, the causes she'd spent thirty years attaching her name to. Sawbuck was a paragraph. A footnote in a sidebar about her son's "quiet venture into fintech." The kind of mention that gets read once and forgotten.

Except it didn't get forgotten.

Someone screenshot the sidebar and posted it. Then posted about posting it. By the time I saw it trending it had been shared forty thousand times — not by fintech people, not by investors, but by the people Ian had always said the platform was for. Gig workers. Immigrants. Women running cash businesses out of their apartments. People who recognized themselves in the description of what Sawbuck actually did.

Inside of forty-five days we had three hundred thousand new sign-ups across fifty countries. Not users who'd heard a pitch. Users who'd found us because someone who looked like them said it worked.

It should have felt like winning.

What it felt like was the walls closing from a different direction. Our infrastructure wasn't built for that kind of load. We spent the next six weeks rebuilding on the fly — two engineers in Uruguay working around the clock, Ian sleeping on the office couch, every line of the seed round burning faster than any projection I'd shown anyone. We held it together. Barely.

We used what was left of the seed round to build Sawbuck's infrastructure: faster payments, embedded trust protocols, frictionless onboarding. The engineering team worked like the walls were closing in. In some ways, they were.

We launched betas in three verticals — subcontractors on a hotel in Baltimore, independent grocers in Jersey City, barbershops in Atlanta. Half of them didn't have a business account when we started. Now they're running their shops through Sawbuck in real time. The results turned heads.

Q was a natural as our chair. I wasn't surprised. But I couldn't always tell if he was protecting me or managing me. His money saved us, the terms were what they were. I accepted them because I needed the runway and because my father's voice was still underneath everything.

Ian stayed focused on the tech. Quiet. Relentless. He's the reason it all works. But I've become the face — on the deck, on stage, in the rooms that matter. Some days it feels like partnership. Other days it feels like theft.

Interest in the Series A isn't any stronger. That's the thing nobody is saying out loud.

Call after call, the same answer dressed in different language. Execution confidence. Technical depth. The team around the founder. What they mean — what they have always meant since Brighton — is that they look at Ian and see a founder who got pushed out, and they look at me and see the person who moved him. And they don't trust the story.

Our remaining projection on my laptop shows six weeks. Maybe eight if we stop hiring. We're not going to stop hiring.

At home, Alex still leaves her light on late. Still at the table with her casebook after midnight. She doesn't ask where I've been. Giving her space — that's how I frame it.

Blake's world keeps bleeding into mine — gallery openings, rooftop dinners, the kind of restaurants where everyone pretends they don't care who's watching. She's magnetic, always framing me in the right light, always talking about the next big thing before it happens.

And Liz is having a moment again. Two films, an AmFlix matriarch, more press than I can count. The CODA piece worked in both directions.

* * *

The conference room on 23 at Sutter Rowe is smaller than the main boardroom — and quieter. No skyline views. Just glass walls, a round marble table, a muted rug. The kind of place where power moves quietly.

I'm on the far side of the table. Across from me sit Philip Ames and Martin Halbridge. I used to sit outside these rooms. Now I'm driving the agenda.

Halbridge flips through the printed Sawbuck deck. He stops on user adaption, then TAM, our Total Addressable Market opportunity. Says nothing. I let the silence work. The CODA piece is there — tastefully placed, impossible to miss.

He sets the folder down, taps the cover twice. "You've built some momentum."

"Momentum follows narrative," I say. "Quimby invested earlier this year with two other family offices. We were oversubscribed at seed. Now we're ready to pull up the Series A to lock in the attention."

Ames sits forward. "Wait — you got Quimby?"

I nod. "Led the seed. Andro is our Chair." That hits.

Halbridge: "I'll be honest. I didn't expect you to get this far so fast."

I smile. "That makes two of us."

"What's the ask?"

"One billion Series A. Straight common, with a preferred convertible tranche on the back for anyone wanting a little more vig."

Halbridge raises an eyebrow. "You're not just testing the market, then."

"Quimby priced us at ten a share — two hundred million cap — when Sawbuck was just a dream. Today we're closer to a hundred a share, pre." I hold his eye. "Subject to your validation."

Halbridge glances at Ames. Something passes between them.

"Twenty million shares outstanding," Ames says. Flat. "At a hundred a share, that's a two-billion-dollar pre-money valuation." He sets down his pen. "You actually think it's worth that?"

"I think the market does." I let it sit. "We're pushing half a million users on the platform. Not downloads — active users running real transactions. The addressable market is eighty million underbanked adults in this country alone. Every point of penetration is worth billions in recurring fee revenue." I pause. "The question isn't whether the valuation is defensible. It's whether you want to own a piece of it before someone else sets the price."

He recalculates.

"We're building the infrastructure for what comes next," I say. "Sawbuck isn't just a product. It's a platform for trust. For operators who've been locked out — freelancers, immigrant entrepreneurs, the little guys. People banks ignore. We give them speed, legitimacy, and control. In one tap."

I pause. "The market's bigger than people realize. But the window's short. We scale now or someone else will."

Ames: "You really think you can put a billion to work?"

"We have to," I say. "We're not catching up. We're laying track."

"That kind of capital draws sharks," Halbridge says.

"Then we swim faster."

Ames gives a dry laugh. "We'd need firm resources for what still looks like a long shot."

"I expect full engagement," I say. "Institutional polish. Quiet precision. No media leaks, no interns writing talking points. This stays internal."

"You'll have full engagement," Halbridge replies. "Assuming we're aligned on economics. Two percent?"

"Two percent. Close it by end of Q1."

He chuckles, low and sharp. "You're either in total control or completely out of your depth."

I nod once. "That's what the best deals feel like."

"Fine. You've got us." He pauses. "I assume you have a preference on who you'd like to lead the deal.

I smile. "I want Zack and his team running point. Start to finish."

Ames squints. "You're serious?"

"Zack's team knows the vertical. They're aggressive. They'll want this win badly."

"Fine," Halbridge says. "You'll have Halloren's team."

I stand, button my jacket. The meeting ends with a handshake and a nod. Sutter's officially on the deal.

As I step into the hallway, I don't look back.

* * *

Corner of 7th and Grove. The lot packed — trucks lined like carnival booths, chalkboards scrawled with names I don't recognize, the smell of cumin and smoke and something sweet. A breeze off the river. I adjust my suit jacket, trying not to look like I dressed for Midtown.

Nico's in sunglasses that cost more than my old Jeep. "You're late."

"You're on time for once."

Darren emerges from the crowd with three tacos and the energy of someone who slept six hours and still did burpees. Behind him the vendor — middle-aged woman, cash register gone, just a phone and a card reader that didn't exist two years ago, handwritten menu, the kind of truck that's been in the same spot long enough to have regulars who know her name — taps her phone to close the transaction. The Sawbuck interface, unmistakable. Nico doesn't notice. I don't say anything.

"They've got kimchi bulgogi on corn," he says, handing one over. "Tell me we're not living right."

I take a bite and let the grease and spice land before I talk. I nod. It's good—messy, but good. We lean against the railing over the East River. For a moment, we eat in silence. Boats move slow against the current. Manhattan looms across the water, gleaming like it knows something we don't.

I clear my throat. "I locked in Sutter Rowe."

Daren looks up, wipes his mouth. "Wait — what?"

Nico lifts a brow. "They must think we're further along than we are."

"We are," I say, holding his stare.

Daren: "You built this."

"I did," I say. No apology.

Nico looks away. "Big swing."

"It has to be," I say. "This isn't about closing a round — it's about setting the story before someone else writes it."

We grab a shaded table. I pull up the deck on a tablet — cleaner visuals, sharper numbers, everything arranged to look inevitable. Then the traction slide. I've folded pilot users into active users.

Daren slides his laptop across the table.

"Active transacting users. Actual." He taps the screen. "Not projected. Not pipeline. What's moving money right now."

The number is three hundred thirty five thousand.

The deck says over five hundred thousand.

"I know," I say.

"I know you know," he says.

He pulls the laptop back. We don't discuss it further.

Daren taps through, nodding. "Design's tight. Retention looks stronger than last week."

"It is," I say smoothly. "I modeled forward — traction post-funding. Investors want to see scale."

"But we haven't hit those numbers," Nico says.

"We're about to," I say. "You don't pitch where you are. You pitch where you're going."

Daren shrugs. "It's not untrue."

"It's strategy," I say. "Storytelling with data."

Nico doesn't blink. "Did Ian sign off?"

"I refined it. He's aligned on the big picture."

"That's not a yes." Nico sets his coffee down. "Ian built the backend that makes those numbers possible. You're quoting his work and you cut him out of the room. You see how that looks?"

"Ian's still a founder —"

"That's not what I asked." His voice is flat. Not angry. Worse than angry. "I asked if he signed off on the number. Because if he didn't, you're out there alone on this. And when it falls apart — and these things fall apart — you're going to be the only one holding it."

I don't answer.

"That's what I thought," he says.

Daren fills the space. "This is why Will's driving now. He sees the arc."

Nico doesn't respond. Just picks up his coffee and looks at the window.

I don't add to it. Let his voice build in the space between us.

Nico finally speaks. "That's a good story." He says it carefully. Then he's quiet.

* * *

Two days later.

Water Street. The floor is already humming before eight — keyboards, calls, the low-grade urgency of a company that hasn't slept enough and isn't stopping.

There's a room off the back that nobody uses before noon — a glass box, six chairs, a whiteboard someone forgot to erase. I find Zack there. Jacket off, sleeves rolled. He hears the door and turns.

"Will Chaffee." Not warm. Not cold. A man deciding which version of this conversation to have.

I close the door. Don't sit. Let him decide whether to stay standing.

He sits. I sit across from him.

"I heard you requested me specifically," he says.

"I did."

"I'm trying to figure out if that's respect or strategy."

"Both. And I don't have time to explain the difference, so let's move."

He almost smiles. Sets down the pen he picked up. "You turned down my offer. Said something about not opting into becoming me."

"I was right. And now I need someone who wants the win badly enough to actually close it." I put the term sheet on the table between us. "One billion. Sixty days. Two percent on close. You run point, end to end."

He looks at the paper without touching it. "You're not here to ask."

"No."

He picks it up. Reads it the way someone reads something they've already decided about — looking for the catch, not the terms

"Some of the numbers in that deck aren't where you're saying they are," he says. "I've seen the data room."

"I know. That's why I need someone who can sell trajectory without losing the room. You know the difference between a story that's ahead of the business and a story that's a lie. I need you to run it like the first one."

He sets the sheet down. "What happens if I can't hold that line?"

"Then we course-correct. But that conversation comes after you're on the deal, not before."

The city sits in the glass behind him, indifferent.

He extends his hand. Not friendship. The handshake of two people who have decided to be useful to each other — on terms I set.

I take it.

"First meeting's Monday," I say. "Come ready."

I walk out. Daren's already at his station. Nico's leaning against the wall with coffee, watching me come out. He raises an eyebrow.

"Done," I say. And keep walking.

* * *

The conference space on the second floor of The Ashford, a downtown hotel that gets everything right without announcing it — warm light, clean angles, floor-to-ceiling windows that make the city look like something worth building. Thirty seats. All filled. The kind of people who don't ask for credentials. They wait for proof.

Zack gestures toward me without fanfare. "Will Chaffee. Founder of Sawbuck. You've seen the press. Now hear the thesis."

I stand. One breath. That's all I allow myself.

"We don't need another neobank," I say. "We need a system that works where banks have never bothered to go."

That hits. It always does.

"We're not a payments app. We're a financial layer — built for speed and legitimacy where trust has never been evenly distributed." I flip to projections. "We're building the rails banks forgot, starting with the guys who fix your wiring and cut your hair."

The door opens behind me. I don't turn. I don't have to. Blake crosses behind the investors like she owns the room — chic in black wool, heels loud enough to announce without apologizing. A few heads lift. I keep on the slide.

"Following our CODA profile, inbound interest has spiked — banks, processors, potential acquirers. We're not selling."

I let it hang. Eyes come back to me. She takes a seat near the end of the table, legs crossed, phone face-down. I glance once — quick, controlled. She gives the smallest nod.

When I sit, Zack gives a single approving nod. Three hands go up. Two more ask to talk after.

It's working.

* * *

The last investor leaves with a handshake and a branded folder. The door clicks shut.

Zack exhales, loosens his tie. "Clean," he says. Banker for approval.

Nico slumps into a chair. "Better than the beating we took all around midtown trying to raise seed."

Daren tosses a Sawbuck pen back into the tray. "I think one of them tried to take a selfie with Will."

"Private room at The Library Bar in an hour," Zack says. "You in?"

"Yeah," I say. "Let's celebrate."

* * *

Three texts from Ian in the Uber to The Library Bar.

Ian: Can we talk tomorrow? Early if you need.

Ian: Just want to understand where I fit in the next phase.

Ian: Will.

I scroll my inbox. Swipe past texts from rowing buddies, article links, investor intros I should care about.

One new message near the bottom:

Dinner at the Voss's tomorrow night. Bring the new suit. Lizzy is coming. East 82nd & Fifth. I'll send details later. —Blake

No emojis. No warmth. No question. The next move, already planned.

I start typing: Can't make it tomorrow. Delete. Rain check? Delete.

I tap a thumbs-up and make it official.

* * *

The room is all low light, dark wood, crystal on every surface. Zack orders a bottle old enough to have its own zip code.

He lifts his glass. “To the kill shot. And the man who delivered it.”

Eyes swing to me.

I raise mine. “To execution.”

The night slides into laughter and blur. Someone from a VC fund arrives with a model on his arm. Zack, at the bar, smiles like he just closed a public offering.

“You hit the nerve and didn’t let go,” he says. “You’re not just trending — you’re compounding.” He lifts his glass. “To Sawbuck. And to the man who made it feel inevitable.”

We clink.

Nico sips slower. “Inevitable is a dangerous word.”

Zack waves him off. “Relax. Will sold the room. It’s done.”

“It’s not done,” I say. “But we’re on track.”

Nico looks at me. “Don’t confuse traction with truth.”

“We’re fine.”

“We’re not fine. We’re performing fine.” He leans forward. “Ian built something real. You’re out here selling a version of it that doesn’t exist yet. When the gap closes — and it will — you’re going to own that alone.” “I’m driving this because someone has to—” “I know why you’re driving it. I’m telling you what it costs.” He stands. “I’m not covering for the number. I want that on the record.” Daren: “We’re close. That’s not nothing.” “Close isn’t the number we’re quoting,” Nico says. Then he walks out.

* * *

I step outside for air. The patio is empty. A line of candles in glass hurricanes along the brick. I loosen my collar and lean on the rail.

Footsteps. Zack.

He stands beside me, quiet. "I meant what I said in there. You're good in a room. Too good."

"That a compliment?"

"It's a warning." He sets his glass on the rail. "You asked for my team. You said this was real."

"It is."

"Then stop selling like you're still trying to prove something to someone."

That one stings.

"Silver-spoon kid playing the underdog," he says. "It sells."

"You don't know a thing about my story."

"I know enough. You grew up loaded. Your mom's famous. You walk into rooms like the world owes you stage time."

"I grew up with money until I didn't. My father lost most of it when I was fourteen. And yes — my mother is Elizabeth Prescott. I'm not going to pretend that didn't open doors."

Zack's eyes narrow. "I worked three jobs to get through Yale. No fallback. No trust fund. No icon with a CODA spread to drop your name at a dinner party."

"You're right," I say. "That's real. I had things you didn't. I'm not going to argue that. But don't tell me the address I grew up in is the whole story."

"No," he says. "I want you to stop pretending it didn't matter."

Silence. "Don't let your ego burn the thing you're actually building." He raises his glass slightly. "You've had your warning."

He goes back inside.

I stay in the dark, jaw tight, the city flickering.

* * *

Inside, Nico sits near the edge alone, sleeves rolled, watching the room.

"You know Ian's not going to call you," he says when I reach him. "The guy who started this with you."

I haven't forgotten."

"I know you haven't." He drains his glass. "That's worse, actually."

Heels behind me. Blake, sliding between us like a blade

"It's still winning today."

He walks.

* * *

Ian's text is still on my phone when I get back to Water Street the next morning. I see him through the glass of the third-floor conference room. Not our conference room — the shared one at the end of the hall that anyone can book. He's alone. Laptop open, a whiteboard behind him covered in architecture diagrams, the focus of someone working through something for hours.

He looks up when I pass the glass.

I stop. Go in.

"Good pitch?" he asks.

"Strong room," I say. "Thirty seats, all filled. Zack ran it clean."

He nods. "I heard about The Ashford. Sounded like a big moment."

"It was."

A silence.

"I would have liked to be there," he says. Not accusatory. Just true.

"It was tight," I say. "Zack's format. He controls the invite list."

Ian looks at me for a moment. The look of someone deciding whether to say the thing or let it go. He almost lets it go.

"I built the platform you were pitching," he says. "I should have been in that room."

"You were in it," I say. "Every slide."

He looks back at the whiteboard. "That's not the same thing."

I don't answer. The hallway hums outside the glass. Somewhere Zack's team is already celebrating.

"I'll loop you in on the follow-up calls," I say.

He nods. We both know I won't.

I walk back out into the hallway. He's already turned back to the whiteboard, marker in hand. Keeps working.

* * *

It's past midnight when I get home. The house is quiet the way it's been quiet lately — Blue at the door, the low classical station Liz leaves running, the particular stillness of a place where someone has been alone for hours and arranged themselves around it.

Alex is in the kitchen. Not studying. Not working. Just sitting at the table with a glass of wine and nothing in front of her, like she came down and decided to wait without deciding to wait.

Something is different. I can't name it immediately.

Her hair is down. That's part of it. Usually it's pulled back — studying, moving, always somewhere to be. Tonight it's down and she's in a sweater I haven't seen before, something soft and dark, and she's sitting with her legs folded under her like she has nowhere to be and has known it for a while.

"Hey," she says.

"Hey." I set my bag down. She's already poured a second glass.

I open the refrigerator without needing anything from it. Close it. Turn around.

She's watching me with the particular steadiness she has — not waiting for me to perform, not filling the space. Just present. But there's something underneath it tonight that isn't her usual register. Something that has made a decision.

"Sit down," she says. Quiet. Not a question.

I sit across from her. She pours me a glass of wine without asking, the way you do for someone you've decided to stop being careful around.

We talk. Nothing significant at first — her contracts professor, a case she's been working through, a story about her sister that makes her laugh in the unguarded way she almost never does in front of me. I watch her face while she talks. The way she uses her hands. The way she looks down when something is funny before she lets herself laugh at it.

The words thin out and she's looking at me across the table and neither of us is filling it.

"Nantucket," she says.

"Yeah."

"I keep thinking about what you said. On the porch."

"Which part."

She looks at her glass. "The part about building from fear." She pauses. "I don't think you're as far gone as you think you are."

"No?"

"No." She looks up. "I think you know exactly what you're doing. I think you just haven't decided to stop yet."

That one sits. I don't answer.

She reaches across the table then — not for my hand exactly, just close enough that her fingers rest near mine on the wood. It's the smallest possible gesture. She's never done it before. She did it once on the boat and once on a porch in the dark and both times she pulled back.

She doesn't pull back.

"Will," she says. Just my name. The way she says it when she means the real version.

I look at her hand near mine. At her face. At the particular quality of the light in the kitchen at this hour and the way she looks in it and the sweater and the hair down and the wine she poured without asking.

I know what this is.

I know what she's offering and what it would cost her to offer it and how many times she has decided not to and decided again tonight that she would.

I start to say something —

My phone buzzes on the counter. Blake's name on the screen.

I look at it. One second. Two.

"You should get that," Alex says. Her voice hasn't changed. But her hand has moved — barely, just enough.

"It can wait," I say.

But I'm already reaching for it. Some part of me already reaching before I decided to.

The habit of it. The momentum.

"Hey," I say into the phone. Blake's voice warm and certain on the other end, already telling me about tomorrow night, another dinner, the people I need to meet, the story that's working.

When I look up Alex is carrying her glass to the sink. She rinses it without hurrying. Sets it on the rack. Picks up her book from the counter.

"Good night, Will," she says.

She doesn't look back.

The door to the back hallway closes softly behind her.

I'm still on the phone. Blake is still talking. The kitchen light is on and the classical station is playing low and Blue has gone to find Alex down the hall.

The call ends.

The glass she poured me is still on the table, untouched.

I drink it alone.

CHAPTER 18

SATURATION

Liz's new house in the Hollywood Hills sits on a ridge built for display — glass walls, infinity pool, every angle designed to catch light. I flew in private. That's new. The yard has been turned into something between a movie premiere and a soft launch.

Liz moves through her guests in full hostess mode, martini in hand, with the ease of someone who has never once questioned whether she belongs.

She spots me and beams. "Everyone — this is my son. Founder of Sawbuck. You've seen the press."

The room is full of people who've made careers out of being seen — directors who greenlight by instinct, publicists who speak in access, producers whose names appear before the title. The kind of LA that doesn't ask what you do because they already know, or don't care, or both.

Then Q's hand on my shoulder.

"Figured Liz would turn this into a spectacle," he says. "You've been all over lately. Hard to miss Sawbuck."

"Not all by choice."

He lifts an eyebrow. "Yeah. It's flirting with saturation." Not judgment. Just true. The kind I haven't heard in months. He squeezes my shoulder. "Try not to get swallowed whole, buddy." Then he's gone.

The noise rushes back in. Marci scans for photographers. Blake loops her arm through mine.

"They're eating it up," she says.

The words leave my mouth fully rehearsed. Legacy. The system forgets. The usual.

I excuse myself to check messages.

Liz's dressing room. Every surface polished to reflect who you're supposed to be.

Blake: Crushing it. Stay 20 more. Then we ghost.

I scroll past investor tags. Then stop.

Alex posted a photo — her sister, tagged, somewhere back home. Sun on a terrace. A street I don't recognize. Caption: Bendición. A yellow heart.

Not for me. It knocks something loose anyway.

In the mirror I catch my reflection — open collar, tailored jacket, a face still trying to look like it belongs here.

* * *

Zack calls while I'm still in the hotel bed, morning light barely crawling across the sheets.

"Stonebridge is out," he says.

I sit up. "What do you mean, out?"

"Reallocating toward hard tech. Cited valuation sensitivity."

"They were in last week."

"Now they're not."

I press a hand to my temple. "They were supposed to anchor."

"We'll plug the gap," Zack says. "Pelham and Weston are in diligence. Quimby's doubling down. We're not dead."

"You said we had momentum."

"We do. This is the middle of a raise. Flinch points." Zack's voice sharpens. "Stay visible. Stay sharp. No founder panic."

"I'm fine. Send me the warm leads by noon."

The line clicks off.

I scroll back to the CODA piece. My face — clean, framed, inevitable.

I close it. Open the deck.

Zack calls it a flinch point.

I call it blood in the water. Everyone smells it.

No time to spiral. I text Nico and Daren: Back in New York tomorrow. Game on.

I sit, palms flat on my knees. Morning light slices the carpet like a countdown I never asked for.

I don't look at Ian's texts. There are three now.

I get in the shower.

* * *

The glass conference room on the twentieth floor hums—Monica and Jamie pulling slides into place, Nico cross-checking numbers, Daren treating the cap table like it might bite.

I walk in and drop my coat on a chair.

Zack doesn't look up. "We ready?"

"Not yet," I say. "But we will be."

The PPM is almost final—fifty pages of glossy narrative, clean pro forma, and the kind of market language that makes people feel behind. I scroll to the term sheet:

$1B raise Pre-money valuation: $2 billion / $100 per share Minimum check: $25M Commitment deadline: January 15

"Lock it," I say. "That date holds."

Zack raises an eyebrow. "That's sixty days."

"That's the window. Scarcity and urgency—every deck, every email, every conversation. January 15, or you miss the wave."

Nico leans back, watching. Daren doesn't flinch.

Zack shrugs. "You're the founder."

He taps his pen once and looks at his team. "You heard him. Let's package it."

Daren pulls up the pipeline on the wall screen. Forty-three names, color-coded. The red tiles outnumber the green ones. That's how it always looks at this stage — more no than yes, more silence than signal.

Zack walks us through the anchors. Langford — private equity, Blake's intro, went quiet for ten days then came back with six follow-up questions.

"That's not a no," Zack says.

"Coventry." He pauses. "Still in diligence. Hasn't moved since the initial meeting. Could go either way."

"Remsen's guys say he wants the chair if he comes in," Nico says.

"Everyone wants the chair," Zack says. "That's not our problem until it is."

"Stonebridge is out," Zack says. He doesn't look up from the screen. "Pulled this week. Focusing purely on hard tech going forward." He scrolls. "Weston's team is deep in the data room — three analysts, two weeks of requests. That's a serious look. And Pelham came back yesterday. They want a follow-up call with Ian specifically. Product architecture."

Dalton Reeve. Bastion — hedge fund, Greenwich, came in through Q, their team just started digging in the data room.

"Langford and Bastion," I say. Between them, potentially a few hundred million. Enough to anchor the round and pull the rest in behind them. Pelham still circling. Weston team is deep in the data room."

Zack looks at me and laughs. "And, of course, Charlotte Voss. She asked you for the offering doc before dessert — practically a term sheet in her world.

The rest gray. Untouched."

"We need one of big guys to move first," Nico says. "Once one of those commits the rest follow."

"Then let's get them to move," I say.

* * *

The mic is vintage—matte-black Shure, gleaming under soft studio light. The walls are so soundproofed even the silence feels produced.

Across from me sits Declan Shaw—Capital Signals. Two million followers. Everyone wants this chair.

"We're here with Will Chaffee," he says, voice smooth, camera-ready. "Founder of Sawbuck. You've seen the headlines. You've felt the noise."

I smile just enough.

"We've had a good run," I say. "But we're just getting started."

"Walk me through it," Declan says. "Banker at Sutter Rowe to one of the most visible fintechs in the country?"

"Honestly?" I say, leaning in. "You stop waiting for permission. You stop asking old institutions to validate new ideas. You build what the market's already begging for."

He nods, like I've confirmed what he already wanted. "And what is the market asking for?"

"Trust. Speed. Fewer gates." I pause. "Sawbuck isn't just a product. It's infrastructure—for the overlooked. We've onboarded nearly five hundred thousand vendors, most of them small operators banks ignore."

Daren's face flickers in my mind—then I move past it. "And that's factual?" Declan presses. "Traction, user adoption stats —this isn't just a story?"

"Multiple pilots converting now. Regional banks embedding us in merchant onboarding. The velocity's there."

I say it flat, like it's already in The Journal.

"So what's next?"

"Series A closes this quarter. Then embedded finance.

Merchant-services expansion. We're not building a wallet—we're building the rails under the ecosystem. This isn't about payments anymore. It's about control."

Declan leans back, sold. "A lot of founders talk big," he says. "You talk built."

The red light clicks off. He reaches across the table. "You crushed that."

"Appreciate it," I say, standing.

In the corridor, my phone buzzes.

NICO: Just listened. You know 500,000 is fiction, right?

I stare at the screen. Type. Delete.

I walk.

* * *

The car service is waiting when I come out — black SUV, engine running, the particular silence of a vehicle that costs more than I used to make in a month. I give the driver the address and watch Midtown slide past the tinted windows.

One Vanderbilt.

The lobby is the kind of space that makes you stand up straighter without knowing why — stone and steel and forty feet of ceiling, the whole building designed to remind you that altitude is a kind of argument. The elevator takes me to the thirty-eighth floor without stopping.

We don't borrow rooms anymore. The Sawbuck office wraps the northeast corner — glass on two sides, the Chrysler Building close enough to feel like a neighbor, the rest of Midtown spread below as though we'd been given permission to look at it. Nico calls it the cathedral. Blake says it photographs well. I haven't decided.

There's cedar-eucalyptus in the air—some consultant said it makes people feel "elevated."

I step off the elevator into glass and concrete silence. Quiet money hums—reclaimed wood tables, staged lighting, two new hires I don't recognize. Everyone looks busy pretending the ship is unsinkable.

Ian's by the lounge. No suit. Backpack slung low. The guy who actually wrote the code that built this thing. He spots me before I can pretend not to.

"Will," he says, stepping into my path.

"Hey," I nod, angling toward the bullpen.

"You really said over five hundred thousand?"

I don't blink. "Directionally, we're close."

"Directionally?" He gives a short laugh. "You mean fiction."

"It's framing."

"You realize I built that tech to help people like my mom. Real people.

Now it's a pitch. A soundbite. A prop."

"It's still the same mission," I say, lower. "We're scaling it."

"No, Will." His eyes narrow. "You're scaling yourself. You cut me out of calls, panels, everything. You turned this into your platform and hollowed what made it human."

"I'm the one raising the capital," I say. "I'm holding this together."

"You're selling something we haven't built yet," he snaps. "And you didn't just edge me out—you made me invisible."

I don't have a comeback. Not one I can say out loud.

"You used to want to build something that lasted."

"I still do."

He shakes his head. "No. Now you just want to be seen as something."

I turn and walk to my office. Glass walls, frosted along the bottom—transparent without actually being seen. I drop my coat on the leather sofa and take the desk: walnut slab, matte, no drawers. No clutter. Just a leather notebook, the Montblanc Blake gave me after the CODA piece, and the latest deck within reach. Always.

* * *

Ian doesn't leave right away.

I watch him through the glass. He's standing where I left him — same spot, backpack still slung low, looking at the office the way you look at something you built with your hands and don't recognize anymore.

Daren goes to him. I can't hear what's said. Ian shakes his head once — not angry, just tired. He unzips the front pocket of the backpack and takes out his phone. Sets it on the counter. Picks it back up. Puts it away.

Daren says something else. Ian is quiet for a moment.

Then: "I knew he'd have to be the face. That was always the trade. You don't get to people like my mother without someone who knows how to talk to the rooms she'll never be in." He looks at the floor. "I just thought I'd still be in the room with him."

He zips the backpack. Adjusts the strap.

"The platform works," he says. "That part's still true."

He says it like a man reminding himself of something he needs to keep believing.

Then he walks to the elevator and waits for the doors.

I look away before they open.

Behind me, a floating shelf holds the version of my life that photographs well. The Quimby commitment letter in a glass frame. A photo of me and Liz at the early launch party. A bottle of Japanese whiskey I've never opened. A silver award from a fintech panel I barely remember. It's someone's life. I'm not sure it's mine.

Recessed lights are programmed to dim at 7 p.m., regardless of how late I stay. The espresso machine hisses when it thinks I'm ignoring it.

One chair faces my desk—armless, hard. Built for posture, not comfort. Out the window: the Chrysler Building one block over, its crown catching the last light, Grand Central's roofline spreading below it, the East River a thin silver line beyond the grid. This view used to mean something. Now it's just the view. I turn back to the office. The art is abstract—Blake's design friend handled it. Nothing personal. Just polish. Everything in here was chosen to signal something. I'm still figuring out what.

I check the time—ten minutes past the hour. On purpose. The team's in my private conference room with Cayden Remick from Weston Ventures. Zack's on Zoom. They've been waiting. Liz once told me it's better to let people settle before you enter the room you're about to own.

Glass walls, brass accents, diffused lighting designed to flatter skin and ego. We call it the Pitch Deck, unofficially. Nico hates it. I like it more every time I hear it. I straighten my collar, adjust my jacket, and push the door open. Let the game begin.

Cayden stands to greet me. Perfect hair. Turtleneck under a blazer. Wrote an op-ed last week on "Financial Empathy as Brand Strategy."

He likes the offering. He nods as he flips through the updated pitch, quotes our LTV/CAC ratio back to me like a love letter.

Nico's in the corner, arms crossed, watching everything. Daren's got his laptop open, ready to go deep.

Cayden taps the printed deck. "I heard your podcast on the way over. You said more than five hundred thousand vendors. The data room shows under three hundred fifty thousand."

"It's a rolling estimate," I say too quickly. "Directionally accurate."

Cayden raises a hand—calm, clipped. "Directionally accurate isn't what we invest on. We don't do hype. We do facts," he says evenly.

Zack leans toward his screen. "We're projecting over five hundred thousand by quarter-end. The podcast was framing trajectory."

Cayden looks straight at me. "You framed it as present tense." "The number's climbing daily," I say. "And the window's closing. If we wait for perfect reporting, we'll miss timing."

He closes the folder, slow. "We're still interested. But we need a revised deck by Monday. Auditable numbers. And a holdback until Q2."

"Understood," I say. He stands. Offers his hand. "We believe in the product, Will. Just don't let your voice move faster than the business underneath it."

I force a smile. Shake his hand. Nico walks him to the elevator.

"Could've been worse," Zack mutters.

"They're not wrong," Daren says softly.

"They see the vision," I say.

"They see it," he says. "They just want to know it's viable." Zack signs off.

Nico's by the whiteboard, arms still folded. Daren's hunched over his laptop, fingers twitching on the trackpad. I'm pacing—restless, wired.

"We're not pulling the number back," I say. "We're contextualizing it."

Daren looks up. "We could split the metric—onboarded versus actively transacting. Clarify the difference without walking anything back."

"No." I stop pacing. "That gives them an out. We reinforce momentum. We give them context."

Nico raises an eyebrow. "You mean spin."

"I mean narrative," I snap. Quieter: "We clarify pipeline. Show conversion. Prove direction."

Daren turns his laptop toward me. "I can add cohort growth—make the trendline read more aggressive."

"Do it," I say. "And we get testimonials. Real ones. Pull vendors who've transacted and get them on camera or quoted. Show impact."

Nico doesn't move. "Half of them aren't under PR release. You want legal in this?"

"No time. Call favors. Comp the next payout batch. Whatever it takes—get the soundbites."

Daren glances at Nico, then back to me. "You think that's enough for Eastpoint?"

"It's not about satisfying them," I say, rubbing the back of my neck.

"It's about keeping control of the story. We give them what they didn't know they needed, before they ask again."

Silence.

"And if they push harder?" Nico says.

I meet his eyes. "Then we move faster."

I turn back to the board, thinking about the next slide, the next call, the next twist in the pitch.

We don't pivot. We accelerate.

"You know what to do." I walk back into my office.

* * *

After the door clicks, I stand at the corner window.

Stonebridge passed last week. Pelham finally caved on us—gave us the smile-with-a-scalpel routine—"reallocating toward hard tech." Now Jay Remsen — chair of Coventry, the largest PE firm in the room — is getting weak knees. But I know the look he gave me. Not risk aversion—doubt.

I can't let that stand.

I grab my phone and text Zack.

I pocket the phone. No time to dwell. Pelion Group's up next—West Coast, late start, always watching the East for conviction.

I take the long table—dark walnut, matte—laptop open, camera framed high enough to catch the abstract art and the leather bench.

I ping Daren on Slack.

WILL: Update the deck. Reflect merchant growth as confirmed.

DAREN: It's not confirmed.

WILL: It will be.

I watch the cursor blink. The lie isn't heavy yet. But it has mass.

Text from Zack: If you want Remsen, he's got a window in 45. Car's out front. Don't be late.

* * *

Jay Remsen doesn't smile when I enter.

He doesn't stand. Doesn't offer a hand. Gestures to the seat across from him.

"Thought we already passed."

"You did," I say. "I'm asking you to reconsider."

"That's not how this works."

"Then let's test the rule."

He studies me—cold, professional—the kind of look that ignores the suit and decides whether the bones are worth trouble.

"You're asking for a billion," he says. "You're two verticals shy of traction, your onboarding UI is half-differentiated, and your compliance stack's unproven."

"And yet Quimby's talking about doubling down. Pelion's serious. Weston's soft."

"Momentum isn't substance," he says.

"No," I say. "But substance without momentum doesn't survive long enough to get funded." I place the PPM and the latest deck on the table.

He flips pages.

"This company will scale," I say. "With you or without you. I want you in because you know what this becomes once it hits velocity."

He taps the PPM. "You'll have my answer by the end of the month."

"The fifteenth."

A silence. "You always this confident?"

"Only when I'm right."

He almost smiles. "We'll see."

I leave without a handshake. Neither of us reaches.

* * *

The office is quieter now. Most of the team's gone, lights dimmed to evening. But Daren and Nico are still here—feet up in Nico's office next to mine, a bottle of Jack already down a third.

Nico's tie is loose, shoes off, staring at the skyline like he's deciding whether it deserves saving. Daren's hoodie sleeves are pushed up, eyes scanning flowcharts he probably doesn't trust.

I step in, drop my bag. "Pelion's gonna move," I say. "You felt that."

"They're sniffing," Nico says. "You fed them enough blood to keep them circling."

"And glitter," Daren adds.

"It's all the same currency," I say. "They're in the game now."

I stretch on the leather couch, glass in hand, let the silence roll—the kind that only shows up after you convince people you pulled it off.

"Coventry?" Nico asks.

"Noncommittal," I say. "Remsen's thinking."

Daren snorts. "Guy doesn't think. He calculates."

"Let him," I say. "I gave him enough."

Nico turns. "You gave him a script," Nico says. "Not the same."

Daren glances at Nico. "That only works if the numbers hold."

"They will."

I laugh, lean forward, and pour the rest into three glasses.

"How long since we actually unplugged?"

"Define unplugged," Nico says. "Last time I asked for a Wi-Fi password was 2018."

"Exactly," I say. "We've earned a bit of a break."

"Where?" Daren asks. "Vegas? South Beach?"

"Too obvious," I say. "We go offshore."

I let it hang.

"St. Barth's."

Nico groans—the kind that means yes. "You serious?"

"Deadly," I say. "Long weekend. Sun, surf, and a signal weak enough to fake disconnection."

"You taking us private?" Daren grins.

"Is there any other way?"

Nico whistles low. "Goddamn. We really are those guys now."

I raise my glass. "For now."

We clink. No one says the quiet part—what happens when the high wears off.

That's for later.

* * *

The jet hums like a secret — smooth, controlled, the kind of quiet that makes you forget the speed under you. We're sprawled across butter-soft leather in a G4. Champagne in crystal. Nico across from me in a silk camp shirt, scrolling villa photos. Daren in back, headphones half out.

I refresh my inbox. Nothing new, nothing reassuring.

"By the way," I say, glancing up from my screen, "we're in a good spot heading into January. Eastpoint's circling. Quimby's in diligence. Coventry is asking for updated metrics."

Nico stops typing. Daren swallows. They know what that means — no one has committed.

But I keep going. "We're close. Right where we need to be."

Half true. Half bluff. The kind that only works if no one blinks.

I lift my cup. Nico grins and clinks.

"You realize most founders are still pitching from coworking spaces," he says.

"Let them," I say. "We're playing a different game."

Daren turns his laptop toward me. "New deck went out this morning. Flagging one thing. '500,000 merchants transacting weekly.' That's optimistic. Actual is about 335,000. Including repeats."

I don't blink. "That line's for where we're landing, not where we are today."

Daren lowers his voice. "Investors are betting on trust, not projection."

"Investors are betting on narrative," I say evenly. "And we're winning."

Nico shifts. "Just don't forget who's holding the dice."

Daren closes the laptop. His silence weighs more than the argument ever did.

Below us the Atlantic shimmers — far, quiet, endless.

Blake sends a photo from her apartment — candlelit skyline, legs tucked under her.

Blake: You boys better land pretty. Don't embarrass me. SPF 50. You're not built for island light.

I snap the cabin — sunlight, Nico mid-smirk, Daren two drinks in.

Will: Coming in hot.

The attendant tops off Daren's champagne. He doesn't look up.

We ride the silence like the altitude. Above it all. For now.

* * *

The villa spills down the cliff like it was poured into the rock. White stone. An infinity pool swallowing the moon. The air burns white. Pool lights under the surface, cell-phone flashes above it, bodies lit from every direction until no one has a shadow. Music rolls like smoke—deep bass, soft edges, too loud to think.

Everyone's barefoot or close to it. Linen. Silk. Heat. Laughter. This is what victory feels like when you confuse it with escape.

Inside: full. Models, investors, plus-ones who've never had to explain what they do. Private chef. An Italian Greyhound. Something powdered in a leather pouch no one pretends not to recognize.

A tray of Negronis floats by. Nico's already found a bottle and no boundaries—a woman in black who used to run PR for a Formula One team.

Daren's in a woven chair by the pool, drink in hand, eyes on everything and nothing.

I find the edge of the patio, glass loose, watching the dark water below. The surf glows faint under the moon. Too beautiful to be real. Which feels about right.

"This is the reward," Daren says, slurring just enough to mean it.

I don't answer. It doesn't feel like reward anymore. It's performance—a simulation of success, dressed in linen and backlit by luxury.

Inside, someone calls my name. Laughter breaks over the pool. A cheer goes up for no reason at all. I let the noise carry me back inside. Let it swallow the part of me that still remembers quiet.

* * *

I wake to quiet. No voices. Just the fridge hum and the ocean pushing through the open doors. The bed beside me is empty. Sheets still warm. A wine glass on the nightstand—lipstick smudged, not red. Neutral. Someone used to being seen without being named.

I sit up. The villa's too bright. Throat dry. Head throbbing on the sea's slow churn. Fragments: her laugh, her hand on my chest, the tilt of her head before I kissed her. Everything after blurs. I pull on last night's shirt and step onto the terrace. The pool is still. A plastic cup floats near the edge. The beach below is empty—wind, water, a line of light like the world didn't notice what we did.

There's a note by the espresso machine. Folded. No name. Just:

Fun night. • C.

I stare a second. Toss it. It isn't guilt, exactly. More like subtraction—like I left something behind and I don't want to name it.

CHAPTER 19

GOLDEN BOY

The jet door opens to gray light and cold air. Teterboro is as always — private, polished, bored with itself.

I walk across the tarmac alone, tightening my tie. Inside the gate a black Escalade idles. Angela steps out when she sees me — She is a tall Black woman in her mid-forties with the kind of face that is expressive when she decides and closed when she doesn't. She fills whatever space she's in — not loudly, just completely - black jacket, boots, hair tight, a small gold cross at her throat and three rings on her right hand that catch the tarmac light. Coffee in one hand, keys in the other. No sign. No clipboard. She moves with a quiet femininity that has nothing to prove.

She clocks my condition and hands me her coffee without a word.

I slide in. Heat already on. Nico and Daren climb in back. She pulls out.

I flip to NYBC on my phone, scrolling.

A headline stops me cold.

SunCoast Bank to Merge with Regional Giant in $3.8 Billion Deal.

The photo is unmistakable. Priya, sharp as ever, flanked by two MDs at Sutter. She's the lead. Her name in the byline.

She did it. They did it without us.

A flicker I won't name. Not regret. Not envy. Recognition. The world I once ran in is moving on.

I swipe past it. Angela keeps her eyes on the road.

"400 Park?" she asks.

I nod.

* * *

Glass walls. Navy carpet. Conference Room 23. I know this room too well.

Zack sits at the head, sleeves rolled, tie loosened to signal urgency. Three analysts line the wall. I take my seat. Nico on my left. Daren scrolling something he doesn't like. Ames walks in last — calm, controlled, a faint smile like he knows the ending.

"We've got a problem," Zack says. No preamble.

I lean back. "Go on."

"Weston just called. Concerns about your user-volume disclosures. They think you're overstating merchant activity. Someone flagged the 500,000+ transacting weekly stat."

"We've explained the growth curve."

Zack slides a folder across. "They want system logs. Transaction-level data. Something concrete."

I don't touch it.

"They're spooked," Zack says. "If they pull, Pelion might follow. If Pelion wobbles, the stack shakes."

Ames speaks. "You were told to stay tight on numbers. Clean. Verifiable."

"The numbers reflect our trajectory," I say.

"Trajectory doesn't close," Ames says. "Credibility does."

Daren shifts. "We can clarify. Reframe the metric. Show net new users instead of throughput."

Zack shakes his head. "No time. Weston's committee is tomorrow."

I fold my hands. Look straight at Ames. "We hold this."

"I think you built a house on narrative," he says, even. "And now someone's testing the foundation."

Silence. Zack watches me, waiting for the version of me that fixes this to stand up.

Nico leans in. "We can pull merchant segments. Filter repeats. Make the five hundred thousand defensible."

"Do it. Today. And Zack — get Weston back on. They're getting what they need."

Zack exhales, half relieved. Ames watches me a moment longer. "Get it clean," he says at the door. "Or get ready to watch it collapse."

As the room clears, Daren lingers. "They're not wrong. The gap between what we are and what you're selling."

"It's a gap we're closing," I say.

He studies me. Not angry. Just tired. "Don't close it so fast we lose what matters."

I don't answer. My calendar is already open. Next meeting. Next pitch.

* * *

The Escalade is already at the curb when I come down. Angela steps out — no expression, no question, just the door.

I stand on the sidewalk. "I'm sure you have other clients," I say.

She gives me a look. "That's correct. Lots of them."

"Drop them," I say. "Full time. I'll make it worth it."

She doesn't answer right away. Pulls her keys from her pocket, turns them once.

"You know what I clear right now? Between all my clients?"

"Tell me."

She does. The number is not small. I don't flinch. "I'll beat it."

"By how much?"

I tell her.

She looks at me the way she's been looking at me all morning — like she's running a calculation I'm not privy to. "I've got a standing Thursday with a cardiac surgeon on Park. He tips well and he doesn't talk."

"I'll cover the Thursday."

"And I drive my route. You tell me where, I get you there. How is my business."

"Understood."

She's still not sold. She's still not sold. I can see it.

"I'm not a yes-man," she says. "I don't do errands. I don't wait in lobbies for three hours while you wrap up a dinner you said would be an hour."

"I wouldn't ask you to."

"You say that now."

"I mean it."

She opens the door. I slide in. She gets behind the wheel and pulls out without another word.

A few blocks later she speaks again. "One condition."

"Name it."

"Sundays are mine. Non-negotiable."

I glance at the rearview. "Family?"

"My grandmother." A silence. "Dementia. Sunday's our day. Always will be."

"Done," I say. No hesitation.

She nods once. Eyes back on the road. The city moves past the windows.

"Another thing," she says.

"What's that?"

"Angela sounds like someone who writes parking tickets. You can call me Angie."

I almost laugh. "Alright, Angie."

At 42nd she speaks again, eyes on the road. "I drive plenty of CEOs.

Founders. Wall Street heavy hitters. There's a look that shows up once the money hits. Like the city owes you its attention."

I watch the traffic. "And mine?"

She pauses. Not unkind — just honest. "You look like someone following a script you haven't memorized yet."

She doesn't smile. But something in the mirror shifts. Close enough.

* * *

Forty-seventh floor of a boutique firm near Bryant Park. Quiet money, not loud. Framed tombstones on the walls. Two partners from Eastpoint Capital — dry as powder, serious East Coast energy. They don't blink unless it matters.

Zack beside me. Nico and Darren in the back row. Blake passed: You've got this.

"Visibility isn't velocity," one partner says.

"Visibility got us in the door," I say. "Velocity's what we're building." I walk them through it — vendor onboarding, enterprise contracts, burn allocation, the banking stack. They listen without moving.

"What's the ask for a board seat?"

"Ten percent of the total raise."

"We're in." Provisional, but in.

Zack nearly smirks. I nod like I expected it.

In the elevator going down he straightens his tie. "First solid yes. Momentum follows momentum."

Maybe. The doors open. Cold air. Midtown noise.

Not yes. Not no. Not yet.

My phone is already buzzing.

* * *

By the time we're back at the office, the sky's gone to slate. Rain threads the windows. The building hums with heat and fluorescent resolve that feels borrowed.

Inside, it's too quiet—the kind of quiet where everyone watches something strain and pretends it isn't. Nico heads to the war room. Daren's already in motion, screens waking, Slack threads lighting up. I drop my coat, unbutton my collar, still hearing Ames in my head. Built on narrative. Bullshit. It's solid enough. It just hasn't caught up yet.

"Pull the segments," I say. "Transacting merchants by week. Unique IDs only."

"We've done it," Daren says, eyes on his screen. "The issue is frequency. Same vendors processing five times in a week. They're counted as five. Weston wants single-instance data."

"We frame it as engagement," I push. "Repeat usage. Retention."

"Will—" Nico starts, stops.

"What?"

"They're not buying a story. Not now. They want numbers."

"We'll give numbers," I say. "We'll just decide how they're seen."

Daren looks up. "You realize that's exactly what they're afraid of?"

"It's positioning."

"It's spin, Will. I've been in this room for eighteen months. I know what we have and I know what that deck says. They're not the same document."

"We're in a fundraise—"

"I know what we're in." He sets the marker down. "I'm just telling you I won't stand up in front of potential investors and call three hundred thirty-five thousand five hundred thousand. I'll frame it. I'll contextualize it. But I won't say the number." A moment.

"Fine," I say. "I'll say it. You think Tap got here by underselling itself?" He looks back at the screen. Doesn't say anything else.

Nico rubs his jaw. "We're not Tap."

"Not yet."

No one answers.

Daren and Nico are debating at the white board. I walk to the glass wall facing the Hudson. New York looks washed out, likes it's waiting for something to give.

My phone buzzes.

Blake: What's going on with Weston? My guy heard they're spooked. Want me to run interference?

I type. Delete. Set the phone down.

Behind me, Daren types faster. Nico paces.

We're still in it. Just.

Then the elevator dings. Footsteps.

Ian.

Hands in pockets. Hoodie. Same scuffed boots. Same quiet calm I forgot he carried. No performance. No posture. Just presence.

Daren glances at me, then back to the board.

Ian stops a few feet inside the room. "I heard you're underwater," he says. Not unkind.

"We're working through it," I say.

He looks past me at the data on the screen. Walks over. Picks up a dry-erase marker. Studies the board.

Then, quietly: "You're not selling the wrong thing. You're just telling the wrong version of it." He starts marking up the whiteboard.

No one speaks.

I step back. Let him write.

* * *

It's close to midnight when I finally leave. The office is still. Nico stayed behind with Ian. Daren's asleep on the couch. I needed air.

Angie's waiting out front. Same spot. Hazard lights ticking like a heartbeat. I slide into the back seat. She doesn't say a word. Just glances once in the mirror, then pulls from the curb like she's been expecting me.

The city's quieter than usual. Rain on the windshield. Wipers slow and steady—the kind of rhythm that makes you think about things you never say out loud.

The river glows back at us, and all I can think about is how close we came. Weston calls out our numbers—really calls them out—and suddenly the whole story feels fragile. Then Eastpoint drops a commitment on us, our first real yes, and for a minute I let myself believe the ground was solid. And then Ian walks in and saves the pitch I nearly broke. Quiet. Precise. Like someone who still believes the thing he built matters. It's been that kind of day—fracture, hope, then truth.

Angie glances at me—long enough to see through it. "You're carrying something," she says.

"I'm fine," I say.

She lets out a small, skeptical breath. "Mhm. And I'm the Mayor of New York."

I look back out the window. Try again. Fail.

The truth sits in my chest like a weight that finally got tired of being ignored.

"I've been treating someone wrong," I say. "For a while."

Angie is quiet. She glances in the mirror, then back to the road.

"What made you see it?" she asks.

I exhale. "He showed up. When he didn't have to. When he should've walked away."

"Those moments hit different," she says. "When someone still shows up after you've been pushing 'em out."

She keeps her eyes on the road.

* * *

I'm back in Greenwich.

Liz is on the white settee with W and a cocktail that's somehow always half full. She doesn't look up.

"I thought I'd find you out saving all the world's hair dressers."

"World's on hold. Checking on home."

She studies me when the magazine finally folds shut. "You've become very polished," she says, almost suspicious. "Maybe a little too polished."

"Polish works," I say.

"And what does it cost?"

I built something that works. People are using it. I tell her that. She listens without answering.

I turn. "I thought you'd be pleased."

It slips out unfiltered. Too much boy still in the man.

"I am," she says. "I just don't say it every five minutes like some people seem to need."

She softens, barely. "I was proud when you chose Colby. I'm proud now. But if you're chasing approval — mine or anyone's — you'll run yourself empty."

"I just wanted you to see what I've become," I say.

"I see it," she says.

She lifts the magazine. The moment passes. For now, that's enough.

I drift down the hall to the study. Sink into the old leather chair. The room smells like dust and old books and a ghost I keep mistaking for memory.

I hear it again. I thought you'd be pleased. I hate how small it sounded. Macaroni art, held up for applause.

Blue pads in, noses my leg. I curl my fingers into the soft fur behind his ears.

* * *

6:52 a.m. The floor dark. Daren already in a hoodie, booting dashboards. Nico at the espresso machine, staring out at a gray city.

I drop my bag. "Anything yet?"

"Sutter won't start calling till eight," Daren says.

Nico: "Love when hundreds of millions hang on voicemail."

I pace. It doesn't help. Ian once stayed until two in the morning rewriting a single function because it didn't feel right. I remember nodding when he explained it. I don't remember when that stopped being the priority.

My phone has been buzzing since six. PitchDeck ran something overnight — unnamed sources, Series A speculation, the kind of piece that either accelerates the close or spooks the room. I've read it four times. I don't know which it is yet.

By noon the round is either locked or we start unraveling.

10:07 a.m. Zack forwards Weston's email.

After committee review, we've decided not to participate at this time. We wish you continued success.

No call. No color. Just a door closing. Somewhere a reporter is probably already writing the pivot version of our story.

Daren swears. Nico sets his mug down hard. I say nothing. But I feel it — the tremor.

By noon, worse. No callbacks. No emails. Not even from Q's office.

Zack's texts stop. We're ghosted.

I call him.

He answers tight. "They're circling. Committees. Second-guessing."

"Push harder."

"You think I'm not?" he snaps. "Keep your phone close. We're not done." I shut my office door. For a minute I let myself see it — the press release we won't send, the team I'll have to face. The version of me that collapses in real time.

Then, 2:03 p.m., it shifts.

Pelion: Confirmed. $100MM. $100/share. Docs to follow. Langford: We're in. $150MM. $100/share.

The room jumps. Nico whoops. Daren validates. "Amazing — $2 billion valuation."

Then it snowballs. Eastpoint. Q's office — three hundred million combined at the $100 price, doubling down from seed without the re-trade in terms my father warned about. Stonebridge pivots back. Bastion. Easton. Grayson. A few West Coast funds chasing the trend.

By 5:11 p.m. we're at $800MM hard. Still nothing from Remsen.

5:16 p.m. Unknown caller.

I step into the hall. "Will Chaffee."

"Jay Remsen."

My breath catches. "We've had a strong showing," I say.

"Depends how you define strong." Jay continues. "You ran a smart process. Got people excited.

Played narrative well." He pauses. "I've also been reviewing concerns. Transaction volume. Repeat rate. Gaps between what's written and what's working."

Heat rises in my neck. "We're closing those gaps. And we have capital to scale into them."

"You do now," he says. Then: "That said—"

Silence stretches.

“We’re in. Four hundred million. Hundred per share, like the others. Full allocation. No syndicate split.” A silence. “Three board seats. And I will be chair. No negotiation.”

“Anton Quimby is our board chair. That’s a committed governance position from seed.”

“Was,” he says. “Before this call.”

“I’ll need to discuss—”

“No you won’t.” His voice is even. Not unkind. The measured quiet of someone who has made this call before. “You’re at eight hundred hard. You’re ninety minutes from close. You need our commitment and I need the chair. We both know it. The question is whether you can accept our terms.”

Silence.

“Our commitment and terms are ready to go to Sutter now.”

I look through the glass at the war room. Daren at the board. Nico still on his call. Champagne sweating on the counter like it already knows.

The chair. Q's chair. The one we structured at seed. "Then put it through."

The line clicks. Call duration: 01:58.

I exhale so hard I almost drop the phone.

I step into the war room. Nico on a call. Daren re-checking the board.

I clear my throat. They look up. I hold up four fingers. Nico lowers his phone.

"Four hundred?"

I nod. "Coventry."

The room goes still.

Zack, still on speaker: "Holy shit. At one hundred?"

"At one hundred," I say.

Nico runs a hand through his hair. "That's the raise. We're over subscribed."

"I said yes to the chair," I say.

Zack exhales. "Of course you did."

No one cheers. No one moves. The gravity of the room changes. Eight hundred million in before five. Now one-point-two billion. Oversubscribed. I should feel triumphant. Instead I feel off-balance, like the moment is too big for me.

Nico hands me a glass. I raise it. "To narrative."

They echo it. "To narrative."

* * *

It's just past seven when the war room empties. I stay behind.

By the time I open my laptop the stories are already running. The Financial Record leads with the number — $1.2 billion, record Series A for a fintech platform serving the underbanked. Ticker, the financial wire service, has the Remsen angle. PitchDeck calls it the raise of the year.

Founder magazine has a draft piece they want a quote for by nine. I don't send one.

One-point-two billion. Founder's equity valued at a hundred million. The number should feel like arrival. All I feel is the weight of the next call.

I open my laptop. The board-composition doc still up, cursor blinking over: Chair — TBD (Quimby). I delete it. Type: Chair — Jay Remsen (Coventry).

The words look neat on the page. Heavier in my chest. I sold a piece of what I built to buy the illusion of control.

Blake calls. I let it ring twice. "Hey." Her voice already in motion — restaurant echo, laughter, curated celebration. "You did it. Remsen's in for four hundred. At one hundred?" She whistles. "You should be popping something top-shelf."

I glance at the untouched champagne. "Not yet."

She keeps going — Summit magazine, a cover idea, dinner at Casa Cruz — while the sound dulls at the edges. On my screen: Chair — Jay Remsen. I end the call and set the phone face-down.

Q's feed on my phone. Same grin. Pacific sunset. Surfboard under one arm. Caption: Never stop chasing the sets.

I scroll to his name. Call.

Q answers before I finish dialing. “Damn, Chaffee. Thought you’d be too busy bathing in commitments to call your boy.”

I laugh, quieter than I mean to. “We closed at one-two. Hundred a share.”

Low whistle. “No shit.”

“Langford and Pelion jumped in first. Brighton, Bastion, Voss, Easton, Grayson all followed. Even Stonebridge, who we’d written off in October came in.”

“Coventry came in for four hundred. Remsen wanted the chair and two more board seats. I let him have it.”

Silence. Longer than the one before.

"You gave Remsen the chair."

"He had four hundred million behind the ask."

"I was always the board chair, Will. That's how we structured it at seed."

"I know."

"You know what my team is going to say. You know what it means for my position with my family LPs when I have to explain why I let four hundred million override a governance commitment I made at seed."

"Q —"

"I'm not done." His voice is different now. The grin gone. "I backed you. Early. When nobody else saw it. Not because of the numbers — those weren't there yet. Because I know who you are when you're standing in a room and you mean what you're saying."

A long pause.

"Did you mean it?"

The screen reads: Chair — Jay Remsen. "Yes."

"Then I'll live with the chair. But Will — the next time something like this happens, you call me before you agree to anything. Not after."

"Understood."

Another pause. Then, quieter:

"You just turned my family's hundred million into over a billion in under two years."

"Right."

"I still hate that you gave away the chair." A moment. "But I hate running meetings more." The grin back in his voice, barely. "Don't make me say it twice."

We hang up.

Air finds me again. Less of it than before.

* * *

The next morning I'm in a blue suit, riding the elevator--wired and weightless. The place buzzing with wins we haven't absorbed yet.

The doors open to glass, light, energy. A new buzz that didn't exist before the raise.

PR has already framed the Summit magazine and Founder magazine covers along the entry corridor — both dropped the same week, both featuring the same photo, both leading with the same number. I keep walking. We're not scrappy anymore and everyone know it.

Nico shows up in a sand bomber that costs more than a used Civic.

Daren's got a new MacBook, new kicks, a custom Sawbuck hoodie in clean Helvetica.

Cold brew on tap. Standing desks. Plants that look alive. Success has a smell—polish and espresso, mostly. We don't say it, but we know: we're not underdogs anymore. We're the show, apparently.

The team packs into the atrium—standing room only. Some clutch coffee. Some already high on the last few months.

The wall monitors flash: Series A Closed: $1.2B. Founder magazine and Summit magazine loop. My face, everywhere.

I step onto the low platform near the screen. Heads lift. Eyes lock. "Two years ago," I start, "this was a napkin sketch in a dive bar." "Now it's a billion-dollar platform backed by the most respected names in capital."

I let it hang.

"That doesn't happen by accident. It happens because you show up early, stay late, and do the impossible in between."

A few nods. A few eyes drop.

"We're not celebrating a finish line. We're crossing a threshold."

"We told the world who we are. Time to prove it."

"This is where it gets hard. This is where gaps get noticed. And this—right now—is when we define who we are."

"People are betting real things on us. We owe them something solid. Let's be worth the faith."

I step down. No applause. Just a hum—adrenaline meeting pressure. Perfect. Applause is for the past. We've got too much to live up to. People scatter — some to Slack, some to espresso, all to the work. A reporter from Ticker is waiting in the lobby. I asked Daren to handle it.

* * *

Nico and Daren find me fifteen minutes later — coffees and bagels, the particular ease of men who have just done something impossible and haven't slept. Nico flops on the couch. "Speech of the year."

"You sounded like an actual CEO," Daren adds. "I almost believed you."

"Glad I fooled at least two people," I say.

For a second we just sit — three guys in the glass box, surrounded by floor-to-ceiling windows and million-dollar expectations.

Daren glances around. "Remember the broom closet we worked out of that first month?"

"Blocked it out like trauma," I say.

"At least the Wi-Fi worked," Nico mutters. "Half the time."

Nico leans forward. "You did it, man. We did it. Walked out of Sutter with nothing but a half-baked deck and a chip."

Daren: "And now we're here."

I let it land. "We're not done. Not even close. But I'm proud of us. All of it."

Nico raises his coffee. "To broom closets."

"And billion-dollar delusions," Daren adds.

"And whatever comes next," I finish.

We tap paper cups like flutes.

For a moment I let myself feel it. It feels solid. We did something real.

* * *

Alex.

Not in the house, not in the hall, not in her usual geometry of this life we've been living in parallel. Here. At Sawbuck. In the city.

She has never done this before.

I stand without deciding to. "Hey there."

Something crosses her face — the smallest acknowledgment that the standing matters. "Hello."

I come around the desk. We hug — not the careful kind, the real one, the kind that says I know you and I've missed you and I don't have the language for the rest of it. I hold on a moment longer than I should. She lets me.

I sit back down.

She takes the chair opposite me. The desk between us again. The way it always ends up. The open laptop, the ordinary evidence of a day that didn't know she was coming.

"You came into the city," I say.

"I had things to do for Lizzy," she says. A small smile. We both know that's not the whole reason.

She has a folder — a contract, a schedule revision. She sets it on the edge of the desk like it's the pretext it is.

"Your mother wants to know if you're coming to the Vanity Fair thing Thursday."

"Tell her probably."

She nods. Doesn't move to leave.

On my desk, face up, is a printout of The Column item — the gossip page that follows money. Nico's handwriting in the margin: not your best angle. The two of us by the firepit, Blake's hand on my arm, both of us caught mid-laugh in the amber light. Sawbuck founder Will Chaffee with Blake Caswell at Friday's Series A celebration.

I reach for it.

Too late.

Alex has seen it. I know she has. I watch her not react to it — the particular stillness of someone who has just received information they already suspected and are choosing not to name.

"I'll tell her you'll be there," she says.

She picks up the folder.

"There's something I want to ask you," she says. "What happens now that Sawbuck is taking off?"

I lean back. "What do you mean?"

"I mean — who do you become? On the other side of all this."

"Someone who built something that matters."

She looks at me the way she looked at me on the porch in Nantucket — not appraising. Something closer to sad.

"And what did you give up to get here?"

I don't answer. The answer is in the room. She can see it.

"That's what I thought," she says. Not unkind. Just clear. The way she always is.

She stands. Picks up her bag. Doesn't make a production of it.

I go toward her. "Alex—"

She stops at the door. Doesn't turn around.

"I know how this ends, Will. You don't have to say it," she says.

Then she's gone.

I sit back down behind the desk. The chair across from me still warm. The city outside still moving. Everything exactly as it was two minutes ago except for the thing that isn't.

I don't go after her.

I'm still sitting there when Daren appears in the doorway. "Ian's here," he says. "Came in awhile ago. Said he didn't want to go through your assistant."

I look up. "Where is he?"

"Conference room."

I stand. Leave the phone where it is.

Ian is at the window when I come in, hands in his pockets, staring down Lafayette like the view doesn't match the thing he wanted to build. He doesn't turn.

I already know this isn't a check-in.

"You didn't have to wait," I say.

He turns. "But have I earned the right to be seen?"

I stop. Look at him.

"I want it clear, Will. Either I'm treated with the respect and visibility I've earned — recognized as the true founder of this platform — or I'm out."

No heat. No drama. Just truth.

I cross to the desk, slow. "The story mattered more than we wanted to admit," I say. "Me as the face. A story the market could believe."

He doesn't blink.

"You're not wrong," I add. "The team just made almost a billion. Your share of that is over two hundred million."

"I know," he says. "I'm not in it for the money." He steps closer, never raising his voice. "I built this because it meant something. I let you run with it because I thought we were in it for the same reasons."

He pauses. "This isn't about ego. It's about standing where I belong. Either I'm there — or I walk. And if I go, I won't bring lawyers. I won't trash the brand. I'll just be gone." A silence. "But I need to be able to look in the mirror. Right now I can't."

I don't answer.

Ian nods once, turns for the door. "I'll expect your decision by end of the week."

He's gone.

I sit behind the desk. The phone still face-down. The chair where Alex sat still across from me.

It feels smaller now.

CHAPTER 20

THE SPECIFIC HOLLOWNESS

A week passes. I'm in every meeting and barely present for any of them. Emails stack. The office buzzes with traction updates and investor check-ins. I nod in the right places, say the right words, play the part I built.

That night most of the team clears out by eight. Nico and Daren stay in the war room — Nico at his screen running transaction volume projections, Daren with headphones on, the playlist bleeding through. I close my office door.

Ian steps in without knocking. I tell myself it's a meeting to discuss vendor usage numbers.

He doesn't sit.

"I gave you the week."

I nod, close my laptop. "You did."

"And?"

I lean back. "We're at a stage where the story matters more than the origin. You know that."

"I do," he says. "But I also know I built this with you. And I asked for something simple — respect. Visibility."

"Ian, you're set for life," I say. "Your equity's worth over two hundred million. Start anything you want. No lawsuits. No headlines. We'll honor everything."

He takes that in. No anger. Just a long breath.

"So that's the answer."

"I'm giving you freedom," I say. "To do what's next without the noise."

"You're giving me a payoff."

I don't respond.

He looks around—the glass, the art, the skyline—then back at me.

"I used to imagine this moment," he says. "Here together, after the raise, after the press. I thought it would feel like we made it."

He adjusts the strap of his bag. "Instead, it feels like I disappeared."

"You didn't," I say, softer than I expect.

"I did," he replies. "And you let it happen." No bitterness. Just truth.

He turns to leave, pauses at the door.

"I hope you find your way back to what started this."

Then he's gone.

I watch the city's reflection in the window, trying to pinpoint when the color bled out.

Long enough for the lights across the river to shift.

Then my phone buzzes. Marci.

NYBC wants you on Squawk Box this Thursday. Live segment. Future of fintech. They're calling you "the new face of trust."

Before I can process that, another message:

Ticker wants a follow-up roundtable next week. Your team. Who's your pick? I set the phone face-down. Pick it back up.

Daren and Nico are still in the war room when I walk back through — burn rate versus the playlist, the particular energy of people who don't know what just happened in the next room.

I stand in the doorway watching them.

"Ticker wants a roundtable," I say. "You in?"

Daren: "Me? Yeah, of course."

"Nico too. And we'll loop in Noah from dev."

"Not Ian?" Nico asks. Too casually.

I shake my head. "Not this time."

Neither of them says anything. But the silence says plenty.

* * *

By Wednesday I need out. Not just out of the office — out of the noise, the interviews, the orbit. I book the last seat on the 7:30 to Nantucket. Angie doesn't ask why.

She gets me there.

Liz's family has had the cottage since before she was born. She offered it without conditions. That was the kindness of it.

April in Nantucket. Still off-season. Still cold enough to layer up and light a fire. The cottage smells like cedar and sea salt. Whitewashed walls. A fireplace that smokes if you don't open the flue just right. The kind of place built for living, not impressing.

No noise. Just water on three sides and a silence you can feel in your chest. I walk the shoreline in a jacket too thin and boots not made for sand. No one recognizes me here. And maybe that's the point.

Text buzzes. Marci: Squawk Box went well. Andrew loved you. Clip is circulating. TechPulse wants a cover. Also — Gala Saturday. Press will be there. Blake says you promised.

Blue curls near the hearth.

I scroll through headlines. My face is everywhere.

The Financial Record: "Sawbuck's $1.2B Raise Signals New Era for Underbanked Fintech."

Ticker: "Coventry Capital Takes Chair Seat in Record Series A."

PitchDeck: "Will Chaffee Is the Face of the New Trust Economy."

Ledger has a profile running Sunday — I haven't read it.

I should feel proud. Instead, I hear Ian's voice from that first night at The Tank: This wasn't about being the face, man. It was about fixing the system.

Back inside, I build a fire and pour a bourbon. I close my eyes, and I'm ten again.

The cottage was Liz's then too — her mother's, really — but my father brought us anyway, off-season, when no one else wanted it.

He poured two glasses of ginger ale and handed me one like it was scotch. We sat on the porch, ocean wind snapping the railing. He didn't say much. Just let me sit beside him, my feet too short for the deck. Every now and then he'd nod toward the surf.

"That sound?" he said. "That's what the world sounds like when it's not asking anything of you."

I nodded like I understood. I didn't. But I remember how quiet it felt. How safe.

I open my eyes.

The fire's burned low. My drink still half full. The world I built shines outward. God's shines inward. I miss the second.

* * *

The loft in Tribeca still smells like new hardwood and fresh paint. Half the art leans against walls. I haven't figured out the lights.

Blake brings a private chef from Blue Hill and opens a '96 Burgundy her father saved for when the big thing hits. She says this is it.

We sit on the floor — duck confit with wooden chopsticks, mismatched glassware — like college again. For a moment, it feels like something might be starting.

Blake's in a hoodie and socks, hair undone. Ten years younger without the armor.

I lift my glass. "To us."

She taps her can. "To a place of your own, finally."

We eat in the good kind of silence — earned, easy.

"Thank you," I say.

She looks up. "For what?"

"The article. The strategy. The push. You helped get us there."

She shrugs, pride showing anyway. "You were already there. I just made the world see it."

I glance around the empty loft. "One day you're begging for meetings. The next you've raised over a billion."

"You made it look easy."

"It wasn't."

She smiles — knowing. "I wonder sometimes if I'm just a mirror," I say.

"Meaning?"

"I reflect what people want to see. Investors, press. You."

She sets her chopsticks down. "Maybe. But you're not just reflecting anymore. You're shaping."

I look away — not because I don't believe her, but because I wish I saw it too.

She brushes my hand. "You know what I admire most?"

"My devastating humility?"

She laughs. "You don't flinch. Even when it's messy."

"I flinch more than you think," I say. "I just do it where no one can see."

She kisses me — slow, unhurried. For a moment I let go of the deals, the numbers, the weight.

Later we lie back on the floor, limbs tangled, the city humming beyond the windows. Not perfect. But real enough for now.

* * *

Next morning, I'm on the water like every other Sunday.

Cold air. Oars slicing the Mianus in clean rhythm. For a few strokes

— wind in my lungs, hands blistering again — I remember who I was before any of this.

"Big raise," Tucker says as we glide past a frostbitten dock. "You finally made something of yourself."

"Like everything you thought would matter does," I say when Graham asks what winning feels like."

It's true. That's the problem.

After, in the lot, they talk ski trips and foundation boards. I pretend to listen. Even here, with people who've known me longest, I'm still performing.

* * *

We're still damp, walking up Greenwich Avenue, when I stop at the Nutmeg Café.

Graham squints at the chipped sign. Tucker peers through the fogged window. Beau shakes his head. "This place? Thought we were celebrating."

"Oh, we are," I say. "You just don't know it yet."

Inside: Formica and sizzling bacon. Burnt coffee. No shame. We grab a booth. Debbie doesn't write anything down. I order a double stack, eggs over easy, two sides of sausage. They hesitate. Then cave. After plates land, even Beau admits it's the best sausage he's had in months.

"You come here?" Graham asks.

"Every chance I get," I say. "Before the clubs. Before the charts."

For a few minutes it's just us. Coffee. Grease. Quiet.

"So," Tucker says, tipping sugar into his cup, "what's next for Chaffee AI?"

"It's still Sawbuck," I say.

"For now," Beau adds.

Graham nudges his plate. "You're the face, right? That's what Blake said at Jake's thing. Will is the face."

I nod. "That's what they tell me."

"Must be nice," Tucker says. "Being worth more than the guy who used to lend you his boat."

I laugh — not because it's funny. Because it's true. And I wonder how long before the guy with the most money becomes the one they trust least.

* * *

After breakfast the guys peel off — Graham to a call, Tucker to tennis, Beau to his fourth renovation. I'm not ready to go back to the city.

A few blocks up sits the classic car showroom I biked past as a kid — when owning one felt like Bond fiction. Now it's a possibility.

Putnam Classic Autos. A black-glass box set behind a hedge on West Putnam. No banners. No pitch. Just glass.

Inside: vintage 911s. A '72 Ferrari Dino. A Jaguar E-Type with butter-soft seats and miles that read like stories.

But it's the Aston that stops me.

British Racing Green. Wire wheels. Wood rim. The exact car my father drove me to school in on Fridays — top down, even in November. His version of joy. The thing he held onto longest before the bankruptcy took everything else.

Then I go inside and buy it.

Not for me.

I'm there for two hours. The paperwork takes forty minutes. The rest of it I spend standing at the window watching the car on the showroom floor, trying to decide if I'm doing something generous or something that will outlast the gesture. By the time I hand over the card I still don't know.

* * *

The parking garage under his building is the kind that exists in every pre-war Brooklyn apartment — low ceilings, the smell of oil and concrete, fluorescent lights that flicker like they're deciding whether to bother. His name is still on the space, hand-lettered on a small sign that's been there since before I can remember.

The car is already there when I arrive. The dealer had it delivered that morning. It sits under the flickering light in British Racing Green, wire wheels catching what little shine there is in the place.

I text him from the lobby. The elevator opens and he steps out into the garage — dark jacket, the deliberate composure he never goes without — and then he sees it and he stops. Not the careful stopping of a man being polite. A full stop. As though something physical has hit him. I watch it move through him. The garage is quiet except for the flicker of the overhead light. British Racing Green in that dim light. Wire wheels. The wood rim just visible through the window. He doesn't speak. He doesn't look at me. He just looks at the car the way you look at something you believed was gone from the world. Then he walks toward it. Puts his hand on the roof. Runs his thumb along the chrome above the driver's door.

I wait.

"You didn't need to do this," he says.

Not thank you. Not I'm proud of you. Not the thing I came for.

His sounds like a man who has received enough in his life — good and bad —to know how to stand still when something moves him.

"I wanted to," I say.

He looks at the car a moment longer. "It's the right color." A pause.

"Your grandfather had one. Before the war."

I didn't know that.

He doesn't say anything else. He doesn't get in. He just stands there with his hand on the roof and looks at it the way you look at something you thought was gone.

I say something easy. It lets us both off the hook. He nods. We stand in the parking garage with the car between us and everything unsaid between us.

* * *

Monday bleeds into Tuesday. Spreadsheets, investor calls, another dinner with Blake where most of the talk is who's flying in for Friday.

I notice it the way you notice weather changing — not when it happens but the moment after, when something is different and you can't locate when it changed.

I notice it on one of my command performances for Liz. Alex passes me in the hallway with a file under her arm and says morning the way you say it to someone in an elevator. Neutral. Complete. Nothing underneath it reaching for anything. She's gone before I turn around. I understand something I have been choosing not to understand for months.

She decided.

Not dramatically. Not with a conversation or a scene or the kind of ending that gives you something to hold. She just — decided. Quietly, in the way she does everything, she looked at the available facts and made her assessment and filed it and moved on.

The available facts were not complicated. The calls I took instead of the ones I didn't make. The Tuesday nights I came home late and didn't sit down. The version of myself I kept choosing — the one that pitches well and photographs well and fills rooms — over the one that played guitar in a kitchen at midnight. She didn't need Blake's name in a headline. She had been watching me choose for months.

She didn't need me to explain it. She never needed me to explain anything. That was always the thing about Alex. She read the room before anyone spoke.

* * *

A few weeks later she is looking for her own apartment. I find out from

Liz, who mentions it without ceremony — Alex has been asking about listings in Riverside. She says it simply, a fact dropped into conversation, leaving the weight of it for me to carry.

I don't say anything.

I open my laptop. Ian's name is off the website now.

The last morning before she moves out I'm at the house early — some errand for Liz, some opinion she wanted. Alex is in the kitchen at six, coffee made, sitting with the window behind her and the early light coming through. Blue is at her feet.

She doesn't know I'm there yet. Blue's tail lifts once and settles.

I stand in the doorway and watch her for a moment — the back of her, the coffee in both hands, Blue's tail lifting once and settling. She's reading something on her phone. She's somewhere else. She has been somewhere else for weeks and I am only now standing still long enough to see it.

I could speak.

I don't.

Standing in the doorway while she sits in the kitchen with her coffee and her dog and her plan and her life — all of it moving forward without me in it — and choosing to say nothing.

I didn't fight for it.

That's the thing I'll carry.

* * *

The call with Meridian Bank takes eleven minutes. Their compliance officer — careful voice, the practiced neutrality of someone paid to find problems — has questions about the KYC verification layer.

"Your onboarding flow has gaps," she says. "The guidance that came out of the CFPB in 2024 changed the threshold for platforms serving your segment. You're below it."

I tell her we're addressing it. That we have engineering resources on it. That we'll have revised documentation by end of month.

After I hang up I hold it — I don't actually know if any of that is true. Ian would have known. Ian would have had the answer. Ian is gone.

I text Nico: We have a compliance problem. Need to talk.

He responds in four seconds: I know.

A week later, Sawbuck crosses a hundred million in transactions. The wire services pick it up before noon. By evening it's trending on financial feeds, whatever that means now. Fresh press follows — TechPulse wants the cover, Ledger is already running the Sunday profile, and Ticker has booked me for a roundtable that Daren and Nico will anchor while I sit at the head and try to look like I'm not reading from a script.

Someone from ops asks if we can slow the rollout. Just until support catches up. I tell them we'll circle back.

We never do.

By Thursday the phone won't stop. Old colleagues. College friends. People who ignored me for years now calling to say they always knew.

Ian's exit is settled. We agreed on terms Wednesday — clean, fair, his equity intact. He shook my hand and didn't say anything else. I keep expecting to feel relieved. I don't.

Nico and Daren drift closer to Zack — drawn to access. Ian is already gone from the floor in every way that matters.

* * *

Friday evening Blake calls it a small gathering. Nothing she touches stays small for long.

The house sits hidden behind hedgerows at the end of a narrow coastal road — shingle-gray and glass-bright, stretching toward the dunes like a secret built to admire itself. The moment Angie pulls through the gates I feel it — sound techs hauling cables, lighting crews adjusting filters, valets sweeping across the façade. Every window glows the same amber tone: warm enough to feel alive, sterile enough to be staged.

Inside, linen and pale oak, candles in hurricane glass, white roses arranged to look accidental. Blake's fingerprints everywhere.

A screen by the bar flashes: 100,000,000 — AND JUST GETTING STARTED.

Guests applaud like it's a coronation.

Cameras strobe against the dusk. LED walls throw my name back at me. For a second I can't tell if they're seeing me or the reflection.

Nico's by the pool, leaning into a conversation he's bored with. Daren's trapped beside a woman in a green dress who runs a media fund. The usual crowd — VCs, legacy money, people who invest in disruption but still dress like the establishment.

Blake spots me through the glass and gestures toward the firepit.

I walk toward the glow. Someone hands me champagne. Someone else calls my name. The hum builds.

Langford finds me first — the particular confidence of a man who just wrote a fifty-million-dollar check and wants to make sure you know he meant it. "Good process," he says. "Clean story. We're proud to be in."

He moves on before I can answer. That's Trevor Langford. In and moving.

Remsen's at the bar — linen suit, drink half gone, smile half real. "Big night," he says, clinking his glass to mine.

"For Sawbuck," I say.

"For you," he corrects. "You built a story the city could believe in. Enjoy it while it lasts. You only get to be the golden boy once."

No threat. Just weathered truth.

"To the last first time," I say. He laughs, already scanning for someone more interesting.

A photographer from the Post catches us by the firepit — Blake says smile, I do. By morning it will be The Column. Blake moves through the room in black satin, arm looped through mine like the headlines belong to her too. "This," she whispers, "is the room where people decide who matters."

For a moment I almost believe her.

Then I catch Nico watching from across the deck, deadpanning into his drink. Daren texting under the table, pretending not to exist.

Dalton Reeve. The brain behind Bastion. The particular ease of a man who has converted every experience in his life into a story he tells at dinner.

He finds me by the bar, drink already in hand, like he's been waiting for the room to thin out a little.

"There he is," he says. We shake hands — the grip of someone who has already wired you nine figures and feels good about it. "Hell of a night."

"You should've seen the room when the wires cleared," I say.

He laughs. Means it. "I told Alton Quimby — this one's different. The story's real." He glances out toward the water beyond the dunes, then back. "You enjoy any of it or are you already onto the next thing?"

"Working on it," I say.

He nods like he expected that. Takes a slow drink. "I'm putting together a trip. Pacific coast. Panama down to Peru. Small group, private vessel." He tilts his glass toward the dark water. "Men who've earned the right to go somewhere the phone doesn't follow."

"Sounds like a pitch," I say.

"It's an invitation," he says. "There's a difference." He lets it sit.

"Blake's already said yes."

I look at the fire. The party hums around us. Somewhere inside, my name is probably on another screen.

"I'll think about it," I say.

He nods like that's a yes. Maybe he's right.

* * *

Later, I tap Nico and Daren on the shoulder.

"You guys hungry?"

Daren looks up. "Honestly? Yeah."

"Good. Let's get out of here."

Nico grins. "You okay?"

"Yeah," I say — meaning it and not. "I just need something that doesn't sparkle."

We slip through the kitchen past caterers, past trays of half-eaten food and a line of staff pretending not to notice us. The glow from the pool fades behind the hedge.

Angie's Escalade idles at the gate. She eyes us as we climb in. "You boys done peacocking?"

"Done pretending," I say.

She shifts into drive. "Where to?"

"Somewhere that doesn't have a dress code."

Nico leans forward. "Murphy's on Dune Road. Locals, cheap beer, no one gives a damn who you are."

"Perfect," I say.

We roll past shuttered boutiques and darkened beach houses. Nico kicks off his shoes. Daren lowers the window. Ocean wind fills the car.

* * *

Murphy's is every dive bar that ever mattered — too loud, salt in the air, a place where no one asks what you do because they don't care.

Nico's two rounds in, trading jabs with a bartender who could kill him with a glance. Daren leans against the wall, studying the floor. We slide into a sticky vinyl booth. Daren joins us with three shots and no questions.

We drink. We don't talk Sawbuck. We talk about the analyst-class guy who quit to open a surf shop in Mexico. Daren's parents finally texting back. Nothing that needs a headline.

Nico leans back. "You good, man?"

"No. But this helps."

"This is where the ride started," I say, settling into the booth.

"Technically," Nico says, "it started when Ian opened his mouth and you started taking notes."

Daren grins. "Nah — when you ordered shots and told us we weren't bankers anymore. We were building something."

"I said that?"

"You said it like you believed it," Nico says. "Made us believe it."

The place gets louder, warmer. A guy argues with a pool table. A woman in a denim jacket sings off-key to a song no one asked for.

"I don't know if it's the booze or the fact no one here gives a damn," I say, "but this I can feel."

Nico: "Low expectations are underrated."

The beers arrive — cold, sweating, unpretentious. We clink bottles without ceremony. No decks. No cameras. Just three guys — broke in the right ways, rich in the wrong ones.

* * *

I wake to sunlight cutting across brick. Blake's call comes before I've finished the espresso.

"You left your own party," she says. No hello.

"It was loud."

"It was the brand launch. Boardrooms, funders, editors notice."

"It was one party."

"It was a signal," she snaps. "I'm the reason this story is flying. I need you focused." She doesn't wait for an answer. "Ticker roundtable Tuesday. TechPulse cover shoot Thursday. Ledger's Next 40 — you're on the list. Vantage Artists wants to build out your speaker profile. Keynote at Aspen Ideas in June. TED is circling."

I close my eyes. Let the litany roll — press and power and performance. All of it.

"You with me?" she asks.

I say the line. "Yeah. I'm with you."

"Oh — and Prism's event is tonight. Glasshouse. I'll get ready at your place. Five."

Click.

Silence again. Different now. Like the loft knows I just lied.

* * *

Blake arrives at five with garment bags and thirty minutes. I let her get ready. I sit on the couch with Blue and say nothing. When she's done I put on the tux and we go.

Once Angie pulls up outside the hotel, I've already rehearsed the smile. I step out. Blake is beside me, silver gown, eyes clocking cameras before her heels hit the carpet. She loops her arm through mine.

"Told you that tux would photograph perfectly."

"Guess you were right."

"I usually am."

The ballroom gleams under chandeliers. Tables glitter with name cards and chilled wine. Everyone's dressed to out-sparkle the ceiling.

A Ticker photographer catches us at the door — Blake angles without being obvious about it. Flashbulbs pop before we reach the table. I'm seated among names that don't feel whole. Every conversation sounds pre-approved. Blake rests her hand on my thigh — a reminder. I nod. Smile. Lift a glass.

They call my name after the foundation president rattles through impact, reach, transformation.

I step to the mic under lights made to flatter, not expose.

"Thank you. It's an honor to be here with the people who make the world move faster and occasionally in the right direction."

Laughter. Applause.

"At Sawbuck, the future of finance is access. Rewriting the rules so everyone gets a seat at the table — even the ones who were never invited."

More applause.

"We're not here because we've arrived. We're here because we're still building. And the most important capital isn't money — it's trust."

They stand.

I step down as cameras flash. Someone from The Financial Record is already filing copy on their phone. The clip will be on NYBC by morning. Liz catches my arm. "That was the version of you the world's been waiting for." Blake leans in, proud. "You crushed it."

I nod. Say thanks.

The version they just applauded — that isn't me. It's the mask I built to make this possible.

I lean toward Blake. "Early call with Tokyo. Need to prep."

She doesn't hide the disappointment. "You're the guest of honor."

"We already made the toast." I squeeze her hand. "You were perfect."

She studies me — knows there's more — then lets it go. "Try not to vanish completely."

"I'll be back before they miss me."

I won't.

The ballroom doors hush closed behind me. Rain makes the city gleam.

Angie idles at the curb, hazards blinking. She's out before I reach the door, umbrella up. "Didn't want to smudge the suit."

I duck under it. Let her walk me to the car.

Inside, leather and quiet.

"Nice night?" she asks, eyes on the road.

"Yeah," I say. "If you like marble and mirrors."

She half-smiles. Keeps driving.

* * *

The text comes two days later.

Dalton: Panama the 14th. Meridian. Blake's confirmed. We could use a third.

I read it three times.

Blake's litany of press engagements running in my head. Ian's name off the deck now — his own decision, or mine, or both, depending on who's telling the story. The platform scaling without him. Liz proud. The parents' world fully inhabited. The round closed.

Everything performed for, finally achieved.

The specific hollowness of arrival.

I pick up the phone.

Will: I'm in.

I turn the phone over and leave it dark.

I sit there for a while. The city moves. The screen stays dark. At some point I stop waiting to feel differently about it and go to bed.

CHAPTER 21

THE COST OF APPLAUSE

The call took four minutes. I made it from the back of Angie's Escalade somewhere on the West Side Highway, the morning still gray, the city moving past the window in long industrial strips.

"Ian's package," I said. "I want it clean. Full vest, accelerated. Whatever the cap table allows, you find the room."

Stephanie Ondrof had been Sawbuck's in-house counsel for eight months. She didn't rattle easily. "That's going to require board sign-off."

"Then get it. Before I land."

A pause — shorter this time. "Copy that."

I ended the call. Set the phone on the seat.

It wasn't an apology. Ian wouldn't have wanted one and I wouldn't have known how to give it. It was just the one thing I could do from a moving car on a Tuesday morning — make sure the man who built the thing got paid for building it. Whether he'd see it that way was his to decide.

Angie glanced at me in the mirror. Said nothing.

The Lincoln Tunnel approach opened up ahead of us. I watched the city fall away behind the glass and thought about the version of this I'd tell myself on the water — that I'd done right by him, that the numbers made it real, that money was how this world kept score and the score was now settled.

I didn't quite believe it.

But I boarded the plane anyway.

* * *

The yacht is called the Meridian. Two hundred and seventy feet. Five decks. A crew of sixteen who move through the corridors with the practiced invisibility of people paid to be present without being seen. Dalton Reeve bought her two years ago and uses her for exactly this: the kind of trip that other men can only describe secondhand.

We fly into Panama City. Blake in linen, sunglasses, the North Carolina in her vowels. Dalton meets us at the airport and drives us to the marina like he's giving us a present, which I suppose he is.

I have been on boats my whole life. I have never been on anything like this.

We cruise south. The Pacific coast of Central America giving way to Colombia, then Ecuador, the water changing color as we move through latitudes. Dalton has a story for every port, every anchorage, every naval checkpoint. He talks about the thrill of remote places, of being somewhere the infrastructure hasn't caught up to the money yet. Blake laughs in the right places. I drink the good scotch and watch the coastline and try to remember the last time I was fully present somewhere.

By the second day I stop trying.

The cocaine arrives the way these things arrive on boats like this — quietly, as part of the atmosphere, offered rather than presented. I partake. It's the kind of decision that doesn't feel like a decision at the time. It feels like the natural extension of where you already are. I hit the head in our cabin and put what's left in my luggage without thinking about it. That's the honest truth of it. I didn't hide it. I didn't plan to carry it. I just put it down somewhere and went back on deck and kept drinking and watching the coastline and the cocaine was in my bag the way a lot of things end up in your possession when you've stopped paying attention to what's actually yours.

* * *

We anchor off a stretch of Peruvian coast on a Tuesday afternoon — small village visible from the deck, fishing boats pulled up on the beach, the quiet of a place with nothing to announce to anyone.

Dalton is in his element. He has binoculars and a story about the last time he anchored here and a theory about why this specific remoteness is more authentic than what you find in the guidebooks. Blake is reading on the upper deck. I am on my second drink watching the village and thinking about nothing specific.

The naval vessel appears from the south.

A patrol boat, gray, functional, flying the Peruvian flag. It comes alongside with the efficient purposefulness of an institution that does not need to hurry because it already has authority. A voice over a loudspeaker in Spanish. Captain Tony, Dalton's captain for the last decade, translates, casual — they want to board. Routine inspection. He's done this before. He waves them aboard like he's welcoming guests.

Four officers in uniform, methodical, professional. They move through the boat section by section. Blake has gone very still on the upper deck. Captain Tony is talking to the senior officer with the confidence of someone whose authority had never once been the second word.

It takes them seventeen minutes to find my bag.

The senior officer holds up the small package and looks at us and says something in Spanish. I don't need to speak the language to understand what's happening. Everything in my body understands before my mind catches up.

Blake doesn't look at me.

Dalton does. His expression shifts — not guilt, not surprise, just the rapid calculation of a man determining what this costs him and whether it can be managed. Captain Tony talks to the officer. Faster now. I hear my name. I hear the word Americano. I watch his face solve the problem as I've watched men solve problems in conference rooms my entire career, assessing, positioning, and deciding what they can absorb and what they need to contain.

I am the thing that needs to be contained.

They put my hands behind my back. The cuffs are metal and they are not gentle about it. I am walked to the rail and transferred to the patrol boat and I watch the Meridian from the stern as the distance between us grows. Dalton is still talking to someone on the deck. Blake has not looked up from her book. The Peruvian coast is behind me. The village is still there on the beach, unchanged, because nothing about this moment changes anything for them.

* * *

I will not describe everything that happens in the first forty-eight hours. Some of it I don't have language for yet.

What I will say is this: every instrument I have ever used — the redirect, the reframe, the voice that makes rooms believe things — requires language. Without language I am just a man in a room. Just a body with a problem. Just another case in a system that has no reason to treat me as somebody.

By the second night I am in a cell in a facility outside Lima, I'm pretty sure, and I understand with complete clarity that I am going to be here for a while and that nothing I know how to do is going to change that.

The cell is roughly the size of a parking space. Concrete walls the color of old teeth. A window near the ceiling — reinforced glass, too high to see through, enough to tell day from night. The smell is bleach over something older that the bleach never quite reaches. Somewhere down the corridor a door closes. Then quiet. The kind of quiet that isn't peaceful — the kind that has a weight to it, the accumulated silence of everyone in this building deciding there is nothing worth saying.

The cell has two bunks. A bunk is occupied.

* * *

He is sitting on the edge of the lower bunk when they bring me in. He looks up when the door opens. Looks at me with the assessment of a man who has processed enough arrivals to know exactly what he's getting.

Then he nods. Once. Moves over slightly to give me the sense of space the cell doesn't actually have. Goes back to what he was doing — which is sitting with his hands resting on his knees, eyes half-closed, not praying exactly but something in the neighborhood of it.

I climb to the upper bunk. Lie on my back. Stare at the ceiling.

This is the ceiling I will stare at for the next six months.

* * *

His name is Mateo Quispe. I learn this over the first week in fragments — his Spanish, my nothing, the slow construction of a shared language from hand gesture and the few words I know and his patient willingness to repeat himself without frustration. He is a compact man, my age, dark hair going gray at the temples. Peruvian in his coloring — the brown of the highlands. His face in repose has a quality I spend weeks trying to name and finally decide is simply the absence of performance.

He runs a coffee shop in Lima. Amanecer. He has a daughter. He is in this cell because a man was trying to lure his daughter online and Mateo found out and did what Mateo did, and now he is here.

He tells me this without anger. That is the first thing I notice. Not resignation — something different. The tone of a man who made a choice he would make again and is living inside the consequence of it without resentment. He protected his daughter. He is paying for protecting his daughter. He would do it again tomorrow.

I have never met anyone like him.

He has almost nothing. The clothes he was arrested in. A small photograph of his daughter tucked into the frame of the lower bunk. A worn Bible with a cracked spine. No money, no connections, no way to make this cell more comfortable than it is. By every measure I have used my entire life to assess a person's standing, Mateo Quispe has nothing.

Not performed happiness — I know what that looks like, I have been performing it for over twenty years. What Mateo has is the real thing. A man who wakes up in a Peruvian prison cell and is genuinely, completely himself. Every day. Without effort.

I have met men who don't feel anger. They're usually performing its absence. Mateo is not performing anything. The anger isn't absent — I watch it move through him sometimes when he talks about the man, what the man was doing to his daughter. But it doesn't live in him the way things live in me. He processes it and it passes and then he is back to himself. Which is the most settled version of a human being I have ever been in a room with.

I keep waiting for the seams to show.

That's what I do with people — I watch for the place where the performance slips, where what someone projects stops matching what they actually are underneath. I've been doing it my whole life. It's the most useful thing my father's world taught me.

Mateo lives inside more uncertainty than my father managed in a lifetime. The cell. The daughter he can't protect from here. The years still ahead of him. The world outside that kept moving without him.

He handles all of it. Every day. Before breakfast.

I don't know what to do with that yet.

But I know what I'm watching. And I know I've never seen anything like it.

I try the version of myself that works in rooms. The one that asks good questions and listens well and makes people feel seen without giving anything away. I ask about the facility, the guards, the food. I frame things. I redirect. I do what I always do when I need someone to trust me without earning it.

Mateo answers each question directly and then goes back to whatever he was doing. He does not mirror me. He does not warm to the performance. He just answers and waits. After three days of this I run out of questions and we sit in silence for the first time and I realize he has been waiting for the silence the whole time.

By the third week I stop telling myself that.

* * *

The yard is a rectangle of cracked concrete behind the facility, fifty feet by thirty, bounded on three sides by a chain-link fence and on the fourth by the wall of the building itself. We are given one hour in the afternoon. Most men use it to walk. Mateo and I use it to play soccer with a ball that is held together by the kind of faith that has no rational basis.

Mateo is better than me. He has been better than me since the first afternoon when he dribbled around me three times and then stopped and waited politely for me to recover my dignity. He doesn't gloat. He just plays. He has a particular move — a small feint left, a cut right — that I have now seen approximately two hundred times and still cannot stop.

The guard on the yard rotation is a younger man. Maybe twenty-five. He watches us from the corner with the boredom of someone whose entire shift is watching other people do things he'd rather be doing himself. He has a name — Jimenez — and I have spent three weeks learning it and using it and learning what he eats for lunch and whether he has a family and how long he has worked here.

I approach him while Mateo retrieves the ball from the fence.

"Jimenez." I keep my voice even. Friendly. Then I try the Spanish I have been assembling for this moment, the specific words I have rehearsed in my bunk at night. "Tengo — una propuesta. Una llamada. Un abogado en Nueva York. El dinero —;" I pause. "Antes de que llegues a casa."

He looks at me. Then past me. Then back at me.

"No entiendo," he says. I don't understand. He says it without inflection, the way you say something that is technically true but more complicated than that.

I try again. Simpler. "Dinéro. Llamada. Una sola vez."

He listens. He has understood. I can see it in the way he holds very still. He looks at me the way people look at you when they have already made a decision and are just waiting for you to finish speaking.

Then he walks away.

I stand there. Mateo has the ball. He is watching me from the center of the yard with the expression of a man who saw everything and will say nothing until I am ready to hear it. We play another twenty minutes. He uses the feint left and cuts right and I don't stop it. We walk back inside.

That night he says: "El guardia." The guard.

"Yes."

"He has a family. He needs the job."

I hadn't thought about that. I had thought about what he wanted. I had not thought about what he could lose.

Mateo closes his eyes. The half-prayer posture. I lie on my back and look at the ceiling.

After a while he says: "You have been in rooms where no one ever said no to you."

It is not a question.

"Yes," I say.

He nods. "That's the problem," he says. And goes to sleep.

* * *

The coffee shop is called Amanecer. Dawn. He opened it eleven years ago, saved for three years to do it, chose the neighborhood because his mother lived there and he wanted to be able to walk to her house before the morning shift. He describes the smell of it — the specific Peruvian coffee he sources from a farm in the highlands, the way it fills the shop at five in the morning before anyone has arrived, the moment each day when the light comes through the east-facing window and hits the counter a certain way.

He talks about it the way I talked about the guitar once, in a room in Greenwich, for twenty minutes, before my father walked in.

With the voice of someone who knows exactly what they are here for.

One night, maybe the third month, he tells me about a woman in his neighborhood. Doña Celia. Old. Walked with a cane. She used to come to Amanecer every morning before he opened — just to sit outside at the table by the door.

"I would bring her coffee before I even had the chairs down," he says. "She never asked. I never mentioned it. That was just — what we did."

After his wife died — Lucía was maybe two — he stopped opening some mornings. Just couldn't get there. The grief wasn't loud. It was the kind that sits in your chest and makes ordinary things feel impossible. Getting up. Turning the key in the lock. Putting the chairs down.

"Doña Celia came anyway," he says. "Every morning I was closed she would sit at that table for one hour. Then go home. She never knocked. Never asked why the lights were off. Just — sat there. Like she was keeping the place from disappearing."

He looks at the ceiling the way he does when he is finding something rather than performing it.

"One morning I came down and saw her through the glass. Just sitting. Cane across her knees. Eyes closed. I don't know why that morning was different. But I unlocked the door. I made the coffee. She came in and sat at the counter and didn't say a word about it. We just — continued."

He is quiet for a moment.

"She died the year before all this," he says. "I didn't know how much I was still opening the door for her until she was gone."

The corridor hums. Somewhere down the hall a door closes.

"She used to call Lucía" — he pauses, finding the word he wants — "la mecha."

My Spanish is good enough by now. The wick.

"She said — a wick is nothing by itself. Just string. But it's the only part of the candle that was made to carry the flame. The candle burns down. The wick was always the point."

He stares at the ceiling. "I still put two chairs out," he says. "Every morning. Her chair and mine. I don't know why. Maybe I'm still keeping the place from disappearing."

I lie on my bunk for a long time after he stops talking.

La mecha. I turn it over in my head the way you turn over something small and heavy, testing its weight. Not the fire you build. Not the performance. The thing that was already there, waiting for something true to touch it.

I think about a boy in a study in Greenwich, guitar in his lap, twenty minutes of being exactly who he was supposed to be before his father walked through the door.

That was always the wick. I just kept reaching for the candle instead.

* * *

I learn his Spanish slowly. He learns my English not at all, which he finds funny in a way that is entirely without mockery. We develop a language that belongs to neither of us — a pidgin of gesture and cognate and the particular shorthand of two people who have decided to understand each other.

The words are Spanish and mostly beyond my comprehension but the quality of them is not. There is no performance in it. No audience being played to. Just a man and a God he believes is listening and the specific intimacy of a conversation that has been going on for decades.

I watch him for weeks before I say anything.

"You believe in all that, in God?" I say one evening. My Spanish by then is enough to have conversations, not enough to be clever in them. Which turns out to be useful.

He considers the question seriously. "I believe in everything," he says. "The coffee. My daughter. The light through the window in the morning. God is in all of it." Mateo looks at me. "You don't believe?"

"I don't know what I believe," I say.

He nods like this is a completely acceptable answer. "Then you are at the beginning," he says. "That's a good place."

I carry that with me.

* * *

The noise dies down gradually. I don't notice it happening — it's the kind of change you only see looking back. The constant low-frequency roar of my own interior life — the deals and the positioning and the narrative management and the performance and the voice that is always calculating and the other voice that is always telling the first voice it's doing the right thing — it gets quieter. Not silent. But quieter. And in the space the noise vacates, something else becomes audible.

I don't have a name for it at first. I just notice it. A kind of pull. Not toward anything specific — not toward action or ambition or the next move. Just toward something that feels like the right direction. The way a compass needle moves without you telling it to.

I think about Gloria Cato in her back room in Crown Heights. The way she moved through her own space. The photograph of a young woman and her infant son. What she said when she came back from the front room about God's plan for us.

I heard it as wisdom then. Beautiful, specific, the kind of thing a remarkable woman says in a remarkable moment.

I hear it differently now.

* * *

Around the fourth month he tells me about the morning he opened Amanecer for the first time.

He had saved for three years. The last year he worked double shifts — the coffee shop where he was a barista during the day, a kitchen in Miraflores at night. He didn't tell his mother how close he was until the day he signed the lease.

"She came to see the space before I had anything in it," he says. "Empty room. Just the counter they left behind. She walked the whole thing. Touched the walls." He pauses. "Then she went to the window — the east-facing one — and stood there for a long time. I asked her what she was looking at. She said: the light is good here. That's all she said."

He is quiet.

"She died the following year. Before I opened. I used to think that was the hard part — that she never saw it. Now I think she saw everything she needed to."

* * *

The fourth month. A Tuesday, I think, though I have stopped being certain of days.

I am sitting on the floor between the bunks. Not for any reason. I did not decide to sit on the floor. I was standing and then I was on the floor and my back is against the wall and the concrete is cold through the fabric of my pants and I am crying in the way that has no dignity to it — not the kind that feels like release, the kind that feels like something giving way that wasn't supposed to.

I don't know what started it. Maybe nothing started it. Maybe it was just the accumulation of what a floor feels like when it's the only thing holding you up.

Mateo doesn't say anything. I am aware of him on the lower bunk, aware that he is awake, aware that he has noticed. He says nothing for a long time. Long enough that the crying works through and comes out the other side.

Then I hear him stand. He goes to the small shelf where he keeps his things. He comes back. Sets a cup of water on the floor beside me — the facility water, tepid, slightly metallic, the water that tastes the same every day.

He goes back to his bunk.

That's all. No words. No hand on my shoulder. No careful framing of what is happening to me and why.

I drink the water.

I sit on the floor a while longer. Then I get up.

I don't know why that cup of water is the most generous thing anyone has ever done for me. I know that it is.

* * *

Five months in, Mateo asks me what I did. Before. In my other life.

I try to explain it. Investment banking. Fintech. A platform called Sawbuck built for people who don't have bank accounts. A founder named Ian Cato who built it because his mother the system had never built anything for.

Mateo listens. He asks a few questions — what does the platform do, how does it work, what did you do to this Ian. That last question is specific and direct and I answer it honestly. Maybe for the first time out loud.

He listens to all of it without judgment. When I finish he doesn't move.

"This Ian," he says. "He built something for his mother."

"Yes."

"And you took it from him."

"I structured it so that—"

"You took it from him," Mateo says again. Not harshly. Just accurately.

"I guess so," I say.

He nods. Sits with it. "What will you do with that?" he asks.

"I don't know. Never really thought about it that way."

"That's honest," he says. He closes his eyes.

* * *

The visiting room is divided by a low partition — not glass, just a table and chairs arranged to suggest a line that everyone understands not to cross. Natural light comes from a single window near the ceiling, the same reinforced glass as the cells.

My attorney is a Peruvian woman named Vargas who was retained by Dalton's people in New York and speaks the precise, slightly formal English of someone who learned it from textbooks. She has a leather briefcase and the manner of a person who has done this before and has decided not to be affected by the doing of it.

She explains where we are. I listen. She uses phrases like "bilateral agreement" and "consular access" and "timeline of six to eight months, possibly sooner." She has a folder with documents. She is competent. She is doing her job.

Across the partition, three tables down, Mateo is sitting with a girl.

She is maybe fifteen. Dark hair, his coloring, his jaw. She is wearing a school uniform — blue and white, a little too big at the shoulders the way school uniforms always are. She has a small backpack that she sets carefully on the floor beside her chair. She sits down and for a moment just looks at him.

He looks back at her the same way.

They don't reach across the partition — the rules are clear about that. But she puts her hand flat on the table, palm down. He puts his hand flat on the table, palm down. Three feet of laminate between them.

La mecha.

Vargas is still talking. I make the appropriate sounds. I watch Mateo across the room. He is asking his daughter something — I can see the question in his face, the specific attention of a man who has one hour and wants to use all of it for her. She answers. He listens. Whatever she says makes him close his eyes for a moment the way he does in the cell when something rings true.

He opens them and looks at her and smiles.

The real one.

I look down at my table. My attorney is saying something about processing times. I nod. I am thinking about a man with nothing sitting three feet from the most important person in his life, keeping his hand flat on the table because rules are rules and dignity is something you carry into the room rather than waiting for the room to give it to you.

Vargas closes her folder. "We'll have more clarity by next month," she says.

"All right," I say.

I look back. Mateo is still listening to his daughter. She has taken a folded piece of paper from her backpack and is showing it to him across the partition — careful, holding it at the edges, the way you carry something that matters. He reads it. Whatever it says, he reads it twice.

Then he folds it back the same way she folded it and slides it across the table to her.

"Guárdalo," he says. Keep it. "Es tuyo." It's yours.

She puts it back in her backpack with the same care.

Vargas stands. Our hour is done.

* * *

Six months in I finally ask him how he stays like this. Balanced. At peace. I describe it because I don't have the Spanish for the thing I mean — how he seems the same every day, not unaffected but stable, like the room doesn't change him.

He thinks about how to answer. This is something I have come to love about Mateo — he does not produce answers. He finds them. There is a difference and the difference is everything.

"I know what I am for," he says finally. "My faith. My daughter. My family." Those things are mine. They don't change." He gestures at the cell, the walls, the gray quality of the light. "This is temporary. Those things are not." He smooths the page with his thumb, the way he always does, like the words need settling before they'll hold.

I stay with that for the rest of the night.

I want to argue with it. I look for the counter — the version where I built something real, where the platform served the people it was supposed to serve, where the intention was always honest even if the execution wasn't. I find the pieces of it. They're there.

They're just not enough.

He's right. I've always known. The guitar. The twenty minutes in my father's study. The way Ian's voice sounded at The Tank when he talked about his mother's laundromat — the quality of a person doing the thing they were made to do. The burning need that surfaces every time I push it down, the way a compass needle keeps finding north no matter how many times you turn the instrument.

I have been choosing the noise.

For too many years I have been choosing the noise.

***

Dalton's connections arrive on a Tuesday morning at the end of the sixth month.

Two men in suits who speak the particular Spanish of people who have negotiated with governments before. Documents. Signatures. The machinery of money and political access doing what money and political access do when applied correctly. A Peruvian official who does not look at me. Forms. A stamp.

It takes four hours. Then someone unlocks the cell door and tells me I can go.

The doorway. Mateo on his bunk.

He has told me about his daughter, who is fifteen now and doing well in school. About Amanecer, the coffee shop in Lima early morning before anyone arrives. About the prayer he says every morning — what it contains, why it doesn't change, what he is asking for and what he is giving thanks for and how the two things have become the same over the years.

I told him about what I want to build. Not the details — I don't know those yet. Just the shape of it. A place for kids who need a room where they can be exactly who they are. Built from purpose rather than momentum. Starting from the inside out. I told him about Ian. About Alex and Blake. Not the things I built with other people's hands and called mine. Mateo listened the way he always listens — without filling the silence, without offering the conclusion before I'd found it myself.

When I finish he says: "Then you know what you're here for."

"Yes," I say. And for the first time in longer than I can name, I mean it without performance.

"What will you call it?" he asked. "The foundation."

I told him.

He was quiet for a moment. Then he smiled — the real one, the one I have been watching for six months. The one that belongs to a man who is at peace with what he is and where he is and what God has planned for him.

"That's too much," he said.

"It's exactly right," I said.

Now I stand in the cell doorway. Mateo is sitting on his bunk praying. The half-closed eyes. The morning prayer that looks like stillness from the outside and is something else entirely from the inside. He does not get up. We have already said goodbye.

But he opens his eyes and looks at me.

"Go," he says. In English. His only English word, learned for this moment.

I go.

* * *

The air outside the facility is the same air that was always there. This surprises me — I expected it to be different, charged, the way the air feels after a storm. It is just air. Warm. The smell of diesel and dust and somewhere underneath it the specific green smell of the Peruvian coast.

The men in suits put me in a car. Lima airport. Miami. JFK.

I sit in the window seat and watch the continent fall away beneath the plane and I think about Mateo praying and waiting to get back to a coffee where the light comes through the window and the smell of Peruvian coffee fills the room.

A man who knows what he is for.

The plane crosses the equator somewhere over the ocean. I've been trying to name what's different. Not what happened — I know what happened. What's different is something quieter than that. I used to think the gap was between what I built and what it was worth. Now I think the gap was always between what I was doing and who I was while I was doing it. Mateo knew what he was for. I'm starting to know what I'm not. That's not nothing. It might be enough to start from.

I know where Alex is. I know that door is closed. I know it with the specific clarity of a man who finally understands what he traded and accepts the cost without asking her to manage his grief about it. She is exactly who she always said she would become. That is not nothing. That is the most I could have hoped for her, even if I am not part of it.

The Atlantic spreads out beneath the plane. Gray and enormous and indifferent and beautiful.

The plane lands at JFK at six in the morning. The terminal is the terminal. The city is the city. A woman at the arrivals gate is holding a sign with someone else's name. The coffee cart in the corner has been there since the invention of burnout.

I take a cab to Tribeca.

I go home.

CHAPTER 22

TRUE THINGS

The cab drops me at the loft at seven-thirty.

I stand in front of my building for a moment with one bag — everything I left Peru with, which isn't much. The city is already running. Delivery trucks. A woman walking a dog. The particular indifference of New York to anyone's return.

The doorman is new. He doesn't recognize me. I give him my name and he checks the list and lets me up.

The loft smells like stale air and six months of nobody. I set the bag down by the door. Don't turn on the lights. Just stand in the gray morning coming through the windows — the water tower across the way — and let it settle that I am actually here.

Everything is exactly where I left it. The couch. The kitchen. The guitar case in the corner I never opened.

The city humming five floors below like it never noticed I was gone.

I shower. Sleep until noon.

When I wake the sun has moved and the loft is warm and I lie on top of the covers and let the quiet work on me the way it does when you've been somewhere very loud for a very long time.

My phone has messages I don't open. Somewhere in the stack there will be one from Blake — or from someone Blake tasked with this — explaining the shape of the story they've been managing for six months. The arrest never made the press. I know this because no one has called me a criminal. Because Sawbuck is still standing. Because Blake Caswell understands that some stories are better buried than told, and she has the access and the patience to do the burying. I don't call to thank her. That's not what this is.

The statement she put out said I was dealing with a family health matter requiring extended leave. She held it for three weeks before releasing it — long enough that the silence itself wasn't news, not long enough for the board to force a replacement. She framed the Series A as validation that the platform could operate without its founder at the helm. She positioned it as proof of institutional strength. It wasn't untrue. That's how Blake works — she finds the version of events that doesn't require lying, and she builds around it until the thing she's protecting disappears into the architecture.

That's not quite right.

I told him I'd been in a cell outside Lima for six months. I told him it had changed the way I see things — not in a way I could fully articulate yet, but in a way I couldn't ignore. I told him the platform still mattered to me. I told him the people it was built for still mattered to me.

"But?" Remsen said.

"No but," I said. "I'm pretty sure."

He was quiet for a moment. "Come back. Look at it from the inside. Then we'll talk."

"All right," I said.

"And Chaffee — I'm glad you're not dead."

It was the warmest thing he'd ever said to me.

* * *

That evening I drive to Greenwich. Not for the house. For Blue.

Hana meets me at the door — no surprise on her face, just the practical warmth of a woman who has been expecting me without knowing when. She says Blue is in the garden. She says there is food if I want it. She goes back to the kitchen.

Blue finds me before I find him. He comes around the corner of the hedge at a trot, sees me, stops. Then he crosses the lawn and leans into my leg and stays there.

I crouch down and put my hands on either side of his face. He is exactly the same. That registers.

Through the sitting room window I can see the back of Liz's chair — she is home after all, reading a script, a glass of something beside her.

I go in.

She looks up. A full beat of assessment, and then something underneath it settles.

"William," she says.

"Hi, Liz."

She doesn't get up. She sets the script down carefully. "You look thin."

"I'm fine."

She studies me a moment longer. "Are you?"

"Yes," I say. And I mean it in a way I haven't meant it in a long time.

She nods. Picks the script back up. "Hana left a bag for Blue in the hall. His things."

"Thank you," I say.

I stand in the doorway. There is more to say — there is always more to say between us — but this is not the moment for it. She knows it too. She has always known when to let a room breathe.

"Come back when you're ready," she says, not looking up.

I take the bag from the hall. Blue is already at the door. We drive back to the city.

* * *

There's a knock at eight-fifteen. I'm not expecting anyone. She's in the hallway in a good coat, a coffee from somewhere nearby in each hand, the expression of a woman who has decided to do something and arrived before she could talk herself out of it.

"I was in the neighborhood," she says.

She was not in the neighborhood. Liz is never in Tribeca at eight-fifteen in the morning.

I step back. She comes in. She hands me the coffee and looks around the loft the way she looks at everything — taking inventory, making assessments, filing it all away. She doesn't say anything about it.

We sit at the kitchen island. Blue settles at her feet, which surprises her. She looks down at him for a moment, then reaches down and puts her hand on his back. She doesn't make a thing of it.

I watch her hand on Blue's back and think: she has always known how to be in a room with something that needed her. She just spent forty years choosing rooms that didn't.

"You look better than yesterday," she says.

"Lower bar than usual," I say.

She nods. Holds her cup in both hands. Outside the windows the city is doing its morning thing — the particular light off the Hudson, the sound of Tribeca waking up slowly.

"There's something I should tell you," she says. I wait.

She looks at her cup. Not performing the pause — actually using it.

"Your father." She stops. Starts again. "What he did to you. Not just the way he spoke to you — all of it. I knew. I told myself it wasn't as bad as it looked, that you were resilient, that men like him didn't know another way." She sets the cup down. "I should have stopped it. I didn't. That's mine to carry."

She doesn't look at me when she says it. That's how I know it's real.

"I'm not asking you to say anything," she says. "I just — I've been carrying that for a long time. And you went away, and I didn't know if you were coming back, and I decided if you did I was going to say it."

The room is very quiet.

"Thank you," I say.

She sits with it for a moment. Then she picks up her cup, realizes it's empty, and looks at it like it has personally failed her.

"Well," she says. "That was thoroughly unpleasant."

Then, almost to herself: Then, almost to herself: "I need a real drink."

She straightens her coat. "Dinner Thursday. Somewhere with a proper wine list. Don't argue."

"I will," I say.

At the door she pauses — just briefly — and puts her hand on my arm. No words. Just that.

Then she's gone.

I sit at the island for a while. Blue puts his head in my lap.

Outside, the city keeps moving, indifferent as ever, the way I used to need it to be.

* * *

I text her around noon. Nothing strategic about it. I'm walking past a coffee place in the West Village where we went once, the winter before any of this started, and I stop on the sidewalk and look at the door and take out my phone.

Will: I'm in the city. Can I buy you a coffee?

Three dots. Then nothing.

An hour later: I'm at work. Sorry.

That's it. I stand there for another minute, hands in my pockets, watching people move through the door of the place without me. Then I keep walking.

I try again ten days later. This time I call. She picks up on the fourth ring, a little breathless, the sound of an office behind her.

"Will."

"Hey. I know this is out of nowhere. I just wanted to—"

"I'm in the middle of something," she says. Not unkind. Just true.

"Of course. I'll let you go."

Then: "How are you?"

And I hear it in the question — not warmth exactly, but something careful. The way you ask after someone you've decided to be generous toward from a distance.

"Getting there," I say.

"Good." A moment. "I have to go."

"Yeah. Take care, Alex."

She's already gone.

I sit on a bench outside the park for a while. The city moves around me. I'm not sure what I was expecting — recognition, maybe. The door opening. Instead I got exactly what I deserved: someone who had already filed the thing, moved forward, was living the life she was always going to live.

The Berklee application folded and put away. That's what this feels like. Some things you don't get to go back for.

I get on the subway and go home.

* * *

In the afternoon I open my phone.

Six months of messages. I don't read them sequentially. I scroll until I understand the shape of what happened while I was gone.

Sawbuck is still running. The platform scaled — the numbers Ian built are holding, the beta verticals converted, the merchant base grew without anyone at the front of the room claiming it. Daren kept the operational side moving. Nico managed relationships. Zack's team handled press with a holding statement Blake drafted — Will Chaffee is taking a leave of absence for personal reasons. Sawbuck's leadership team remains fully operational. Clean. Managed. The story continued without the face.

Blake comes to my loft around five. She arrives with wine and the particular energy of someone who has been holding a lot together and is ready to set some of it down. She looks good — she always looks good — but there's something underneath the surface that is genuinely glad to see me. Not the press strategy version. The real one.

We sit on the terrace with the wine and the last of the October light. For a while we are just two people glad to be in the same place.

I ask questions. I am present in the way I haven't been present with her in a long time — maybe ever.

She notices.

"You're different," she says.

"I've heard that a few times since I've been back."

She watches the light change. "Different how?"

I think about how to say it. "The performance isn't available the way it used to be. I keep reaching for it and it's not there."

She watches the light go golden behind the hedges. "Is that good?"

"I think so," I say. "I'm not sure what it means for everything else yet."

She hears what I'm not saying. She's always been good at that. But this time she doesn't let it sit. She reaches toward it.

"I would do the NYBC segment," she says. "Your PR team thinks this week. It's the right moment — you're back, the platform is scaling, the narrative writes itself. This version of you — the founder who went quiet, who came back changed — that's a better story than anything we had before. Peru becomes the turning point. The transformation. Will Chaffee, rebuilt."

She says it with the specific precision of someone who has been drafting it in her head since the plane landed.

I recognize it.

"That's good," I say. "That's really good."

She almost smiles. "I know."

"But I'm not going to do it that way."

She sets her glass down. Reading me. "What does that mean?"

"It means Peru isn't a narrative device. It means I'm not going to walk into a studio and make six months of losing myself sound like a hero's journey."

She's quiet. I watch something move through her — not hurt, exactly. More like the particular stillness of someone recalculating. She has been doing that since she was twenty-two years old, walking into rooms that didn't expect her, finding the angle. It has never failed her.

"I can't manage a version I can't frame," she says finally.

"I know."

"I'm not saying that as a threat," she says. "I'm saying it because it's true. What I do — what I'm good at — requires a story with edges I can work with. I can't make something shapeless compelling."

"I know," I say again. "That's not a criticism."

She holds the silence for a long time. The woman who walked into Liz's house in Greenwich and earned the room without me in it. Who sees power clearly and has never once pretended not to.

"You know what the frustrating thing is?" she says.

"What?"

"I think this version of you is actually more interesting." She picks up her wine. "I just can't sell it yet. The market doesn't have a category for it."

That's Blake — the compliment and the limitation arriving together, inseparable, because for her they have always been the same thing.

We finish the bottle. We talk about other things — her work, a trip she's thinking about, a piece she wants to write that has nothing to do with anyone she knows. We are kind to each other. We are honest with each other in the specific way of two people who understand that something is ending and are choosing to let it end without declaring it.

She leaves before dark.

At the door she pauses. She turns back. For a moment she's about to say something that would reopen it — I can see the sentence forming, the angle, the frame. She's been doing this her whole life and she can't quite stop.

Then she doesn't.

She kisses my cheek instead. "For what it's worth," she says, "I think you're going to be interesting to watch."

Not okay. Interesting. That's still Blake, right to the end — she can't give you the ordinary version of anything.

"Thank you," I say. And mean it for all of it.

Then she's gone.

* * *

I go into Sawbuck early the next morning. No announcement. No prepared remarks. I just show up the way I used to show up — early, before the floor gets loud, coffee from the cart on the corner.

Daren is already in his office. He looks up when he hears me. There's a half-second where something crosses his face — relief, and underneath it something older — and then he closes his laptop and stands. We shake hands. Then we hug.

"You look different," he says."

"I am different."

He nods like he already knew that. "Coffee's fresh. Terrible. Same as always."

"Perfect," I say. We head into the bullpen.

He pours two cups and we sit at the long table where we used to brainstorm at midnight. The floor is quiet at this hour. Just the building settling around us and the particular hum of a city that never stops.

"Six months," he says. Not a question. Not an accusation. Just the weight of it, acknowledged.

"Six months," I say.

He wraps both hands around his cup. "You don't have to tell me anything."

"I know." The whiteboard is still up. Still has the market map from before I left. Someone drew a line through the original TAM number and wrote a larger one. The platform kept growing.

Daren looks at me. "Are you back?" he asks. "Really back?"

"I'm back," I say. "But not the same version."

He nods slowly. Sips his coffee. "The platform needs you. The team needs you." He stops.

"I know," I say.

"Okay," he says. And opens his laptop.

* * *

Nico arrives at nine. He walks past three people eyes on his phone, drops his bag, grabs a coffee — and then sees me standing by the window.

He stops.

It moves through him. Not surprise exactly. More like the thing that happens when you've been bracing for something a long time and it finally arrives.

He walks over. Stands in front of me. We hug — the kind that doesn't need explaining. Then, quietly: "Peru?"

"Peru," I say.

"Prison?"

"Six months."

He exhales through his nose. "Cocaine?"

"That's the headline version."

He looks at me for another beat. He picks up Daren's coffee, takes a sip, makes a face, sets it back down. "You look like someone who got humbled."

"That's accurate," I say.

"Good," he says.

He wraps both hands around his mug. "Okay then." He walks to his desk. Sits down. Pulls up his screen. "Welcome back, man. Try not to disappear again. It's annoying."

I almost laugh. It's the most Nico thing he could have said.

* * *

I take the F train to Court Street on a Wednesday afternoon without planning to.

No call ahead. No reason I could name if someone asked. Just the particular pull of a direction that has been waiting.

He answers the door, shirt pressed. Of course. Three in the afternoon and the shirt is pressed. That never changes. I used to read it as performance — the careful maintenance of a man pretending to be more intact than he was. Now I just see a man who irons his shirts. Some things are simpler than the story you build around them.

"Will," he says.

"Hey, Dad."

He steps back. I come in.

The apartment is the same — the quiet of a space organized around solitude so long it has become its own kind of order. The Aston Martin keys are on the side table. He has kept it there. I notice it and don't say anything.

He makes coffee without asking. I sit at the small table by the window and watch him move through the kitchen — the deliberate economy of it, everything in its place, the particular care he has learned by making a small life feel sufficient. He has been doing this for eighteen years. Getting up. Pressing the shirt. Making the coffee. Tending what's left with the specific dignity of someone who had made a small life sufficient and wasn't asking anyone to admire it.

He sets the cup down in front of me and sits across.

We talk. About nothing important — the Yankees, something he read, a restaurant on Atlantic Avenue he's been meaning to try. He holds the cup in both hands — that same deliberate grip. His hair is fully white now. His hands are his father's hands — the same broad knuckles, the same deliberate grip.

I look at him across the table and I think about Mateo Quispe sitting on the edge of a bunk in a cell outside Lima. A man who protected his daughter and paid for it and would do it again tomorrow. A man who wakes up in a concrete room and is genuinely, completely himself. Every day. Without effort.

I think about what it costs to be that.

My father had a line about faith — the one I carried without examining for twenty years. "Faith is for people who can't handle uncertainty."

I think about Mateo waking before sunrise in that cell. The prayer he said every morning — not because certainty had been given to him, but because he had chosen something to return to. He was the steadiest person I had ever been in a room with.

I don't know what I believe. But I can no longer say it the way my father said it. Something happened to that certainty in the sixth month, and I haven't found it since.

My father lost his father's company. He lost it through his own decisions and then watched his father watch him lose it and then he went to a small apartment in Brooklyn and started pressing his shirts every morning and kept going. He kept going with nothing to show for it except the going. No audience. No return. Just the daily decision to keep tending something that had already fallen apart.

I have been reading that as failure my entire life.

Sitting across from him now, watching him hold his coffee cup in both hands, The understanding arrives whole: it isn't. It is the hardest thing I know. It is harder than the round. Harder than the pitch. Harder than the rooms and the performance and the story I built to avoid ending up exactly here — in a small apartment in Brooklyn, tending what's left.

He didn't know how to pass anything down except the reaching. The hunger. The belief that the next thing would be the thing that finally held. He gave me that the way his father gave it to him and his father before that — not a gift exactly, not a curse exactly. Just the inheritance of men who want too much and know it and can't stop wanting.

He punched me on a terrace when I was sixteen years old. He said things that carved specific grooves in the way I understood myself. He failed in front of his father and his son simultaneously and never recovered. He loved me badly and meant it.

All of it true. All of it the whole picture at once.

I don't say any of this out loud.

He refills my cup without asking. He tells me something about the restaurant on Atlantic Avenue — the octopus, apparently, is worth the trip. He says it with the specific enthusiasm of a man whose pleasures have gotten smaller and more precise and genuinely better for it.

I watch him and I put it down.

Not forgiveness as an event. Not ceremonial. Not named. Just the slow settling of something I have been carrying since he sat on the terrace above me with his drinks and his damage and his love that didn't know how to land.

I put it down.

I drink the coffee. It's good. It is just coffee.

"The restaurant," I say. "Let's go sometime."

He looks up. Surprise moves through his face — underneath the old habit of not showing it. Then it settles.

"Yeah," he says. "Let's do that."

We sit a while longer. The F train passes somewhere below. The amber lamp. The Persian rug. The keys on the side table catching the afternoon light.

I stand to go. We shake hands at the door — the same careful distance he's always kept. His grip holds.

"Take care of yourself," he says.

"You too," I say.

I take the stairs down. The lobby. The street.

The afternoon is ordinary. Brooklyn doing what Brooklyn does. I walk to the subway without hurrying.

On the F train back I watch the dark of the tunnel and feel the particular lightness of a man who has put something down and is not going to pick it up again.

Not healed. Not resolved. Just done carrying it.

That's enough.

CHAPTER 23

FULL DISCLOSURE

I wake early. Soft gray over 10th. Emails stack. Calendar full — NYBC, product, press, Zack. I should dive in. I lace up instead.

West toward the Hudson. Past galleries and coffee windows, sun knifing between buildings. Music, breath, footfalls, the dull rhythm of a city that never stops asking. By the West Side Highway I'm soaked. The skyline bends behind me. The river opens ahead. Little Island floats like a dream the city kept. I slow at the rail. River smell. Rain in the air. Heart pounding — earned, not panic. Mateo prayed every morning before the world asked anything of him. I never understood that until now. From here the city hums on without me. Tomorrow's interview: The Making of Will Chaffee. Trajectory, market strategy, founder narrative. The prep notes might as well be ad copy. I'm supposed to talk about what's next. Growth. Scale. More of the same. I practice answers. They already sound rehearsed. A ferry horn cuts across the water. Wind lifts, cool and sharp. No panic. Just clarity for once. The water moves — gray, alive. I let it. Tomorrow they'll put me under lights and ask what I've learned. I already know what I'm going to say.

* * *

The next morning the city feels too clean — streets rinsed, glass winking sharp in the sun.

Studio lights are always colder than you remember.

Times Square. Same glass walls, same skyline looping behind the blue ticker crawl.

Blake stands off camera, headset in one hand, coffee in the other, surrounded by Sawbuck's handlers. Cam, my media coordinator, scrolling analytics before the segment even starts. Emily from PR whispering with a young producer. Two analysts from finance, polished and buzzing.

"Remember," Blake says, touching my sleeve. "Steady energy. Hit the growth story, the mission, the partnership pipeline."

Cam: "Avoid any comment on the Fed's liquidity stance. Don't confirm the valuation leak."

"Got it." My throat's already dry.

In the makeup chair I listen to Cam run through the talking points one more time. Growth trajectory. Partnership pipeline. The Series A as validation, not beginning. Don't confirm the valuation leak. Don't comment on the Fed's liquidity stance.

I know all of it. I've said all of it. The sentences have been in my mouth so many times they've stopped having weight.

The makeup artist dabs at my forehead. The studio lights are the particular cold white that makes everything look like evidence. I catch myself in the monitor — the navy suit, the practiced stillness, the face that reads as certainty from twelve feet away.

Six months ago I was in a cell in Peru with nothing between me and the ceiling. Mateo on his bunk with his hands on his knees, talking to God in the conversational tone of someone for whom prayer was just talking, and had been for years.

And now I'm here. Under these lights. About to say the sentences again.

Emily from PR appears at my elbow. "Two minutes. You good?"

"Good," I say.

She nods and disappears. Blake catches my eye from behind the cameras. She holds up a thumb. I nod back.

The floor manager counts down from five. I square my shoulders. The ticker glows:

SAWBUCK CEO WILL CHAFFEE ON DISRUPTING CONSUMER FINANCE

Three. Two. One.

The red light clicks on.

* * *

"Joining us now is Will Chaffee, founder and CEO of Sawbuck Technologies," the anchor begins.

"Thanks for having me." Smile rehearsed.

"You've been called one of the fastest-growing platforms in the country. What's driving Sawbuck's success?"

Easy. "Access and efficiency. We're building financial tools for people long ignored by traditional banks — helping them build equity and credit from the ground up."

She nods. "You closed a record Series A, a two billion-dollar valuation. Remarkable traction for such a young company."

She flips back a page. “Before we get to that — you were largely absent from public view for about six months. There was a statement about a family health matter. Can you speak to that?”

Behind her I see Blake go still.

“It was a personal matter,” I say. “I needed to step back. The team held it together.”

“Would you say the company suffered during that period?”

“Every company suffers when its founder is absent.” I keep my voice even. “The team is why we’re still here.”

She holds my eye for a half-second longer than the question requires. Then she nods and moves on. Cam gives Blake a small nod. Crisis contained.

For now.

Behind her, I catch my reflection in the glass — perfect posture, crisp navy suit, a man assembled from certainty.

"It's a team effort," I say. "We built something that meets people where they are."

"Sounds like purpose drives your work."

"Purpose and performance," I answer. The words come easy. Too easy.

Blake nods. Cam gives a thumbs-up. The lights stay cold.

She flips a page. "You've talked before about your family's legacy. How has that shaped this next chapter?"

Legacy. There it is.

I could give the clean answer Emily wrote. For a second I see my father in the reflection — not the man he was, but the man right before everything tipped.

"I think we all want to make our mark," I say carefully. "For me, it's about creating opportunity where there wasn't any." My breath won't finish itself. I try again. "My father believed in that too. But he mistook it for approval. Thought success could fix what was broken. I did too."

Blake freezes. Cam stops typing.

"And did it?" the anchor asks.

"My father—" I start, then stop.

I'm aware of Blake behind the camera. I'm aware of Cam's tablet. I'm aware of the ticker running below the shot and the producer in the booth and the twelve million people who might be watching a man in a navy suit talk about fintech on a Tuesday morning.

And I'm aware that none of that is available to me the way it used to be.

In the cell outside Lima, Mateo used to say: you already know.

You've always known. You just keep choosing the noise instead of the answer.

The noise is right here. All around me. The lights and the prep notes and Blake's thumb and the sentences I've rehearsed until the meaning left them.

And the answer is also right here.

"He was a good man. Kind. Smarter than he ever got credit for. He wanted success — not for the money, but for what he thought it would fix. But it wore him down. He lost himself trying to keep up. Became someone I didn't recognize." A breath. "And I watched it happen and swore I never would."

The anchor waits.

I glance at the glass wall. My reflection stares back — the suit, the logo, the loop of my own image.

And I realize I'm looking at him.

"I used to tell myself I'd never end up like that," I say. Quiet now. "But the truth is — I'm halfway there."

The anchor blinks. The anchor blinks.

"There's a man named Ian Cato," I say. "He built Sawbuck. The platform, the architecture, the original idea — he built it for his mother's laundromat in Crown Heights because the banking system had never been designed for her. I walked in with capital and connections and I told his story better than he could in a room full of investors and I let the world come to believe it was mine." I stop. "It wasn't. Not in the way I've let people believe."

The studio is very quiet.

"The numbers we took to market during the Series A—" I pause. "Some of them were where we were going, not where we were. We dressed projection as traction. And I knew it. And I kept talking. After the round closed, compliance gaps with our banking partners surfaced that we never disclosed."

Cam has stopped moving entirely. Emily has gone pale. Blake is very still.

"I'm not saying Sawbuck doesn't work," I say. "It works. Ian built something real. The platform is real. The people using it are real. Gloria Cato's laundromat on Nostrand Avenue is real." I look at the anchor. "I just stopped being honest about what I contributed and what I took."

She blinks. "Would you like to—"

"I think that's enough," I say.

"Okay," she says. "We'll cut to break."

The red light dies.

The handlers swarm — damage control, next steps. None of it sticks.

Blake crouches beside the chair. "Hey. Look at me. We'll frame it as emotional honesty. Founders struggle. Vulnerability is—"

"It wasn't vulnerability," I say. "It was just true."

She studies me. The version of this she can manage is already assembling in her head. I can see it.

I pull the mic off my jacket and stand.

Behind me the studio door opens — Cam calling my name, Emily with a notepad, Blake trying to keep her voice even. "Will, just wait — let's debrief before you go—"

I don't stop. Past the cameras. Past Cam calling my name. Past Emily with the notepad. Past the security desk where a man I've never learned the name of nods at me — a habit that survives everything — and I nod back.

A production assistant catches me near the exit — late twenties, headset crooked, soft voice. She reaches for the mic pack at my waist, careful, like she doesn't want to name what just happened.

"Sorry," I mutter, stopping.

"It's okay," she says. "You're fine."

She works the clip loose. The cable slides free. Velcro. Plastic. Nothing dramatic.

"You want some water?" She's already holding a bottle out.

I take it. My hand's shaking. She notices and doesn't react.

"Happens to everyone," she says. "Live TV's weird like that."

She finishes packing the mic, tucks it into her pouch, looks up at me — not curious, not impressed. Just present.

"For what it's worth," she adds, quieter, "you didn't say anything wrong."

I meet her eyes for a second. Long enough to register that she means it.

"Thanks," I say.

She smiles once. Small. Professional. Kind. Then she steps aside so I can pass, already turning back toward the set like nothing remarkable just happened.

But it did.

* * *

My phone is ringing. I don't look at it.

I stand for a moment. Times Square humming around me, the screens cycling through their advertisements, someone's face fifty feet tall on a building across the street.

The performance is over.

Not because I decided to end it. Because it stopped being available.

That's the difference. That's what six months in a cell with Mateo Quispe actually did — not a decision, but the removal of something I had been using so long I'd stopped noticing it was a tool. The thing that found the angle. That made the room lean in. That turned the true thing into a version of the true thing that served me better. Gone. Not by choice. By six months of watching a man who never needed it — and realizing what that meant.

I stand there long enough for three cabs to pass and a food cart to open and a couple to argue briefly about something that resolves before they reach the corner.

Then I call Angie.

Outside, the city blazes. Traffic hums. Screens already flashing the story I just cracked open.

Angie is double-parked on Sixth. Hazards on. She doesn't ask how it went. I'm sure she already knows — watched it on her phone in the parking garage. She opens her arms once, briefly. I let it last a moment. Then I get in the car.

We don't talk for three blocks.

"Where to?" she says. "Home first," I say. "Then I'll figure out the rest."

She nods. Changes lanes. That's it.

I look past the glass — the cars, the billboards, the noise I built my life around.

* * *

Inside, the loft smells like stale coffee and cologne. I strip off the suit, toss the tie onto the couch. The mirror catches me mid-motion — white shirt open at the collar, pale under the light.

I throw a few things in a bag. No suit. No laptop. Jeans. A hoodie. A beat-up copy of East of Eden.

Blue watches from the doorway like he knows.

"Come on, buddy," I whisper. "We're going for a ride."

* * *

Back on the street, Angie pops the door.

"Where now?" she asks.

I think about Blake — still in the studio probably, already working the phones, building the managed version of what just happened.

I think about Ian. The mic pack on the floor of the break room. The dashboard he rebuilt so the numbers would be defensible. Coming back when he didn't have to.

I think about Mateo talking to God the way you talk to someone in the room. A man who knows what he's for.

"West Fourth," I say. "The F train."

Angie meets my eyes in the rearview. She doesn't ask why.

She just drives.

CHAPTER 24

FINDING THE LIGHT

Angie drives north up Sixth. There's a small wooden cross hanging from the rearview — rosewood, worn smooth. She's had it as long as I've known her.

Angie's Escalade idles at the curb. The same station she always has on–one from Harlem. She doesn't turn it down when I get in. She drives in silence. At my building, she asks: "You want me to wait?"

"Yeah. Won't be long. Or I will. I don't know."

She nods. Parks at the curb. Doesn't say anything else.

I took the F train.

I could have had Angie take me. There's something about the F train to Brooklyn that belongs to this — the specific underground light, the way the car rocks and the people around you are going somewhere else entirely and don't know where you're going and that indifference is its own kind of permission.

At Carroll Street I get off. Walk the three blocks.

He answers, shirt pressed. Of course.

He looks at me the way he always looks at me — the assessment running, the calculation of what version of this visit he's receiving.

"Will," he says. "I wasn't expecting you."

"I know," I say. "Can I come in?"

He steps back. I come in. He gestures to the sofa and takes the chair across from it — the arrangement of every conversation we've ever had in this apartment.

I sit. He picks up his coffee. The room is very quiet. Outside, the F train passes somewhere below, the sound traveling up through the building the way it always does.

He looks at me for a long moment without speaking. I know what he's seeing — the Chaffee jaw, the height, the build that came from Big and skipped a generation. He has his father's eyes but not his frame. I got the frame.

He sets the cup down.

He has never been a man who asks.

He sits across from me — the dark jacket, the white hair. The watchmaker's precision he brings to every gesture, every cup held just so, every room entered as though he has already decided how it will go.

His eyes are darker than mine and they have been somewhere mine haven't been yet.

"I need to say something to you," I say. "And I need you to let me finish before you respond."

Something moves in his face. The machinery running. Then he nods once.

"You hit me," I say. "More than once. I was a child and you hit me and you called me things that I carried for twenty years without knowing I was carrying them." I keep my voice level. "You made me afraid of you. And then I spent my whole adult life trying to earn something from you that wasn't available. Your approval. Your pride. Anything that would tell me I was enough." I pause.

The room is very quiet.

"That's what I came to say. Not to hurt you. Not to start a war. Just to say the true thing, out loud, in a room with you, because I've been saying it to myself for thirty years and it's time."

He is still. The coffee cup in his hand, held with that watchmaker's precision. His eyes on the Persian rug.

Then he says: "I don't know what you're talking about."

Not anger. Not defensiveness. Something closer to incomprehension — the specific response of a man who has been telling himself a story about who he is for so long that the alternative is not just wrong but genuinely unrecognizable.

"I was hard on you," he says. "That's what fathers do. You turned out fine."

I don't argue. I don't produce evidence. I just stay. That's what I learned in the cell — you don't have to win. You just have to say the true thing and let it exist in the room.

We sit.

The F train passes again below, the particular vibration of something enormous moving underground. Then it fades. Then it's just the room again.

My father is looking at the Persian rug. The one from the Greenwich study that Liz didn't want after the split. He kept it. Of course he kept it. It's the only thing in this apartment that remembers the larger life.

I think about sitting in this chair as a boy. The same chair. The same rug. A different city, a different version of everything, but the same distance between us. That distance was always there. I spent thirty years mistaking it for the normal distance between fathers and sons, then another few years understanding it wasn't normal, and now I'm sitting in this apartment on a Tuesday morning trying to name it out loud and watching my father not be able to hear me.

The F train passes again.

He says nothing. Long enough that I stop expecting him to speak.

Then he sets the cup down.

"My father," he says. Slowly, like he's finding the words in a language he hasn't used. "My father ran the factory in Bridgeport. You know that. What you don't know—" He stops. Starts again. "He didn't believe in saying things. What he believed in was that you showed up and you worked and you didn't complain and if something was wrong you fixed it. That was the whole philosophy." He goes somewhere else for a moment. "I never heard him say he was proud of me. Not once. Not when I graduated. Not when I married your mother. Not when I built the company up from nothing." He looks at his hands. "I thought that was just how it was. How men were."

I don't say anything.

"I wasn't trying to break you," he says. The words come out careful, deliberate, the way words come out when a man is not used to saying true things and is trying to do it anyway. "I was trying to make you ready. For a world that—" He stops. "I thought the world was harder than it turned out to be. Or harder in the ways I expected. I didn't understand the thing I was doing—" He picks up the cup. Sets it down again without drinking. "I didn't understand what it was doing."

It is not an apology. It is not the full accounting. It is a crack in a wall that has been solid for forty years and the crack is small and the wall is still mostly standing.

But it is something.

I look at my father — the white hair, the coffee cup held with precision, the Persian rug beneath him from a house he built and lost and has been living without ever since. A man who trusted no one and controlled everything and lost it all anyway. A man who learned from his own father that silence and hardness were the only currencies available to him. A man sitting alone in a small immaculate apartment at ten in the morning with a scotch glass and a son he doesn't know how to see.

The great grandfather's nameplate coming off the wall. The math finally stopping working. The thumb pressed to the eye.

He is also that man. And I am also this man. And somewhere between us is the question of whether the pattern stops here or keeps going.

"I'm not here to punish you," I say. "I'm not here to make you admit something you're not ready to admit." I lean forward, elbows on my knees. "I'm here because I've been waiting for your verdict my whole life. Whether I was enough. Whether you were proud. Whether I finally did the thing that would make you lean forward the way you leaned forward in that diner." I hold his gaze. "I'm done waiting for it."

Something shifts in his face. Not anger. Older.

"That doesn't mean I'm done with you," I say. "It means your verdict on me is not my verdict on myself. Those are two different things and I've been treating them like the same thing for thirty years."

He is quiet.

"I spent my life waiting for a verdict from you," I say. "I'm done waiting." I stand. "The Cos Cob pub was real. The mornings on Halcyon were real. I'm not throwing those away." I look at him directly. "But your verdict on who I am is not my verdict. Not anymore."

He doesn't stand. He stays in his chair with the quiet of the apartment he has maintained with absolute precision since the larger life fell away.

"Will," he says.

I wait.

He opens his mouth. Closes it. Then back at me. The machinery running. The performance assembling. And then — for just a moment — the performance not arriving. Just a man in a chair looking at his son.

"The car," he says. "The Aston." A pause. "I drove it last week. Up to the reservoir and back." He picks up the cup. "It drives the way I remembered."

It is not I love you. It is not I'm sorry. It is not the thing I came for.

It is a man telling his son that he drove the car his son gave him to the reservoir and back. Unprompted. In a conversation about damage and inheritance and thirty years of distance. He could have said anything. He chose to tell me about the drive.

And it is the most honest thing he has said in this apartment in years. Maybe ever.

My father is not at peace. He is a man sitting in a small immaculate apartment with a coffee cup and a Persian rug and a car he drives to the reservoir and back. He is doing what he can with what he has. That is not enough. It was never enough. But it is something. And the gap between nothing and something is the only gap that can ever be crossed.

"Good," I say. "That's what it's for."

He is quiet for a moment. Then, almost to himself:

"My father wanted me in the business. I had — other ideas. When I was young." He picks up his cup. "There was a program. Peace Corps. I'd already filled out the application. We had a band in college — nothing serious. But I thought —" He stops. "It doesn't matter what I thought."

"What happened?" I ask.

"He needed someone on the floor. The factory was struggling." He sets the cup down. "I stayed."

He doesn't say it like a man who was wronged. He says it like a man who made a sensible decision forty years ago and has never quite finished making it.

I think about the guitar in his study. I never asked about it. He never offered.

We are more alike than either of us has been willing to say.

"That explains the guitar, I guess."

He looks at me. A long moment. Then he nods once.

I stand.

He doesn't stand. He stays in his chair — the white hair, the watchmaker's stillness, the room that has held its shape for a long time.

"I'll call you," I say.

He nods once. The way he does when he means it.

I let myself out.

The elevator. The lobby. Court Street in the November cold, the F train audible somewhere beneath my feet.

Angie is at the curb. She doesn't say anything. Just opens the door.

I slide in. The leather warm from the heater. The city moving past the window. The cross hanging from the rearview. It's always there.

I feel the specific weight of having said a true thing in a difficult room and is now sitting in a car on Court Street in Brooklyn carrying all of it — the anger, the love, the grief, the small opening in the wall, the handshake that wasn't warm and wasn't cold.

CHAPTER 25

WALKING FROM THE EDGE

It's quiet for Manhattan — the kind of stillness you only notice when something inside you finally stops spinning.

I pass a red-brick church on 22nd, heavy wooden doors cracked for midday prayers, and a memory finds me uninvited.

I'm in a pew at the church we hardly ever attended in New Canaan — ten, maybe eleven — near the back, legs swinging above the floor. Christmas Eve. The kind of cold that makes the air sound different. I don't remember why we went. My father said the place was full of phonies. But that year something cracked between them — loud enough to scare even her. Instead of champagne and jazz records, she pulled me into the car and drove us to St. Mark's. Said the choir would settle our nerves.

Candlelight. The velvet hymnals. The priest's voice rising over O Come, All Ye Faithful.

And the stillness — just before the Eucharist. A man stood to read a verse I didn't know but never forgot:

The light shines in the darkness, and the darkness has not overcome it.

It echoed in the rafters like truth.

My mother cried. Quietly, but I saw it. And for one instant I believed anything could hold this mess together.

I stop outside the church and stand there a moment. I don't go in. I just let it sit.

Then I keep walking.

* * *

By the time we reach the gate the clouds have thickened. Angie's got her rings on — all of them, which I've learned means she's in a good mood. The cross swings from the rearview when she turns. She eases to the shoulder. "You want me to wait?"

"Yeah. Won't be long."

Cold air. Wet leaves. Granite and quiet.

I walk the path alone — hoodie damp, sneakers caked in city soot. No flowers. Just breath and memory.

I stand there a long time. Not speaking. Not praying. Just letting the silence meet me halfway.

The stone reads:

William Hayward Chaffee II

September 4, 1927– June 17, 2013

He built what he was given and gave what he could

My grandfather. The man whose father's nameplate came off the wall while my father pressed his thumb to his eye in a downtown office and tried not to make a sound. The man who ran the factory in Bridgeport and believed silence was a form of strength and never once said proud to his son.

I look at the moss gathering around the edges of the stone.

"You were doing what you knew," I say. "That doesn't make it right. But I think I understand it now."

I kneel, wet grass cold against my knees.

"You handed something down," I say. "Through my father, to me.

A way of being that said silence is strength and hardness is love and the worst thing a man can do is need something. Three generations carrying it. Passing it forward without knowing what we were carrying."

The wind shifts. A crow calls somewhere beyond the trees.

"I'm done carrying it. Not because you don't matter. Because I need my hands free for what comes next."

I think about my father in his dark jacket in the Brooklyn apartment. The Aston in the parking garage. The way he said it drives the way I remembered — the most honest thing he'd said in years. The factory. The nameplate. The man who ran it who never said proud to his son who hit his son on a terrace in Greenwich and watched that son spend thirty years trying to earn it back.

"I forgive you," I say. "Both of you. The one who started it and the one who passed it on." I press my palm to the cold stone. "I don't think you knew what you were doing. I think you were just men who never learned another way." A long breath. "Neither did I. Until I had to."

The tears come quietly. Not dramatic. Just real.

I stay until they pass. Then I stand, brush the wet grass from my knees, and look at the stone one more time.

"It stops here," I say.

I turn and walk back toward the gate. Angie sees my face when I come out and opens her arms once, briefly. I let it last a moment. Then I get in the car. “Westchester,” I say.

She nods and pulls out without a word.

* * *

Forty minutes later we're at the gate. Island Express. A small commercial prop to Nantucket — twelve seats, half full. I find a window. Blue settles under the seat in front of me without being told. I don't check my phone.

As we land in Nantucket the sky is gray, fog brushing the edge of the dunes. The air smells like salt and cedar.

I breathe it in.

The cottage creaks when we open the door. Blue runs the perimeter like he owns it. I don't turn on the lights. I drop my bag, sit on the bed, and let the silence come find me.

* * *

The light wakes me before the sound does. Then I hear the waves.

Blue stretches, yawns, shakes his collar. I pull on jeans, an old sweater, and follow him outside.

The air cuts clean — salt and pine. Gulls drifting low over the dunes. We walk toward the water. The sand damp and smooth, dark ribbons where the tide pulled back overnight.

Blue runs ahead in wide loops. I let him go.

I sit on a driftwood log, watching the tide breathe in and out — steady, indifferent. I think about my father. How maybe he wasn't chasing money so much as chasing proof. Proof he mattered. Proof he could fix what his own father broke. Maybe he just never found the right way to begin again.

Blue trots back, drops a shell at my feet like an offering. I pick it up. Cracked down one side but still holding light in the curve.

"Good find," I tell him.

He leans against my leg.

The sun breaks fully above the surface, gold spilling across the water.

"Let's go," I whisper.

We turn up the beach, moving with the wind.

* * *

Inside, the cottage is quiet except for the ocean against the rocks and Blue's slow breathing at my feet. The fire's low, mostly embers.

I've been staring at the guitar on the chair across from me for an hour.

It feels strange, lifting it again. The strings are old, rough on the fingertips. I tighten one, twist the tuner, strum softly. The sound wobbles, then steadies — thin, true enough.

Blue lifts his head, ears twitching. "Yeah," I murmur. "It's been a while."

I set my phone on the table, hit record. No mic, no filters — just air and wood and whatever I still remember.

The song comes slow — a melody I started years ago and never finished. Something about leaving. Maybe returning.

Halfway through, the wind presses against the window, carrying salt and pine. I close my eyes and let the notes find their shape.

When it's over I let the silence sit, then press stop.

Blue shifts closer, resting his head on my foot.

I replay the track. The sound's rough, uneven — but underneath, something holds.

I save the file without a name.

Put the guitar on the chair, kill the light, and step outside barefoot on the splintered deck. Salt on my skin. The ocean against the rocks.

My father was wrong about a lot of things.

But the thing he was most wrong about wasn't the company or the money or even me.

He was wrong about God.

He was wrong about Jesus. He was wrong about the Bible. He said faith was for people who couldn't handle uncertainty. He said smart people learned to settle with not knowing.

He was wrong.

I know because I sat in a cell for six months with a man who handles more uncertainty before breakfast than my father faced in a lifetime — and that man was the most at-peace human being I have ever shared time with. Not performing peace. Not medicating it. Not buying it with money or status or the particular numbness that comes from drinking through the hard parts.

Living inside it. Every day. Because of something he believed and my father dismissed as fiction.

I think about what Gloria Cato said about God's plan for each of us.

He was wrong to stop. That's what I think now. He was wrong to hand me his stopping like it was wisdom.

I don't know what I believe yet. Not fully. Not in the way Mateo knows — a lifetime of the same conversation, the deep groove of a faith that's been tested and held.

But I know what I saw in that cell. I know what I felt in that church at ten years old before I learned to be too smart for it. I know that the stillness I've been running toward on this beach, in this cottage, in the silence after the guitar stopped — it isn't empty. There's a presence in it.

Something that was here before I arrived and will be here after I leave.

My father got a lot of stuff wrong. But this was the one that cost him most.

I don't intend to make the same mistake.

I lean against the railing, staring into the dark, and say it quietly — to no one and to everything.

"God. I don't know what I'm doing."

Quieter.

"Help me."

Not because I expect lightning. Because I have reached the place where my own strength runs out and something deeper has to take over.

The stillness answers. Not with clarity, not with thunder. With a kind of release.

I breathe in — sharp, ragged — and something gives way.

I've been bowing to the wrong things for a long time. I'm tired of the noise.

I sit back against the railing and let the tears come. Not loud. Not cinematic. Just steady.

I call my father from the cottage porch. It's early. The fog is still on the water.

He picks up on the second ring.

"I'm leaving Sawbuck," I say.

"Leaving." Not a question. Testing the word.

"Resigning. End of the month."

He processes it. I watch the water while he does.

"You're sure," he says.

"Yes."

He is quiet for a moment. "I spent forty years trying to build something that would last," he says.

"I know," I say.

"You built the thing I was trying to build," he says. "You actually built it."

"I built a version of what you were chasing," I say. "That's not the same thing."

A long pause.

"No," he says quietly. "I suppose it isn't."

I stay on the porch until the fog lifts. Then I go inside and make coffee.

* * *

Two days later I'm in row 26, middle seat, knees pressed to the tray table. No upgrades. No champagne. Just the hum of engines and a bag of pretzels.

The guy next to me snores against the window. A kid across the aisle colors with a broken crayon, his mother asleep beside him.

I watch the kid work. He's trying to stay inside the lines with what he has left. I lean back, close my eyes, and know exactly what I'll do when we land.

Q meets me at the water with a board under each arm and the particular ease of a man who has decided that joy is a discipline.

"Rookie," he says, handing me the longer one.

We stay out for two hours. I fight the water for most of it — wrong angle, wrong timing, the old instinct to force things. Q doesn't give advice. He just keeps paddling back out, and eventually I stop fighting and start reading, and twice I find the break just right and the board goes and for a few seconds there is nothing else.

When we haul in he's grinning. "There you are."

We sit on his deck with beers, the Pacific going gold and then dark. I don't ease into it.

"I'm done, Q. I'm leaving Sawbuck."

He doesn't answer right away. He drinks. Looks at the water. I wait for the objection — the money, the timing, the board, the terms.

Instead he leans back. "Not surprising, man."

He's quiet. Then:

He looks at the water for a moment. "You know what I found? The office side and the foundation side — they're not as different as people think. The capital still moves. The decisions still matter. But the why changes." He turns his cup in his hands. "That's the part that gets easier. Not the work. The why."

Something releases in my chest. "Yeah?"

"Quart." He turns to look at me directly. "I've known you broke. I've known you chasing every shiny thing. I've known you when you forgot who you were." He shakes his head. "The guy I love is underneath all that. The kid who played guitar too loud and gave a damn and could laugh at himself when he was wrong. That's the guy I wanted to survive this."

I look at the ocean. "I swore I wouldn't become him. My father. And the more I ran from it the more I was doing exactly what he did — reaching for the thing that was supposed to prove something and couldn't."

"You're not him," Q says. "Not close. He let the world break him. You've been breaking yourself, which is different. You've still got a choice. You always have."

I stay with it. The waves come in whether I watch them or not.

"Maybe that's what scared me," I say. "Having the choice."

Q nods once. He doesn't try to finish it. That's always been the thing about Q — he knows when a silence is doing work.

We clink bottles. The sun goes all the way down.

"You're a good friend," I say.

"Yeah, well." He tips the bottle. "Don't make me say it back."

* * *

"Jay. Calling because you deserve to hear this directly."

"I've been waiting," he says. Not unfriendly. Just measured.

"I'm leaving Sawbuck," I say.

"We can defend this, Will. The board has talked it through. What you said on air — it's defensible. The numbers are complicated but they're not criminal. We can build a narrative."

"I know you can," I say. "I'm resigning anyway. End of the month. I'm selling my block to Anton."

A silence. "Quimby."

"Yes."

"That's not what I expected to hear."

"I know."

Jay exhales. "All right. I'll need a week to prepare the board." He pauses. "Don't do any more interviews."

"Understood."

His tone shifts. "The company lost ground while you were gone. The board was concerned. We managed it. Then your people managed the Peru situation — the PR mess, the framing, the noise. That took months.

We were almost through it." He stops. "Then you went on television and burned it down."

"I told the truth."

"You told the truth on a Tuesday morning in front of twelve million people without giving your board or your investors or your legal team twelve minutes of warning." His voice goes flat. "That's not courage, Chaffee. That's just a different kind of recklessness."

I don't argue. He isn't wrong.

"Sixty days," he says. "Make the handoff clean. Give the company a fighting chance at surviving what you just did to it."

"All right," I say.

We say goodbye. He hangs up first.

* * *

Marcus calls at seven the next morning — Marcus Webb, my attorney since before Sutter Rowe, the only lawyer I trust to tell me the truth before he tells me the options. His voice has the particular flatness of someone who'd been up since four with bad news and had already rehearsed how to deliver it. "Coventry's counsel has already filed a complaint. SEC referral is likely. The settlement window is narrow and closing. You should know — the number we're looking at is not the number you were looking at yesterday.'"

I tell him I understand.

He tells me he'll have something more specific by noon. We hang up.

I set the phone on the counter.

The number. Not the number I was looking at yesterday. I run through what that means. A settlement to make the SEC referral go away. A buyout to let me and the problem I created go away. Everything I built, transferred at a discount, in exchange for the right to leave quietly.

That's what walking away costs.

The loft is quiet. The city outside does what cities do at seven in the morning — indifferent, continuous, already somewhere else.

Then I call Blake.

She picks up on the second ring.

"I know," she says. Before I say anything.

"Can you come?" I ask.

A pause. Long enough that I think she might say no. Long enough to understand what it would mean if she did.

"Yes," she says. "Give me an hour."

I do.

I call her from the loft that afternoon.

"I need to see you," I say. "Can you come by?"

She reads the register the way she always does. "I'll be there in an hour."

* * *

She arrives in forty minutes. Good coat, composed — but there's something underneath it that didn't finish assembling in the car. She's been with me long enough to know when a conversation is going to cost something.

She comes in, looks around the way she always does when she arrives — quick inventory, everything noted — and sits on the leather couch. She doesn't take off her coat.

"You recovered from the interview," I say.

"Still dealing with the fall out," she says. "I know you're stepping down, Will. Remsen called me this morning." She looks at me directly. "What did you do, Will?"

"I said what was true," I say. "On camera. About Ian. About the numbers during the raise. About what Sawbuck is and what it isn't."

She is very still.

"The clean version wasn't available anymore," I say. "I tried to reach for it and it wasn't there."

The window. The Hudson below. A long moment passes.

She is very still.

"Did you know it would land this way?" she says. "When you said it on air."

"Yes."

"And you did it anyway."

"Yes."

Blake studies me. Not long. Just long enough.

The woman who built the story that got us here. Who never once pretended to be something she wasn't.

"I've been managing your story for two years, Will. I believed in most of it." She looks at her hands. "But I knew. I knew." "The story was real," I say. "I just wasn't."

She already knew. Needed to hear it confirmed.

A long silence. The candle on the side table — fig and smoke, the one she brought once and never took back. The Hudson through the windows, moving.

"I don't think you're wrong," she says finally. Softer: "I just don't think I can follow you there."

That's the truth. The most honest thing either of us has said in this relationship, maybe.

She stands. Picks up her bag.

At the door she pauses. Looks at Blue briefly. Then at me.

"Take care of yourself," she says.

"You too, Blake."

The click of her heels fades down the hall. The door closes softly. I don't move. The candle keeps burning.

Blue pads in from the hall and sits at my feet.

"We're really doing this," I say.

He leans into my hand.

* * *

The statement goes out Friday morning. Clean, controlled, the language Remsen and I agreed on — founder transition, strategic evolution, gratitude for the team. The kind of language that says nothing while covering everything.

Somewhere in a federal building in lower Manhattan a file with my name on it is moving between desks. I don't think about it directly. I think about it the way you think about something you can't afford to examine.

By noon it doesn't matter. The headline version writes itself anyway.

Sawbuck Founder to Step Down Amid Turbulence. Face of Fintech Walks Away. The crawl underneath: sources close to the company cite internal tensions, questions about leadership, the Peru absence still unexplained publicly.

The talking heads run with it — burnout, scandal, breakdown, a carefully worded segment about the NYBC interview where I told the truth on camera and the market responded by dropping our valuation six points. Someone calls it a self-inflicted wound. A crisis of confidence, says another. Nobody calls it what it is.

I watch it from the loft with the sound on for exactly twelve minutes. Then I mute it. The city outside keeps moving. The Hudson. The lights coming on across the water as the afternoon goes dark.

In the corner, my guitar waits — dusty, strings dull. I haven't touched it since the cottage. I lift it, sit on the couch, press a chord. It's out of tune, rough — the note pushing through the quiet of the room like something that has been waiting. The sound isn't clean.

It's mine.

CHAPTER 26

LA MECHA

It's a cold dark morning, the kind that makes Tribeca feel like a different city — quieter, the streets still finding their shape for the day.

I pull on sweats, lace up, clip Blue's leash. He's already at the door before I have my second shoe on, doing that low impatient whine he saves for mornings when he knows we're going.

The elevator opens into the lobby. Marcos at the front desk nods. I push through the glass door and the air hits — sharp, clean, the Hudson carrying something off the water that smells like the start of things.

Blue pulls left toward the river. I let him lead.

My phone buzzes in my pocket.

Liz: I saw the news. I hope you know what you're doing.

That's it. No follow-up. No question.

I don't reply. Just head out into the city.

I open a blank message and type as Blue picks up our pace:

Coffee? Same place.

I don't expect a reply. For a while, nothing. Crossing Madison, the screen lights:

Tomorrow, 8.

* * *

Same table in the back. Same hiss of steamers. Maybe I'm the thing that's different. Ian shows ten minutes late, backpack over one shoulder. No suit. No pitch. Just him. He hesitates, then sits without hello.

"Appreciate you coming," I say.

He peels the sleeve off his cup, eyes on the cardboard. "You said coffee, not a eulogy. Get to it."

"I crossed a line," I say. "I know where."

He finally looks up. Not angry. Just tired.

"I watched the NYBC thing," he says.

"I know."

"You said my name four times." He looks at his cup. "The architecture. The mission. Crown Heights. All of it." I look at my hands. "My phone didn't stop for three days."

"Good calls or bad?" I ask.

Something moves at the corner of his mouth. Not quite a smile. "Mixed." He wraps both hands around the cup. "There was one from a woman in the Bronx. Said her daughter used Sawbuck to start a cleaning business. Said she wanted to thank the person who built it." He looks up. "She asked for you. I told her I was the engineer. She said that was good enough."

I don't say anything.

"You didn't have to do that," he says. "On camera. Like that."

"Yeah I did," I say.

He nods slowly. Then the tiredness comes back into his face — not anger, just the weight of everything that happened before the NYBC moment. Before any of it.

"You didn't just take the idea, Will. You took the friendship that came with it. That's the part I can't get back."

It hits. I don't dodge. "You're right."

He huffs a small laugh. "You always wanted to be right." He leans back. "Thing is, I'm glad Sawbuck isn't mine anymore. It was born from something personal. You turned it into whatever that became. Maybe it had to. Maybe I couldn't have carried it." I start to speak. He holds up a hand. "Don't. This isn't forgiveness. This is me telling you I'm not angry anymore. Just done."

I nod. More than I expected. Less than I hoped.

We sit another minute. He stands, slides the strap over his shoulder. Doesn't say goodbye. He just goes.

* * *

The place just feels good. Not curated or cool — just right. Like it always has.

The neon still buzzes over the door. Same worn floors. Same low ceiling stained by time. I step inside alone and the warmth hits like a hand on my shoulder.

Mumford's on the speakers — stripped down, no pretense. I slide into our booth near the back.

The bartender catches my eye. He doesn't ask. He remembers.

Second booth from the window, leather cracked at the edges. A nick in the table shaped like an ampersand — Nico pointed it out once, said it felt poetic. I run a thumb over it and exhale.

A beer lands in front of me. High Life, cold.

The door creaks. Nico walks in first, then Daren. No speeches. They slide into the booth like it's a ritual.

We order burgers and more High Life. No shop talk. No push.

"This place saw us before the headlines," I say. "Before decks and press and power plays. Just three guys trying to outrun the grind."

"And now?" Nico asks, eyes on his glass.

"Now I'm the one walking away from the race."

Daren breaks the quiet. "So that's it? You're just out?"

I swirl the beer, don't drink. "Yeah. I'm out."

"Jesus," Nico mutters. "I figured sabbatical. Not bonfire."

Nico leans back. "Explain it, because right now you sound like the guy in a viral post about leaving Wall Street to open a surf shop."

I laugh.

"You changed lives," Daren says.

"I hope so. But I wasn't living mine."

Nico is quiet. Then: "You were always better when you stopped trying to win."

It's the closest thing to a blessing he'll ever give.

"So what now?" Nico asks.

"I don't know. No one asks what I'm doing tomorrow."

Daren grins. "So we're finally opening that taco truck in Red Hook?"

"Only if it has a full espresso bar and no investors."

They laugh — clean, easy.

"I know this isn't what you signed up for," I say. "But I need you to know I'm grateful. For all of it. For both of you."

We drink. No toast. For the first time in a long time, the silence between us isn't pressure. It's peace.

We step into the night. It's quiet — the way endings should be. Daren claps my back. Nico lingers at the door. We don't hug. We don't need to.

I head downtown alone.

* * *

It's a Sunday. Her day off. She showed up anyway.

Angie and I loop the Reservoir. No suits. No headlines. Two New Yorkers with coffee and nowhere to be.

Rhinestones on her cap. Yankees sweatshirt tied at her waist.

"You still rich?" she asks, side-eye over the lid.

"Rich in clarity," I say.

She snorts. "Please. You're still a little bougie."

"Not wrong. I'm learning."

We walk on.

"You okay now?" she asks.

I think. "Getting there."

She bumps my shoulder. "Keep going, Boss."

I don't flinch at the nickname. I laugh.

My phone buzzes. I put it in my pocket without looking at it.

"How you doing?" I ask.

"Pretty good," she says. "Just saw grandma." She brightens. "She remembers the hymns. Every word. Doesn't always know where she is — but she knows every word." She says it matter-of-factly, no weight added. "That's okay with me."

At the gate she slows. A new Escalade idles at the curb, chrome bright in the late light. Windows down. Temp tags taped to the glass.

She eyes it, then me. "Nice ride. You finally trade that old Jeep in?"

"Nope."

"Don't tell me—"

"Keys are in the cup holder," I say. "You earned it."

"Will—"

"Angie." I cut in, gentle. "You kept me pointed forward when I didn't deserve it. Least I can do."

She exhales, shakes her head, a smile breaking through disbelief. "You really are a piece of work."

"Working on it."

She hugs me — quick, firm — and climbs in. The engine hums low.

"Try not to drive it like you're late for church," I say.

"No promises, Boss."

Chrome flashes once and she's gone.

I stand until the sound fades, then turn back toward the water, the city wide and breathing around me.

* * *

The conference room is glass and steel, perched high enough to make the city look like a model. This used to give me a rush. Now it just feels like distance.

The lawyer slides the documents across the table. "Once you sign, Mr. Quimby takes the block at the agreed-upon price. You will fully exit."

The agreed-upon price. Forty cents on the dollar from where Sawbuck was trading the morning before the NYBC segment. Q didn't negotiate hard. He didn't have to. The market did it for him.

Two documents. The Quimby block transfer. And beneath it, the Sawbuck settlement — SEC cooperation agreement, disgorgement of gains above a threshold Marcus spent three weeks negotiating down to survivable terms. I pick up the pen. Cool in my hand. Heavier than it looks. For a second I see my father's wrist over bankruptcy papers, the way he wouldn't meet my eyes. That same silence. That same quiet surrender. But this is different. He was losing something. I'm letting something go.

I sign.

The ink soaks in like it's been waiting.

No speech. No photos. Just a signature and the particular sound of a conference room when a decision has been made and there's nothing left to say. The money is already spoken for — a new foundation. La Mecha. First investment: Camp Create. A place for kids to find what I buried.

The lawyer studies me. "You're sure?"

"I'm sure," I say. "This time it's mine."

I step into the hallway and call Q. He picks up on the first ring.

"It's done, Q," I say.

A moment. Then: "Good. Now go do the thing you were actually supposed to do, Quart."

I don't look back when I leave. There's nothing in that room I need anymore.

* * *

La Mecha takes a year to build properly.

Not fast. Not with a press release and a ribbon cutting. Quietly, the way Ian built the original platform — because someone needed it, because it pointed toward something real.

Two missions.

Camp Create — for kids who need to make something that is genuinely theirs. Music. Painting. Writing. Film. A place where the only question asked of you is what you want to say. Me going back to the moment my father silenced me on that terrace and making sure it doesn't happen to someone else.

The Bridge Program — training and capital for local entrepreneurs. Barbershops, bakeries, food trucks, flower carts. Anyone with a dream and the grit to try. Seed money, coaching, connection between talent and opportunity. Gloria's laundromat on Nostrand Avenue. The fifteen-year customer. The sixty million people the system was never built for.

Named after the daughter of a man in a cell outside Lima who had nothing and was the most balanced person I had ever met. A man who knew what he was for.

Mornings are simpler now. No office, no driver, no texts screaming for attention. Just me and Blue walking into town. Some days the shelter — sorting coats, restocking supplies. Others, patching drywall at the old rec center, painting walls. No one asks where I worked before. They smile when I show up.

That's enough.

* * *

I cut the engine on the old Jeep and let the ticking settle into the quiet. Gravel crunches under my boots as I take the stone steps. I'm not here to perform.

Inside, she's in the sitting room — where she always is. Pale shawl, one hand on an open script, a half-finished tea cooling beside her.

"I saw the article," Liz says, not looking up. "La Mecha."

I nod. "It's small. But it's something."

She finally glances over. Her face is older than I remember. Not softer — more tired. The mask is still there. She just isn't holding it as tightly.

"I didn't start it to prove anything," I say.

"I know," she says. And for once, I think she does.

I drop into the armchair across from her, elbows on my knees. I let the silence breathe.

"You look better," she says.

"I am better. I spent a lot of years trying to make sense of the two of you," I say quietly. "Who I was supposed to be. Who I wasn't allowed to be."

She closes the script with care. "And now?"

I exhale. "Now I'm not trying to make sense of it."

A long pause. No performance. From either of us.

"I used to worry you'd become him," she says.

"I did," I answer. "For a while."

She doesn't flinch. She nods.

"I'm not asking you to like it," I say. "Just to hear me."

She looks toward the window, blinking against the late light. "I'm trying."

I stand, lean down, and kiss her cheek. Lavender and linen.

Then, as I reach the door, her voice follows.

"I remember the fireflies."

I don't stop.

But I smile.

* * *

The camp opens the following summer along the Hudson in Garrison. Twenty kids, aged ten to sixteen, two weeks, a farmhouse with a studio in the barn. Guitar. Piano. Voice. Film. Writing. A place where the only thing asked of you is that you make something genuinely yours.

The first morning there are eleven of them.

They come in off the van in ones and twos — some with bags, some without, most wearing the particular stillness of people who have learned not to expect much from a new room. They sit where they're pointed. They don't make eye contact right away. That's fine. Neither did I, at seventeen, the first time someone put me somewhere I didn't ask to be.

His name is Darius. He's sixteen and he has a sketchbook he keeps pressed flat against his thigh like he's not sure yet if it's allowed. One of the staff had flagged him — talented, she'd said. Also angry. The kind of angry that comes from being told the talent doesn't matter.

I know that kind.

I pull a chair up across from him. Not behind a desk. Just two chairs, facing.

"What's in the book?" I ask.

He weighs me. Then he opens it.

The drawings are precise and alive — cityscapes, mostly, but with something off about the geometry. Buildings that lean. Stairwells that spiral into nothing. The kind of work that's doing something the hand doesn't fully understand yet.

"These are good," I say.

He shrugs. "People say that."

"I mean it specifically." I point to one — a rooftop scene, a figure at the edge, the city falling away below in careful cross-hatching. "This one. The perspective is wrong on purpose. That's a decision, not a mistake."

He looks at the page. Then at me. "Yeah." "What do you want to do with it?"

He takes his time with it. Like the real answer is being weighed against the safer one.

"I don't know," he says. "Nobody ever asked me that."

The barn is loud with the sounds of the first morning — chairs scraping, introductions being made, someone laughing too hard at something that probably wasn't funny. The ordinary noise of people not yet sure if they're safe.

"You don't have to know yet," I say. "That's why you're here."

He nods. Closes the sketchbook. But carefully — the way you close something you plan to open again.

The guitars are out of tune and nobody cares. A couple of kids strum beside me, a beat behind, a chord off, and it still holds — messy, alive. Their voices crack in all the right ways. The fire snaps, shadows dancing over sketchpads and notebooks smeared with paint and lyrics.

Blue is curled behind me, chin on paws, ears twitching at laughter and the snap of a stick.

I keep playing, thumb brushing the strings, quiet enough to hear the kids instead of myself. That's the point now.

For once I don't feel like I have to lead or impress or fill the silence.

I already belong.

The song spills into the night — uneven, perfect — and the fireflies rise with it.

On the last night of the first session, I play for them.

Not a performance. Just me with a guitar in a barn, playing the melody I recorded alone in the Nantucket cottage — the song about leaving and maybe returning, the one I saved without a name.

Halfway through the second verse, I see him.

My father. Standing at the edge of the barn door, still dressed, hands in his pockets, watching.

I almost didn't invite him. I wrote the text three times and deleted it twice. The third time I sent it before I could think about it again.

He came.

I didn't explain it. Just the date and the address and: if you want to come.

I didn't know if he'd come.

He came. Pressed shirt. The Aston in the gravel lot. He didn't bring anything. He just came.

I keep playing. Don't stop, don't acknowledge him, don't make it a moment. Just play. The kids are watching my hands on the strings. The fire snaps. The barn smells like wood and summer and something beginning.

Outside, the field is alive with fireflies — small gold flares blinking in the dark.

When the song ends I let the silence sit. The kids are quiet in the way kids are quiet when something real has just happened in their presence.

A girl of twelve asks when I learned to play.

"A long time ago," I say. "And then I stopped. And then I started again."

"Why did you stop?" she asks.

I think about the terrace. The instruction not to play in the house. The twenty minutes of being exactly myself before anyone told me who to be instead.

"Someone told me it wasn't serious," I say. "And I believed him for a while."

She looks at the guitar. "Do you still believe him?"

"No," I say. "Not anymore."

She smiles — the uncalculated smile of a person who hasn't yet learned to curate herself for rooms — and goes back to her friends.

I look toward the barn door.

My father is still there. He nods once — small, almost imperceptible. Not pride exactly. Older and quieter than pride.

I nod back.

He stays for another hour. Before he leaves he shakes my hand in the gravel outside the barn. "Good work," he says.

He turns to go, then stops. For a moment I think he might say something else. He doesn't. Whatever it is, he keeps it.

Just that. No more.

I watch him go from the gravel. It is what it is — a man in a pressed shirt who drove out from Brooklyn to a barn in the Hudson Valley and stayed an hour and said two words.

Not the thing I spent thirty years waiting for. But the thing my father had available, given freely. I let it be that.

* * *

Morning air at the station smells like rain and steel. Camp dust still on my bag. Trains run quieter up here. Even the announcements sound far away.

The platform's mostly empty. A woman with a paperback. A man tapping his phone. A kid with a guitar case.

And me.

A boy waits near the edge. Seventeen, maybe. Shoulders hunched, hoodie too thin for the morning. Clutching a folder like armor.

He reminds me of someone I used to be.

I walk over and shrug off my coat. Hold it out. "Here. You'll need it more than I do."

He blinks, then takes it. "Thanks."

The train shows in the distance. I don't check the time.

The doors slide open. The boy boards, still wearing my coat. I step inside, let them close.

I find a window seat. Let the coatless boy fade into the crowd. Rest my head against the glass.

We pull out of Garrison — past brick facades and lawns, past station signs I used to count like rungs. I don't count now. I watch.

At Grand Central I come up into the main concourse. The ceiling. The light. The particular noise of ten thousand people moving through the same space without touching.

Near the subway entrance a man about my age stands alone, collar up, eyes on the middle distance. He looks how I used to feel — half here, half gone.

He lifts his head. Our eyes meet.

I nod. Small. Enough.

I take the stairs down.

* * *

The La Mecha offices are on the second floor of a building that used to be a hardware store. You can still see the ghost of the old sign through the paint on the window. The stairs creak on the third step. There is no reception desk.

Sofia has the paperwork laid out on a folding table — two copies, flagged with the small yellow tabs that mean sign here. She is twenty-six and runs the foundation's legal intake on a salary that would make Blake laugh and that I think about every morning when I sit down at my own desk.

"First one," she says. Not ceremony. Just fact.

The pen.

The grant is for fourteen thousand dollars — six months of programming for eight kids at the Bronx site. It will pay for materials, for the two instructors, for the van that picks them up on Tuesdays. It is not a large number. It is a specific number. That's the difference from everything I spent the last decade doing, where the numbers were large and general and connected to nothing you could hold.

I sign.

Sofia countersigns. Slides one copy into a manila folder, hands me the other.

"That's it?" I ask.

"That's it," she says. "The money moves Thursday."

The page is in my hand. My name at the bottom. The number in the middle. The names of the eight kids somewhere in a file I haven't read yet but will.

I think about Mateo — the cell, the coffee shop story, the way he described the regulars in a language we were both improvising. About the way he described the regulars — not as customers, as people. Their names. Their orders. The specific way he said: they came because they were known there.

That's what the number is for.

I fold the copy once and put it in my jacket pocket. Sofia is already back at her laptop. The stairs creak as someone comes up from the street below. Through the painted window the afternoon light comes in gray and clean.

I don't feel like I've arrived anywhere. I feel like I've started.

A few things still find me.

Liz calls sometimes. Usually mornings, when the house is too big and the silence too loud. Her voice is lighter — less sharp. She doesn't check the room before she speaks anymore.

Blake's name drifts across my feed — panels, galas, perfect lighting. She looks consistent. I hope meaning finds her in all that shine. She earned it, in her way.

Alex passed the bar. She's doing entertainment law now — protecting artists the way nobody protected her when she was working for Lizzy. She is exactly who she said she would become. I don't reach out. I honor her by not making her part of this story's ending. She was never my ending. She was my education.

Ian never replied to the email I sent after the coffee. That's okay. Some conversations don't circle back. They just end. His name appears in a PitchDeck piece from three months ago. A profile — not of Sawbuck but of Ian specifically. The engineer who built the platform's core architecture. The founder who created something for his mother's laundromat in Crown Heights.

The piece quotes him talking about the mission in the voice I recognized from The Tank — not the pitch, not the deck, not the raise.

Passion and purpose. The real reason he built it.

Someone finally asked him the right questions. I should have been the one asking.

I read it twice. Set it down.

Q checks in. Sends verses, not advice. Be still and know. He says I sound lighter. I tell him I'm trying.

Mateo's sentence ends next spring. I've written to him twice. The second letter I told him about the foundation. His reply came on a single sheet of paper, three sentences in Spanish. I had it translated. The last line was: God does not give you the future you planned. He gives you the one He planned.

Gloria said the same thing to me once, in the back of a laundromat in Brooklyn, in a language I didn't understand. Two people, two languages, the same sentence — word for word. I heard it the first time. I just wasn't listening.

Nico moved west — consulting for a startup that seems to actually care about people. Daren's teaching analytics at Columbia. Priya sends kid photos every few weeks, captions full of exclamation points. No one follows up. Somehow, we are all okay.

* * *

The guitar stays out of its case now.

At night, when Blue's asleep and the cottage goes quiet, I set a mic on the kitchen table. The guitar feels right in my hands in a way it hasn't felt since I was sixteen in a study in Greenwich, playing for nobody, playing for everything.

I hit record.

I used to think momentum was the point. Keep moving. Keep building. Keep the story going forward and eventually you'd arrive somewhere real. I believed that for twenty years. I built a life around it.

It was a lie.

Not because forward motion is wrong. Because I was moving toward the wrong thing, at speed, without stopping long enough to ask what I was actually for.

Mateo knew the answer before I asked the question. He found it in a cell outside Lima with nothing left to perform for and no audience to perform to. Just a man and the quiet and whatever was in the quiet waiting to be heard.

I don't know what I believe yet. Not fully. But I know what I heard when I finally stopped.

I hit record.

Nothing fancy — just a melody that's been waiting for air. It's rough. I leave it that way. The chord fades.

I'm just a man with a guitar, in the quiet, in the evening, exactly where I'm supposed to be.

— END —

www.ingramcontent.com/pod-product-compliance
Lightning Source LLC
Chambersburg PA
CBHW030537130726
48054CB00020B/77

* 9 7 9 8 9 9 6 1 6 5 9 0 2 *